Blues For A Dying Nation

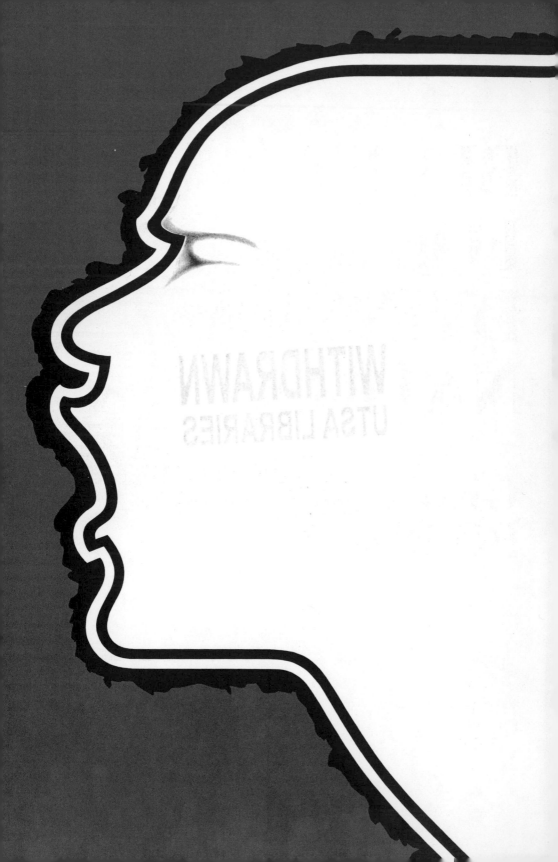

BLUES FOR A DYING NATION

GERALD ROSEN

THE DIAL
PRESS
1972

for Charlotte

With special thanks and appreciation to Karen Kennerly

Dr. Howard Levy (upon being released from federal prison after having served time for refusing to train the Green Berets): "I've noticed in myself and in others who left before me that it's hard to feel joy. David Miller (the first draft-card burner) and Don Baty are still back there. Every once in a while you remember that you've left them behind."

PRE-GAME
SHOW

Commercial

At the White House today, President John Sun (the first Oriental to hold this high office) warned that America is up against a crafty and ruthless foe.

"The Oriental mind is different from that of the American," the president declared. "The Oriental has no respect for human life.

"And I can speak with authority on this matter," the president added, "because I'm one myself."

"Ain't no motherfuckin machine gon make no fool a Moms! No *sah!* Not Moms! I waren't bo'n yestiday ya know."

We are in line at the toll booth gates. One lane to the right of the line which is being blocked by Moms. I'm sitting in the back seat, reading General Eisenhower's joke book, *At Ease: Stories I Tell to Friends.* I'm going into the army, I guess. But through the dense, sweet smoke which fills our little car, over the edge of the page, I can't avoid the pull to the periphery. I watch her. Her movement lures my eyes toward her—toward activity.

"I put one fuckin dollah in this fuckin machine and I ain't movin one fuckin step till I gets my change."

We move ahead one notch in our chain.

She slams the door of the ancient wreck she is driving. "No sah, I been round too long for them to pull that kinda shit on me!"

As she mounts the toll booth basket in the automatic change lane, she lifts her dress to spread it over the edges of the basket rim. I can see the enormous black balloons revealed as, her back toward me, she lowers her soft bulk onto the basket.

My wife Edith, who is driving, searches for change to pay our toll. She isn't aware of what's about to occur. Next to her, on the front seat, slouches our friend Warren, stoned. Staring down at his toes.

The toll basket is made of silvery metal, pocked with rows of tiny circular holes. Through these little apertures I can see Mom's flesh, in blackheads, protruding.

Then, with her feet up off the ground, her knees pressed against the toll booth wall, squatting on the silver basket, she begins to piss.

Edith pays our toll.

"No sah! Moms waren't bo'n yestiday."

Edith shifts into first.

"Moms ain't gettin taken by no fuckin machine!"

We rumble and whine away from the toll booth gates. The geese begin to honk their horns at Moms. Over my shoulder, on the small movie screen at the back of our Volkswagen, I can see my black Dale Evans, riding into the distance on her metallic mount, her arms flailing in circles above her head, swinging twin lassos which aren't there, while she continues to piss into the machinery, yelling like hell.

I turn to the front, but I can still hear the brass ensemble playing in the background as the bank tellers in the booths thumb frantically through their little green books: *Rules and Regulations of the Massachusetts Turnpike Authority.* They are seeking the proper guidelines for action.

SECTION 17—CRAZY SPADES

A. Shitting.
B. Pissing.
    1. On Highway.
    2. On Soft Shoulder.
    3. On Officer of the Law.
    4. On Innocent Denizens of the Open Road.
    5. None of the Above.

Edith shifts into fourth, perfectly.

"Oh, wow!" (Warren has discovered some new fact about his foot.)

The speedometer levels off at fifty. I turn back to the jokes—back to Ike.

FIRST QUARTER

Literature is news that STAYS news.
EZRA POUND

He who fights the future has a dangerous enemy.
SOREN KIERKEGAARD

Commercial

Vice-President Herbert Hubert, on a fact-finding tour of South-east Asia, spoke to one of our reporters on a dirt road in the back country near Danang, South Vietnam. "You see, Marvin," he said, "someday, and I hope it's not going to be too long from now, in fact I *know* it's not going to be too long from now, roads like this will be a thing of the past in Vietnam. When peace and prosperity return to this war-torn, brave little nation, I know, and I know the president and the American people will back me up when I say this, I know that American engineers and American know-how and materiel will be here, here in Southeast Asia, and they'll build a whole system of highways, a whole network of new roads all across this brave little nation, so the villagers of South Vietnam can move into the twentieth century, along with their allies in the rest of the free world, where they so rightly belong.

"And not long after that, Marvin, not very many long years after that, do you know what they're going to have here in the provinces of Vietnam? Do you know what I guarantee they're going to have, Marvin?"

"What's that, sir?"

June day. Afternoon. Submerged in the wood, the road winds through dusty curtains of filtered sunlight. It emerges at the edge of a small concrete bridge.

Over the page top, sitting on the high bank of the river's far side —buildings. Houses. A kind of suburban development.

"Look!" Edith says, pointing at them. "That must be it."

And on the bridge rail, poised above the skipping water's glitter, Tom Sawyer.

Skin burned orange-brown. No shirt. No shoes or socks. Ragged dungarees sheared at the knees. Hair bowled around the front of his dome, sunbursts out into rusty gold ringlets which cover his ears. Fire.

Fire in his face. In his imp freckles. And in his laugh, as he grins open toothed, eating the air. Fire in his sparking eyes as he tight-rope walks the iron rail toward the center of the span.

Only I spot him. (Edith steering carefully, searching for the sign which points to the entrance of the base; Warren absorbed in his attempts to fold Edith's map—giggling.)

As we pass, he turns into a glowing seraph, suspended above us in space, arms spread out wide, moving to give him balance. Like wings.

He peeks a smile at me from under his bangs, loses his footing, and falls. Off the bridge.

BULLETIN

And This Little Piggie...Gone!
AUCKLAND, New Zealand (Reuters)—The little toe is on the way out because of tight shoes. Dr. S. R. Bob, an American foot specialist, told a New Zealand conference that in 10,-000 years man will have only four toes on each foot.

C A M E R A   O N E

"Stop! Stop the car!"

"What?"

"STOP THE CAR!"

Brakes jam. Pavement grips at the tires, ripping off their treads. Filling the air with burned rubber smell. I reach over Warren's shoulder to throw open the door. His seat is pushed forward by my thrust, crushing him against the dashboard. I burst out of the car and throw my body, like a cat in a bag, over the rail and off the bridge.

"He can't swim! Warren, he can't swim!"

SPLAT!

BULLETIN

> **Man Denies His Death**
>
> WORKINGHAM, England (UPI)—After the local newspaper ran an obituary on James White, a councilor, Mr. White telephoned the Town Clerk and said, "I may have been in the hospital for 13 weeks—but I'm a long way from dying.

CAMERA TWO

I felt her strength before I saw her. Even while flailing, I remembered not to fight. Even while choking up gag water from my throat I remembered not to fight. I surrendered to my saver and I faded out. Faded into my own sea.

CAMERA ONE

I am lying on my back. I open my eyes. Two legs straddle my body. Above me. From my low angle of vision her length is exaggerated beyond her true height.

Black bikini bottom. Wet and shiny. Clinging satinlike to her skin. Gripping her crotch. Firm, twin flesh peaks above, caressed by wet black tight cloth. Between, her face looks down at me. Smooth sun-copper skin. Large strong white teeth. Sleek dark hair. Like wet silk, hanging.

"Beginners should learn to swim before they try to dive."

Her voice is warm honey—like Southern Comfort rolling over her tongue. Copper and silver flash of a smile. She shakes her head in wonder, anointing me with the spray from her hair. She walks away—toward the base.

The elastic bands of her bikini bite the supple flesh of her buttocks. Climb up the crack of her ass. The wet black daub of cloth seems carelessly stuck on her—like a gummed sticker. An after-thought to satisfy the law. And to affront it.

And the copper doesn't quit. No band of modesty. No point at which darker public skin becomes white and private. No line of shame. Just constant copper, broken only by the tiny triangle of black, pinned at her hips, and the strands of dark string stretched across the breadth of her back and over her shoulders, taut with the weight of the large breasts which they strain to support. She never looks back.

Behind my head, many-freckled laughter. "You almost drowned!"

I cough up some water. Raise myself to a sitting position.

"Hello, Tom Sawyer."

He giggles.

"Can *you* swim?"

"Sure," he says. "Cal taught me. Last year."

"Cal?"

"Sure. She's the one that pulled you out. She's the best swimmer around here. Better than anyone."

He moves around me, looking me over. As if I were a beached whale (discarded upon the shore).

"She can swim better than David. He can't swim to save himself."

"Who's David?"

"Oh, he's my father. He's a Negro. I am too. Could you tell?" He smiles and holds out his thin freckled arms.

"You know, now that you mention it, your skin *is* kind of dark for a redheaded, freckled person. But it's hard to tell."

He beams. "Well I am. David and I are the two Negroes in our family. And Sibyl is the white one."

"Sibyl?"

"My mother. She's not a Negro. What's *your* name?"

"Jake. What's yours?"

"Jo. Little Jo is what they call me on the base."

"O.K. Little Jo it is," I say. "Does your family live on the base?"

"We did. Now only Sibyl and I live there."

Behind us, the sound of a scurrying plod. I bend my neck and watch the heavy hips bounce as the loose brown skirt and yellow schoolteacher blouse, ruffled, puff down the bank to-ward us.

Following Edith, dangling from a hook, loose Warren flops and bobs along. Mainly hair. Over a foot of it. Like black nylon, hanging straight down to his shoulders. Covering his ears and most of his cheeks, like drapes drawn open to reveal the windows of his eyes. Thin, hawk-face Warren. Gentle. Long nose peering out. A beak on which horn-rimmed glasses rest, their supporting arms piercing his hair veil to reach his ears.

Edith is excited. "What the hell is wrong with you! Are you an idiot?" Her adrenalin is speaking. "You're a fool. That's what you are. A stupid fool! With your crazy heroics. What a lot of crap!"

I'm too spent to reply. I stare and breathe.

"What are you trying to do? Kill yourself showing off?"

"He couldn't see that chick, Edith," Warren says, puffing.

"We'll he's damn lucky that *she* saw *him*, I'll tell you. If that big . . . *thing* hadn't of pulled him out right when she did he'd be swimming underwater right now."

"That was Cal," Jo says to her.

"Well whoever she is, he can thank his lucky stars that big shouldered butch was around. . . ."

"What's a butch?" Jo asks.

"Oh . . . never mind," Edith answers. Then, in a fit of frustration and rage, she fists her hands, stamps her heel into the ground, twice, and begins to sob.

"What's the matter with you, Jacob?" she cries, shaking her head from side to side. She takes the dirty handkerchief Warren holds out to her and wipes the tears from under her eyes. "What's the matter with you, anyhow?"

"Is Cal a butch?" Jo asks, turning to Warren. "She was in the Olympics."

Warren ponders for a moment and then, staring at the ground in front of his feet, he says quietly, "I think she's beautiful."

CAMERA TWO

When we returned to the bridge the car was in the same position in which we had left it. Diagonally swung into the curb, doors still open flung. Jo was with us.

"Come on, kid, we'll give you a lift home," Edith said.

"I'm not 'kid.' I'm Little Jo."

"O.K. Little Jo," she said. "Where do you live? . . . What the hell is *this*?" With the toe of her shoe she nudged a small yellow object which had been lying on the road, near the curb. "Damn it, Warren, will you learn to be more careful!"

It was a roach—from the joint Warren had been smoking.

"That's my fault," I said. "I pushed Warren into the dash. Anyhow, let's forget it. We've had enough hassles for one day."

As we got into the car, Little Jo said, "Do you guys smoke? We do. But I'm not supposed to tell anybody."

"O.K. kid, you direct and I'll drive," Edith said, shifting into first. On her face, a look of exasperated wonder.

CAMERA TWO

"Oh, wow! Is that the place?"

"That's it, Warren," Jo said.

"Oh, man! A log cabin. Hey Jake, dig—a log cabin."

"I see it, Warren."

"Oh, wow. Thoreau. Abe Lincoln. A fireplace. Writing on a shovel in the weak light. What a gas! I can't believe it! A log cabin."

The cabin really was made of logs. It was a tiny structure that seemed almost toylike. Perhaps because of the uniform precision with which the logs had been selected and cut. And the caulking of bright white mortar which ran in neat parallel strips between the logs along the entire length of the cabin.

"Come on in. Follow me," Little Jo said, entering the cabin.

"Did your father build this place?" I said to Jo, marveling at how tightly it had been constructed.

"Are you kidding!" he laughed.

Once inside we came upon an incredible scene. Trash. Piled all over. About three to four feet high in most places. Not garbage rinds and eggshells but broken things. Chairs without legs, television sets without picture tubes, chests of drawers without drawers. Clothing piled on top of everything and, in the corner, blocking the stove, an unbelievably grotesque looking ancient dentist's chair, complete with the remnants of what once must have been an early model x-ray machine.

Through this motley disarray a narrow path threaded, and we followed Little Jo along it, walking Indian file to a clearing in the far lefthand corner of the room where a well-worn king-size mattress, which almost filled the free space, was set on the floor. Seated cross-legged upon it, wearing square-rimmed Ben Franklin spectacles and reading Hermann Hesse's *Siddhartha*, was a large, light-skinned Negro. Except for his glasses, he was completely nude.

He looked up and smiled. "Make yourself at home," he said, pointing to the mattress and putting away the book. "Oh, don't mind me," he added, when he noticed Edith staring at his naked immensity. "It's hot as hell around here in the summer."

His body appeared soft and flabby, as if it had fallen into an unhealthy state of perpetual desuetude.

"I see you've met Peter Pan," he said, pointing to Jo. "I'm his father. David. Pull up a seat."

He moved over to make room and we sat down on the mattress.

"You look like you took a flip in the dip, man," he said to me.

"He thought I was drownding, David. He jumped off the bridge to save me. Cal had to pull him out."

"You could've done worse, man," David said. "Cal is somethin else. That big chick turns me on. . . . But look man, one good turn deserves another. How about some grass?"

"Fine with me," I shrugged. "Edith?"

"I don't have to ask my man over there with the hair," David said, smiling at Warren. "I know *he's* not going to pass up a portion of Hanoi Gold served in my own special giant Turkish hookah."

Warren smiled back at him from under the folds of his hair.

"Hey Jo, where's that hookah?" David said. Then, to me: "I can't find shit around here since my old lady went on this collecting jag."

"Here it is!" Jo cried, lifting it out of an old toy chest which was missing its top. The hookah was a lovely artifact resembling a cut glass vase in the shape of a large light bulb, the globed end truncated to provide a flat surface on which it stood while the elongated stem rose upward, supporting the hand-carved wooden bowl like a flower. At the base of the bowl was anchored the coil of woven fabric through which the smoke was inhaled.

CAMERA ONE

From a cigarette pack on the floor beside the mattress, David shakes out some of the oregano-like, sweet green weed. He stuffs it into the intricately worked hardwood bowl at the top of the hookah, tamping it with his index finger.

"Man, we might as well enjoy it," he says. "This is the last of the just, the last of the good."

He lights the pipe, taking an exaggerated drag until he swells up like Hotei. Then, with the benevolent pride of an inventor presenting his latest device to mankind—still holding his breath—he begins the passing of the hookah hose around the circle. By this time Little Jo has lost interest in the adults and is involved in the trash somewhere on the other side of the cabin.

"Well?" David, the proud papa, asks with a smile. "Was I putting you on or is this stuff dynamite?"

"You weren't kidding," I say, and I mean it, for really good grass, like hash, can start you into the stratosphere right away. Instantly.

Warren, who has little flesh and less control, is already out there, just beaming now, not speaking. "My man over there is somewhere else," David says, digging Warren with a quick glance and then winking at me. Glowing.

"This is excellent," Edith says, reclining back upon one elbow, her skirt tousled carelessly above her knees revealing the loose flesh of her heavy thighs. "Just excellent."

Inside of me a warm balloon of expansive air is dilating. Trying to raise me off the ground. At the same time I feel heavy. Heavy and lethargic and loose. Real heavy.

"Man, gravity's got me," I giggle. "Gravity!" It's impossible to sit up straight. The pull of the earth is too strong and the earth in my body answers it—agrees to come back. I topple and roll over on my side. The giggling begins to reflect on the mirrors around me.

"Hey!" David says, in his soft bass voice, "That man's not kidding. Gravity's got him for sure." He chuckles and begins to shake. "Gravity has got him bad."

At this, Warren, who's been holding in his last drag, cracks up, laughing and coughing the sweet smoke out of his nose and mouth in choking spurts. "Gravity's got Jake, Edith," he says, still gagging on his laughter. "Gravity's got Jake in his clutches."

I am magnetized. Glued to the floor by the ballast of my body. Feeling just fine. Sticking fast to the earth. Small and alone forever in the vast of spacious emptiness. A universe of warm winds from nowhere. And I feel fine, just fine to be in gravity's grasp.

"Gravity's got our car too," Warren giggles. "Got it in its clutch."

Edith breaks up. Shatters into laughter. Hold me mother earth. The world begins to accelerate its spin, and I feel the tug of my own particular pathway out, my unique and fatal tangent which waits up ahead. Unseen. To pull me off. Hold me.

I roll over and rest facing the ground. Alone and facing down. Arms out wide. Making a T with my body. Palms down. I hug the ground. Spinning. Hold me, earth. Clutch my hug and cool the balloon within my skin which would lift me away like a soaring kite on an invisible force stream, into nowhere. The night.

"Well, well, looka here," David says. "It's my man."

I shake off the skin of the vision. Break through the bag of night and see David reach his hand toward a wiry black man (about twenty-five years old) who has just navigated his way through the trash maze around us.

CAMERA TWO

"This is my man Walter. Walter Qwalters. Heavy conga player, black-belt karate freak, and business manager of our underground paper, *The Railroad.* Walter, meet some fine new friends. This one stretched out on his stomach here took a dive off the bridge to save Jo and got himself the bonus of being pulled out by the number one chick in all of Christendom." David smiled at his own words, and at Walter. "Walter knows who I mean, don't he now," David added, beginning to tickle the underside of Walter's chin with his index finger.

With a flash move Walter smacked the hand viciously away from his face. David, feeling the sting, staring at the sore fingers, said quietly, "Well, well. I guess Walter *does* know who I mean at that. O.K., take it easy, man. Pull up some mattress and take a toke of some of this good stuff."

Walter pushed away the hose which David offered.

"Not today, man. Where's Sibyl? I want some speed."

He sat down. Walter could not be called colored because black is defined as the absence of color. And he was really black. Compared to Warren's unsuntouched skin his face shone like black keys on a piano. He wore beautiful leather sandals, carefully and complexly laced around his dark ankles. Tan slacks, well tailored and tight. A brown and gold dashiki. Shades.

"Where's Sibyl? I'm not fuckin around, pops."

"Take it easy," David said. "She'll be here in a minute. What's going to happen to your reflexes if you keep eating that shit?" He smiled ironically toward me and said, "Who's going to be my second in command when Armageddon day comes around?"

At this, even Walter smiled.

"Armageddon, my ass!" he said. "He talks big, but he's so fuckin fat and depressed it takes a goddamn derrick to get him out of the cabin to take a shit," he laughed.

"I'll be there when the day comes around."

"The hell you will, pops," Walter said. "But I love you just the same. The man got ahold of you too soon is all. He got his chains into your brains."

Then Walter turned off his smile and looked at me.

"What're you doing around this hick territory? You look like city to me."

"We are," Edith answered. "Warren and I are from Philadelphia and Jake grew up in the Bronx. We've been living together in Philly for the past few years."

"We were on our way to Fort Ellis," I added. "I'm supposed to be working at the hospital there for the next couple years."

Walter continued to look toward me.

"He was getting drafted," Edith explained. "We were going to go to Canada and then Jake thought he ought to go to jail and then . . . well we really didn't know what we were going to do when they offered him this direct commission thing. He works at the hospital and gets officer's pay. It will be just a nine-to-five job."

"You a doctor?" Walter asked.

"He's a writer," Warren said.

"I'll be in hospital administration," I said. "It's because I got a degree in business."

"You don't look like a businessman to me," David said.

"I'm not. In fact I've never really held a full-time job. I've been working as a part-time movie projectionist for the American Friends Service Committee and reading a lot and writing some stories and poems."

"Then I guess you *are* a writer," David said.

"Well I've never been published. . . .",

"What difference does that make," Walter said. "David, here, wrote a lot of heavy stuff and he never got published. That don't mean he's no writer."

"That was a long time ago," David said. Turning to me, he asked, "You working on anything now?"

"Well, I think I'd like to write a novel about the army when I get out. I hope to write the notes for it in my spare time."

"Good luck," David said, somberly.

"You'll need it," Walter added.

"I thought of writing a book about revolution. Something really far out and fanciful. I want to call it, *The Dark Ages Dawn.*"

"David was gonna call his book, 'Sons and *Mothers*', Walter laughed. "How come you took business in the first place, man?"

"He started in physics," Edith said. "Then, when he found that it wasn't relevant to what he wanted, he got out, but his parents were footing the bill and they demanded that he study something with practical value."

"So I switched to business because it was the easiest," I said.

"You two married?" Walter said, nodding toward Edith and me.

"Yes," Edith replied. "We got married in Philly two years ago."

"What about hair here," Walter said, pointing to Warren. "He married to you too?"

"Only in common law," I said, and Warren smiled and even Walter loosened up a bit.

"Well you're gonna be sorry," Walter said, "real sorry. Sorrier than you can imagine."

"I don't expect to be happy. But shit, it's only nine to five. And I'll be at a hospital. Helping people. It's not as if I'm going to Vietnam or anything."

"Suppose they send you," Walter said.

"I'll cross that bridge when I come to it. I can always go to jail. But I might be lucky enough to spend my entire time at Fort Ellis. The sergeant at the recruiting station where I signed up said that for two years its doesn't pay for them to send me overseas."

At this David began to chuckle.

"Something the matter with Fort Ellis?" I said.

"It's not that," he said. "It's no worse than any place else. I was just amused at your quoting a recruiting sergeant is all."

"Well I certainly didn't believe everything the recruiting sergeant told me, but this seemed to make sense."

"Jake," David said, "let's just say a recruiting sergeant isn't in the honest business, that's all. He simply isn't paid to pursue the truth and announce it."

"He didn't seem like too much of a scholar." I smiled.

David didn't return my grin. "That's one way of looking at it, man," he said.

C A M E R A   O N E

"David's had his own experience with recruiting sergeants, ain't he now," Walter says. "David's had his own little run-in with Fort Ellis."

David seems disconcerted. "Well . . . I did have a bit of a taste of army life. . . ."

Walter quickly moves in on David. Face to face. "And it killed you, pops," he says, his voice getting louder and tighter. "And it killed you. When you went into the army you were dynamic, man. *Dynamic!* But you know what you are now. Now, with your hookah and your hash and your Buddha . . . and your fat ass. Man, you're static. That's all you are. Static! . . . And that ain't nowhere, pops."

"Were you in the army, David?" Edith asks, bluntly.

"Well, I guess I was there for a while . . . and maybe Walter's right. I can't say I've been the same since I got out."

"Got *thrown* out!" Walter says.

"Well I guess Walter hit the mark again. . . ."

"You know it, I did. And you been depressed ever since. One contact with the man and he cut off your balls and put them up your ass and you been glued to the ground ever since." Turning to me: "I mean you shoulda seen this cat before Whitey got his hands on him. He was beautiful, man. He was a leader. And now . . . well you can see where he's at. I mean I still love him—he's still a beautiful cat—but he's not together, man. All this consciousness expansion and acid and grass, day and night, it ain't nothing but a lot a shit. Cause he *knows* the truth. He don't have to find it. He's seen it, man. He's been through it. And he knows what he has to do, too. Don't you, pops!"

He puts his right hand under David's chin. David has been looking down toward the mattress in front of him. Walter lifts up David's head and shouts into his face: "Don't you, pops! Don't you! Don't you!"

David's eyes moisten and fill. He tries to avert Walter's stare, but Walter keeps shouting vehemently into his face, "Together!

Right? Together! We gotta put you back together. Then we gonna act. Right? Together . . ."

And then another voice: "Oh shut up, Walter darling. Must we be subjected to these religious diatribes every time you come here to cop some crank? This is becoming intolerable. Simply intolerable. Leave poor David alone."

The voice has come from out of the trash, over near the door. Then, following her words into the room, appears (I shake my head to clear it—to see straight) a nun. Or a woman, wearing the habit of a nun.

"Don't mind Walter, kids," she says, "he's really a dear but he gets this way when he wants some of my powerful medicine. He begins to see visions of Africa—'Oh dark Mother Africa'—arising after centuries of sleep to crush her exploiters, the dark power of the black masses casting an ominous cloud shadow over the white world.

"And get this, because this is the wildest of all, who does he see as leading these mighty hordes? None other than our own David. Poor, sweet David, who, God knows, is about as white as I am and who's been stoned for so long he can hardly move. Well, poor David is going to lead a band of wild niggers and burn down Tara, which Walter saw in 'Gone with the Wind,' and which, God knows, is the closest poor Walter has ever been to the South."

She throws back her nun's hood and reveals her hair, which is orange and stringy. She swings it free like a dog shaking off water. Her skin seems never to have touched the sun. Ghastly pale, it picks up the blue from the tiny veins beneath its surface and the orange tint of her hair. And she is, she *really is* wearing a nun's habit. And she's carrying a two-legged object that was once a chair. She turns to the piles of junk and searches . . . for the right place. Then she finds it and, turning the chair to the proper angle, she sets it down with concerned precision upon a rubber tire which is lying on top of a tilted old table.

"Oh, wow!" Warren says. "Found objects! Living in a work of art! I don't believe this. It's all too beautiful."

David smiles again. "You kill me, man," he says to Warren, slapping him on the back.

Warren coughs and Sibyl says, in an astringent tone, "Oh, we're not interested in art around here. Once we were, but now we're only interested in power. Isn't that so, Walter?"

CAMERA TWO

"Jesus Christ," Walter said, shaking his head from side to side in impatient displeasure.

"Isn't that so, David?" Sibyl continued. "Art is decadent. Only power is generative of new forms."

She had a hint of an English accent. It was not easy to isolate her meaning from the rapid babble of her words. I'm not certain she was clear herself. She seemed kind of scattered in her brains—bright but elliptical. A bit off the beam. Her eyes were set in deep sockets and loomed green. With her thin angular face, reddish cast, and black habit, she reminded me of a witch from the dark world of children's books. The last of the three weirds, gone senile at about the age of forty.

"Mommy, why don't you give Walter what he wants?" Little Jo called from over by the stove.

"Yeah, Jo's right. Just give me what I came for and I'll split and you can philosophize all you want. You can help the Buddha find his Bo Tree for all I care." He nodded toward David who was smiling once again.

CAMERA ONE

Like a nut cracker, Sibyl bends herself in half to get to the bottom of her habit, reaches under it, and begins to lift it up. Knees, thighs, hips, waist, small breasts. Doesn't stop until it is crumpled and bunched up beneath her chin. Her bony frame and body revealed. And her underwear. Black brassiere above a pair of men's jockey shorts.

From inside her bra she takes a tiny metal aspirin box. When she straightens up she raises her chin and her black gown falls back into place. She opens the tin over Walter's extended hand and we watch about eight small green pills fall out onto his palm. They are shaped like hearts.

"Is that speed?" Edith asks.

"It's dexamyl," Walter says. "It's what them straight chicks in the suburbs take to turn themselves on. Only they call it weight-reducing pills."

"Use it well, child," Sibyl says, "because there's no more where that came from. Not since the narcs busted Cowboy and Gypsy's pad last night."

CAMERA TWO

Walter looked up at her, the edges of his mouth pulled back and up to form the puzzled half-smile of incredulity. He turned to David.

"It's true," David said. "I think they got our number now, man. So I'm afraid the game is up."

"The game is up, my ass," Walter said. "We'll just have to find another source." He then placed half of the pills on his tongue, swallowed, and began to rise. "The paper sure isn't making a fuckin nickel since you began to meditate on the universal hash can."

David laughed.

Walter continued, "You won't laugh so much when the chief finds out what's happening. I'm telling you, pops, the chief is gonna be pissed. And then you'll be out of bread yourself, so you better get with it soon, static-man, or you're gonna be living the life of the spirit by necessity cause you ain't gonna have a dime to get a shine."

He began to make his way to the door through the trash. "All they can do is put you in jail, pops, and that ain't much worse than the funny farm where they're gonna hatch you for sure if you don't get on the ball and wake up."

As he left the cabin, Sibyl shouted after him, "We can take care of ourselves, thank you. So don't you worry about David. I'm quite certain we can do without your ever so frequent advice and your...." Her voice trailed off as she was distracted by something in her collection which seemed out of place. She knitted her brows and, squinting at various objects from different angles of perspective, she became absorbed in the rearranging of a section of her tangled heap of junk. Trying to get it right.

"Don't mind Walter," David said. "He isn't always like that. Some days he's a bit salty is all. I guess I disappointed him some . . . I guess I really did."

BULLETIN

Zini Indian Rain Dancers 'Cause' Unslated Downpour

GALLUP, N. M. (AP)—The Zini Indian rain dancers did their thing at the annual inter-tribal Indian ceremonial here.

When they walked off the stage, a thunderstorm struck, drenching the 6,000 pale face spectators.

Officials said that they were uncertain whether the rain dancers would be invited to perform at next year's cere-monial.

CAMERA ONE

"Mommy, I'm hungry!" But Sibyl is into her collection and doesn't hear. *"I'm hungry!"*

"Oh, be quiet Jo, you see I'm busy." She picks up an empty orange crate. "You know we can't cook here, now that the x-ray machine is blocking the stove." She places the wooden crate on the sink, wedging one of its sides under the cold-water faucet.

"Well I'm hungry!"

"Why don't we go out and eat?" I say. "I'll be making money soon. I'll treat."

"That might be a good idea," David says. "Why don't you folks take Jo along with you. I don't go out much anymore. Less hassles that way."

As we wend our way to the door, the three of us and Little Jo, picking our holes like slow-motion halfbacks, Warren turns back and gives David a wave. David, who's just taken a long drag from the water pipe, nods pleasantly. Then he says in words shaped in smoke, "Hey, you folks plan on spending the night here when you get back. We can work it out. Sibyl and Jo will stay back on the base. No sense throwing away good money on a shitty motel."

Reaching the doorway, Edith turns and says to Sibyl, "Want us to bring you back anything?" But Sibyl is busy crossing the room, carrying a bookcase without any shelves in it on her head. She doesn't answer.

BULLETIN

A GUNMAN KILLS 2, WOUNDS 3 IN SPREE

PARKERSBURG, W. Va., Aug. 20 (AP)—A former marine apparently used combat tactics early today nn a shooting spree that left two persons dead and three others seriously injured, the police said.

The suspect, David L. Grimm, 25 years old, of Parkersburg, was arraigned on a charge of murder after the police aested him at his home, Police Chief Gale Smith said.

The shooting spree began at about 3:3; A.M. at Ada's Club, a downtown nightspot.

The police said the gunman apparently left the club, tossed a gas device—possibly a grenade — into the building and picked off its occupants with a rifle as they fled.

Killed were Charles Hardman, the owner of the club, and William Plant, who may have worked at the club. Aother person was wounded.

Cheif Smith said Grimm then walked one block to the rear of the Parkersburg National Bank, where, "out of fright or something," he wounded Lawrence Palmer, an employe of American Courier Company, who was making a delivery.

Two blocks away, the chief said, Grimm shot a passing motorist, who was in fair condition in a city hospital.

CAMERA THREE

When we lived in Philadelphia we would often get stoned and go out to get some food. Edith and I would order the most interesting or foreign sounding dish on the menu and share it while Warren would stick to his special favorite—vanilla ice cream smothered in hot fudge sauce.

Sometimes, we would talk about our future together. Edith would expand upon her plans for revolutionizing public education, Warren would tell us about new dishes he was planning to cook for us and new records he was going to buy, and I would scheme aloud about my plans for writing. But after I had signed the papers at the recruiting station we no longer talked about my future. Warren's comment that you could get stoned anywhere and live in your own world was about all that any of us could say.

For, besides random half-forgotten images gleaned from war novels and movies, none of us knew a damn thing about the army. We knew of Vietnam—of places like the imperial palace of Hué and Cam Ran Bay—but we knew next to nothing about the army itself. Until I actually joined up we had never heard of the base to which we were assigned.

CAMERA TWO

As we drove away from the cabin I sat in the back seat, alongside Little Jo, watching the rerun, in my mind, of the memory-movie of my rescue. It had all happened so quickly, so unexpectedly, that it was difficult for me to focus on anything besides the imprinted image of the incredible chick who had saved me.

The hard, clean lines of her face against the dark luster of her hair. The imposing stature of her athlete's body, with its firm flesh-curves pushing against the restrictions of her little swimsuit —which was all that kept her ripe body from being nakedly embraced by the warm June air.

And the allure of the insolence in her smile. As she turned her virtually bare body and walked away from me.

I couldn't keep from asking Little Jo if he knew anything more about Cal, but because Edith kept interrupting him to ask directions I was only able to learn that she was in the WACs and that she was an officer.

We were still slightly stoned when we reached the roadside restaurant. Edith and I sat down at a table. Warren told Little Jo to order some vanilla ice cream with hot fudge for him and he went into the men's room. Two crew-cut types seated at another table with their fat assed, high-haired dates (who were wearing slacks), whistled maliciously at him as he passed, but he didn't pay them any notice. The men made joking remarks about him but their laughter seemed forced—unnaturally loud and uneasy.

Little Jo took our orders and went up to the counter to place them. He seemed to know everybody who worked in the place. The busboy waved to him and the fellows behind the counter kidded with him, calling him by name.

"He must eat here all the time," Edith said. "Hamburgers and Cokes. He's awfully thin. Just skin and bones really. Someone should take better care of him."

"He seems to take pretty good care of himself."

"He's awfully young to be on his own so much. He's funny though. Did you hear when he called Warren an owl in the car? I hope he didn't hurt his feelings, because it is true that Warren looks like an owl with those big glasses on his nose."

The men's room door slammed and Warren returned to the table. "Hey, did you hear? Jo called me an owl on the way over here," he said. "What a groovy kid! It's true. I was just digging myself in the mirror. I *do* look like an owl."

"What do you think so far, Warren?" I said. "I mean about the whole scene up here."

"I think it's going to be great, Jake. I really do. I'm just happy to be here with you two. In Massachusetts. I'm happy to be alive."

Little Jo brought back the food and we ate it slowly. Just hamburgers and french fries with ketchup. But the benevolent grass had opened the buds on our tongues. We savored the taste. And when the food was all gone we felt a kind of sadness, as if we had just seen a friend off on the train. After a weekend of warm winter love.

And it was the first day of summer.

BULLETIN

FATHER CAN'T HAVE TOWER KILLER'S GUNS

Special to The New York Times

AUSTIN, Tex., Oct. 20—A state court today turned down a suit by Charles A. Whitman Jr. of Lake Worth, Fla., to get possession of the six rifles and pistols his son used to kill 14 persons from atop the University of Texas tower in 1966.

Mr. Whitman filed suit in State District Court asking for the guns, describing them as "things of sentimental value," and also for $8,000 to cover burial expenses and loans he made his son.

CAMERA TWO

On the way back to the cabin I said to Edith, who was driving, "Hadn't we better drop Little Jo off at the base? David said he and Sibyl were going to sleep there tonight, and it's getting dark."

"I can come back to the cabin," Jo said. "I don't feel the least bit tired."

"What do you think?" I said to Edith.

"It's all right with me," she shrugged. "How are *you* feeling, Jake?"

"Why do you ask?"

"Well, you looked a bit apprehensive for a while back in the cabin. When David and Walter started talking about the army."

"I guess I am. . . . But we'll see. We'll find out soon enough."

"I certainly hope so," Edith said. "But speaking of the base, where do you and Sibyl stay when you sleep there, Little Jo?"

"In our house."

"In your house?" I said.

"Sure. Where else?"

"But I thought David was thrown out of the army?" Edith said.

"He was," Jo said. "A long time ago."

"Well, then how can you still have your house there?" Edith asked.

"I don't know," he shrugged.

"Don't they have a Post Housing Office or something, that takes care of these matters?" I said.

"Oh, that got blowed up a long time ago."

"About how long ago?" I asked.

"Oh, way back. Just before they throwed David out."

"Well that explains it," Edith said. "The records must have been destroyed in an explosion. If they had duplicated their records on tape in a central memory bank at another location slip-ups like this wouldn't occur."

"Jo," I said, "you said *they* blew it up. Who's *they*?"

"I don't know," he smiled.

BULLETIN

Soccer Fans Riot in Italy
Five Hours; 45 Are Hurt

TORRE DEL GRECO, Italy, May 26 (AP)—Hometown fans in this South Italian community resented it when a visiting soccer team tied the local squad yesterday in a minor-league game. The ensuing riot lasted five hours and 45 persons were hurt.

More than 1,000 spectators tore down a metal fence in front of the stands, invaded the field and besieged the visiting players, the referees and newsmen in the locker room.

The police fled under a hail of bottles and stones. Reinforcements arrived from Naples, but even with clubs they couldn't disperse the fans. Finally, two armored cars arrived and the crowd disappeared.

CAMERA ONE

Back at the cabin. Dark now. David asleep on the mattress. Still nude. Curled up like a fat walrus fetus.

He wakes as we approach. Rubs his eyes. "I must've dozed off."

"It's been a long day."

"That's the grass talking, Jake," he says. "Whenever you smoke, the slow-motion camera takes over."

"But when you film slow motion," Edith says, "you have to make the film in the camera move faster."

David smiles. "Now you're talking, Edith." He rises to a sitting position and stretches his arms out above his head. "You folks just make yourself at home. We've always got room here for good people."

"Looks like your room is kind of limited," Edith says, nodding toward Sibyl's collection.

"So are the good people," I say, and we all grin.

"Hey, David, there's one thing I want to ask you."

"Shoot, Jake."

"How come, without even knowing who we were, you broke out the grass before? Isn't that kind of dangerous? Trusting strangers the minute you meet them."

"Oh, it wasn't you I trusted. It was Little Jo. He wouldn't have brought you here if you weren't right."

Like a little lantern on the edge of the mattress, Jo beams.

"He may be pretty mature for his age," Edith says, "but he's still a child."

"Let's just say that it seems to me that childhood is an invention of those who oppress us," David says, yawning, as Jo lights up again. "You see, without the invention of the concept of childhood you couldn't have its opposite."

"Adulthood," Warren laughs.

"You know it," David says, quietly. "Adulthood has been keeping people in chains since the Middle Ages. So we just never started that kind of shit in our cabin here. Jo's as free as the rest of us, I guess. And we don't keep anything from him."

David reaches for the hookah, which is filled with ashes of burnt grass. He manages to get it lit long enough to get a single short drag and then he looks up at Edith, trying to read her face in the dim light of the small electric bulb suspended from the ceiling, which is rapidly losing its battle for the cabin to the encroaching darkness of the night. "Am I going beyond you, Edith?"

Edith, on her hands and knees upon the mattress, hesitates pensively, and then begins to crawl slowly across, stalking Little Jo. "I'm afraid so," she says softly, without taking her eyes off her prey, until she's upon him with a leap and is tickling him madly while he rolls around beneath her, trying frantically to escape and squealing with glee.

BULLETIN

Blind Man Kills Wife
DETROIT, Aug. 19 (UPI)—An elderly man, blind for 15 years and fearful of prowlers, shot twice toward a noise in the hallway off his bedroom early Tuesday and killed his wife, who had risen before him. The police said John Boggan, 69 years old, told officers he did not know he had shot his 73-year-old wife, Mary, until he heard her moan after the second shot.

CAMERA ONE

Morning. Not as clear as yesterday. Sunshine. Some haze, maybe smog, in the air. Just the three of us again. Approaching the base. I'm in the front this time. Warren in back. Edith driving.

At the gate to the base, a kind of toll booth. Out pops an MP. (It says so on his shoulder.) He waves us to a stop. Six stripes on his arm. He looks at our bumper for a second. Then, apparently not finding what he was seeking, he circles the car. Like a camera on a dolly.

Approaching the driver's window, he says, across Edith to me, "State your business on the base, please."

"Yes, sir," I answer. "I just accepted a direct commission and I'm supposed to report here today. To get housing and sign in, I think. Sir."

"Name?"

"Klinger, sir. Jacob F. Klinger."

"And you were given a direct commission?"

"Yes, sir."

"Then you're a second lieutenant, right?"

"Yes, sir. I guess so, sir."

"Then why are you *siring* me, sir?"

Edith looks toward me. She seems to think I know the answer.

I guess it's because of all those stripes on his sleeve. Can it be that simply by signing my name on a piece of paper, handed to me by a stranger in an old building on North Broad Street in Philadelphia, I've already earned more than those six stripes this man wears? He probably won them for bravery in action during the Battle of the Bulge or something. During World War II. When I was just a baby.

"Sir?" he asks, again.

Edith continues to stare at me expectantly. As if I'm supposed to know what's up. I figure I'd better change the subject. "Do I proceed to the hospital first or to my house?"

"Your house, sir? Oh, your *quarters!* Yes. I'll guide you to your quarters, sir."

By God, I have earned more stripes than he has. And just by studying accounting.

"I'll just slip into the back, sir. Next to your sister."

Oh, God!

"I'm not his sister," Warren giggles. Edith catches the germs of his laughter and begins to quiver. My guide turns to me. Stern, but perplexed.

"I'm sorry, sir, but we cannot allow just *anyone* on the base. Whoever or whatever the aforementioned party is. It is the responsibility of the MP at the gate to ascertain the identity of all parties endeavoring to enter or leave said base, impeding their egress or transgress until said identity of said party, and the function of said party, is ascertained."

"I'm his pet owl," Warren says. That does it. He and Edith are now hysterical beyond control.

"Sir?"

"O.K. Quiet down." (My first command.)

"I'm his houseboy," Warren says, as he and Edith fight to bite back their laughter.

"Well, that's different," the sergeant says. (Of course. That's it! He's a sergeant. *They* have the stripes. Officers have something else. . . . Bars! That's it. I'm beginning to get my bearings now.)

The sergeant pulls out a small green covered booklet, puts on a pair of clear-rimmed spectacles, and begins to follow his index finger down the pages with his eyes, his lips silently moving, he seeks. . . . and finds what he's looking for.

"Ah, here it is, sir. *Oriental Houseboys.* If said party on the back seat is, in fact, a boy, and is Oriental, I will be able to allow him to proceed onto the base, sir."

"Oh, he's a boy all right. I'll guarantee that," Edith says, and she and Warren begin to giggle again, as the sergeant pinks with blush and I redden.

"Now cut that out! Come on, this is serious," I say. "I don't want to get off on the wrong foot."

"And being a linear descendant and present incarnation of Matsuo Basho, the seventeenth-century Japanese poet and monk, I can certainly qualify as an Oriental," Warren adds.

"Be *serious*, Warren," I say.

"O.K." Edith laughs. "That's enough, Warren." Then, turning to the sergeant, she says, "But you certainly must admit that he does qualify to proceed."

And the sergeant, slightly flustered, answers, "Yes, ma'm. I . . . [a quick glance down at his finger on the page] Yes. . . . Yes, he does qualify to proceed."

I lean forward to open the door and the sergeant climbs into the back, squeezing himself against the right side of the seat to get as far away from Warren as possible, while sneaking repeated quick glances at him in amazement.

"O.K., ma'm, proceed straight ahead if you will. I'll tell you when to turn," says the sergeant, who is now so squashed away from Warren into the corner of the Volks that I begin to fear he'll soon burst out through the side window.

Edith shifts into first and the car struggles forward.

"Just straight ahead please, ma'm."

And then there's a silence within the car until, over the motor's grinding moan, Warren cannot resist adding a single last word.

"Hoot!"

BULLETIN

Would Impeach High Court
Special to The New York Times
MONTGOMERY, Ala., June 4
— State Senator W. G. Mc-
Carley introduced a resolution
Wednesday calling for impeach-
ment of the entire United States
Supreme Court and declared,
"If we don't do something, I'm
going to take my gun and do
something." He assailed Court
decisions in obscenity cases.

CAMERA TWO

After driving about an eighth of a mile along a wooded, blacktop road, we came to an opening in the growth which revealed, on the left, a group of ivy-covered, red-brick buildings—a kind of campus setting.

"That's MACE," the sergant said.

"What?" Edith said.

"MACE. The Military Academy for Communication and Espionage. The army spy school, ma'm."

"For a minute I thought this might be the place where they manufacture the chemical mace," she said.

"Oh no, ma'm," he smiled, "the army doesn't make mace. That's private enterprise."

"It is?"

"Yes, ma'm. A group of civilians came up with the idea for that cute little number. Built themselves a nice business around it."

On the right we passed a golf course. A large imitation Greek-revival building stood at its edge. Its tall frontal columns and portico gave it a southern flavor.

"That's the new officers' club, lieutenant. You'll be a member of that."

I nodded, with exaggerated interest.

"Just straight ahead please, ma'm. And then a right turn at the approach to the next intersection."

Edith caught my eye, signaling that she wasn't quite sure of what he meant. I looked to the front and she continued to follow the road, reached the intersection, and turned right.

We returned to a tree-hooded road and after about a quarter of a mile we reached a long curve on which the trees began to thin. A suburban housing development came into view.

C A M E R A   O N E

"Stop! Stop this vehicle!" the sergeant shouts. "STOP THIS VEHI-CLE!"

Edith squeals the car's wheels. The sergeant flies forward onto the back of my seat and neck. The squeal then yields to a whine. A loud whistling scream.

"Hit the dirt!" the sergeant shouts toward the roof of the car. "Take cover. Incoming!"

He reaches over my shoulder and throws open the door. "Take cover!"

BOOOMP!!!

Trees crack on our left as splinters and spectral bits of fire fly by.

"Incoming! Take Cover!" the sergeant yells, as if he were commanding an entire company of men spread over the area of a football field, rather than the three bewildered people whom he alternately pushes (because of the danger) and pulls (because I'm an officer) to the side of the road and into a ditch.

SCREE-E-E-E. . . .

"All in the area. Take cover!" he shouts at the sky as, just like in the movies, we leap into the ditch and nestle our faces into the cool soft dirt.

BOOOMP!

Like mad eagles, swooping, they scream down. Eagles out of control. In crazed radar-jammed dives down after prey. But continuing to accelerate in never stopping sweeping falls until all their majestic beauty and force is lost in soft pillow-tossed bursts of blood and feathers. The world's natural soaring king plops flaming apart in an anticlimatic

BOOOMP!

That's all. Booomp! But the earth shakes as the fire begins to wail and the screeching eagles howling down at invisible speeds become meteors of falling fire and explode against the ground like burning paper bags filled with water.

SCREE-E-E-E. . . . . . . BOOOMP!

Making craters in the earth.

I peek over the edge of the road. I must see. And, apart from the others, I am given a private arc to hear. To trace the flame of its fall. To hear it ride the rainbow down. To its end. In the housing development. In a single home, brick and neat with tended lawn and, to greet the guests, a brightly painted plaster statue of a smiling black Uncle Tom in front. Fishing. With a plaster fish hanging suspended from the wire at the end of his protruding rod.

And as the house flies apart, like a brick balloon burst from within, I watch the fish on Uncle Tom's line. Swaying gently, helplessly, in the hot wind that was once a warm home.

And pieces of the history of the house glide gracefully by. There goes part of a see-through oven door. And a window frame. And a single boot. And bricks fly through the air—blocks that were once the cells of a house. And the severed head of a large toy doll. And pieces of glass and wood and, no doubt, silk.

While I continue to watch the black angler's fish. Suspended. Even after the holocaust. Dangling forever from dark Uncle Tom's rod.

"Sir!" the sergeant cries. "Please. Put your head down."

The sergeant, Warren, and Edith are slightly lower than I am, their heads snuggled into the roadside bed. Eyes down, bodies taut, like children determined to hold their breath until they turn blue. Hugging the earth, the skin-soft side of the ditch.

SCREE-E-E-E . . . . . .BOOOMP!

I pull my head down and listen to the sounds of tearing apart around us. The ripping and flinging and screeching falls. Until, although I can still hear the resonance of the din within my head, I realize that it has stopped. The earth has ceased its quaking and, as before a storm, the air is still. I peer over the side of the road toward my fish. It is still on the line. Still.

BULLETIN

L. I. Veteran Is Fined $50 For an Upside-Down Flag

Special to The New York Times

HEWLETT, L. I., Oct. 15— A businessman here who raised an American flag in an upside-down position to signify his belief that the country "is in a distressed condition" was arrested and taken to a police station in handcuffs today for flying the flag illegally. He was fined $50 in First District Court, Mineola.

CAMERA ONE

The stillness around us shatters like broken plate glass as we all begin to move at once. Dusting and slapping our clothes and shaking the burnt cotton-fog out of our heads.

Edith is the first to speak. Indignantly. "What's going on here, sergeant? What's the meaning of this?"

The sergeant straightens himself out, smoothing his stiff, starched shirt and fixing his hat, which, though spattered with dirt, has remained on his head throughout the confusion. "It's Him, ma'm. He's infiltrated the village. . . ."

"Who the hell is this 'He,' sergeant?"

"Ma'm?"

"Who's this 'He' you're talking about?"

"Why, ma'm, it's *Him* . . . the enemy. . . .The B.C."

"Who?"

"The B.C., ma'm. He's all around here. We've got to use our superior firepower to flush him out. He's a ruthless and determined foe, ma'm"

"Wait a minute!" Edith says, startled to full height. She whitens with incomprehension. "You mean that was us?" Turns to me. "This is inconceivable . . . Jacob. . . ." Turning back to the sergeant, "Those were *our* bombs?"

"Shells, ma'm. Those were ours. . . . It's the B.C., ma'm. It's the only way."

"But they landed *here*. They could have killed us." She points to the ruin of the house. "And there! Look down there! We bombed down one of our own houses."

She begins a series of fitful, little, furious sobs. "Look at that carnage, sergeant. You mean to say we did that? What can you say for yourself? Go on! Speak up!" she cries at him, exasperated. "What do you have to say about *that*?"

The sergeant lowers his head and, with an almost reverential deference, replies, "That's war, ma'm."

CAMERA TWO

"He joined the army to avoid the war and he gets poor Warren and me right into the middle of *this*," Edith said, her hands held out in front of her in the direction of the wrecked house, palms upwards, as if she were presenting us with the bloody evidence on a tray.

"Oh, it doesn't shock me," Warren said.

"You mean you don't care?" Edith asked.

"Well I'm not going to waste my energies building ladders over the clouds to see if the sun's still there on overcast days, if that's what you mean. What was here yesterday will return tomorrow. Or the day after."

"Well that's really profound. . . ."

"You know what your problem is, Edith?" he said, "The radio plays fifty-five minutes of rock an hour but you only come into the room for the five minutes when they give the news and weather. You're too precious to waste yourself like that."

"Well that's just grand," she said. "I must say, that's just grand. The whole world is breaking apart and that's just what we need: cracker-barrel philosophy."

CAMERA ONE

Warren puts his arm around Edith's shoulder and they move over to the car and begin to check it out for damage. Instead of joining them, I walk toward the broken house. It would have been easier to wait and drive the couple hundred yards but my attention is fixed upon the vortex of the destruction and I walk directly toward it. The sergeant follows along behind me.

The bang of a slammed screen door pulls the focus of my attention to the house next to the wrecked one. Out bursts a man in uniform (no hat) who runs recklessly into the still smoking debris. Wafting on the fresh morning breeze, his short greeting card reaches the sergeant and myself (still unseen) as he rushes into the newly made pit: "Motherfuckers!" Bitten out through tightly clenched teeth.

As we approach the ruin he emerges, carrying, like a flag draped over his extended arms, the limp body of a child. With a solemn efficiency, he bears it across the lawn to his own house and disappears into the doorway.

I can't say whether it's a boy or a girl. Alive or dead. I couldn't see the face.

I pass some broken china and the guts of a dead clock. I look down at my feet and I stop. The sergeant continues to walk toward the remains of the building. But I stop. For down on the ground in front of me is the doll's head which I had seen fly out onto the lawn. Where the neck of the doll has been severed from its body, there are stains made by splashed doll's blood. I now know the sex of the child which the soldier carried into his house. It was a girl.

CAMERA TWO

The Volkswagen chugged up to the foot of the lawn. I bent down and picked up the head. Held it out in front of me, cradled in my hands.

Edith yelled from down on the road, "The car's fine, Jake."

Then a running woman, wildly agitated, appeared. She rushed by the front of the car and up the lawn to me. Where she stopped. And wailed a horrible cry. And began to punch at my face with little fistfuls of woe while she howled.

I did nothing. My hands were full. I was shocked into passivity by this cloudburst of grief.

Then, out of the next house ran the soldier without the hat. He grabbed the maddened woman, spun her around, sharply cracked her face with a smack, and held her as she collapsed.

Finally, I moved. I began to walk toward the neighboring house, following the soldier who half-carried, half-dragged, his sobbing sack. On my arm, like a football, I toted my present of pulp and skull.

C A M E R A   O N E

We pass near the sergeant who is shaking his head from side to side and muttering to himself. "That's the price we have to pay for peace. . . . He'll pay for this."

A short woman (the hatless soldier's wife, I gather) opens the door and helps him to carry the deflated woman who punched me (the decapitated child's mother?) into the living room. I follow. The soldier looks at me and nods toward the topless corpse on the couch. A thin torso which couldn't have spent more than seven or eight years on the earth. I read his gesture and carry the severed head (whose blood still oozes thickly through my fingers) over to the sofa, on which he has placed the soon to rot young body (whose cells are still alive) and I set my gory ball back on the shoulders where it once belonged.

There is an empty chair in the far corner of the room. I sit on it while the soldier (he's an officer—I can see the silver bar on his collar) turns the mother over to his wife.

His wife is high cheekboned and brown skinned and the flatness of the front of her face says that she is an American Indian. She is holding a cup of whiskey up to the lips of the mother, whom she has seated on an old easy chair.

The officer walks over to the couch, which is now widely stained with blood. His uniform is blotched in several places with scablike red spots. Suddenly, he perceives the dark liquid on the fingers of his right hand. He stops, with a jerk, and, while staring fixedly at the child's corpse (at the two unequal halves), he deliberately inserts his finger tips into his mouth, one by one, and sucks off the sweet thick red sauce.

When he finishes he stands there. Not moving. My eyes are drawn along the line of his gaze to my hands, still bowled as if supporting a heavy ball. And like a fade-in and fade-out I begin, alternately, to see, and then not to see, the image of the severed head which still weighs heavily. Moving into focus and out. When I bend to kiss its bright lips they fade into my own fingers, from which I lick off the blood jam. Deliberately. While the officer watches. And the mother sobs in her chair across the room, unseeing.

When I look up, we resume the reading of each other's eyes, until he says, "I've got to change clothes and get down to the clinic. Got some crazy people to attend to."

He begins to walk out of the room toward the back of the house, stopping to say to me over his shoulder, "I think you better go and pick up your sergeant out on the lawn. He won't enter an officer's house if he can help it."

"Oh, you know him?" I say, as he enters the bedroom.

"No."

BULLETIN

Unrest Laid to Boredom

WASHINGTON, Sept. 27 (UPI) —Gov. Daniel J. Evans of Washington said today that one of the prime causes of campus unrest was not the draft but "the boredom of as much affluence as exists today." In a broadcast interview he said that he believed the young were disturbed by "things coming easier and perhaps less challenging."

CAMERA TWO

I looked across the room at the soldier's wife. She was still comforting the mother (holding the woman's head in her hands and stroking the hair). With a nod toward the door, she signaled that it was all right for me to leave.

I walked out the door and sure enough, like a faithful horse without need of a hitching post, there stood the sergeant on the lawn, waiting for me.

"We can proceed to your quarters now, sir. It's right next door. You share this duplex with Lieutenant Rainey," he said, pointing to the name under the doorbell behind me.

I waved to Edith, who was standing with Warren at the edge of the debris, next to the car. "Bring it up here: We have the other half of this house."

And the sergeant and I walked across the front of the single-story, ranch-style building to meet them at the driveway on the other end.

As soon as Edith and Warren had unfolded themselves out of the car again, the sergeant exhaled a sigh, clapped his hands together, and said, "Well, let's get on with it," and he started up the cement path which led from the driveway to the front door. Edith didn't follow.

"At least He didn't get your new quarters, lieutenant. Like they say, every cloud has a silver lining." He noticed that Edith hadn't moved away from the car. "Thank God for little things, ma'm," he said. "Your quarters weren't touched at all."

"Our government asks no quarters and gives no quarters to the forces of evil," Warren said.

I had to laugh. Of course the sergeant didn't get it, but I was surprised to see that the expression on Edith's face didn't change. She looked as if she had inadvertently turned a corner somewhere and stepped into a painting by Hieronymus Bosch.

She was not yet ready to dismiss the topic of her previous questions. "Sergeant, now that we've calmed down a bit, would you mind once more explaining what we've just witnessed?"

And the sergeant, calmly and methodically, like a teacher with a slow pupil, began again. "Well, you see ma'm, the B.C. have infiltrated into many high positions in the village. There is reason to believe that He has a large underground network of spies and saboteurs operating right up to, and even within, the boundaries of the base. So we've got to unload on him at periodic intervals. To establish our control over the perimeters of our position."

"But . . ."

"Why don't we just let it go for now," I said. "It must have been some mistake. We'll find out about it tonight on the news."

"Oh, this won't be on the news, sir," the sergeant said, quietly. "PIO won't release this."

"PIO?" Edith said.

"Post information officer, ma'm. He won't give this to the press. This could hurt our morale and help Him."

"Him?"

"The enemy, ma'm. News like this could lend aid and encouragement to the enemy."

"To the B.C.," Warren added, with exaggerated didactic seriousness (as if trying to help the sergeant to get the simple facts of the matter across to an impractical female).

Then he smiled. And in spite of everything that had happened, he and Edith began to giggle nervously once again, while the sergeant looked Warren over, suspiciously. From his hair and owl face, down along his six feet of 140-pound, long boniness. His pink shirt with stitched collar (which he found on South Street, in the black section of Philadelphia), his dungarees (which Edith bought for him), and his twenty-nine-cent thongs (which he bought for himself with money earned babysitting).

The sergeant was memorizing him for future reference.

C A M E R A   O N E

The sergeant says, "Here comes my car. If it's O.K. with the lieutenant I'll run along now."

I realize that he's talking to me, so I tell him, "Sure sergeant. Thanks for everything."

"My pleasure, sir," he says, and then he throws me my first salute. And holds it. . . .

In my embarrassment, I turn to Warren, but he just gives me the hint of a sly cat-smile, so there is nothing else to do but salute the sergeant back. Which I do. Awkwardly.

But he doesn't seem to notice my uncertainty. He comes out of his salute with a snap, says, "Good luck in your new career, sir," and climbs into a khaki Ford, with a red light on its roof, which has just pulled up next to us in the driveway. The driver backs the car down onto the road and they roar away.

"Let's get some of this stuff out of the car," I say to Warren. Edith goes into the house to look around.

As I lift up the front hood of the Volks, to get at the trunk, I hear the sound of a phone ringing nearby.

"Here, Warren, you take these clothes and I'll . . ."

"Jake!"

It's Edith in the doorway.

"Yeah?"

"Jake . . . I know you won't believe this, but there's a phone call for you. . . . It's your mother, Becky."

"I don't believe it."

I turn back to the car and Edith shouts, "Jake! I'm not kidding. It's your mother. There's a telephone on the kitchen wall and your mother's waiting to speak to you. It's long-distance, Jacob."

"But. . . . But how did she get the number?"

"That's what *I* asked. All she would say was, 'Don't think it was easy, young lady. Don't think it was easy.' She's kind of excited, Jacob. You'd better speak to her."

"I won't."

"But Jacob . . ."

"I won't speak to her. She can't follow me around like this."

"But . . ."

"Edith, I *won't* speak to her! There'll be no Jewish mothers in this novel!"

"Jake, be serious."

"I *am* serious. I will *not* answer that phone. The Jewish novel is dead. She was born too late."

"Jake . . . she's waiting."

"I'm not kidding."

"But I have to tell her *something.*"

"Tell her to call Philip Roth. Tell her this is *my* novel and she can call all day, she's not getting into it."

Edith is exasperated. She turns toward the door.

"And Edith, tell her not to get any ideas about having your mother call, either."

"But her mother isn't even Jewish," Warren says.

"Makes no difference. The psychological novel's dead too."

Edith tries once more. "Jacob, be serious," she calls from the doorway.

"It's passé," I shout up to her. "The last great writer of psychological fiction died thirty years ago."

I've got her now. She's still angry but her curiosity is getting the better of her rage. She stands there, hands on her hips, and then she says, wearily, "O.K. . . . . I'll bite. Who are you talking about?"

"Sigmund Freud."

"I give up," she groans and reenters the house, slamming the door behind her.

"Come on, Warren, let's get this show on the road," I say, handing him some clothes and picking up a carton of books. To carry up the path. Into our new home.

BULLETIN

'Pushy' Woman Routs Thief
HOLLYWOOD (AP) — Miss Lucy Denarigny, alone in her dry-cleaning shop here one day, looked up to see a gunman, who demanded money. "I don't have any," she replied as she walked toward the door. The man went, too. She shoved him out the door. He ran to an automobile, leaped in and drove off.

CAMERA TWO

While Edith deflected my mother, Warren and I brought in most of what little stuff we had packed into the Volks. The army had sent an enormous moving van to our apartment in Philadelphia and most of our belongings were in the truck. It was scheduled to arrive the following day. I had never realized how little we owned until I'd seen our things inside that cavernous van. They seemed pitifully small there. Like the furnishings of a doll's house.

Finally, Edith got off the phone. She said that my mother was almost maddened by my refusal to talk to her. That she was terribly upset about my entering the army. But I wasn't really interested. Because my mother had been even more upset when I talked of going to Canada or to jail. "Just do your duty," she told me, "and in a few years it'll seem like a dream that never happened."

But what was shattering my mind was the image of that headless child, lying on the couch on the other side of our common wall. Warren said, "What else can you expect? When you enter a crazy house, you've got to learn to expect that the people will act crazy," but even he couldn't hide the fact that he had been disquieted.

Edith revealed her discomposure in spurts of nervous bitchiness. At one point, when I was speaking of the dead child, she turned on me, saying, "A lot you did to stop it." Then she began to speak of me to Warren, as if I weren't in the room. "He complains about events but he does nothing to deal with them. No, all he ever does when something overwhelms him is rap about the modern novel or about his writing. Honestly, ever since he left accounting school, whenever he's had to confront something he can't understand or control, he's turned to his writing . . . or at least to the *subject* of writing, since besides his damn diary I can't see that he's done any writing of his own to speak of."

I didn't answer her because she began to weep and I knew that she was sorry she had sounded off. And perhaps, too, because I recognized the truth of what she had said. Anyway, we were interrupted by the clacking of what sounded like a giant egg-beater. We ran to the door. A helicopter was hovering over our front lawn. In a net, it lowered down two men dressed in white, with red crosses on their sleeves. They followed the Indian woman into the house and returned with the little girl's body, which they plopped into the cradle of the net that hung from the helicopter on a coil—like an umbilical cord.

Then the dead girl's mother ran out, screaming, and she clutched the net and would not release it. The Indian woman recognized the problem, fetched the girl's missing head from the couch, and gently laid it into the net with the body.

At this point the two aidmen left to examine the corpse of the wrecked house, but the mother became agitated again and, before the Indian woman could stop her, she leaped into the net along with her daughter's trunk and head. The men in the hovering chopper didn't know what they could do, so they hoisted all three of them up.

And because of the noise of the helicopter's engine we couldn't hear the sounds of the mother's wails as she rose into the sky in the net. But we could see her pasty face. And her tear-puffed eyes. And her distorted, wide-open mouth.

And it was like watching the frightful mime of an old silent horror movie. It really was.

When we closed the door again, only Edith spoke. She said, "Well, this has been quite a morning, I must say."

BULLETIN

A Socio-Economist Finds U.S. Culture Heading to Its Doom

EVANSTON, Ill. (Religious New Service) — American culture very likely cannot change in time to prevent its utter destruction, a noted socio-economist told a seminar of 100 religion reporters and editors.

Dr. Robert Theobald, addressing a Conference on Issues in Religious Journalism held at Northwestern University, said that this is an almost certain prospect because "much of our unconscious analysis is still based on a belief that conditions will remain stable."

He warned, however, that American culture had become irrelevant to its environment, a condition which, he said, historian Arnold Toynbee had termed as a cause for "inevitable collapse."

CAMERA ONE

Morning. My first day. Up with the alarm at six fifteen. Edith gets up too. I dress in a suit and tie and while I'm combing my hair in the bathroom I can hear the clatter and bustle of activity coming from the kitchen. Warren's in there with her.

Yesterday afternoon we drove to town so that they could buy some food to bring back to the house. I went into a book and greeting card store where I bought an army officer's guidebook which I read last night. I also stopped at the barber shop where I was given the shortest haircut I've had since I was a kid. And my head feels naked now. Vulnerable.

"Happy Birthday to you . . . ," they sing as I enter the dining room. Warren is standing on the far side of the army table which was in the house when we arrived. He's holding a brightly colored, iced cake. On a platter.

"Happy Birthday to you. . . ."

I walk up to the table and count the candles.

"Happy Birthday, dear Jacob. . . ."

There are thirteen.

"Happy Birthday to you."

"What's this?"

"What do you think?" Warren says.

"It's not my birthday, that's for sure."

"It's for your *bar mitzvah,*" Edith volunteers.

"Your *second bar mitzvah,*" Warren quickly adds. "The secular one."

"Today you are a man," Edith says.

"Yeah, today you join this man's army," Warren says, giggling along with Edith in shared delight. "Make a wish and blow, Jake."

I hesitate for a second. Then I lean over the table and blow out the candles in a single forced breath, after having made a wish. The right kind of wish. Necessarily secret because of its being too broad to be born into articulation.

Edith removes the stilled candles and we eat the cake for breakfast along with instant coffee. Except for Warren, who drinks his favorite tea instead. Formosa oolong. He's brought a little package of it along with him from Philadelphia.

Like all birthday parties, this one eventually comes to an end. None to soon. And I walk out into the morning. Into the dawn of my adult life. And there isn't a cloud in the sky.

BULLETIN

Impatient Man Sends Blank Check for Taxes

BOISE, Idaho, Nov. 8 (UPI) —Ray Sander got so frustrated figuring up his taxes that he sent the state a blank check.

"That's all there was," said Secretary of State Pete Cenarrusa. "Just the check. Nothing else. There was no letter of explanation—nothing." Mr. Cenarrusa called Mr. Sander at the restaurant and tavern he operates in Culdesac and asked him what was going on.

"It's just for everything," Mr. Sander said. "It's for everything I owe the state. I just haven't got time to do all this bookkeeping."

CAMERA TWO

As I started up the car I was surprised to find that my mind was preoccupied with a single question: How long would it be until I saw Cal again? Little Jo had said that she was an officer in the WACs. Perhaps I would meet her at the hospital. The possibility of seeing her again made me impatient for my first day in the army to begin.

Ellis Hospital was not far from our quarters. I drove there, guided by a map which the sergeant had left us. When I reached my destination, however, the sign in front of the building read: "Ellis Service Station."

It was the right name, Ellis, and pictured beneath it, I recognized the staff with wings on top and the snakes entwined around it, as the medical caduceus. But I was puzzled, for it should have been a hospital.

The building itself was an old, single-storied structure, built on stilts. Its immense length made up for its lack of height. It extended parallel to the road for a distance of about three football fields.

I entered the building via the main entrance and turned into the first office on the left. I must have startled the little WAC who was tending the desk, for she quickly straightened up in her chair and tried to hide a paperback book by covering it with her left arm.

Then she looked up. She was one of the few American Negroes who are absolutely black. Her skin was as smooth as ivory. And her teeth white and perfect when she smiled. Which she did when she saw me. She relaxed, and sat back in her chair, revealing the book she had been reading. It was Flaubert's *Sentimental Education*, in translation. She couldn't have been more than eighteen years old.

"I'm Lieutenant Klinger."

"Oh, Jacob Klinger. We've been expecting you. One second, please," she said, as she rose from her seat. "The colonel will want to speak to you."

She picked up her book, smiled again as she placed it in the top drawer of her desk, and walked into the adjoining office. Through a glass window in the wall, I could see her speaking to a man in a business suit with two silver bars on each shoulder. He rose from his chair, squinted a peek at me through the window, nodded knowingly, and entered the office beyond his, the third in the line.

Through the glass of two windows I watched him confer with a corpulent, silver-haired man who wore a silver leaf insignia mounted on each of his shoulders. He too walked up to the window in the wall, looked me over, and went into the office beyond.

In a minute, he bounced out of the fourth office and into the captain, who bounced out of the third office and into the WAC, who bounced out of the second office and into the cue ball.

"You can go in to see the colonel now, lieutenant. He's waiting for you."

"Just step this way, lieutenant," she said, as she walked over to a strange looking object in the corner of her office. I had never seen anything like it before. It had four wheels and it resembled the kind of movable beds (or tables, perhaps) which the hospitals use to wheel patients to and from surgery. Only it wasn't flat on top, but rather boxlike. As if a kind of telephone booth had been mounted on the table top of the cart. Or a confessional.

"Just lie down here, lieutenant, and I'll wheel you in."

"What?"

She shrugged her shoulders and gave me an I-only-work-here look. Then she grasped the two bicyclelike handlebars at the rear of the cart and tipped it forward until it reached about a forty-five degree angle and the foot of the box rested on the floor. She was able to do this because the forward two wheels of the cart had been set about halfway back under its base, rather than at the front.

I walked around to the foot of the cart to lower myself in, but before I did I noticed a large sign which had been affixed to the outside of the foot of the box. On it there was neatly painted a single word. IN.

When I lowered my body into the box and crossed my arms on my chest I couldn't help but feel that I had lain down in my own coffin. And that it had always been waiting there just for me. At that precise point in space. And time.

But when the WAC leveled me out and wheeled me by the interested faces of the two officers in the intermediate offices, I felt more like I was in a baby carriage.

There was no window in the wall of the colonel's office. There were, however, two doorways, separated by a vertical wooden pillar, between his office and that of the heavy, light colonel, which preceded it in the row. Each had a small sign above it. IN and OUT. I was pushed under the sign marked IN.

And then dumped in the fourth office. It was larger than the others and plushly furnished with rugs and plastic covered arm-chairs. It seemed to be the last office in the line, for in the far wall there was only a single small door, which appeared to lead to a closet or to a private bathroom, perhaps. A large mirror filled the top half of the door. Next to it stood a tall bookcase filled with army manuals.

Behind a huge desk (which was proportionately bigger than the lieutenant colonel's in about the same ratio as the lieutenant colo-nel's was bigger than the captain's) sat a man in medical whites with an eagle on each shoulder. The colonel.

"Hello, lieutenant." He reached over the desk, stretching to grip my hand, "Glad to see you made it. We've been expecting you. My name is Dr. Creetner. Have a seat." He pointed to a steel-gray-colored chair which faced his desk.

"I wear two hats around here, lieutenant," he said, proudly. "I'm chief of old Ellis here," he patted the top of his desk as if it were the neck of his faithful horse, Trigger, "and I'm post surgeon." As he said this, he pointed across the room to a hat rack, on which there hung two hats. But they both looked the same to me.

And on the wall, above the hat rack, there hung a flag. It pictured the medical caduceus above the motto, "Conserve the Fighting Strength."

"Yes," the doctor said, leaning back in his chair, "if the balloon goes up, I'm in charge of all medicine in New England."

He then proceeded to ask a few perfunctory questions—when did we arrive and how was our trip. He was about sixty years old, with a square-chinned face and short light hair, which was quite thin and neatly parted. His handshake had been unduly vigorous and there was a kind of withered toughness about him. One could imagine him in the role of a high school football coach. Or better yet, as a former high school coach, who, after seven consecutive losing seasons, had been kicked upstairs to head the school hygiene program.

"I'm sure you'll fit right in here, lieutenant. . . ."

On the wall to my left there was a series of large, framed photographs, one above the other. On the bottom, I recognized Doctor Creetner. Above him another doctor in white, with a star on each shoulder. Next, there was a general, in military uniform, with three stars on each shoulder. Then a general sporting four stars and, above him, an oriental in a business suit. The commander in chief. President Sun.

"That's the chain of command, lieutenant," the colonel said, with pride. "Oh, lieutenant, I meant to ask you, did you ever play any sports?"

"Well, I did quarterback a . . ."

"Good, good. You'll be our new recreation officer. . . . And, lieutenant, do you have any questions?"

"Well sir, I do think I have a few. The first is, well, I thought I was to be working in a hospital, but . . ."

"Oh, yes. . . . Well, lieutenant, hospital is just one of our functions in this new modern army. You see, things change fast nowadays, and you've got to keep a step ahead of the tide of progress or it'll wash over you is my motto. Yes indeed, we've come a long ways since the day of the foot soldier, lieutenant. Yes indeed, we certainly have. . . . You see, son, we perform a service function in this new army. That's why, a few years ago, when they closed down old Ellis Island—you remember that, lieutenant?—I volunteered to fill in the breach."

He selected one pipe from the dozen or so standing in his pipe rack and lit it with a series of quick sucks.

"What do you thing happened to immigration after they closed Ellis Island, lieutenant?"

"I hadn't really thought about it, sir. . . . I guess I thought most immigration ended back in the twenties. . . ."

"Yes, yes," the colonel said, impatiently, "that's what most people think. But when Uncle Sam slammed the door it bounced back a ways, and we've still got thousands of them slipping in every year. Critical skills, relatives, Mexicans, P.R.'s. And there's where we fit in, lieutenant. Most people didn't appreciate the job that was still left to be done. *Somebody* had to process all those greasers. So, since somebody had to do it, and since service is our function, lieutenant, I volunteered.

"Our name was already Ellis Hospital, so it was just a matter of changing "Hospital" to "Service Station." I suggested it to the general, up at Post Headquarters one day. He ate up the idea, and quicker than you could say Jackie Robinson, we were in business."

He punctuated his statement with a slap on the top of his desk.

"So you process immigrants here now, sir?"

"And not just some immigrants, son. *Every* immigrant to Uncle Sam's sunny shores has to stop right here at Dr. Creetner's lighthouse. And we perform other service functions here at Ellis, too, but no time for that now . . . got too much work to do. . . . Paperwork piles up on you nowadays." He reached over to an enormous pile of papers stacked on the floor against the side of his desk, removed the top sheet, and began to read it, moving his lips as his eyes followed his finger across each line.

"Doctor, can I ask just two more quick questions?"

"Shoot," he said, looking up from his papers.

"Well, in the first place, what about my uniform? I was wondering about the uniform requirements here at Ellis."

He straightened up in his seat and smiled. "Oh, yes, uniforms. Well, lieutenant, I think I have some good news for you. We don't wear uniforms anymore here at Ellis, son. This is a new army now. Uniforms are becoming a thing of the past. The public just doesn't keep up with what the army's doing these days. This isn't World War II, you know."

He relighted his pipe.

"No, lieutenant, you'll find no uniforms around here. We wear dark blue three-button suits, light blue shirts, dark blue ties in the style of the season, dark blue sox, and black shoes. . . . You had one more question?"

"Yes, sir. My main job. Will it be in accounting?"

"Didn't I tell you, lieutenant? You're our new troop commander."

Astonished, I was about to say, "Troop commander?" when a rapid hammering or pounding began to sound on the small door to the colonel's bathroom. The colonel pursed his lips in exasperation, shaking his head from side to side. "What now?" he muttered.

The racket continued, the tempo of the banging increasing steadily.

"Just a minute. . . . Just one cottonpickin minute," he said, as he rose from his chair and went to open the door, still muttering frustrations under his breath.

The open doorway revealed a small, tile-floored bathroom, and in it, to my amazement, behind a tiny desk set between the sink and the toilet, sat a dried-up old woman, still swinging the cane which she had been using to pound against the door.

"Mother, how many times have I told you . . . ," the colonel began, but she interrupted him with a downward crack of her cane against the top of her little desk. Then, without saying a word, she lifted the cane and pointed it toward me.

The colonel followed the line of the shaft with his eye. Got the point. "Oh, yes, lieutenant . . . take a haircut, will you? That kind of thing's O.K. if you play the violin, but in this man's army we like to be able to separate the women from the men."

His mother's prune-wrinkled puss changed into the shape of a tight, little smile.

C A M E R A   O N E

But my eyes are drawn toward the door. Toward the small door which the colonel has pulled open. It has been completely swung open so that it rests against the colonel's bookcase of army manuals. So that I can see its back side.

And through the top of the door, through the glass of which it is composed, I can see the rows of manuals on the bookshelves. I can see right through the top half of the door. And that's how his mother was able to see me. The top half of the colonel's bathroom door is a one-way mirror.

The colonel closes the door on his mother, straightens his tie and white medical jacket while looking at his reflection in the mirror, and returns to his desk, saying abstractedly, "Honestly, it's a wonder I can get any work done here at all, what with all these interruptions every minute."

He sits at the huge desk. "Where was I, lieutenant. . . . Oh, yes, we were about through for today, weren't we."

"Yes."

"*YES!*" he shouts, leaping up so fast he knocks over his chair. "*Yes!* What do you mean, *Yes*, lieutenant. Where do you think you are? . . . Back in school? . . . It's yes, *sir*, lieutenant. Got that? Yes, *sir!*"

"Yes, sir."

"Well don't you forget it. Don't get tough with me because you're educated, lieutenant. You won't get anywhere in this man's army that way, let *me* tell *you*."

His furious face fills with bloody hue. "Don't get high-hat with me. I'm an M.D., lieutenant. I went to school too, you know. Don't ever forget that, lieutenant. Just don't get high-hat with *me*."

He sits back down. But he doesn't remember that his chair has been overturned. So he doesn't stop going down when he reaches desk level, but drops out of sight behind it. He falls right on his ass.

Soon the colonel has gotten back together with his chair and is again seated at his desk, a bit calmer but still flushed. He presses a black button on his desk top and says, "Now go on out of here, lieutenant, and get down to business."

"Yes, sir." I rise and salute. He salutes back, remaining seated. Then the WAC appears with the surgical cart. It seems to be the same one, except for the sign on the front, which has been changed: OUT.

She tilts the cart forward by lifting the back, and I lay my body into the box once again. As she begins to wheel the cart around, the colonel says, "And lieutenant . . ."

She stops. "Yes, sir?" I say, as she raises the handlebars again, so that I can see the colonel.

"You will inspect the enlisted men in their barracks, tomorrow morning. Any questions?"

"Yes, sir. One last one."

"What now. . . ."

"Sir. . . . Where are they?"

"The enlisted men?"

"No, sir. The barracks."

He gives me a look of impatient bewilderment. "Why, right where they've always been, lieutenant," he says. "Right where they've always been."

And as the WAC lowers her end of the cart and begins to wheel me from the room once more, I see him rise from his desk and turn to the mirror on his bathroom door with a look on his face which says, "You see what I have to put up with around here?"

CAMERA TWO

The WAC told me where the enlisted men's barracks were. She also directed me to the hospital barber shop, which was in a room off the hopsital PX. I stopped in the PX, bought two gold bars, and pinned them on, using a mirror on the wall to help to line them up in the right place on each shoulder.

Then I walked over to what I had supposed was the hospital barber shop, but when I entered the only person there was a middle-aged nurse.

"Oh. . . . Excuse me, ma'm. I'm looking for the barber."

"I *am* the barber, lieutenant," she said. "Have a seat. Name's Smith. Delilah Smith. The boys call me Smitty."

"O.K., Smitty," I said. And I had a seat.

BULLETIN

Hair Issue Appeal Planned

HOUSTON, Nov. 8 (AP)—The regents of San Jacinto College say that they will carry to the United States Supreme Court, if necessary, their fight for the right to suspend any male student wearing long hair or a beard. The regents voted Monday night to appeal the ruling by Federal District Judge John V. Singleton Jr., who issued an order temporarily reinstating Carlos Calbillo, 20 years old, o Pasadena, as a student at the college.

CAMERA TWO

When I returned to our quarters, Warren greeted me with a shout: "Hey, Edith! Jake's been scalped."

Edith came into the hallway and joined Warren in staring at my head. I wanted to tell them what had happened but I couldn't really get it together. I was able to circle what I meant but not to approach it. Finally, I gave up. I secluded myself in the bedroom and began to try to write it down. In my diary.

Warren was a help to me in one respect. When I had nervously complained about the inspection I was supposed to make the following day—that I hadn't the slightest notion of what I was expected to do—he told me about a program on TV that evening, called *The Captain.* It was about an officer who was in charge of an infantry company. He suggested that I watch it instead of the football special which was on at the same time. "If it's all the same to you, Jake, I'll give a yell when it comes on." I didn't object.

Warren knew a great deal about all aspects of popular culture. He would usually spend his afternoons smoking and listening to the stereo. Either to the FM or to records. In the evenings he would smoke and watch TV. Except for his trips to the movies, or to visit his friends, he didn't go out very much. He loathed the sun.

In Philadelphia, he had done most of our cooking and housework. He was an excellent cook, but the thing he did best was befriend people. In fact, he was a kind of professional friend. He had nothing but time and he was slow enough in his life's pace to be able to listen to anybody. He thought about the problems of his friends a great deal and was usually able to help them. While he was not always able to provide them with "answers," he did extend to them a sympathy and sincere interest which often proved to be almost as valuable.

It was for Warren's sake that I was so delighted to have run into David on our first day. I knew it wouldn't be easy for Warren to make many friends around the base. His friends ranged from those who would admit their problems to those who cherished them. But he never had much luck with people who were certain they had no problems.

When the show came on the TV, Warren called to me from the living room. I went in and sat down. Edith was watching, too. Knitting.

Before I had a chance to get settled in my chair I saw what was wrong and stood up. "Warren, dammit, this show's about the marines!"

He wasn't at all nonplussed. "What's the difference?"

"What *is* the difference, Jake?" Edith asked.

"It's too complicated to explain."

"Well, why don't you watch for a while, anyway," Edith said. I sat down again and Warren passed me a joint.

"No thanks. If I'm going to watch, I might as well watch."

Edith took a drag. And then, sure enough, the captain went into the barracks and inspected his men.

"You see, Jake," Edith said, "it's easy. Just do what *he* did."

At this, Warren looked even more content than he usually did.

"But this is the *marines!*" I said.

"Who knows the difference?" Edith said. "Just do what he did, Jake. These shows have technical advisors."

"You don't understand, God dammit. I'm not *in* the marines."

Edith stopped moving her needles and knitted her brow. "Jacob, how can you be so stupid? Everyone on this base is watching this show at this very minute. So who's going to know what's *really* right? If you act like the fellow on TV, I'm absolutely certain they'll think you're doing just fine."

"But Edith . . . you don't understand. . . ."

BULLETIN

'Bang!' Bang!' Scares Thief
FREEPORT, Iowa (AP)—When
a holdup man entered the Freeport General Store and demanded money, Mrs. Jack Tellford,
the store owner, pointed a finger at the unarmed robber and
shouted "Bang! Bang!" The man
fled.

CAMERA ONE

A sergeant, about fifty-five years old, gray haired, crew-cut, with clear-rimmed army spectacles resting on a bright bulbous nose, leaps up to attention as I enter my office for the first time. He salutes, with such exaggerated formality that I smile. But he continues to salute, getting stiffer and reddening from the strain. I salute. He begins to breathe.

On his sleeve there are six stripes with a diamond in the center. He is Sergeant O'Mara. My first sergeant. And he is proudly pointing to an empty picture frame on the wall. Above it there are five photographs. The same five I saw in the colonel's office.

"The blank is for you, sir. I got the office all ready for your arrival. We knew of your ETA last week."

"Oh. . . . What about the fellow who was here before me?"

"That was Lieutenant Dunbar, sir. A fine young officer. I broke him in. I've broken in twelve different COs in my time. Both as first sergeant and as acting first sergeant when I was only an SFC."

"Conscientious objectors?"

"Pardon me, sir?"

"COs?"

"Oh," he smiles. "Commanding officers, lieutenant."

"But I thought Colonel Creetner was the commanding officer around here."

"He is, sir. But he's the commanding officer of the whole hospital. You're just the commander of the enlisted men who work in the hospital. You see what I mean, lieutenant."

"Not exactly."

"Well it's really very simple, sir. You see, as CO of the hospital, the colonel has a staff of officers beneath him. This includes people like the chief of surgery, the chief nurse, the personnel officer, the registrar, the hospital supply officer and several others. And as troop commander, you're on the colonel's staff. Do you read me so far, lieutenant?"

"Well, you're coming in a little clearer now."

"I'll give you an example. Say there's a private who's an x-ray technician. Well, during his working hours he's responsible to the radiologist who runs x-ray, and this radiologist is a young doc who's under the chief of surgery. But for all nonmedical matters—for all of his life outside of his nine to five—this private is under your command. I mean for things like training, discipline, pay, and recreation.

"You see what I mean now, sir? You're the private's old man, and the colonel is your old man."

"I think I'm beginning to get the picture, sarge."

"I knew the lieutenant would. It's just a matter of time."

"But what about the previous old man of this outfit? That Lieutenant Dunbar. Was he discharged?"

"Well, that's the pity of it, sir. He was in for a career, regular army and all, and a fine officer he would have made too, I can tell you that, but it was during the attack on the airfield. . . ."

"*What* attack on *what* airfield, sergeant?"

"I'm sorry, sir. I forgot. You couldn't have known of it."

He sits down at one of the twin desks. They face each other, their fronts touching, the two rectangular, metal tops forming a square. "Would the lieutenant like a seat?" he says, pointing to the chair facing him. "That's your desk, sir."

As I sit down, he continues: "It was about a month ago, lieutenant. The colonel, Colonel Creetner. . . . Did you meet him sir?"

I nod yes.

"Well, the colonel called in a mortar barrage and we took some heavy losses that night."

"He called in a mortar barrage on our own airfield?"

"Yes, sir. The colonel's an old soldier, sir. That's the toughest decision an officer ever has to make. To call in a barrage on his own position in order to save it. But like I said, sir, the old man's been in the army a long time. . . ."

"But he's the *hospital* commander!"

"Oh, he's a lot more than that, lieutenant. He's the post surgeon, too."

I must look puzzled, for the sergeant adds, "And he and the chief of staff are like this," holding up his index and middle fingers, entwined like the snakes on the caduceus.

With a false, saliva-swallowed composure, I ask, "But what about Lieutenant Dunbar?"

"Oh yes, the lieutenant. Well he was O.D. that night, sir, and like the number-one old man he was, he wanted to be with his boys when the heat was on. So he jumped into one of the ambulances the colonel dispatched. . . ."

"The *colonel* dispatched the ambulances?"

"Yes, sir," the sergeant says, surprised. "The old man's a doctor. Didn't you know that, sir?"

"Yes, I did. . . ."

"Well, sir, if I may say so, don't let anyone tell you the colonel neglects his medical duties because he's taken on some others. No, sir, I was with him in France. The colonel and I are like that" (entwined fingers).

"The colonel must be a pretty busy man."

"The finest, sir. The finest. He's an inspiration to us all. I was with him in France back in '45. He was only a captain then. Working in an aid station. And I was just a corporal. . . . Ah, sir, those were the days."

He straightens up in his chair. "I had a buddy then, sir. Jewish fellow, like yourself. Corporal Ginsberg. Greatest guy you ever want to meet. I like the Jewish people, lieutenant. The Jews and the Irish. You tell me now, sir, what two peoples have added so much to the world? . . . For such small nations, I mean."

"But to get back, Sergeant O'Mara. . . ."

"Oh, yes, sir. Well, Ginsberg and I are outside of Paris. In the suburbs, you see. And we're looking for a place to use as a battalion aid station, back behind the troops advancing into the city. And Ginsberg was a bitch on wheels—oh, he could bitch, that Ginsberg. About all the tail we were missing in the city and how we always miss out on the real action, when, just then, we come upon this big fancy mansion which Ginsberg says looks like as good a spot as any for an aid station since there wasn't a soul in sight, and we both figured there'd be more fucking than fighting once our boys got into the city, anyhow.

"Well Ginsberg, he walks up the lawn to the house, goes over to the garage, and he calls down to me, 'Jack! Jack, look here! What's this now. *What . . . is . . . this!*' And he throws open the door of the garage and there, staring us right in the face, is a silver-gray Rolls-Royce.

"Well, lieutenant, all the way to Paris we'd been liberating stuff, you know. Bottles of wine, clocks, cameras—whatever the hell we could get our hands on and carry away. Taking back what we could of the Frog's World War I debt to Uncle Sam, don't you know."

He winks at me. "But lieutenant, I never, I never in a million years will forget when Ginsberg, he looks over at me, and he says, 'O'Mara. . . . O'Mara, old man, we are going to liberate a Rolls-Royce and drive it to Paris.'

"Well Ginsberg was wild, lieutenant, but he wasn't any dope. You'll go a long way before you'll find a Jew who's a dope—"

"But what about Lieutenant Dunbar going to the airfield?"

"Holy Mother of God, where was I? . . . Oh, yes, the lieutenant went up to the field just when the confusion began. You see, they wanted to get the B-52s off the ground. . . ."

"So they wouldn't be hit by the mortars?"

"Well, partly, sir, but it was mainly because the B.C. were rumored to still be in the area and they wanted to get the big babies into the air to unload on them. You see what I mean?"

And I *was* beginning to see. "To bomb the airfield. Right, sergeant?"

"Right, sir," he lights up. "You're catching on fast."

"And the lieutenant was killed by a bomb from a B-52?"

"I'm afraid not, sir. That's were the tragedy comes in. You see, at night, with mortar rounds falling and everyone scattering here and there and the big B-52s taxiing around and taking off one after the other, you can't hardly see the little planes at all. The single-engine jobs they use for spotters. So, with all the lights and confusion, the lieutenant, he just leaped out of his ambulance and right into the propeller of a small scout plane."

He shakes his head sadly, and says, "One thing sure, sir. The lieutenant, he didn't feel no pain. That blade just tore him apart. . . . It took them quite awhile just to get him together. And funny thing, the ambulance he drove in out to the field, well he came back in the same ambulance. Only he wasn't up front with the driver this time . . . no, sir. . . ."

"That was pretty bad."

"Yeah . . . and that's not the end. That scout plane must've been jinxed or something that night, because later, as he made a run real low over the field, one of the big five hundred pounders from a 52 up at forty thousand feet that he was spotting for, well one of these big babies hit this little observation plane and took it down with it, right into the main runway of the field. Well sir, that made a crater that it took engineers awhile to fill, I'll tell you that. For three days all B-52 missions had to be flown out of Logan Airport in Boston."

He sighs and begins to rise. "Well, we'd better go, sir. They'll be waiting for us to inspect the barracks."

As I join him at the office doorway, he adds, "The poor old man. . . . Such a young fellow and planning to get married this summer, to a wonderful girl, too. The daughter of an admiral. He introduced me to her, once. Oh, he wasn't one to pull rank, not Lieutenant Dunbar, sir."

"That's a pity," I say, as we leave the office.

"Yes it is, lieutenant," he answers, in a lumpy voice that resounds along the narrow corridor which runs to the barracks. "But like they say, when a propeller has your number on it. . . ."

CAMERA TWO

I hated to admit it to myself, but the inspection went as well as Edith and Warren had said it would. When we arrived at the first barracks (which was located in a converted hospital ward) a buck sergeant, with a meaty sack-face and bag eyes and an enormous pot belly, snapped to and saluted and shouted into my face while staring over my shoulder, "Barr-hacks one, ready for inspect-shun, *sir!*"

The only thing worse than bad gin is bad gin that's spent the night in someone's mouth. I was almost knocked over by the stench of the sergeant's breath. Only Dante could have walked through this man's mouth and lived to write about it.

But what was even more disconcerting was hearing Sergeant O'Mara introduce me to Buck Sergeant Mooney as, "The new old man." Mooney, the forty-year-old buck sergeant and human miasma pit, smiled a goofy smile, and by God, when you couldn't smell him, his face had a certain charm. It was the large spaces between his few remaining teeth. And his defeat.

Mooney had not made it in the army. There was at least that much to say for him.

So I went on with the inspection, picking out simple things that could be wrong, whether they really were or not. Things you couldn't argue with. Like dirty equipment, for example. Who can say whether a footlocker is dirty or not. Or whether a man's belt buckle is adequately shined.

And I stole a few tricks right from the captain on TV. I noticed the two sergeants smiling at each other approvingly whenever I revealed one of these TV specials.

Sometime later, at the log cabin, I told David about this, and about Edith's theory that things became real by virtue of their appearing on TV. He wasn't surprised. "It's like sports," he said. "You can argue with an umpire or a referee on the rules, but not on the facts. That's where he's got you by the balls. There's no appeal on the facts."

"As long as I play it safe on the rules?" I suggested.

"Well, Jake, I don't guess I went far enough," he said, scratching his head. "In the army, I don't guess there's any appeal on the rules either."

BULLETIN

BANK ROBBERY GIVES CHILEAN POLICE FITS

SANTIAGO, Chile (UPI)—Their search for two bank robbers who stole $25,000 has given the Santiago Detective Division nothing but trouble.

Three detectives trapped the bandits in a third-rate hotel, but the fast-drawing gunmen got the drop on the police and escaped. The detective in charge was summarily dismissed.

A short time later, three other detectives shot a man they believed to be a suspect in the bank robbery. The man turned out to be Hernan Cortez Calderon, a Government Agriculture Department official. Mr. Cortez Calderon said he had fled in the belief that the three unshaven detectives were muggers. He sued the police.

Still later, at Concepcion, Chile, detectives boarded an airliner and dragged off a passenger as a suspect in the robbery. The "suspect" turned out to be Judge Gabriel Fernandez of Aruaco Province.

CAMERA THREE

So that's the way it went for a few days. I would get to work early in the morning and return late in the evening, leaving me just enough time for a few drinks and a record or two before I went to sleep. To prepare me for the next day.

And I began to appreciate the enormous supply of energy that is necessary for being a baby. For a baby is a mad empiricist adrift in a new world. A scientist without a science. Because the aim of science is to supercede empiricism by building bridges of theory over the craggy facts. But a baby is right down in there. All the time. In the gully of reality. Exploring it a foot at a time. And that's the way I was. And that's why I was so weary, I guess.

Because I couldn't find the logic behind it all. The general formula that could be applied to each specific case as it arose. Instead, I could only learn by memorizing each particular occurrence. And my knowledge would only be applicable when one of my experiences happened to be a repeat of another I had previously memorized.

Of course there were army regulations. But that's what I'm talking about. They seemed a random collection of rules, any one of which could have been reversed without having any effect on the system as a whole. But I suspected that maybe it was me. Maybe it was my own shortsightedness which blinded me to the governing principle or natural basis of the world in which I lived. I was not certain about where the fault lay.

So I went to the hospital and exhausted myself doing the step-by-step best I could, while Sergeant O'Mara told me of his adventures in World War II and did *his* best to "break me in." And, surprisingly enough, the other officers were quite willing to teach me what they knew. Like Americans in a foreign country, they were most generous in their efforts to help one of their own.

Any hopes I had for meeting the fascinating woman who had rescued me were disappointed. Though I was made aware of her presence on the base by a poster which I saw on several bulletin boards. And on the walls of the company barracks as well.

It advertised classes in self-defense. But it was dominated by a large photograph of Cal and a soldier who was outfitted in complete battle dress. She was facing the camera and smiling her great, wicked smile as she threw the soldier to the ground with a judo hip toss. And all she was wearing was that tiny black bikini.

When I went to the post photographer to get my picture taken for the chain of command photos on my office wall, I spotted Cal in another large picture which had been taped to the studio wall. It was a float in a parade carrying a big sign: "Join the WACS and See the World." Above the sign was a large globe with the continents and oceans painted on its surface. And posed on a small flat area, up near the North Pole, stood my statuesque rescuer, her body covered only by a little two-piece suit made of leaves. In her right hand she held aloft liberty's torch. And in her eyes, a glint of hidden knowledge.

I must have stared at the photo, for the sergeant who ran the studio said to me, "Man, that big captain is *too* much . . . if you don't mind my saying so, sir."

BULLETIN

Heater Rings Telephone
WOODBRIDGE, England (Canadian Press)—A policeman reported that every time he switched on the immersion heater in a water tank in his new house in this Suffolk community it made a neighbor's telephone ring.

CAMERA TWO

The sun set late in July. Even in Massachusetts. One evening I was able to leave the office after only an hour of overtime—Warren and Edith were not home when I arrived.

So I sat in the backyard by myself, sipping on a can of Narragansett beer. On the grass, in my dungarees, watching the sun set itself down on its soft bed of night. Listening to the stereo. I had turned the speakers around so they sent their sounds out of the windows. My back was toward the house. I faced west.

"Mind if I join you?"

It was our neighbor, the psychologist who had carried the child out of the wreckage. The one with the Indian wife.

"I'm Len Rainey. My wife Jeannie's in town so I'm alone right now."

He was carrying a can of beer.

"Sure, have a seat. It's your lawn. We just got here."

"It isn't mine, it was here when I came, too. But I'll sit down just the same." Sitting. "That Bach?"

"Yes. The Third Brandenberg Concerto."

"I like Bach. I like Dylan first. And rock, and jazz. Though my wife's the real jazz fan. But I really dig Bach."

"So do I. I dig rock and the blues, but Bach has something that I really need at times. I'm not sure what it is, but today is sure one of those times."

"You're learning about the base," he said. "I can see why you need music."

"Like Jim Morrison says, 'Music is your special friend . . . til the end.'"

"Well don't worry about it too much. You'll get used to it. They all do."

He looked into my face with a fixed glare.

"I don't know," I said. "It's pretty weird. I feel like a German entering the Auschwitz Museum—the one German who really didn't know."

We watched the sky for a while, listening to the music. Then I spoke: "Maybe Bach provides the solidity I need. A retreat from confusion and chaos into some kind of order. Like putting a steel helmet on your head when the world begins to fall on top of you."

Len didn't say anything, so I continued: "I mean Bach had a real faith in order. You can hear it in his music. God kept taking away his children and he kept answering with music that was divine. Each grave must have seemed like a hole in the universe that Bach felt he had to fill with the substance—with the structured solidity —of his music. And he *would* fill it. Only to have another kid die."

"It must have seemed like he was living in a bad dream."

"And Shakespeare had it, too, that faith. I mean when I go to a play by Shakespeare it's like when my mother goes to a wedding. As soon as I get seated I begin to cry. And I don't think it's the fate of any of his characters that causes it so much as the staggering recognition of his belief in underlying order, in structure. Imagine, that a guy like Shakespeare, such a really great guy who saw so much, could still write about the good prince who comes out at the end of Romeo and Juliet and tells everybody where it's at."

Len didn't reply. "I don't mean to bombard you," I added, "but sometimes I feel that I can only find what I'm thinking by trying to say it."

"Oh, that's O.K. I'm used to it."

"You mean this is your job?"

"No. Just that I *am* used to it by now. I didn't mean that disparagingly. Although it *is* my job. A lost of people have their expectations raped when they first arrive here. But they get used to it, all right. The house they carry inside their heads gets shattered at first. But it's only a matter of time until they rebuild it in tune with the prevailing mode of architecture here."

"What style is that? American army modern?"

For the first time, he smiled.

"Are you a psychiatrist?" I asked.

"I'm not an M.D.," he said as he stood up. "I'm a psychologist. A Ph.D."

"Aren't they pretty much the same? Except that only an M.D. can prescribe medicines?"

"Pretty much. But I've got some medicines of my own."

He turned and began to walk toward his house. "You ready for another beer?" he called back over his shoulder.

"Sure."

He brought out two cans of cold Schlitz. "I didn't mean to turn you off, before," he said. "Actually, I dig Shakespeare, myself. Especially when I'm feeling down. That whole age fascinates me. As I see it, what they had, and what we lack, is momentum."

He sat back down on the grass and continued: "Do you know how momentum is defined?"

"Mass times velocity?"

"Right. And Bach had it. He was big and he kept moving. Like a big fullback, who can move, hitting a stationary tackler on the goal line. Bach was headed for that end zone, baby, and if you got in his way that was your tough luck. And if you jumped on his back he was prepared to carry you along." He sipped at his beer. "I think that's what we sense about him, and what we lack—his momentum."

"I see what you mean. . . ."

"Sure. Because all we have is inertia. The whole mad world is moving while we sit on our fat asses and watch it roll over us. And the bigger a person is, the more inertia he's going to have to overcome before he can get moving again. Even a single death can stop a man who isn't moving."

"Sometimes a single death can really prove insurmountable. When the Spanish killed the king of the Incas, they killed an entire empire. Sometimes a death can stop history."

"And sometimes it can *start* it!" he flared.

We sat and listened to the music for a while. Then I moved the conversation back to Bach. "I see what you mean about momentum. Each of Bach's lines seems to imply the next. He's willing to bet on the chance that he'll be able to keep moving ahead."

"Right. Like a fullback. If he's not already taking the next step in his head they'll nail him before he gets to it. But Bach's reckless. He *flies* ahead. He's not afraid to commit himself to movement because he knows the alternative is death anyway."

"Hey, I can get behind that." I set my beer on the grass. "And Shakespeare does the same thing."

"Right. In the end Hamlet has to act, because his action was implicit from the start. It was present in the momentum of his words. And Shakespeare's reckless too. He's willing to risk everything to make it to the end zone."

"But it's not easy to do that today, Len. Sometimes it's hard to even believe in an end zone any more."

"We'll see it, when the time comes. But we've got to get moving first. We've got to borrow some of that momentum. It's like facing a football team with a huge front line. We've got to get outside. We can't confront them directly. We've got to go around. And we won't be able to see the goal posts until we've turned the corner. We won't be able to see the end zone until we're already in the clear."

He slacked back onto the lawn and after taking a quick sip at his beer he added hurriedly, "But let's drink up and enjoy the sunset."

He didn't say anything else. And neither did I. For I got the feeling that he had said more than he'd intended to.

BULLETIN

Nude Strolls on 5th Ave.

A 24-year-old woman walked naked for about five blocks on Fifth Avenue yesterday, then entered St. Patrick's Cathedral at 50th Street. She was removed from the cathedral at 1:30 P.M. by policemen, taken to the East 51st Street station house and then sent to Polyclinic Hospital for psychiatric examination. The police said she had a history of mental illness.

CAMERA TWO

About a minute after the record had ended and the turntable turned itself off, the quiet was interrupted by a cry.

"Dr. Rainey! Dr. Rainey, come quickly!"

Running and stumbling acorss the grass, from the next house, came a young, big-bottomed woman wearing purple slacks which seemed to have been designed to exaggerate her worst feature— her dumpy hips. Her hair was studded with curlers and she looked like a hysterical radar transmitter running toward us.

"Oh, Jesus, what now!" Len said, as he slowly lifted himself up off the lawn. "It doesn't pay to help anybody around here. If you slip once you're committed. You're defined as a fucking 'helper.' "

"Dr. Rainey," she said, breathlessly, "down at the enlisted men's quarters. They just called me. They couldn't get you. It's all crazy. Can you please go?"

"O.K. Calm down," Len said. Then to me: "Hey, I forgot. Jeannie's got the car. Can you give me a lift over?"

"Sure," I said, to his back, for he was already on his way to my car, followed by the puffing Samaritan.

"It's right at the corner of MacArthur Road and Freedom Drive, doctor. A woman had a nervous breakdown and locked herself and her son in the house for three weeks. They were discovered by a team of counterinfiltration personnel who were making investigations of suspicious circumstances on the base."

We reached the driveway. "You just go on back into your house, Donna," Len said. "I'll go down there with . . ."

"Jake," I said. "Jake Klinger."

"I'll go down there with Jake," he said, in a confident tone which seemed to calm her.

CAMERA ONE

We pull up to the house and walk in through the open door. Inside, it's incredible. Except for the fact that the walls are in place one might think the place had been bombed. Dirty laundry, trash, garbage, old food scattered all over the place. Dead furniture fractured and strewn like the useless hulks in an automobile graveyard. And the smell. Shit. Shit on walls. Shit on the floor. On the furniture and on the trash. And urine. In bowls and stained into the rug. And rotting food.

We wade through it into the living room, where, in the middle of a group of clucking hens who must be the neighbors, he sits, with legs crossed, staring rigidly into space, like a small, frail, freckled Buddha. It's Little Jo.

The bevy of wives are all talking at the same time. One says, "She's all right, Jo. Your mommy only meant it for the best. She did it for your own good. She only wanted to protect you."

Another says, "The medics took her away to help her. Soon you'll both be fine."

One turns to Len: "His mother told him ghosts and devils were after them, doctor. She locked the doors and pulled the curtains to keep the demons away. She was only trying to help him, doctor."

Len moves forward briskly, forcing a path through the crap and wives. He goes right up to Little Jo. Face to face.

"You know who I am, Jo?"

"Yes, Len," he whispers, in a hoarse, small voice.

"Good. And you know what happened here, Jo?"

"No. . . . I'm not sure. . . ."

"Yes you do, Jo. You really do."

"I . . . I don't. . . ."

"You do. Your mother went beserk. She went nuts—freaked out. You know that, Jo. Sibyl went crazy. But you're O.K. Your mother flipped out is all. Isn't that so?"

Little Jo opens his eyes wider and looks directly at Len. He says nothing but tear beads begin to form at the corners of his eyes.

Len grasps his thin shoulders. "Sure you do, Jo. It was your mother. She freaked out." And then softly, he adds, "Isn't that so, Little Jo?" And he stares into Jo's eyes as if they were windows on an infinite sky. "Aren't you O.K., Jo. Wasn't it your mom who went nuts?"

"That's a harsh word," Jo says, quietly.

"But it's true, isn't it?" Len says. I can see him relax.

"I guess so. . . ."

"Sure. It's no crime to go crazy these days. But you're O.K. And all along you knew those demons and devils were in Sibyl's head, didn't you?"

"I guess so."

"Sure you did. Hey, Jake, help him to find a few of his things. Jo, you'll come home with me till we get you straightened out. O.K.?"

"O.K."

SCREE-E-E-E

"Hit it!" Len yells.

BOOMP!

The concussion throws Little Jo off the table and he screams as a gash opens over his eye. The hens begin to flutter about. "Get down, ladies!" Len shouts, but they run excitedly out of the house and scatter.

SCREE-E-E-E

Len and Little Jo and I are down. Down in the urine, still damp. Down in the human feces and rot.

BOOMP!

And then the choppers come in fast. Over the tops of the trees. We see them through the picture window.

"Jo, quick, get under the table!" Len says. Jo crawls underneath. "Jake, help me!" Len says, and I join him in hurriedly piling garbage around the table and onto Little Jo."

The door opens with a kick and three gas-masked soldiers come running in, bayonets at the ready.

"Who goes here?" their leader shouts.

"Who goes here, *sir!*" Len says, quickly.

"Oh . . . sorry sir . . . ," the leader apologizes sheepishly. "Back off, men. This area is friendly," he says, and they head back out the door.

As they pass through the doorway, the leader turns around and says to Len, "Sorry, sir. Heat of battle. . . ."

"Quite all right, soldier. Carry on," Len says.

But the corporal, instead of leaving, snaps to attention, clicks the heels of his combat boots together, and salutes.

Len returns the salute. "*Carry on,* soldier!"

"Yes, sir." He leaves.

"Stay down, Jo," Len says to the garbage pile under the table.

Little Jo raises his head, knocking off half his cover. "O.K., Len."

Len shakes his head and smiles.

Outside, through the picture window, I watch the three men who left our house join about ten others in front of the house across the street. There is a woman in the doorway, weeping and talking rapidly to the men in the gas masks. She is cradling a baby on one arm and carrying a portable TV with the other as she expostulates with the soldiers.

Then three of them seize her and drag her onto the lawn as two others run into her house, carrying what appear to be five-gallon cans.

It is surprising how beautiful even an ugly house can be, as it burns to the ground on a clear night in early summer, just after the sun has dropped below the horizon. When its rays continue to be bent into view by the atmosphere of the earth, rouging the skin of the world.

CAMERA THREE

So that's the way it went. In spite of the bombings and maimings my days took on an aspect of sameness. If one lives on an island that is hit by a daily hurricane, even that will eventually submit to the harness of routine. Every day, things blow down—you do your best to keep them up. The fact that different things are falling doesn't really change the basic pattern of diurnal disintegration.

I made inspections. I signed papers. I helped to dispatch ambulances to the areas of the base that were being shelled or bombed, and sometimes, when they returned, I even joined the corpsmen in carrying the bloody victims into the hospital—the actual and potential corpses. (It was often difficult to tell them apart when they came out of the old, boxlike ambulances which Sergeant O'Mara called "meat wagons.")

But as the days turned into weeks I found myself becoming more and more depressed. The shelling of the officers' quarters had been stopped. Rumor had it that the colonel's mother had objected to the aftermath of the attacks as "unsightly and not in keeping with dignity befitting the family environment of commissioned officers." Still, Edith grew more irritable every day. Warren said I was exaggerating Edith's pique, but I felt that she thought that I could do something about what was happening around us.

Warren, of course, just kept saying, "Forget it." He continued to cook, to read movie magazines, to listen to the Boston rock station on the earphones, and to smoke a great deal or trip out every once in a while. He seemed, at times, to be the only person on the base who was truly happy. In many ways, he seemed never to have left Philadelphia.

I felt increasingly helpless. And I began to have a recurring dream. I was on a rug that was repeatedly jerked from under me, in different directions. Since I couldn't predict which way the rug would move, I couldn't compensate for its motions.

All I could do was to stay down. On all fours, like a baby. For I was certain that if I tried to stand, I would be jarred off my feet and would fall. So I seemed better off on my knees, although it took all of my energy just to maintain myself even in that position. And I felt the frustration that babies feel. And the impotent rage. And always, I was completely nude. Except for a soft cotton diaper.

BULLETIN

Lack of Complaints Decried

INDIANAPOLIS, (AP)—Robert Beckmann Jr., director of the mayor's complaint department, complained that there were not enough complaints to keep his five-man staff busy.

C A M E R A   T H R E E

When I saw Cal again it was even more exciting than I had imagined it would be. If my memory can be trusted, that is. For by that time, after I had spent so many hours dreaming and fantasizing about the woman who had held me against her and carried me out of the river, I found her sheer physical presence so compelling that I could not easily concentrate on what she was saying.

And her energy—the magnitude of her vitality and decisive force—served to overwhelm me. And confuse me. Like static electricity collecting on the edge of a soft fur, all the sex in the atmosphere around us appeared to be drawn to her being, to glow and crackle on the surface of her body, daring one to release it with a touch. Threatening me with her nearness.

She exuded a hot sensuality which charged my body by robbing blood from my brain. But I was too enthralled by her to care.

CAMERA ONE

Saturday afternoon. My first sergeant and I are at our desks, catching up on some paperwork. And watching a taped rerun of the Super-Bowl on the TV which he has moved into our office from the company day room.

O'Mara leaps to his feet and snaps to attention as she enters, but before he can say a word, she barks, "At ease, sergeant." This deflates him, like a pinprick releasing his sucked-up breath. "You can go now. The lieutenant and I already have known each other."

"Yes, ma'm," the sergeant answers, with a hint of shyness in his voice. He closes the door behind him as he walks out, leaving me alone in the office with her.

"Sit down," she says, with a sudden friendliness in her voice.

"Yes, ma'm."

"And can that 'ma'm' shit, Jake. Unless there are GIs around, that is. . . . You look surprised. Didn't you think I'd know your name?" She smiles. "I've got business with you, Jake. It seems we're going to be partners."

She takes off her WAC cap, pulls a few well-placed bobby pins, and lets the cool, black hair fall down the sides of her face. I can feel its sleek touch along her cheeks.

"But first an introduction is in order. My name is Taylor. Captain California B. Taylor, commanding officer of the WAC detachment here on the base. My girls call me Cali."

"Kali?"

"My men just call me Cal. Not these faggots around here, that is. . . . The colonel and his boys. . . . They usually call me Captain Taylor or ma'm. And that's fine with me. But you just call me Cal. Little Jo's told me about you."

"Oh, that's where you got my name. You've seen Little Jo."

"Not lately. But I spoke to him about you a few days after our embrace in the water. He's a bright kid. I taught him to swim last summer."

"You ever been to their cabin?"

"Their 'quarters' you mean? No, I don't think he ever spoke to me about his folks. . . . What are they like?"

"They're O.K. . . . I . . . I guess I should thank you for pulling me out that day."

"Don't mention it. It gave me a chance to show off. I've worked on my body for a long time and I enjoy showing it off—and using it." She casually removes the jacket of her uniform and sets it across the back of Sergeant O'Mara's chair. Underneath it she is wearing only a white, see-through blouse. No bra. And her breasts are tight skinned and full. They seem to thrust upwards, like plants reaching toward the sun.

A touch of slyness appears in her eyes. "I might even have enjoyed wrestling around with you in the water," she says, as she sits down in the sergeant's chair. "I hope you're not shocked by my frankness."

"Well, I am a bit surprised. . . ."

"There's no need to be, Jake. I'm not interested in shocking you. I'm just a realist. That's all. And my body's the source of my power around here. So I'm not too concerned about hiding it."

"But why are you telling *me* all this?"

She leans back in her chair, putting her long legs on the desk. I can see the lines and hollows of development in her thighs and calves. "Because I'm convinced that our fates are irrevocably linked. When I kidded with the sergeant before—telling him that we *knew* each other—I wasn't completely joking. We met in the presence of Death, Jake, and his white heat fused us together in a way that time can't corrode. I know it. . . . I can feel it. Pacts made in the presence of Death are not alterable. When I held you there in the water, when I grasped your body and I felt your flesh, still warm and alive, something was consummated. Something was consecrated, Jake, and I think it was a bond between us. It was very exciting for me. . . . Sexually exciting."

"Sexually?"

"Yes. Sex is related to death, Jake. You know that."

"You mean in the sense of orgasm as death? That death is a part of sex?"

"I mean that sex is a part of death. That death may be the ultimate fuck."

"Well, that's pretty heavy. . . . But I will admit to you Cal, I've thought a lot about you since that day. I don't remember many of the details of what happened, but I can't deny that I felt that I did know you in some way . . . in a more intimate way than I've ever known anyone before. But I don't know. . . . I've been pretty mixed up about a lot of things lately."

"You don't have to play dumb with me, Jake. You know what's

going on around here as well as I do. I'm not sure how this all came about, but I do know that I can see what's happening. And you do too. We didn't ask for this, but we're on the field and we have to play the game. . . . And Jake, I play for keeps."

"I'm not sure I follow you."

"Come off it. Look, I can get away with anything around here. I'm the only woman officer on the base, and, for that matter, the only real woman in the whole damn army. And they can't figure out how to handle me. From privates up to generals, I've got these babies by the balls because they've never seen a piece of ass in uniform before.

"These creeps only know what they've been trained to know, and they know that I'm the most woman they've ever seen. And I don't hide that fact. I'm everything they've been trained as men to want. And I'll tell you something else," she stands and stretches the muscles in her legs, "I'm also what those babies really want. I mean *really* want, deep down in those dark caves beneath the starched surfaces of their little minds."

She reaches for a shelf high up on the wall and stretches her back by pulling down on it. Like a lithe, wild creature, a healthy animal, with cat grace and allure. The most beautiful being I have ever seen. And tall. Easily over six feet in her heels.

"And that's all you want, Cal? Power?"

"I'm a realist. Power's all there is. And I play to win."

On the TV, the crowd roars as a fullback runs into the center of the line and is thrown back for a loss. Cal reaches over and switches off the set. She sits back down and looks across the desk at me. Fixing me with her eyes. Until I feel that I must speak.

"You talk a lot about 'playing' and 'games.' Do you understand football. . . ."

"Do I! Baby, I screwed an all-American quarterback for two years in college. I don't care if I never see another football again. What a waste!

"Oh, I don't mean he wasn't beautiful," she adds. "Or at least he was potentially beautiful. He could have been such a beautiful man. . . ."

"What happened?"

"He finally chickened out, like everyone else. He could have been governor of the state, but he was afraid to get into a man's game. He couldn't face the facts. So when he got a big offer to play pro ball in Canada, he decided to stay with the boys on the playing field—the big boys who get paid to act out the myths of their emasculated fans. Football fans are even more afraid of the reality outside the stadium than the faggots who play are."

"The reason I brought it up is that I've found myself thinking in metaphors of sports and games lately. And it seems to me, if we look at what's happening to us in football terms, that maybe our problem is that we won't be able to see our goal—to see the end zone—until we're already in the clear. . . . Maybe it's a question of having faith. . . ."

"Oh, Jake," she shakes her head in a mixture of sadness and impatience, "don't you see? The goal posts are down. I told you before that we were on the field and we had to play, but what I didn't get to say was that there is no more end zone, and the first down markers are gone as well. And the field is full of guys who still like to think that they know where they're going and that there's a clearly marked goal they can eventually reach. But in some dark part of themselves, they know this is no longer true. So they begin to thrash out in desperation."

She leans over the desk toward me. "Don't you see, they can't live in a world in which there is no goal line and they're going to hurt anyone who's willing to try."

"That could make it pretty rough on the other team's quarter-back."

"It *is* rough. Everything's rough now. Everything's a forced choice between unsatisfying alternatives. Except one."

"What's that?"

"Except fucking up the bastards who are trying to hurt you."

"What?"

"Don't you see the beauty of it, the justice? They won't let go of the old game, with end zones, and yard lines, and neat referees, and cheerleaders who go down for the home team when they win. So we use that final limit of theirs, that last blindness, to fuck them up and get power for ourselves. Because we can see. We can forget about the end zone. We don't need it. We win on each play. Because each play *is* the game now, Jake."

"What you mean, *we*, white man?" I answer, feebly imitating Tonto in that old gag about him and the Lone Ranger finding themselves surrounded by Indians.

"I'm not kidding, Jake. Your fate is tied to mine, now. I know it is."

"Well, *how* do we win? Give me an example."

"O.K. Take this afternoon. I report to the colonel regarding the WAC detachment, see."

"And to his mother."

"Ah, you know! That's *it*, Jake."

"Well . . ."

"Well, I won't go into the whys and wherefores of the matter. That's not my bag. But all I do is walk in there and subtly threaten to approach the colonel in front of his old lady."

"Aggressively or sexually?"

"Both, baby. They add up. They turn his fear of his mother into fear of me. First, I open up my jacket, see. And then I stretch to put my tits out in front of him, but at an angle where gramps can't see them. And all the while he's sputtering and blushing like an old maid who's walked into the men's room, because he can't admit to himself that I know gramps is behind the mirror. That makes him even more scared of what I might do. He's convinced himself that I'm not hip to the old bag."

"Hasn't she ever come out when you were there?"

"Are you kidding? She knows she can't scare me. And he knows he's got no power over me, either. Have you ever heard of a WAC officer being court martialed? It isn't possible, baby, because in the old game women are innocent."

"And you're beyond that game?"

"Right. And they can't consciously face it . . . but they can't resist me."

"Why's that?"

"Because, unlike the women who are still playing the old game, I'm willing to take care of myself. They feel safe with me because I never ask any of them to be a man. Because I can face the truth about this goddamned army—there isn't a man in it."

"Then how do you get power over them? Over the colonel? You think he's physically afraid of you?"

She looks carefully into my face. "What he's afraid of is the possibility that I may reveal the existence of the new game that we're covertly playing. That I may break out of the old man-woman game in front of gramps and end the pretense that nothing's changed. Because if I do, the jig is up. He senses that. And he senses that I know it. So we have a little unwritten truce, the colonel and I. I don't fuck up his head and he doesn't fuck up my career. He'll give me anything I ask for."

"The way you were talking before, you seemed to picture yourself as the girl of his dreams. Of all their dreams. A kind of new American dream girl."

"I am, baby. Like a creep who's afraid of heights dreams of the Empire State Building. The colonel's afraid of me, but at the same time he knows that I'm the only one who's strong enough to give him what he really needs."

"Freedom from gramps?"

"Freedom from the entire old game. But he's not strong enough, yet, to openly give in to me."

"Or weak enough."

She smiles. "I think he loves me, Jake. Someday, I wouldn't be surprised if we were to get married, the colonel and I."

"You're kidding!"

"You think so?" she says, with her smile turned half-ironical, half-cunning. "He's a widower, you know."

"What *are* you?"

"Come on, we'll talk about it over some coffee." She stands up, straightens her blouse over her breasts in front the office mirror, puts her jacket back on, and turns to the door.

I follow her out into the hallway, where she turns to me and whispers, "Don't forget. Call me ma'm in public. I outrank you, you know." She winks at me and we begin to walk in the direction of the hospital snack bar.

BULLETIN

Police Drive on Kissers

RIBEIRAO PRETO, Brazil (AP)—"Kissing and embracing on a public street is a crime," Police Chief Edgard de Siqueira Meirelles explained in launching a new campaign in the name of virtue.

C A M E R A   O N E

Before I can object, she pays for both of our coffees. "My treat, lieutenant," she smiles.

We sat down at a little table in the corner, apart from the other people.

"That's two I owe you, captain."

"Two?"

"The coffee and my life."

"Why, lieutenant," she says, with a trace of approval in her uplifted eyebrows, "you're more conscious than you let on. And that's going to make it more difficult for me, because the only debts I can collect are unconscious ones. They never get paid off."

"Well, maybe you can hook me by teaching me how to swim."

At this, she looks pleased as a warm kitten. I can almost hear her purr. "You'd like a better look at me in that bathing suit, wouldn't you, lieutenant?" Before I can answer, she touches her finger to my lips to silence me, and then she runs the backs of her fingers along my jawbone, starting under my ear and moving forward so gently I can feel the electricity sparking from her nails to my skin.

"Seriously," I blush, "I . . ."

"I'm always serious, Jake. Because I told you I don't expect the game to end, don't think that I don't play for keeps. I'll teach you, Jake. In the indoor swimming pool. I'll arrange everything. The WACs will have the pool once a week when it reopens in the fall. That'll give you a couple months to get into shape to impress the little girls when you swim with them."

"Look, Cal. Really. Be serious. Why do you give yourself to these schemes and fantasies? You're playing with the Devil. The army can't hold you if you resign. Why don't you just pick up and leave? Go into the town. You're smart. You're more than just good looking. You'd have it made."

"Well, Jake, you wanted to be serious, so I'll lay it on the line. It's because there ain't gonna be no town, no more," she says, in some kind of a fake dialect. "Cause this here base is gonna destroy the town, and what it don't destroy, it's gonna run. And Cali ain't gonna be run by this here base, baby, cause when it happens Cali's gonna be *on* the base. And *she's* gonna be running *it.*"

"You can't be serious!"

"I am. Dead serious. The sideline markers are down. The grandstands are down. Every fucking container in this whole fucking country is broken. And I'm the only one with the guts to face it."

"But that's an exaggeration. This base isn't the world. The colonel isn't in charge of *everything.* He has bosses too. Take away his technology and he's nothing. Why the scientists . . ."

"The *scientists!* Jake, Wake up! Haven't you been in the hospital laboratory? What do you think they do in there? Test urine samples? Every scientist in the whole fucking country is working for the colonel or his bosses. There is no appeal. The scientists are the biggest faggots of all. They're just a bunch of overgrown babies. All they want is to be allowed to spend their lives in a playpen with lots of shiny, new toys."

"I can't believe that."

"The base is the future, Jake. I'm betting my life on it. And the colonel, that absurd, ridiculous fool, has access to all the power that man has been able to devise. Socrates, Bacon, Newton—he's never heard of any of them, but they've all helped to put the weapons in his grubby little hands. He's got it, Jake. That's all there is to it. And I'm going to get it."

"But why tell *me* all this?"

"I have a feeling about you, Jake. I know I can trust you. I was fated to save you from the river that day. I'm sure of it. And I have plans for you. For the two of us."

"For the three of us, you mean."

"Oh, the colonel." She smiles. "Well you could say that."

CAMERA TWO

She took a last sip of her coffee and set the cardboard cup down on the table. "I've been checking up on you, Jake. On your personnel records. With your friends. With your wife."

"Edith? When did you see Edith?"

"You can ask *her* that."

"This is crazy. Cal, you've got to stop this. The colonel is a sick man. He needs a doctor."

"He *is* a doctor." She rose from the table. "But I've got to run. I'll be seeing you, kid. I've got to get across the street to the WAC detachment."

"But what about our business? That business you mentioned."

"Oh, that. It can wait til tomorrow."

She turned to leave.

"Your hat!" I called after her. "It's in my office. Aren't you supposed to wear a hat when you walk outside in uniform?"

"Me?" she said, with a surprised smile. "Jake, be serious!"

And she walked out the door. When I turned back to the room

I noticed that there were no other women in it. And every eye had been on Cal. In fact, it was only when the soldiers started talking to each other once again that I realized that, as she walked out, the entire snack bar had fallen into a complete silence.

BULLETIN

> The story that Mrs. Aristotle Onassis threw a newspaper photographer to the ground with a judo flip here Sunday was denied yesterday by a witness and by a friend of the former First Lady.

CAMERA TWO

That evening, when I returned from the hospital, I found Edith alone in the house. In the kitchen, cooking dinner. I mentioned to her that I had met Cali once again.

"Oh, it's 'Cali' now, is it." Her face turned sour.

"Why, Edith, I think you're jealous." I began to pinch at her ass, chasing her around the room.

"Stop it, Jake! Stop it!"

"Not until you get sweet again."

"I'm hardly jealous of that big dyke. Jacob, stop it!" she said, slapping at my hand and beginning to giggle.

"Well don't be so uptight about it." I stopped pinching her. "Where did you meet her?"

"Oh, it was at the Wives' Club meeting. She gave some damn lessons in self-defense."

"So?"

"So, she asked if I would volunteer to help, and then she threw me all over the stage for about twenty minutes. I'll say one thing for that bitch. She can back up what she says. I wouldn't want to run into her in a dark alley some night."

"Well . . ."

"Well, she made up afterwards, asking me all kinds of questions about us . . . about you, especially. I guess she really isn't that bad.

I just don't think anyone likes to get tossed around like a toy in front of a hundred people. I believe Warren was really taken with her."

"Warren!"

"Yes. Didn't you know? . . . I guess you were at the hospital that night and we didn't see you afterwards. Warren went to the Wives' Club meeting with me."

"And they let him?"

"Well, there *was* a fuss, but that's where this Cali, as you call her, entered the picture. She said that as far as she was concerned, Warren could stay, and anyone who felt differently about it could make a simple test to prove whether or not he was a woman. They all looked at Warren, and they saw that he wasn't about to stop anyone from removing his pants, so they let him stay. In fact he won the door prize. A frozen turkey. Didn't he tell you?"

"Warren hasn't been saying anything lately. I think he may be the first astronaut to be lost in space."

"Well, we ate it last Thursday. Remember? That was Warren's turkey he roasted for us."

"Where is Warren these days? I hardly see him anymore."

"He's been spending a lot of time over at David's cabin. And he goes next door a lot. Jeannie plays jazz records for him."

"Warren knows everybody," I said. "He has a bank book full of friends wherever he goes. I don't know how he does it."

"He demands nothing, Jacob. People like him. . . . Oh, I should mention. . . . I don't think Len likes him too well."

"He doesn't object to him seeing Jeannie, does he?"

"Oh, no. He doesn't mind that. In fact I think he's rather glad that she has someone to keep her company. After Jeannie lost her baby last year. . . ."

I started.

"Oh, you didn't know that either, did you? Warren and I have had so much time on our hands for the last few weeks, I guess we've found out a lot of things we haven't told you. We hardly ever see you anymore. You're the one who's been gone. Not Warren."

"Well, it's tough to begin a new job without any training. They drop all this responsibility on your head. It's ridiculous—a lot of paperwork and crap like that—but I've got to do it. I thought it would be a snap but it's become a full-time thing. I don't even seem to be able to find the time to read anymore. But there's nothing I can do. . ."

"But what happens to *you*, Jacob? What do *you* become?"

"It's only two years."

"I hope so," she said, as she beat up an egg in a bowl. "I certainly hope so."

"What about Jeannie?"

"Oh, she's really so depressed, Jacob. She sits around the house all day. Listening to the blues. I can hear it through the wall. All afternoon. And there's one in particular. Warren says it's John Lee Hooker. 'The Tupelo Flood.' She plays it twenty times a day. The same part, over and over again."

"What's that?"

"You know the record?"

"I think so. The one about the whole town was 'stroyed'?"

"That's it. Well, she plays this one part again and again. Where the people say, 'Lord have mercy. You the only one we can turn to.' And she sips on a bottle of Old Grand Dad."

"Is she a full-blooded American Indian?"

"Oh, yes. No doubt about that. Warren and she often talk about it. She's a Mohawk. From Brooklyn."

"You're kidding!"

"No, seriously, didn't you ever hear about that colony of Iroquois in Brooklyn? They work in construction."

"That's right. I did read about them. They work highsteel, don't they?"

"Yes. And apparently they drink a bit, too. If Jeannie's an example, then they're a lost people, Jacob."

"Well, what about Len? He doesn't seem lost. Is he an Indian?"

"That's the funny part, Jake. Nobody knows. Jeannie is very open with Warren. . . ."

"Who isn't?"

". . . But even she says that she isn't really certain. She met him in Brooklyn. He claims Indian descent on his mother's side, but no one knows for sure. He won't talk about it to anyone."

"He looks like he might be part Indian."

"It's hard to tell. Even Jeannie can't be sure. She says that he claims he's an Indian and that's all right with her. He's been very good to her . . . but now he's gotten involved outside. . . ."

"Well, I think Warren should be good for her. Does he turn her on?"

"Sometimes. She's not straight, if that's what you mean. But she seems to prefer her Dad. She says she doesn't want to be happy.

She just wants to drink up her dead baby's sorrow."

"Was it killed in an attack?"

"No. The attacks on the officers' quarters were something relatively new. The women were commenting on it at the club. Last year the attacks never came this far. They think it's because we're close to the river. Though, lately, they've pretty much stopped around here."

"I noticed."

"A major's wife told me that they're concentrating on the town more. That the B.C. have regrouped there."

"The B.C.!" I said, angrily.

She dropped her arms to her sides and suddenly her eyes began to moisten. "Oh, Jacob, Jacob . . . do something about it. . . . You're an officer. You're in this crazy army. Do something. . . ."

I wiped the tears from her cheeks. "I don't know what to do, honey."

"Well, speak to somebody. If that Creetner's nuts, appeal to his boss. To the general. I don't know. Do *something.*"

"What can I do? Look at Len. He's been here over a year. He's a short-timer already. Getting out next spring. What's *he* done?"

"Oh, who knows about Len? Sometimes I think he's as nuts as the rest of them. Now he's become a goddamn scout master or something. Spends all his time with his teenagers. That's why he was cold to Warren."

"Why?"

"He told Warren that it was just fine for him to come around in the afternoons and keep Jeannie company. In fact, he appreciated it. But he asked Warren if he'd mind not coming around in the evenings. I don't believe he thinks Warren's good enough to be around when he's with his scouts, precious little things. Well, Warren got the message."

"Does he still go over there in the afternoon?"

"Oh, sure. In fact, to tell you the truth, Jacob, I don't really think Len offended him that much. Len has a kind of disgruntled stubbornness that makes him hard to dislike."

"Well, I'm surprised to hear that about him and Warren."

"Oh, maybe I made it sound like more than it was. He's been friendly to Warren . . . when the scouts aren't around, that is. In fact, that's Len now."

She nodded toward the wall which the two apartments in the house had in common. Through it, we could hear Bob Dylan being played at a high volume. "Ballad of a Thin Man." "Why don't you go over for a while. Dinner won't be ready for half an hour. Maybe, by then, Warren will be back."

"That's a good idea."

Len opened the door; I followed him into his living room. Dylan's singing filled the house.

And over the speakers' blast, I heard a shout: "Hey, pops! Long time no see."

It was Walter Qwalters, the young, militant black man I had met at David's cabin that first day. He bounced up, "Give me five, daddy," his palm laid out flat in front of me.

"Good to see you, Walter."

"I see you two know each other, already," Len said. "I've got to keep better track of things around here." He turned toward the kitchen. "You want some Dad, Jake? Or how about a beer?"

"That Dad sounds fine."

"O.K. It's on that table. Help yourself. I'll get some ice."

I went over to Jeannie, said hello, and poured some bourbon into a tumbler. Jeannie was seated on an easy chair on one side of a small table. Her eyes were wide open, like those of a small child, and her face held a quiescent expression which was belied by the way her left hand gripped the arm of her chair, like a frightened spider. Sitting on the other side of the table was a boy of about seventeen. He had extremely long, soft, blond hair, and with his slim face and delicate features, he could easily have passed for a girl.

"Can you pour me a little of that, too, Jake," Jeannie asked. I half-filled her glass and, noticing that the glass of the young boy was also empty, I asked, "You want some, too?"

"Hold it, man," Len said, as he passed in front of me and dropped two ice cubes in my glass. "That's Tommy. One of my scouts. He doesn't get anything but ginger ale."

Tommy began to protest, but a sharp look from Len quickly silenced him.

"Len you are too much!" Walter shouted from over on the couch, where he was half sitting, half lying, with a glass of bourbon in one hand and a joint in the other. *Too fuckin much!*"

"You don't like it, you know what you can do, *sport!*" Len flared at him.

"Hey, easy now, pops," Walter said, rising to a tense, sitting position. "Just take it easy now, man."

"I don't need your advice, *Whitey!*" Len shot back. And this remark, directed at coal-black Walter, was so ludicrous, that Jeannie cracked up, and Tommy and I couldn't help but laugh too. This might have made Len even angrier if Jeannie hadn't gotten up and stood behind him, circling her arms around his waist as she kissed his hair.

"Take it easy, Len," she said. "Walter's right. You're getting too jumpy."

"You know what he's getting to be?" Walter said, in a calmer tone. "A disciplinarian. That's what. A dis-ci-pli-nar-i-an." No wonder words are often linked with magic. What fascination they hold for those who don't deal with them, on a serious level, very often.

A-BA-RA CA-DA-BARA

"A dis-ci-pli-nar-i-an," Walter said again, with a pleased look on his face, like Adam naming a new species. "And today, that ain't shit, daddy," he added, his voice suddenly tight again. Jeannie began to caress Len's hair, but he seemed cooler now.

"O.K. I won't push it, Walter. I'm getting another beer." And he went into the kitchen.

"He's too much!" Walter said. "He talks anarchy, but he won't even let Tommy here take a taste."

"Leave him alone for now," Jeannie said softly, as she sat back down in her chair. "He's got it rough. Don't forget, he's got to go in there and deal with them every day."

"We'll just wait and see," Len said, coming back into the room with a fresh mug of beer in his hand. "We'll just wait and see what Walter can do when the underdogs get the ball."

The phonograph turned itself off and we sat in silence until someone called my name. It was Little Jo. He had been in the bedroom, reading. He carried the book in his hand, a finger marking the place. *Huckleberry Finn.*

"Jo!" I said, happily. "I didn't know you were here."

"He's going to stick around with us for a while," Len said. "With all the confusion around here, they'll never miss one little boy. We're going to teach him ourselves. Keep him away from the crap they pass off as knowledge at the base school."

"I've got to get back to my reading now," Little Jo said, in his most serious and scholarly manner. And he looked so cute with that look on his face and the book in his hand, that I couldn't help but grin as he walked out of the room. And when I looked over at Jeannie, I saw that she was following him with her eyes, and that she was smiling too.

Len went over and put on another Bob Dylan side. This time from *Blonde on Blonde,* which was my favorite. As the music filled the hollow of the room once again, Tommy got up from his seat. "I'd better split," he said, giving a perfunctory wave of his hand to nobody in particular and heading toward the door. Saying, "Later," to Walter, as he passed.

"Right, baby," Walter said, putting his roach into an ashtray and standing up. "I'd better make it, myself." He pushed his fist playfully against Len's arm. "Hey, pops, don't take it to heart. I was just putting you on."

"It's O.K., Walter," Jeannie said, rising.

Walter turned to leave. Then he looked back and said, "Hey, Jake."

"Yeah."

"I need to speak to you, man." A quick glance toward Len. "In private."

"O.K. But I don't get much free time. My job is just a lot of shit but it eats up the hours."

"Well, pops, you just speak to your Uncle Sam, and if he'll let your white ass off by around midnight tomorrow night, you just drop on by the Harlem. I'll be there." And as he walked out the door, he shouted back, "Jeannie'll tell you how to get there."

After he left, Len turned up the sound, took a long pull at the bourbon, and washed it down with some more beer. "That bastard is going to push me too far, one day."

"Oh, he's just Walter, that's all," Jeannie said. "That's just the way he is."

"Well I don't trust him," Len said. And then he leaned against the wall with his head in his hands and muttered quietly to himself, "Got to hold on . . . Got to wait."

> *Oh, mama, can this really be the end,*
> *To be stuck inside of Mobile, with the Memphis blues again.*

The doorbell rang. Len ran over to the stereo and turned it so loud the bass boom reached out and massaged the organs of our bodies. He sprung drunkenly toward the door. Jeannie signaled me to follow him.

At the door, sheepishly, stood Sergeant Adams, the MP who had escorted us to our quarters the first day. "Sir," he shouted, "sir, we

have a complaint, I'm afraid." He was in the impossible position
of having to politely reprimand an officer on the officer's home
grounds while having to shout to be heard. He had to shout
meekly.

"Sir, I'm afraid we had complaints from the neighbors about
your noise."

"I CAN'T HEAR YOU, SERGEANT," Len shouted over the
music. "THE HI-FI'S TOO LOUD."

"BUT, SIR. BASE REGULATION 1776 SAYS THAT VIC-
TROLAS MAY NOT BE PLAYED OVER AN AMPLITUDE BE-
FITTING THE COMFORT AND AURAL PROCLIVITIES OF
THE NEIGHBORS."

"I CAN'T HEAR YOU SERGEANT!"

"BUT, SIR . . ."

"THE HI-FI'S TOO LOUD."

"BUT . . ."

Moving up to sergeant and shouting, viciously, into his ear, "I
CAN'T HEar you," his voice trailed off as the turntable rejected,
leaving only the resonant silence in the air.

Jeannie came up behind us. "Thank you, ma'm," the sergeant
said, and for some reason, he saluted her, clicked his heels together, did an about face, and headed down the path to the road.
He was so anxious to get back within the confines of his little booth,
he looked like a Charlie Chaplin figure, heading for the horizon
with jerky, shit-in-the-pants steps, wanting to run but trying
to stay within the heel-and-toe limits of Olympic walking race
rules.

All three of us had to smile, it was so absurd. And after we closed
the door, we all laughed together until the sound of our laughter
was drowned out by a tremendous roar. Overhead. A swarm.

"That's the B-52s again," Len said, suddenly grim. "You can't
even hear yourself laugh anymore." Jeannie pulled herself into
him. She was so short, he could look right over her head. He patted
her hair.

"Sometimes I think we're trapped in a horror movie," she said.

"Or a painting," I said, sadly. "A Guernica."

Jeannie held herself against Len, shivering in the chill of the
giant bombers' vibrations. "Where tonight? Where now?"

"I think I'd better run," I said, as the roar increased. "Dinner's
probably ready by now."

"O.K. We'll see you," Len said, still stroking Jeannie's black hair.
"Oh, Jake, don't say anything about the kid's being here."

"Little Jo? You know I wouldn't mention that."

"Oh, I know *that*. I mean Tommy," he said. "Tommy Creetner."

C A M E R A   T W O

"Well, just in time," Edith said, when I returned. "I'll have dinner on the table in a minute."

Warren came smiling out of the living room. "Hey, some good sounds. I was listening through the wall."

"How's it going?" I said. "I heard you had a little hassle with Len."

"It was O.K., Jake. He's got a right to live his life."

"I can't understand it. Len's not straight. . . ."

"Oh, no. Far from it. But I can dig his point. It was after I told him that I drop acid. He doesn't want me near his scouts. That's all. I can understand it. But I still think Walter is right."

"Walter?"

"Oh, yeah, he knows everything that happens around here."

"What's he say about it?"

"He says you can't keep kids away from tomorrow. Cause that's where they live. They'll get the acid, whether I turn them on or not."

C A M E R A   T W O

At dinner, we continued to speculate about the relationship between Len and the kids on the base for, apart from the fact that he had become some kind of scoutmaster, even Warren really didn't know much about it.

As we ate our vanilla ice cream with hot fudge sauce, I said to Warren, "I forgot to ask Jeannie. Do you know of a place in town called the Harlem?"

"Oh, sure, that's the Hotel Harlem. You go down Main Street to the big liquor store and make a right into a kind of alley. I don't think it has a signpost. The Harlem's about four blocks down on the left. What's up?"

"Walter asked me to meet him there tomorrow night."

"That'll be the Moor Room. Walter hangs out there. It's around the far side and downstairs."

"You been there?"

"I went there a couple times with Jeannie. In the afternoon. They've got a good box. All jazz and blues. Lots of hard bop. There's a piano, too. I think they have some live music at night."

BULLETIN

Tanzania Bans 'Soul Music'
DAR ES SALAAM, Tanzania (AP)—American "soul music" is the latest product of "alien culture" to be banned in this East African capital.

C A M E R A   T W O

After dinner, we went into the living room and spent the evening watching some of Edith's filmloops. She had bought a special projector on which she showed them. Once started, a film loop would run indefinitely, like a dog chasing his tail. Edith played tapes of sound montages along with the films. The best was a loop of a beautiful sea bird, a tern, diving into the sea for fish. The tern would get itself moving along some rocks, gain speed and take off, and slowly climb until it spotted its prey. Then it would simply flip over, fold back its wings, and drop into the sea like a bomb.

It was fascinating to watch because of the way the tern pulled its body and wings into the form of a W, with its head attached to the bottom center, as it dropped through the air. It resembled, quite closely, the shape of the new American fighter bombers which we often saw in the sky over the base, providing tactical support for the troops out on search and destroy missions in the local area. And the resemblance was not merely coincidental, of course. Mother Nature had been experimenting for thousands of years to perfect that diving form.

Warren, who was sitting on the floor and smoking grass, couldn't get enough of it. "Oh, wow! Let it go on," he exclaimed. "This is all we need . . . forever."

And I think he meant it. Although it's difficult to put yourself into someone else's concept of forever. The film loop, which ran about a minute, held my attention for an hour, but after about sixty cycles I was ready for a change. I suggested that I be allowed to pick the music and, when Warren and Edith agreed, I put on a record: The Byrds. *Turn, Turn, Turn.* It was a double bad pun, and both Warren and Edith groaned in unison as soon as the record began to play. But actually, it wasn't a bad choice. The tern's flight-dive had a kind of cyclical perserverance which fitted well with the lines from Ecclesiastes.

After a few more cycles I grew impatient once again. Yet I knew what Warren meant. Often, when I was tired, I would feel that there just wasn't enough good music to last a lifetime. That there just weren't enough great works extant to satisfy one for very long. But whenever I felt less weighted down by depression, I would find that the situation had flipped over. That a single great work was sufficient. I would pick a record and play it over and over again, and each time I would find new areas of joy within it. There is hardly ever enough time to get into and fully explore any one of the last great works of Mozart, much less to run out of music. But you have to really get inside the music and move around. If you're too tired to get moving, the music will seem drab and small, because you won't get much higher than the basement of Mozart's house.

After the movies, Edith went to bed and Warren took out a collage on which he had been working for some time. He would paste the clippings and photos onto a sheet of clear plastic and, when this was covered, onto each other. And if the edges of some of the clippings began to curl up off the backing, it only pleased him more. "That's the point of a collage," he said. "It reaches out of its element and into the world."

The interesting thing, to me, about Warren's collage was that it went on and on. He just continued to cut and paste, and with each new clipping he stuck on, it all changed. For that's what his collage was all about. Not clippings, but relationships.

Warren would spends hours alternately working on, and then examining, his collage. Like the film loop, it seemed that it could go on forever, and in that sense, it was outside of time. Well, almost, because finally the weight and bulk of the papers would cause the collage to sag and begin to fall apart. Warren, of course, drifted with the tide as usual, referring to his work as "An Oldenberg Soft Collage," but I noticed one day that even *he* finally acknowledged the effects of time and the existence of historicity, however briefly, by purchasing another sheet of plastic and beginning again.

BULLETIN

Fire Extinguishes Itself
CRANSTON, R. I. (AP) — A fire in a lounge helped put itself out. The blaze started in a waste basket behind the bar, the police said, and generated enough heat to break a water pipe.

CAMERA THREE

And that night, when I tried to write about what was happening to me, to detail the events of the day in my journal, the daydream intruded. The dream which would grow to haunt my mind like a ghost in an age-hollowed house. And I found it impossible to break the bubble which enclosed me. Impossible to write about my life outside of the dream. So I wrote about the dream:

Imagine that World War II is hopelessly lost. Imagine that America is falling and that it's in the last stages of collapse. It's just a matter of days.

And that you've volunteered to do your part in spite of the imminent defeat. And that you've done what you could. Served on a destroyer in the Atlantic, going without sleep for days on end, to prolong the final national agony of military defeat.

And that your ship is finally sunk, and you find yourself floating in Ishmael-solitude on cold Atlantic's vast top.

Then imagine that a ship appears. And comes up to you. After you'd given yourself up. After you'd resigned yourself to a forever sleep in your cold cradle's rocking wet lull. And then imagine that the boat is a German torpedo boat, and that its captain offers to save you. (Remember, America is falling, the water is numbing your body away from you, forever.) But there is one condition. You must volunteer to serve the Third Reich in a kind of junior executive, administrative position. There are no more prisoners of war. Only if you'll serve will you be saved.

Imagine that the captain tells you that the bloody deeds will be finished with the paranoia of the war. Imagine your answer. You might decide to become a hero unsung. You might make a speech about good and evil, and then choose to drown. Imagine your answer to the captain's offer. You might refuse. You can imagine that.

O.K. Now imagine that the boat which pulls up has only one occupant. A German movie goddess, whom you've watched on the screen. The most beautiful woman, with the most desirable body you've ever seen. And you are cold, in the water. And she is warm and tanned on the ship. And she is wearing a bikini and her skin is radiant and smooth. And her eyes are alert and keen. And as she talks to you, she bends down and the swell of her breasts threatens to roll out over tiny top of her suit. And she smiles at you with vibrant, lusty desire.

And she offers you the same proposition. Except that you will live with *her*. And make love to *her*. And have her beside you in a warm bed of perfumed linens each night when you go to sleep. And remember, you are lost and chilled by cold Atlantic's deep. And that above you, you can see her flesh and eyes.

And it isn't a choice of America or sex, because you are drowning and America is lost. And it isn't a choice of the Jews or sex, because you are drowning and the Jews are already dead. And she says she isn't really a Nazi. Just a luscious hipster who wants you to love her and beckons to you and smiles. And then lies down on a soft bed and pillow which rest on the deck of her ship. And all you have for support are Atlantic's chilly billows.

I mean really imagine it. Imagine her as looking like a continental movie star. An Ursula Andress, beckoning to you from a downy bed. And you are drowning. How strong would your hatred of Nazism be? Would it be so easy to choose to drown? You can always die. But at that moment, at that singular moment in time, when she smiles and calls, would it really be possible to refuse? Can you imagine yourself saying no?

Or can you more easily imagine *willing* the fall of America and the death of the Jews, if it would only bring such a moment about.

BULLETIN

Florida High Court Upholds A Ban on Use of Marijuana

TALLAHASSEE, Fla., Dec. 3 (UPI)—The Florida Supreme Court unanimously upheld to-day the constitutionality of sta laws prohibiting the use or pos-session of marijuana.

"Since marijuana, in addition to harming the individual, is a threat to society as a whole, we have no difficulty in up-holding its prohibition by the state," said the decision, written by Justice Joe Boyd.

C A M E R A   O N E

The following day. I open the door to my office. Cal is already seated in my chair, with her feet up on the desk. Wearing leather boots which fit snugly around her calves. A miniskirt that reveals her thighs. And a tiny, sleeveless sweater, far too tight. Her nipples push against the fabric, threatening to tear it. In her left hand, she is holding a biography of George Frederick Handel which I had left in my desk.

Sergeant O'Mara leaps to his feet as I enter and this time he leaves immediately, without waiting to be asked.

"See how quickly they learn," Cal says, nodding toward the door as the sergeant closes it behind him.

I sit in O'Mara's chair. "I hear you threw Edith around a bit."

"Yes." She smiles. "I hope I didn't hurt her too badly."

"I thought your methods were more subtle."

"With men they are."

"And with women?"

"With women physical force is often enough. Not so much to

hurt them as to disorient them. To pull them down off their pedestals."

She leans back in her chair. "That's what I did to Edith. I just rolled her around a bit. Whenever she was about to plant her feet I just pulled them out from under her. It isn't a question of pain, really, but of shame. Every woman in that audience was thanking her lucky stars that it wasn't she who had to deal with me. And each was just as thankful that her husband wasn't in the audience, in any case."

"You know, Cal, I've met a lot of strange characters since I came here, but in some ways you seem the least real—in the ordinary sense of the word. More allegorical than real."

"Maybe you're reading that into me, Jake."

"I don't know. . . . But maybe you *are*. . . . Maybe you're the Devil."

She doesn't smile. She merely straightens up in her chair and looks at me. "I don't know, Jake. I really don't know what I am." She leans back again. "But I'll tell you one thing: if women rule this hive—which they do, Jake—then there isn't a man in it who wouldn't be better off with me as queen. Because what's the alternative? Grandma Creetner?"

"And the wives fear that their husbands would like to swear fealty to you and end their reign as crown princesses?"

"That seems to be the case. They sense that they only seem tall because their husbands are so short. But if I topple them . . ."

"Do the wives hate you?"

"Not really, Jacob. They do at first, but they seem to come to an unconscious understanding that they remain in power at my behest. And they eventually become kind of grateful to me."

"Grateful?"

"Yes. I really believe they do. They fear me, but I think something has been happening to these women. Even before they came here. I'm a pragmatist, Jake. I didn't make the times but it seems that I'm perfectly suited to them. 'The man of the hour' as another age might have put it."

"But the wives . . ."

"I don't pretend to understand it, but I trust my observations. And one thing I've sensed consistently on this base is that as far as the wives go, there isn't one who wouldn't secretly like to leave her husband if she could move in and make a home for me."

"That's ridiculous!"

"It's true, Jake. This is a new ball game and I can't let old definitions like 'women,' or 'men,' or even 'egotism' keep me from facing the facts."

"*Egotism* is right! This whole thing is one vast ego trip. I can't believe it."

CAMERA TWO

She placed my book upon the desk. "You like music?"

"I love music."

"Well, then you must know enough about it to be able to think for yourself. I'm sure of that."

I looked away.

"Now don't blush, Jake. That's exactly the point of what I'm trying to say. Look, you're not blind enough to think that if a piece is popular it's necessarily bad."

"Right."

"You know that a work like Handel's Messiah really is great, even though all the two-legged absurdities that surround us profess to like it and roll it out each year with the mistletoe and the fruit cake."

"Sure."

"Well do you know what Handel is supposed to have said after he wrote it? He said that he felt it was divinely inspired."

"I know."

"Well you might give that statement some thought before you ever blush again when you're complimented. Because I've thought about it, and to me it is the most humble statement a man has ever made."

She stopped and lit a long, cigarillo-type, thin cigar.

"You see, Jake, Handel knew a great deal more about music than either you or I ever will. He knew that he had given birth to something divine. He couldn't ignore that fact, because he knew too much. He was too great a realist, so he did the only possible thing. He gave the credit for it to God."

She took a long drag on the cigar and blew the smoke out into the room. "Don't you see? Don't you see how humble that was? That it was the most humble act possible for man to make."

"Then . . . then you think you are . . . that your powers come from God. This is incredible! The analogy doesn't hold."

"I'm subordinate to the authority of the facts. It may be a lamentable choice, but at this point in history it's either grandma or me. And I think I can win. I think I've been given the power to make it *me*."

"You. . . . Maybe you *are* the Devil. Because you're not God. . . ."

"I didn't say I was God. Quite the contrary. . . ."

"You're not kidding, quite the contrary. You're in league with the Devil. And you, *you* profess to believe in God."

She took her cigar out of her mouth and placed it, still burning, in an ashtray on the desk. Then she turned directly toward me, set her palms down firmly on the top of the desk, and said, with a depth of sincerity, and perhaps even humility, which I had never heard in her voice before, "Would it be so strange, Jake . . . would it really be so strange, to find that the Devil believed in God?"

CAMERA ONE

The silence in the office is interrupted by a rumbling in the hallway which grows progressively louder and stops when it reaches our door. Sergeant O'Mara knocks and enters.

"What the hell is that, sergeant?"

"It's a secret message, sir. For the commanding officer from the colonel."

"Which commanding officer, sergeant?" Cal snaps. "I'm a commanding officer, too."

"Begging the commander's pardon, ma'm. It's for the lieutenant."

"Which commander, sergeant?" Cal says.

"Ma'm?"

"Which commander's pardon are you begging?"

"Ma'm?"

"Never mind, sergeant." She winks at me. "Dismissed!" The sergeant does an about face and leaves the office.

"A secret message?" I walk out into the hallway. There, mounted on a wheeled dolly, stands a steel safe. About four feet high. And around it are four privates who have apparently pushed it over to the office. And one corporal. I speak to him.

"Corporal, what *is* this?"

"It's a secret message, sir."

"Then what's the combination?"

"I'm not allowed to tell, sir. It's a secret."

"And," I say, despairingly, "the secret message is in the safe, no doubt."

"That's right, sir."

"Well how in the hell am I supposed to read it, if it's in the safe. This is insane! Honestly, I'm . . ."

I'm interrupted by a hand on my shoulder. I turn around to see Cal's smile.

"You boys weren't ever given orders about the combination, were you now?" she says to the privates.

They all begin to speak at once. "You!" she points to a short, light-haired private with a pimpled complexion.

"No, ma'm. We weren't even given the combination."

I smile, triumphantly, but too soon, for she says, "Well, what is it?"

"Two left to seventeen, one right to thirty-four, left to eighteen, ma'm," he answered.

"Wait a minute!" I shout. "Corporal, how does this man know the combination?"

"Well, sir," the corporal answers, apologetically, "we deliver secret messages all the time, now that the counteroffensive has begun. And we only have one safe. So it would be kind of difficult for the men *not* to know the combination. This is all we do, sir. Every day. And all of us are college graduates, sir."

"You are?"

"Yes, sir," he answers, proudly. "That's why we've been put into G-2."

"G-2?"

"Yes, sir. Intelligence."

I turn the dial. The safe springs open and I take out the message. It is on a form that is pale green in color. Almost an exact copy of a bank check. In the space for the date, "September 22" has been stamped. And in the place for the money figures, "4:00 P.M." Next to "For" it says, "One visit to Colonel Creetner," and alongside of "To," "Payable to the Bearer—Not Negotiable." In the lower righthand corner a machine has stamped the colonel's signature.

"Any return message, sir?" the corporal asks.

"Yes."

"Written, oral, or rectal, sir?"

"Rectal?"

"Yes, sir. It's actually a subcategory of written. You write the message on a small piece of paper and we insert it in a suppository which we shove up a private's ass. It's something new, sir. Quite secret, actually. Awfully hard to detect."

"Oral, corporal," Cal says. "But secret. He'll tell it to blondie over there."

The private she spoke to earlier steps forward and places his ear to my mouth. I turn to Cal and she says, "Well, lieutenant, don't just stand there. Whisper it into his ear."

So I whisper in the private's ear, "O.K. I'll be there."

"Thank you, sir," he snaps to attention and salutes.

And then it begins to happen again, almost as if Cal has arranged it as a didactic exercise for my edification. The corporal approaches the safe and slides out a plate from under the top which reveals a series of small holes which go down through the steel, right into the heart of the safe. Then the private to whom I have entrusted the message crawls into the safe, assuming a kind of fetal position so as to be able to fit. The corporal clicks the door shut behind him, spins the dial, and takes the place of the missing soldier at one corner of the safe. We watch as the four young soldiers push and guide the rumbling safe back down the hall which leads to Colonel Creetner's office.

"Fine young men," Sergeant O'Mara says, walking over to the supply room. "Goes to prove brains aren't out of place in the service."

Cal and I return to my office.

"Do you know what this is all about?" I ask.

"In fact, I do. It's that business I mentioned to you yesterday morning."

She sits in my chair and lights another thin cigar. "You see, you, Jacob Klinger, are going to be commander of the WAC detachment."

"You're joking!"

"No, I'm afraid not. It's no longer possible to exaggerate reality."

"What do you mean? . . . What are you talking about?"

"I'll be more explicit. There's no WAC detachment on the TD. . . ."

"TD?"

"Honestly, Jake, you've got to learn these terms. Know your enemy. You've got to get your head inside that gate that your body passed through last June. Or else you'll be helpless here."

"What's a TD?"

"Table of Distribution. It tells which positions are authorized for staffing the hospital. How many people will be assigned here, what their rank will be, and their MOSs. That's Military Occupational Speciality—what job they each do."

"Well, where do I fit in?"

"That's just it. You *do* fit in. You're on the TD. You see, this hospital was built in World War II to last five years. That's why it's in such shoddy shape, incidentally, and is falling apart. But what's happened is the basic TD hasn't changed in all these years, while the composition of the hospital staff *has* changed, and in a way not envisioned by the original designers of the TD."

"What's that?"

"It's simple. The TD says nothing about WACs. So that gradually, as the women began to replace the men (as the army insists on calling them) it became evident that a WAC commander was needed. So they sent me."

"But you're not on the TD."

"Right. And nobody around here wants to bring up the subject of the TD because it gives a lot of high-ranking slots to the hospital, which, in the present, technically peacetime, state, it might not deserve."

"And me?"

"You, therefore, are still official commander of all the enlisted personnel working in this hospital, half of whom are now WACs."

"So what do we do?"

"It's just technical, really. I run the WAC detachment, but you do the signing of official papers, like morning reports and payrolls, for instance."

"That should be easy enough."

"And there's even a bonus for you, Jake. You get to administer company punishment. I'll bring the girl in front of you and stand behind you and make the decisions, but you have to be there while I hear the evidence. And when I've decided, you announce the decision. Won't that be fun, Jake?" she adds, slyly.

BULLETIN

'Diva' Lives as Star At Bavarian Hotel-- Till She Has to Sing

Special to The New York Times

BONN, May 27 — She billed herself as Maria della Metastasia, the grand diva from Milan's La Scala Opera, and lived the life of a star for a month in a Bavarian resort hotel. But when the manager finally persuaded her to sing for her supper, she hit so many false notes that he called the police.

The police of the town of Wunsiedel disclosed today that Maria della Metastasia was really Maria Bittner, 43 years old, of Kassel, a one-time choral singer who had been jailed before for fraud.

Miss Bittner is in jail again, on charges of having swindled a total of $1,675 out of the Crown Prince of Bavaria Hotel and several cosmetic and dress shops in Wunsiedel.

CAMERA TWO

That night I drove into town. Turned right at the liquor store onto a narrow, blacktop road, stripped with gravel and sand on each side rather than sidewalks. There were no street lamps. Only the lights from houses sporadically softened the darkness. After about four blocks, I saw, up ahead on the left, a building which was three stories high with a red neon sign hanging from its front wall. HOTEL HARLEM. There were several cars parked in front, so I stopped and parked on the gravel, about a block away.

CAMERA ONE

I turn off the car lights and the street darkens. Lock the car and walk gingerly toward the hotel. As I pass a thin alley between the hotel and the house preceding it, "Hey, man," comes out of the black.

"What?"

"Hey, man, I need some change to make dinner. You got thirty-five cents?"

In the pocket of my pants, two coins. Both quarters.

"Here," I take out one of the coins. "Here's a quarter. That ought to start you on your way."

He takes the quarter, looks it over in the dim light as I turn away. A hand on my shoulder.

"I said, man, I need thirty-five cents."

"Look, I gave you a quarter. . . ."

He moves out of the alley. A glint of steel flashes in the thick gloom. A straight razor. From out of his sleeve. He backs me against the wall, holding the razor low, at his hip. His bright eyes reflect off the blade.

"I said *thirty*-five, man. Not *twenty*-five."

"O.K. You've got me. Take it easy. Don't get excited." I reach into my pocket and hand him the second quarter. "Here. This is the only other coin I've got."

"O.K., man. That's a little bit better. Now we're getting down to business."

He folds the razor and places it in the breast pocket of the old sport jacket he is wearing. From out of the same pocket he removes another object. A pair of clear-rimmed army glasses. God only knows where he got them. He puts them on and brings his left hand out of his baggy pants. It's full of small change.

"Now let's see now," he says. "Put out your hand here, man." I place my hand in front of him, palm up, and, one by one, counting each aloud to himself, he places upon it a nickel and ten pennies.

"Now that's a little more like it," he says, as he puts the remaining coins back in his pocket and fades back into the blackness of the alley.

CAMERA TWO

I located the door to the Moor Room on the far side of the hotel and went in. It was ill lit, but there was something warm about it. Congenial. What light there was, was soft, and the smoke in the air seemed to float on the sounds of a bluesy ragtime coming from an old upright piano on the far side of the room.

The club consisted of a square room with about a dozen tables arranged in three rows on the floor and a bar against the wall on my right which ran almost to the righthand corner of the room. I looked for Walter, but even as my eyes began to open to the dark, I couldn't see him. Finally, I spotted him at a separate table set over in the righthand corner in the space beyond the end of the bar.

"Hey, pops, you made it. Sit down and take a taste. What'll it be? Dad?"

"Fine with me."

"Hey, Red. A double Dad on the rocks for my man here. And hit me again, too."

"Right!" shouted the bartender, a light-skinned Negro with kinky, reddish hair.

"Well, you found the place," Walter said.

"Yeah. Warren told me."

"He's somethin else," Walter said. "He's been coming round David's place a lot. We all dig him. I mean he's pretty spaced, but he don't bother nobody. . . . He don't bug you. That's what we like about him."

"That's why everyone likes him. Wherever we go."

"I mean, man, he's pretty far out, but he ain't afraid. It's cats that are scared you got to watch. Cause if the man can scare them, he can use them. . . . Against you. You dig?"

"You can't scare Warren with jails. That's for sure. Because he doesn't believe *the world* is real, much less jails."

"Too much!" Walter laughed. "But whatever it is, he's O.K. He's been going for walks with David, lately."

"Oh, yeah?"

"Sure, man. David's been getting out once in a while since Sibyl . . . well you know what happened to Sibyl. She got hatched by the boobies."

"I'm hip. The meth finally took its toll."

"Well, who knows? She lived, she did her thing, and she finally lost. That's about it for any of us, man." He leaned back as the bartender placed a drink in front of him and then set a big double in front of me.

"Hey, Red, this is my man, Jake. Jake, Red."

Red didn't extend his hand. He looked at me like a man examining a snake to determine if it's poisonous.

"He in the army?" Red said.

"Sure, man. They're the ones who took his hair."

"Well, if you don't mind, I'll get back to my job." He turned away.

Walter grabbed his arm. "Red, I said this is my man. He's O.K. He's one of us."

Red turned to me and extended his hand. Mistrustfully. "Well, if you're O.K. with Walter, I guess your O.K. with me."

We shook hands. Red relaxed.

"That's better," Walter said. "Jake'll be around from time to time, man. I want you to take good care of him. He's one of us."

"O.K. Walter," he said, and left our table.

Walter sat with his back to the corner of the club. From his vantage he could see anyone who entered or left the room. My back was toward the club. But I could see the pianist playing the blues now. It was a woman, and she began to sing:

> *When my baby don't love me,*
> *My morning are fill with rain.*

I turned my head and looked over my shoulder at her. Sitting at the old upright. She was a huge, middle-aged black woman, wearing a long, thirties, black gown. And when she turned toward me, as she sang, she caught my eye, and she gave me a smile. And in the light it wasn't easy to tell. But I was almost sure it was her.

It was her. It was Moms.

"Well," Walter said, "I'm glad you got to come. It ain't good to spend too much time on the base. They'll fuck up your head. Like they did David's."

"I'm hip. Did you say David's getting out of the cabin once in a while?"

"That's right, pops. Here and there. But best of all, he's writing."

"I didn't know David still wrote."

"There's a lot you don't know yet, pops. David can put words together. He's really got the gift, man, but when he's stoned all the time, he pulls up the mat and shuts the door."

He sipped on his drink. "Oh, I don't say he'll be rude. That's not David, pops. He'll smile and he'll always hear you out. But when the fire's on his joint, the fire inside him is out. He'll bullshit with you, but he won't *do* a goddamn thing."

"How come the change now?"

"I don't know. Time, I guess. And that Colonel Creetner."

"David knows Colonel Creetner?"

"Who don't, pops? Since they started bombing the town, he's public enemy number one around here. Everybody and his brother knows he's behind these raids."

"He's just a bureaucrat. . . ."

"Man, where you been? Ain't you heard? The colonel's the one who's pulling the strings now, baby. The general ain't been seen in two weeks. Fact is, Creetner told the old man (he began to imitate the colonel), 'Sir, I have ascertained there is an infection in the body politic. As a medical man, I am, of course, trained in curing infections, and as head of the service station, I feel I should be given authority and concomitant responsibility to treat this social disease.' And, pops, he's been in charge ever since. Like I said, the general ain't been seen."

"But that's nuts, Walter."

"I'm hip, dad."

"But how do you know all this? . . . I mean his exact words to the general."

"It's my business to know, man. I got sources. (He pronounced it 'sauces.') I'm a newspaper man. And that's why I wanted to talk to you."

"But what about David? Does he know the colonel? I mean personally."

"Well, he thinks he does. Let's put it that way. He thinks he does."

"What do you mean, *thinks?*"

"It has to do with when David's head got fucked up. He ain't exactly clear about it, pops, but he's sure that Creetner was involved. He just can't remember how. But he says it was right before the shrinks ejected him from the ball park. Before he got the heave-ho from the base. He thinks the colonel had something to do with it . . . with his head. He can't remember what, but it was enough to get him going again once he heard it was the colonel who was bombing the town."

"Did he say that?"

"He said it was just the noise. Said he couldn't hear the music on his radio because of all the noise of the planes and the bombs. But I know different. You take it from Walter, that David's dynamite . . . when he can get himself together. That's why I want to talk to you. Make you a proposal."

"What does David have to do with me?"

"For one thing, you're both writers, right?"

"Well, I have done a little. . . ."

"Don't be modest, man. You got brains. We all can see that. This ain't the establishment, pops. We ain't gonna put you down. We know you can write, if you get into it."

"I still don't see . . ."

"Look, you heard of our paper, *The Railroad*. Well, you don't think it supports itself, do you? This ain't New York City, pops. We don't get that kind of circulation around here."

"How *does* it support itself? Warren gets it every week, but there are hardly enough Warrens in this area to pay its expenses."

"You seen my other paper on the stand, man? *Sado-mask?*"

"That's *your* paper?"

"That's right, pops. You know Irving Fieldman, the editor? And the twelve other names on the masthead? That's me, dad."

"What? Which one?"

"All of em, pops. All of em. I'm Irving. I'm Pamela Cabot Lowell. I'm J. Arthur Node. I'm all of em, man. I own that paper 100 per cent. And I fill all the positions myself. That's how we support *The Railroad*. *Sado-Mask* makes the bread and I put enough of it back into *The Railroad* to keep it running. It's means and ends, pops. And *Violence*, too."

"*Violence!* That's your paper, too?"

"One hundred per cent, pops." Walter smiled, and not without a hint of pride. "Saul Pishkin, the editor of *Violence*. . . ."

"That's you, too?"

He smiled.

"I can't believe this, Walter."

"I'll show you later, dad. They're all the same to put out. I use the kids who work on *The Railroad* to help me set up and lay out the other two. Same printers, same distributors. It's simple, dig?

"And I pay them," he added. "I pay them for their work on the two money-makers and that frees them to work on *The Railroad*.

And it frees them from their parents. And from the state—or from its agents, the fuckin corporations. It gives them some bread and it gives them the time to do their thing. I'm supporting half the heads in central Massachusetts, and David's my source of raw materials, pops. Words. I can get pictures but you can't run a newspaper without words. And David's been my supplier."

"But I thought that he hadn't been writing."

"Not for *The Railroad,* pops. Not for *The Railroad.* But who do you think has been giving me my stories for *Sado-Mask?*"

"David?"

"None other. And that's why I wanted to talk to you. You see, man, since the colonel began to increase the noise level in this here town, David's begun to write again . . . to really write. For *The Railroad.* And his energy is beginning to come back now. So we can't afford to lose him again, see. We need all his energies to go into *The Railroad* where they'll really count. And that's where you fit in."

"Me?"

"That's right, dad. We want you to take over *Sado-Mask.*"

I began to object but Walter silenced me. "Not the business end, or the layout, pops. We'll take care of all that. We just want you to turn out some stories. Two stories a week to keep us going while David writes *The Railroad.*"

"But I can't write that kind of shit. . . . And who's this *we* you keep talking about? You sound like Queen Victoria."

"Well, let's just say the *we* is the B.C. Or its leaders, at least."

"Come off it, Walter. You know there is no B.C. And there never was."

"There *was* no B.C. You're right, there. But that don't mean there ain't gonna be any B.C. In fact, you might say Colonel Creetner is in charge of our recruiting drive."

"Wait a minute. . . . My head is spinning."

"You've been isolated too long, dad. Hey, Red!" Walter called, pointing to our empty glasses.

"I can't write for that rag, Walter."

"You can't *not* write for it, pops. Because we don't have nobody else."

Red placed the fresh drinks in front of us.

"Look at it this way, dad. You're not for censorship, are you? You don't think people should be cut off because they're freaks for something unusual?"

"No. . . ."

"Well, you can pick up the standards of our paper. They're gonna read this kind of shit, whether we give it to them or not. At least this way you can expose them to decent writing. And besides, you'll be able to keep your hand at your trade. Keep your pen sharp for when you do your own writing."

"But, man, I *am* writing. I'm writing a journal. That's why I can't do this. I hardly have time to do *any* writing, much less this kind of stuff."

"Come in here with me," Walter said, and without looking back he walked across the floor of the club and into a small adjoining room.

C A M E R A   O N E

A chaotic place. Photos, proof sheets, rulers, jars of glue, typewriters, piles of underground newspapers all over. Revolutionary posters on the walls next to nude shots from *Sado-Mask*. The smell of incense. Young people scattered about and sitting on a couple of old couches. Walter introduces me.

To a young black girl with an Afro haircut. Named Foxy. She's sitting next to a wild-looking white boy, rapping about how her parents weren't really mean, just demented.

To the wild boy, with the hair spread out around his head like a bonnet of steel wool. His name is Rainbow. He speaks beautifully and is open and friendly toward me immediately.

To a lovely blond girl with the longest, most beautiful hair I have ever seen. Down to her ass. A Godiva coat of fine gold softness. Her name is Flower. "Good to see you, Jake," she says, with a smile. "We need all the help we can get."

To an efficient looking girl in the corner. Hair pinned up, rimless glasses, slouching on the floor. Reading an English language newspaper, printed in Cuba.

And to others. Black and white. Girls and boys. All friendly to me. Talking animatedly and working on the layout of the newspaper.

And Walter shows me around the room. All three newspapers are produced here. More of a club room than an office. Roaches in the ashtrays. Music on the radio from the FM rock station in Boston. Books. Nice faces. A cozy place.

We talk to the kids for a while and then split to let them concentrate on getting out *The Railroad.* As we pass Flower, I glance once again at her hair. And again she smiles to me. She is working on a cartoon. A crudely caricatured face of President Sun.

C A M E R A   O N E

When we returned to our table, Moms was still singing.

You a deepsea diver. . . .

"They're a good bunch of kids, Walter."

"They're O.K. They got enthusiasm and they're getting more aware every day. But they need David. You see, pops, even more than the paper needs David, the kids who put it out need him. He puts their world together for them. But if he ain't writing, he ain't available. Nobody home, dig?"

"I don't know, Walter. . . ."

"You got to, man. We got nobody else to turn to. I told them you were one of us. Are you, dad? Are you one of us? Because you're sure not showing it, working for the man. . . ."

"I'm in the medics!"

"So's Dr. Creetner, man. And you're working for *him.*"

The door which led to the street swung open with a loud crash.

A face stuck itself in, shouted, "The man!" and disappeared into the darkness outside.

"Come on, Jake!" Walter shouted.

But I didn't move. Stunned into immobility by the image of the face which had appeared. It was the guy who had held me up in the alley.

"Come *on,* Jake," Walter said, pulling me sharply to my feet and leaping over the bar. "In here!"

I followed him through a trap door into a small sub-basement hidden beneath the bar. The door slammed over our heads just as the screaming began above us. And running and shouting and things breaking.

I looked around me. In the light of a single tiny electric bulb, I could see the outlines of the small room we were in. And near me, about ten other faces. All men. All black.

"What's happening?"

"It's a raid, pops. Part of your boss's strategy."

"They better not catch me here," I whispered. "It'll be my ass."

"Look, man, if they catch any of us here, we've had it. You're nothing special."

"Where are the women?"

"They're upstairs. Just keep cool and be quiet."

After a while the shuffling and movement over our heads came to a stop. And then the blues began to sound again on the piano.

"O.K." Walter said. "All clear."

We filed back up the stairs and into the room. Chairs were strewn about like cut flowers. Tables turned over, glasses and bottles broken.

Only Moms was left. And she was playing so beautifully it was hard to believe that she had seen anything happen. Playing "Red Sails in the Sunset" in a jerky, soft manner, punctuated by little runs of incredible speed for such an aged, heavy woman. And she held back before every run—before many of the vocal lines, too —as if to catch her breath before attempting another mad dive into the ocean after a treasure which no one could see and only she could imagine.

Anyone can race his fates. But it takes the courage and daring of an artist or a madman to give them a head start.

> . . . *sail in the sunset*
> . . . *mind me of you.*

"Where are the women?" I said to Walter.

"They've been picked up. For rehabilitation," he said, with marked irony.

I followed him into the back room. What had previously been mere chaos was now wreckage. Typewriters smashed, posters and pictures torn off the walls and ripped up, files overturned. As if a cyclone had singled out this one little room as the target of its fury.

"Compliments of your boys," Walter said. "Compliments of the doc."

"What do you mean by rehabilitation?" I said, straightening some overturned furniture.

"What do you *do* all day?" Walter said. "Where is your head, man? Ain't you seen the detention camp over at the south end of the base? Over near the lake."

"No, I'm so busy at the hospital. . . ."

"Well it's there, baby. But don't worry about the chicks. They won't hold them too long. Just a week or so. Some lectures, forced showers, short haircuts. . . ."

"For the *women?*"

"That's what I said. That's rehabilitation. But they get off easy. It's the men who get their ass kicked."

"How come?"

"Suspected B.C. They think any man they can get their hands on has all the secrets of the B.C."

"But there aren't any secrets . . . or at least there haven't been."

"That's why no one's ever talked. But every time they raid somewhere and don't find anything, they respect us all the more. . . ."

"Because they think your people are so loyal and your nonexistent plans so well concealed."

"You go to the head of the class, pops."

The back door opened and the black girl I had met earlier peeked in.

"It's O.K., Foxy," Walter said. "They're all gone now. They get anyone?"

"We got out as fast as we could, but Flower tripped over the paper cutter and Rainbow went back to help her and I think they both got picked up."

She was highly excited and when she sat down on a chair which I had put back on its feet, she began to quietly sob. Walter went up to her and lifted her head so her eyes met his. "Don't you worry about Rainbow," he said. "He can take it. They ain't gonna keep him too long over there. They don't have the room. So don't you go crying because you're thinking about my man Rainbow."

"I wasn't," she said, wiping her eyes with a handkerchief she took out of a pocket in her jeans. "I was thinking about Flower's hair."

Walter and I went back into the club. Moms wasn't singing. Just quietly playing some improvised variations around the chord changes of "Willow Weep For Me." And her notes were light as butterflies and so lovely it was as if, like Foxy, she too, had been quietly weeping, but in Mom's case, the tears only appeared in her music.

Our table hadn't been touched and we returned to it and downed the remainder of our drinks while still standing.

"You ever hear of a French guy named Sar-tray?" Walter asked.

"You mean Jean Paul Sartre?"

"Right. That's the one. Well I don't read much—I'm nonlinear—but David told me something this cat said that made a lot of sense."

"What's that?"

"He said if you stay in the army long enough, you'll eventually become a soldier."

"Look, Walter, you don't have to go on. You've won. I'll write your stories."

"I knew you wouldn't let us down. We need you, pops. And I'll tell you something else."

"What's that?"

"I think you need us."

"Maybe so, Walter. We'll see. I'll try it. I'll do your stories."

"Good. If you can get two of them to me by Sunday, we'll be able to get to the printer in time to be on the stands by 2 P.M. on Tuesday. This business is wilder than you think, man. If we're not on the stands on time, my office is full of cats complaining and yelling like mad. You don't know, man. Phone calls, telegrams. These cats don't joke about *Sado-Mask*. They wait for it, man."

He put his glass on the table. "You know," he said, only partly in jest, "sometimes I think I'm performing a public service.

"It's a weird world," he added. As I reached for my wallet, he caught my arm. "Hey, dad, this one's on me." And as he released my arm, he explained, "I have a charge account here, man. I write it off my taxes."

BULLETIN

Short Life for Newsmen Indicated in Polish Study

WARSAW, Nov. 29 (UPI)—
Polish studies indicate journalism is becoming one of the
most hazardous professions for
life expectancy and health, the
Polish news agency reported
this week.

CAMERA THREE

So that's the way the summer went. Living with the roar of giant bombers overhead, the blood and paperwork at the hospital, and the music at home. And dreams of Cal.

Toward the end of the season, Warren and I spent many eve-nings out on the patio, watching the sun set in the west, smoking some grass, and listening to records. One singer in particular, whom we listened to a great deal in those days, was Tracy Nelson.

And often, after it got dark, we would stay out there and watch the campfires in the distance. On the field between our house and the river. It was Len and his scouts. The group was composed of teenagers of both sexes. "Army brats."

And always, I would think of Cal. In the little time I could find for my journal, I would dream about her thighs. I would dream of the slope of her back into the small. And of the way her ass looked from the side. And of her holding me and pulling me from the current. Of how it must have felt.

And she began to accompany me about in my mind. To domi-nate my thoughts. She clung to me, hung onto me from the inside. Her breasts, thrusting out against the little sweaters she wore. The curve, along which her narrow waist reined in the wealthy blos-som of her hips. The way her hair shone, when tiny droplets of water sparkled in it and fell from its ends.

And I would walk the hospital halls each day, hoping to see her —to see what pieces of cotton, wool, or felt she had hung on her body that morning. Just to meet her. To hear her speak. Just to see the looks of envy on the other officers when she smiled at me as we walked down the hospital hall. Together.

And I dreamed of an end to the pulls. To the strains and tugs which were tearing me apart. Of being one again. With myself. With her. Together.

And she haunted my imagination and inhabited my dreams. As I got up in the morning I would think of Cal. And when I inspected my men I would think of Cal. And when I sat at my desk at work and when I would try to read or write at home I would think of Cal. And when I fucked Edith I would think of Cal.

And sometimes I thought that all I really wanted of either life or eternity was to be fucked by Cal. Then I could be happy again, happy like Warren, if I had her to take care of me, and my oppressors would be impotent, and my life enclosed within a bubble of ecstatic joy, if only I could choose to go along with Cal. To be with her. To give in to her. To submit.

SECOND QUARTER

I felt like maybe they forgot to tell me something,
that this was the way we fought wars and everybody
knew but me.

SGT. MICHAEL BERNHARDT
*(The soldier from Company C
who refused to take part in the
massacre at My Lai, South Vietnam.)*

Commercial

President John Sun announced today at the White House that he has formed a new task force for a massive assault on the smuggling of marijuana into the United States from Mexico.

The project will be called Operation Interception. The president admitted the project will cost many tax dollars and might offend some of the citizens of the great republic to the south of us. But he stated, "No price is to great to pay to stamp out this nefarious weed which is corrupting the moral fiber of the nation's youth."

To counteract any bad publicity and ill will which the project may generate in the Alliance for Progress nations, the president announced the possibility of a State Department tour of Latin America by Xavier Cugat and his orchestra.

In a surprise conclusion to his announcement, President Sun informed the press that to head this vital program he is bringing in his brother from California, Nick Sun.

The scenery offstage changed, but inside the hospital, the weather was always the same.

The one aspect of army life, in either peacetime or war (if these two states can any longer be separated), which has been least adequately portrayed by the media is the boredom. The insistent, unrelenting boredom that sticks to life in the army like a viscous liquid.

For the actual fighting never really goes on for very long. And besides fighting, their is very little for the army to do. Of course they can train for the fighting, but that too becomes a bore rather quickly. So most of the officer's time is spent sitting around, trying to think of things for other people to do.

Like supervising the moving of everything on Ward 26 to Ward 54, or, a few months later, of everything on Ward 54 to Ward 26 (each project having been justified by a cost-efficiency study which demonstrated its economic advantages). This type of assignment would usually be given to the first officer whom the colonel, or one of his chief assistants, ran into in the hallway. So I arranged to stay out of the hallways as much as possible, only venturing from my office when there was a chance of seeing Cal.

But I had trouble filling my time. Sergeant O'Mara was a good first sergeant, and he usually got things done to the point where all I would have to do was sign my name to the paper he presented to me. Of course I would pretend to scan it, so as not to discourage him, and I would praise his efficiency and effectiveness, but I found I could not get myself to read the documents, which were written in a legalistic language that was unintelligible to me. Army regulations were written in this language too, and I couldn't read them either. So I depended on what the sergeant said, spiced with whatever I could pick up from "The Captain" on TV.

Since I was spending most of my free time filling my blood with alcohol or my lungs with the smoke of the Indian hemp, I had done little of my own writing. Often, I would try to work in a notebook while sitting at my desk. But it was too difficult. I was surprised to learn that, unless I could, with complete confidence, forget my external position and turn in to explore my mind, I would never be graced with the power to rise above my public self in my writings.

I had to wear my blue-suit self at all times in the hospital. I had to be prepared to defend this self at a minute's notice. At the ring of a phone. I had to be ready to put myself back on, to wear myself as if it were a disguise. So I could never fully take it off.

I could never fully be anything else. As long as I had to remember who I was supposed to be, I could not draw upon the resources of that other, larger self, which I strove to bring into being through my writing. *In* my writing.

My imagination was continually pinched by the niggardliness of my surroundings. And because, as an officer, I had to maintain a certain specific gravity, I could not fly. But what I *was* able to do, and what I finally did do, was write my *Sado-Mask* stories in my office, on army time. There was no problem about falling into the rut of formula in these pieces, for I was writing about obsession, and that's essentially what obsession is—a love affair which cannot rise above the rut of formula.

I remember writing one about a public figure, an author and TV personality, who receives threatening letters and is eventually driven to hire a bodyguard. Of course, all the private detectives and bodyguards in town are busy guarding the luminaries attending a right-wing political convention (or attending the convention themselves—although this fact was not included in the story), so the agency can't provide anyone, except . . . well, there was one person left, a woman karate instructor whom the agency had been forced to hire because of the state's equal opportunity laws.

The author-personality accepts, and slowly his bodyguard begins to gain power over him. He can't reveal his trepidations for fear of damaging his public image, upon which his success as an author-personality is based. Furthermore, he fears that his bodyguard may do him physical harm, perhaps even kill him, if he speaks out. And since he has no living relatives, he is obsessed by the thought of his pain-wracked or even dead body, lying on the floor of his apartment for days before it's discovered. And he loathes worms. And he dreams of them eating the soft tissues of his corpse.

So he yields. He rationalizes this by saying that, after all, he *was* lonely, and he does get good protection. And the letters *do* stop, although he comes to suspect that it was his bodyguard who had been sending them. But in truth (as the reader is made to see) he enjoys his new situation. He stays safely at home with her all the time (except when he goes on TV), does the cooking, is free of threats, and he even helps his bodyguard to stay in shape by letting her practice her judo and karate on him (so she'll better be able to protect him, he explains to himself). These nightly practice sessions are described in graphic, tactile detail, of course.

I wrote this particular little tale between morning report and my eleven o'clock lecture to a class of GIs on defense against germ warfare. The lecture was actually a great deal more fictitious, and probably more original and inventive, than the story, because I knew a hell of a lot more about obsession than I did about god-damn germ warfare.

I began the lecture by offering to take on any bellicose germ in the house, provided he would stand up and fight like a man. Nobody laughed, of course, because I was an officer. It wasn't that they held back their laughter as a matter of principle or deference to rank; rather it was their inability to conceive of the fact that an officer might attempt to say anything really witty or absurd. It simply had never occurred to them.

When I returned to my office after the lecture, I mailed my story to Walter. But not until after I had signed the story with a nom de plume that I had invented for myself—a name which I used on all my stories and which was rapidly becoming familiar to thousands of my fans all over New England: I called myself N. Ovid.

BULLETIN

Quotation of the Day

"A spirit of national masochism prevails, encouraged by an effete corps of impudent snobs who characterize themselves as intellectuals." — Vice President Agnew,

CAMERA ONE

Morning. I am driving to the hospital. There is a commotion out back. Some of my men are in the woods behind the service station section of the building in which the immigrants are processed. I turn off the main road and drive over to investigate.

There, commanding the men, is Lt. Col. May Grainger, the chief nurse. About fifty-five years old. Pockmarked, pale, flat face, like an uncooked pancake. Thick glasses. Dumpy body on bare bowlegs. She is wearing a track suit and sneakers. And the men are in their underwear.

She explains. She had been jogging around the hospital at dawn, just as she always did, when she saw a man spying at her from the woods. As he was a member of the Negro race, and she had been raised in Alabama, she knew that his intent was sexual. So she sprinted over to the company barracks and ran inside, shouting, "O. K., men! Drop your cocks and grab your socks!" Just as she had planned, the men leaped right out of bed, thinking it was the first sergeant. Without giving them a chance to dress, she led them out into the woods on the double to search for the pervert, but by that time he was already gone.

She calls off the search, sends the GIs back to the barracks, and then thanks me for the use of my men. I tell her that it wasn't anything, really, but she insists on getting a letter of commendation from Colonel Creetner for me until she is interrupted by sounds of song emanating from the service station. A chorus of voices with Spanish accents singing, "Colombia, the Gem of the Ocean."

"What's that?" I ask.

"Oh, that must be the new group of South American immigrants. They came in last night. From Colombia."

She smiles sweetly and begins to bounce her head in time with the song. Then, right there on the road, in her track suit, she begins to wave her arms, as if she were conducting the music. When the song ends, she turns and jogs off down the road.

And as I get back into my car, I hear the immigrants from Colombia swing into their next number—an almost unrecognizable version of "Roar, Lion, Roar."

CAMERA TWO

At four o'clock I entered the offices of the hospital headquarters. I was greeted by the smile of the cute, little black WAC. The one I had spoken to on my first day at the hospital. Way back at the beginning of summer. On one of the longest days of the year.

"Hello, lieutenant."

I was less nervous than I had been when I had first met her. As a consequence, I could see more. And I noticed the texture of her skin. A smooth, lovely ebony cover for her body.

"Hello, Private Washington," I said, reading her name tag on the breast of her jacket. I handed her the green check.

"You got the colonel's secret message, I see," she said, laughing.

"Yes . . . I did." I stumbled over the words in my reply, because her laughter startled me. She was the first person I had ever encountered in the army who had laughed at it.

I felt myself immediately open up to her. A flow of warmth. Perhaps that's what man is. *Homo ridens.* The animal that laughs.

"Do you mind," I asked, "if, when nobody's around, I dispense with this 'private' stuff and call you by your name?"

"I'd like that, lieutenant. It's Lorraine."

"Thanks."

I picked up a book from the top of her desk. It was a Modern Library edition of Proust. *Swann's Way.*

"Do you read a lot, Lorraine?"

"Well, I did before I was in the army. I'm just getting started again. I never went to college, but I read all I can. I like books, I guess."

"This is pretty heavy stuff to begin with."

"But it's good," she said, earnestly. "It's good, isn't it, lieutenant?"

"Yes, it's good, Lorraine."

She smiled again. "The guy who loaned it to me said that Proust was great, but that he was a *yenta.*"

I broke up. "A *yenta?* Is he Jewish, this guy?"

"No. He's a spade like me. But we're both from New York. There, everybody's Jewish."

"I'm hip," I grinned. "Should I go in to see the colonel, now?"

"He's giving a briefing, but there's nobody in the light colonel's office, next to his. Why don't you go in and wait in there?"

"O.K. Fine." Turning to the colonel's office, I added, "It was good talking to you, Lorraine."

She rewarded me with another smile.

"Oh, lieutenant," she called after me as I passed through the entrance to the adjutant's office, "can I ask you one more thing?"

"Shoot."

"This Proust, do you think that he spends too much of his feeling on himself?"

"No. . . . No, I don't think so. Because he's concerned equally with all his characters. He cherishes himself, but no more than he cherishes each of the other people in his book."

Once again, I was privileged to witness her smile.

"Lorraine," I asked, "the guy who gave you this book, is he on the base?"

"Oh, no," she said. "He was here once, but he's outside now."

I entered the adjutant's office and quietly walked through it into the office of the executive officer.

The lights in both offices were turned off, but the door to the colonel's office was slightly ajar and a reddish glow came through. I peeked in and saw the colonel, in front of a large map of the area, holding a pointer and lecturing to about twenty men, sitting in straight-backed chairs. The entire scene had an infernal quality to it, as the red lights soaked everything in a thick, sanguine dye.

On one side of the colonel stood the executive officer (the XO) holding his required tools—chalk, eraser, etc. The colonel would turn to him periodically, hold out his palm, and yell out the name of the needed object, and the XO would vigorously slap it into the colonel's palm while repeating the name.

"Chalk!"

"Chalk!"

"Eraser!"

"Eraser!"

"Pointer!"

"Pointer!"

On the other side of the map stood the adjutant, who, in accordance with a memorized program, turned the next map down at the instant it was required, like the page turner for a concert pianist.

As I silently watched this scene for a few minutes, the true strangeness of it began to hit me. For more bizarre than the lighting and the presentation was the content of the colonel's talk. It gradually became so clear to me that I could not resist understanding it—the colonel was briefing pilots on a bombing mission which was to be carried out that evening. And the target upon which the planes were going to drop their scarlet gifts was Mount Mercy—the town hospital.

Suddenly the meeting ended. The pilots jumped to attention at the adjutant's call and the colonel said, "Dismissed, gentlemen. And God speed you."

I leaped into an easy chair. The pilots tramped by me, but the XO jumped when he saw me.

"Colonel! Colonel, sir! The lieutenant's out here. He's been in my office. During the *meeting!*"

The colonel appeared stunned at first. Instinctively, he turned to his mirror, but then, with resolution, he spun back again and said to the XO, "I'll handle this, Marvin. Dismissed."

"Yes, *sir,*" the light colonel snapped, and he waddled out of the office.

"Come in here, lieutenant," the colonel commanded, his skin red with the reflected glow of the bulbs. "And close the door behind you."

"Yes, sir."

"Sit down, lieutenant." He pointed to a chair next to his desk and he bent down to his intercom box. "Private Washington. Get in here!"

Lorraine quickly appeared in the office. The colonel began to pace around the room as he yelled, "What do you mean by this, Private Washington! You knew that was a top-secret briefing. What do you mean by letting anyone into these offices during a secret briefing!"

"I'm sorry sir," she said quietly.

"Sorry isn't enough!"

"He had a pass, sir. For four o'clock. With your signature on it, doctor. I felt it carried the full weight of your personal command."

"Aghh!" the colonel cried. "Dismissed. Dismissed, private. Don't let this happen again."

After Lorraine had left, he continued to stomp around the room in angered frustration.

"What can you do with them?" he shouted. "How can you run an army when you've got to rely on *them*?"

"Privates, sir?"

"*Niggers,* you imbecile!" he moaned, pulling at his hair. "Niggers!"

Then he began to calm down a bit, and as he sat in his chair, he said, in a more normal but still despondent voice, "Niggers . . . privates . . . what's the difference, anyway?"

He filled one of his pipes and lit it. His spirits seemed to rise. "Well, lieutenant, what do you think of these red lights? Pretty snazzy, ay?"

"Yes, sir. What are they for?"

"What are they *for*?" he leaped up. "What's the matter with you, lieutenant! Don't you ever go to the movies? They always brief the pilots in red light before they go out on a mission." To the mirror: "What are they *for*? That's a good one!" To me: "Don't they teach you anything in college?"

He sat down again and seemed calmer once more. "Pretty authentic, don't you think?"

"Yes, sir."

"Good, good. About our business. . . . I guess by now you've ascertained why I called you here today. About the WAC detachment, you might say."

"Yes, sir."

"Good. Captain Taylor told you?"

"Yes, sir."

"Well, that's O.K. then. Fine young officer, Captain Taylor. Descended from a great general. Goes to show you that breeding and heritage will out."

"A general?"

"Yes, lieutenant. Zachary Taylor. Didn't she tell you? President Zachary Taylor."

"No, sir. . . . She didn't mention it."

"Well, she's not the one to mouth off, lieutenant. But she's a fine officer. Gets things done."

"Yes, sir."

"Look, lieutenant, as long as she informed you we might as well get to this other business. You heard about this counteroffensive we were planning here?"

"I couldn't help overhearing, colonel."

"Call me doctor, will you, lieutenant."

"Yes, doctor."

"Well, you'll have to stay here at the service station until the mission is carried out. Routine security precautions, you understand."

"Yes, doctor."

"And we can use you, besides. We'll have a lot of work to do tonight. A *lot* of work."

He rose from his desk and began to walk back and forth across the floor behind it, nervously rubbing his hands together. His eyes glowed with anticipation. He glanced over to the mirror.

"Yes, yes, it'll be just like old times. The infectious diseases wards will have to be opened again. And the operating room will be back on full schedule, like in World War II. We'll be doing real medicine around here again. Old people, young people . . . we'll need all the help we can get. You stick around, lieutenant."

"But sir—doctor . . . surely you're not going to bring the patients here from the town hospital. . . . You're not going to actually bomb Mount Mercy?"

"What do you think we're going to do, lieutenant? What do you suggest those pilots drop on the hospital? Get well cards?"

"But sir . . . I guess I just . . . I hadn't realized. . . ."

"Wake up, lieutenant. That's war. That's the price we have to pay. That's why the soldier always opposes war. He knows the price, son."

"But sir, this is a hospital. Old people, sick babies. . . ."

"You *see* what we're up against, lieutenant. An enemy that will hide behind the shelter of the red cross. He knows no limits, son. . . . Oh, he's a treacherous foe. Treacherous."

When I sat there without answering, he added, "But we'll get him, lieutenant. Don't you worry about a thing. We'll get him." Then he sat down and commanded, "Dismissed."

As I rose to leave, he said, "You'll eat at the mess hall, lieutenant. Stay with the light colonel and the adjutant until the attack commences. Then report to outpatient to help sort the casualties as they're wheeled up the ramp."

"Will that be all, doctor?"

"Colonel! This is the army, you know."

"Yes, colonel."

"Dismissed!"

C A M E R A   O N E

I go to dinner with the light colonel and the adjutant. Before we reach the mess hall, I ask the fat XO if I can stop in my office to call Edith, to tell her I won't be home for dinner.

"I don't see any harm in that, do you Herm?" he says to the adjutant.

"No, sir," the captain replies. "After all . . . it's his *wife.*"

"You go right ahead, lieutenant. We'll just wait out here for you in the hall."

C A M E R A   T W O

I went into my office, closed the door, and dialed our home number. Warren answered.

"Warren, it's me," I whispered. "Put Edith on, fast."

"O.K.," he whispered back, and giggled. Then I heard him calling Edith, in a loud, simulated, hoarse whisper. She came to the phone.

"Edith, it's me," I whispered.

"Jake?" she whispered. And I could hear Warren cracking up with laughter in the background. Then she whispered, "Warren, shut up," and she, too, began to giggle.

"Edith, this is serious," I whispered. "They're going to bomb Mount Mercy tonight."

"Jake . . . you can't be serious. . . ."

"I *am.* I only have a minute. You've got to let them know."

"But how?"

"I don't know," I whispered.

"Jacob, you've got to be kidding. . . . But even if you aren't, they won't evacuate the hospital on an unfounded tip. They have seriously ill people there. They can't just march them into the street like a school fire drill."

"Edith, that's not enough. You've got to do something."

"Me!" she exclaimed, now fully serious. "Me! What can *I* do? It's your army. It's your stupid colonel, *You* do something."

"I'm stuck here. I have to run."

"I can't do anything, Jacob. You're the husband. . . . You're the soldier. *You* do something."

"Edith, I can't. I have to hang up, now. They're coming."

"Well, dammit Jacob, how can you. . . ." Click.

"Everything O.K., lieutenant? You look disturbed," the light colonel said.

I forced a smile. "Women!" I said. "Sometimes they'll put a soufflé over the national interest."

"I know how it is, lieutenant," the XO said.

"Don't we all," added the adjutant.

So we all smiled a "that's life" at each other and went over to the mess hall. I wasn't surprised to find that in spite of the events of the day, the light colonel's appetite was unimpaired. He had double servings of potatoes and dessert. I wasn't all that hungry, myself.

BULLETIN

Pentagon Issues Rules For Political Activities

WASHINGTON, Oct. 4 (UPI)—The Defense Department ruled Wednesday that members of the armed forces could display political stickers and join political clubs but could not serve as club officers or march in political parades.

CAMERA TWO

That night was unforgettable. It was not just the wounded people, nor even the fact that the wounded were civilians—of all ages. But that they were sick *before* they were wounded.

This led to an incredible turmoil. Trying to patch up people who were already crippled. Taking casts off people to treat them and then putting on new casts. Attempting to keep the infectious disease cases separate from the rest. Trying to save a terminal cancer patient who had had her legs blown off. Picking the bits of metal out of the body of a child with cerebral palsy.

Continuously working. In a mess of stench, tears, shit, blood, urine, and human rot. And always there was wailing. A chorus of groans and cries emitted by people in pain.

But perhaps the single image which impressed itself most forcefully on my mind was that of a man who wasn't hurt at all. He was in his late twenties, small, bearded, with dark, gentle eyes. And he was looking for his wife of one year. An auburn-haired girl, twenty-two years old. She had been in the maternity ward at Mount Mercy.

As I checked in patients and dispatched ambulances back into town, he stood at my side, watching them wheel the patients in and nervously telling me about his young wife. She was a sabra, born in Israel, and an honor graduate of Radcliffe, in Cambridge, where he had met her three years before. He said she could be recognized by a mole above her upper lip, on the righthand side.

Because he was talking, it was I who saw her first. On a table being wheeled up the ramp by Lorraine, the colonel's secretary, who had shown up in civilian clothes soon after the casualties started coming in and had volunteered to help. I saw the mole. And the bright auburn hair. And a face that was full and kind. An Old Testament face. And her skin. So smooth and olive-rich. . . . How lovely it must have been when it still had fresh blood being pumped through it.

"Rabbi," I said quietly, grasping his shoulders. Holding him up.

Lorraine stopped the table in front of us. In the confusion the body had not been covered with a sheet. All it wore was a surgical gown.

The rabbi began to wobble. I put one of his arms around the back of my neck and held him. Then, after an indeterminate silence, he spoke. "The baby," he said, weakly. "The baby . . . the baby . . ."

A nurse from Mount Mercy who was pushing another cart into outpatient overheard the question. "She miscarried, sir," she said to me.

"Where . . . where is it?" the rabbi said in a voice that was almost shy.

"I don't know, sir," the nurse said, avoiding the rabbi's eyes. "The wall of obstetrics was blown out. Everything was burning. The ceiling began to fall. We were lucky to get out alive. . . . Oh!" she straightened with a jerk and blushed. "Oh. . . . Oh, I'm sorry, I'm so sorry. . . ."

"That's O.K., ma'm," I said. "Why don't you just wheel the rabbi's wife over to the temporary morgue on Ward 41. I'll watch the other body til you come back.

The nurse wheeled the body away and the rabbi regained his balance and stood up unsupported.

And then he began to speak. To start a sentence. But he was unable to finish it. He was unable to give form to the sentiments which, as a rabbi, he thought he ought to express.

"Well," he began, "well . . . well. . . ." Until he broke down in tears.

And that was the highlight of an impossibly eventful night. That was the coda to the wail and blood and disease and scurrying stench which surrounded us.

Finally, Lorraine took the rabbi's arm. "Rabbi," she said gently, "you just come along with me. We'll get you a little schnapps."

As she led him back down the ramp, she said quietly, "Goodnight, lieutenant."

"Goodnight, Lorraine," was all I could answer. I couldn't say, "Goodnight, rabbi." No, under the circumstances, I really couldn't do that.

CAMERA TWO

When I returned home, late the following afternoon, Jeannie and Warren were there, listening to an old Lester Young record of mine.

"You dig Prez, Jeannie?" I said, as I entered.

She smiled.

"I knew you would."

"Lester was in the service, Jake," she said. "During World War II."

And as I entered the bedroom to change out of my blue suit, I heard her say to Warren, "And after he got out he was never the same."

The front door opened and slammed.

"Here's a pizza!" Edith cried. "Jake? You home? Celebration, everybody! Celebration!"

I pulled on my jeans and went back inside. "What's up?"

"I got a job."

"With Telecation?" Warren asked.

"That's right." Edith beamed. She put the pizza on the big table in the area of the living room which served as a dining room. "Hi, Jeannie, there's plenty for you, too. Come on everybody, sit down and eat while it's still hot."

"What's Telecation," I asked.

"Haven't you ever heard of them, Jake?" Warren said.

"They're great," Edith said. "It's just what I wanted. The farthest-out people in town. All bright guys from Harvard and M.I.T. And their into the same things that I am. Programmed learning. Audio-visual. Multimedia. Oh, Jacob, it's just what I was looking for."

And Edith glowed—but then a cloud passed over her face. "But look at me going on like this. After what happened last night. I'm sorry about that, Jacob. Maybe we shouldn't be celebrating."

"After last night we need a celebration," I said.

"Oh, Jacob," Edith said. "Look how tired you are. I'll bet you didn't get a wink of sleep all night. . . . And you were right, you know. We were able to do something."

"You were?"

"Well, we couldn't stop it of course. But when we told Jeannie, she packed us into her car—Len was working last night, too—and we drove to Mount Mercy and helped in the evacuation after the attack."

"You did?"

"Yes. But it was mainly Jeannie. You should have seen her."

We all looked at Jeannie, and I realized how silly it is to speak of Indians as being red. For Jeannie was blushing, and, with the blood coming up to the surface of her face, I was able to glimpse a hint of what her skin would have looked like if it had really been red.

"We all helped," she said.

"Oh, no," Edith said, pointing to a homemade bandage on Jeannie's forearm, which I hadn't noticed before. "You should have seen her, Jake. She burned her arm."

"Jeannie!" I said. "You should have gotten that taken care of."

"We already *were* at the hospital, Jake," Warren said.

Then Edith resumed the narrative: "It was at obstetrics, up on the third floor. The floor of the ward fell out. Did you hear about that, Jacob?"

"I heard the ceiling was falling."

"Well, the ceiling burned, but it was the collapse of the floor that cut off the new babies from the rest of the hospital. No one could get to them, because, besides all the smoke and flames, there was only one steel girder going across from the accessible part of the building. So Jeannie simply tightrope walked it, back and forth, carrying out a baby at a time. That's all."

"Jeannie!" I said in amazement.

"It wasn't really anything," Jeannie said, blushing again. "Any Mohawk could have done it. For some reason, we're not afraid of heights."

There was nothing else to say. I just ate my pizza and looked in wonder at this pretty, short, even somewhat squat, drunken Indian, sitting across the table from me, shyly nibbling on a single slice of pizza and not taking another out of sheer regard for the appetites of her hosts.

"Well, what about your job?" Jeannie said to Edith.

"Oh . . . it's really too good to be true. You should see the office. Modern furniture made of the latest plastics. The newest tape and projection equipment. And the reception room! Op paintings and a big Pop sculpture —a five-foot-high roll of toilet paper. It's simply too much."

Then she quieted and turned toward me. "Oh, Jacob, don't spoil it. . . ."

"I haven't said a thing."

"I know what you're thinking, though. And it isn't true. They're really nice, Jacob. And they're hip. I'm sure they all smoke. And they have a connection with a plastics company. . . . They're getting everyone who works there a plastic hemisphere, ten feet in diameter. You put it in your backyard. It's tinted and it serves as a sculpture. But if there's a bombing attack, you get under it, Jacob, and it will withstand anything but a direct hit."

"I don't want a plastic bomb shelter in my backyard, dammit!" I shouted.

Edith began to weep. "I knew it," she said, appealing to Warren and Jeannie, "I just knew it. You can't please him. . . . Nothing I do is right."

Jeannie said quickly, "He's just tired, Edith. . . . Don't worry. It's just that he's been up all night."

"That's right, Edith," Warren said. "It sounds fascinating to me."

Then they both looked at me.

"O.K. O.K., you win. . . . I'm sorry, Edith. . . . I'm tired. These bombings get to me, I guess."

"It's a good firm," she said, through her tears. "I don't want a bomb shelter either. . . . We won't accept it, that's all."

"It's not the bomb shelter. . . ."

"Oh, Jacob," Edith implored, "can't you do anything? Can't you bring them to their senses?"

When I didn't answer, she returned to the subject of her job. "We'll do good things. You'll see. This generation is screwed up, but we'll be reaching out to the young people. Educating them for change. In fact, that's what I'll be doing, Jacob. I'll be working on programmed learning on television for the prespeaking babies— ages one to two."

She looked at me and she began to weep again. Before I could say a word, Jeannie flashed a stop sign at me with her eyes. Then Edith gathered herself together, and said, with a quiet seriousness, "Don't you think we have a chance, Jacob? The adults are beyond repair, but don't you think we have a chance to get to the young with technology?"

"Yes," I said. "I think you do."

"There!" Jeannie quickly interjected. "You see! He was just tired. That's all. Your job will be just fine."

"They're good people," Edith said. "They really are. They're into sensory awareness and all the latest things. One of the secretaries told me that last year, in order to introduce an I.Q. test they developed for preliterates, they had a nude fish fry, with electronic music and a light show projected on the guests."

After we finished the pizza, we quietly sat around the table, sipping on espresso which Edith had made, grinding the beans herself.

"Jeannie," I said, "do you mind if I ask you a personal question?"

"Of course not, Jake."

"Well I was wondering. . . . Is Len really an Indian?"

She took a last sip from her little cup before answering, "Len says the Indian is an invention of the white man."

"How so?"

"Well, there isn't just one kind of Indian. There are as many Indian cultures as there are white cultures. Or at least there were, until the whites saw to it that many of the cultures became extinct. There was as much difference between the Incas and the Sioux of the plains as between the Turks and the Swedes, for example."

"But Len, he's from Brooklyn, isn't he?"

"Yes, he is. That's where we met. In high school. My family moved there from upstate New York so my father could work high steel when I was just a baby. Right before World War II began. Did I ever tell you about my father, Jake?"

"No."

"He enlisted during World War II. And he returned from the Pacific in 1945, but he left his legs on Iwo Jima. He'd been in communication with some of the other Iroquois we knew. They would speak in Mohawk over the radio and the Japanese couldn't translate it. When he came back he stopped going out of the house. He had a pension and he wouldn't take a job. Once you've worked high steel, you don't have much interest in opening up a newsstand in the subway.

"That's when I first heard jazz. There were some spades living next door and my father used to listen to records and drink with them. When Charlie Parker began to record, my father became Bird's greatest fan—would listen to him for hours at a time. He finally drank himself to death in 1955."

"And Len?" I asked.

"Oh yes, Len," she smiled. "I really don't know. Len says he has Indian blood. He grew up with our people and he can speak some Seneca. But I really don't care. When we met, he was fifteen and living with an aunt who was white. He said he was an orphan."

"I guess we'll never know," Edith said.

"I guess not," Jeannie said. "But we're sure going to have some Indian activities around the base this fall."

"What's happening?" I asked, taking the joint from Warren's outstretched hand.

"Len's got base approval for his Indian scout group," she said. "They're registered on the base list of officially sanctioned recreation activities for teenagers as 'the King Phillip Memorial Society.' And they're going to get support from the funds set aside for the base teenager club. I think it was Len's patriotic pitch and the Ph.

D. after his name that did it. You know, American Heritage kind of stuff."

"Oh, wow!" Warren said. "Judo!"

Edith looked puzzled by this statement, but she turned her attention to the joint I passed her. Jeannie smiled at Warren to indicate she dug what he was saying.

And we spent a pleasant evening together. Listened to the *Stabat Mater* of Giovanni Battista Pergolesi. Got wrecked. Forgot about the war for a while. And wondered about what other unutterably beautiful music Pergolesi might have written, had he lived to be twenty-seven.

After Edith went to bed, Len came by, looking for Jeannie. He was slightly drunk and sipped at a glass of whiskey as the four of us watched a TV program about hypnotic research which Warren wanted to see. They hypnotized a guy and told him his girlfriend was in the room with him. While he was holding a conversation with her (with an empty chair) they actually sent his girlfriend into the room. Then the doctor said if your girl is standing here, she can't really be in that chair too, can she? And the subject looked confused for a while, and then answered, simply, that she *was* in the chair. So the doctor said that would mean that she was in two places at the same time. And the subject smiled sheepishly, and he said that's right. That's what she is.

When the show ended, Warren switched off the set and asked Len if he ever used hypnosis in his work.

"Sometimes. But only to find out things. I don't believe in substituting a new set of hypnotic commands for the old ones."

"Which old ones?" I said.

"Those of the culture. The culture's value system. The dos and don'ts they set in kids' heads to keep them on the culture's approved path for the rest of their lives. Like a gyroscope that pulls them back whenever they try to deviate. I'm not into substituting one hypnosis for another. That's Telecation's bag."

It was late and Jeannie was already half-asleep but Len continued, heatedly, "They're into hypnosis just like Creetner and the boys. Only they think *they* aren't hypnotized. But that's where they're wrong."

"Len, don't you think it's time we went to bed?" Jeannie said.

"Underneath, they still dream of becoming heroes by coming off the bench and saving this society in the last minutes of play," Len said, as he rose from his chair. "They don't realize that this country was stolen from my people—that's America's original sin. This land was a paradise—an Eden—until the Americans arrived. With their whole fucking hypocritical unnatural value system. Their snake knowledge of *their* good and *their* evil. Their whole sick culture. It's rotten to the core. Cancerous. It can't be changed. It has to be extirpated."

Jeannie took him by the arm.

"Do you think the American form of culture is hypnosis?" I asked.

"All culture is hypnosis. There's nothing magic about hypnosis. It's just a state of heightened suggestivity. And kids are more suggestible than you can imagine."

"But what about Indian culture?" I said.

"It's *cultures*, not culture. But the cultures were mostly small, rather than unwieldy, particularly in the area now called the United States. And because they weren't based on an original sin, they weren't unconsciously suicidal. They mainly let the kids alone. Until the white man came, Mother Earth provided for everyone's needs and people had an independence, a looseness, which favored growth and life."

"Len . . . ," Jeannie appealed, gently turning him toward the door.

"America is the most uptight, guilt-ridden nation on earth," he said over his shoulder as they left. "This society isn't looking for a hero to save it. It's looking for someone to put it out of its misery. It's in love with death, Jake. Every new gyroscope that's implanted in a baby's brain is just one more pull toward automatism and rigidity. And the ultimate rigidity is death."

As I locked the door behind them, I turned to Warren and said, "He'll regret that speech in the morning."

"I don't know," he replied.

CAMERA THREE

So that's the way it dragged on. Day after day. And often into the night. Most nights were easier than the night of the Mercy Hospital raid, however; usually the patients we admitted were merely wounded rather than wounded and diseased.

But here and there I was able to find some time for relaxation.

Cal arranged for me to have Tuesday afternoons off for my swimming lessons. Because of the way she conducted them, however, these sessions were usually more embarrassing than relaxing.

First, she insisted that I wear a nylon bathing suit which she had bought for me, although I wasn't comfortable in it because I felt it was too tight and too brief. Of course, although all the WACs wore modest, one-piece tank suits, she always made an entrance in one of her bikinis, of which she seemed to have an inexhaustible supply. They tended to fall into two categories, based upon the way they fitted her ass. Some were wide and low, revealing an inch or two of cleavage at the top; others were narrow and high, covering the top of her ass, but working their way up the crack to reveal the luscious swell of her cheeks and the curved hollows where they met her thighs.

Then she would enter the pool and hold her arms out at water level, with her palms upward. I would lie across them, so that one supported me beneath my hips and the other across my chest. Then she would instruct me and support me as I kicked my legs and stroked with my arms and we moved back and forth across the pool. In front of all the WACs.

And her mischievous nature didn't help matters either. Often, when there were a lot of WACs around, she would slide one of her arms down beneath me, as she supported me, and would covertly move her hand to my crotch and gently stroke me with her fingers as I tried to swim. As soon as she felt me getting hard, she would release me and say in a loud voice that the lesson was over for the day and that I could leave the pool now, while smiling at me, knowing that I would be ashamed to leave the pool with a hard-on almost bursting through the little bathing suit she had bought for me.

After a few weeks, in which I had made little progress, if any, she further decreased whatever powers of concentration I had been able to maintain by appearing at the pool in just the bottom half of her bikini. After this I didn't learn a thing. But I couldn't stop going to the pool, every Tuesday afternoon, regardless of anything else I might have done with the free time. I learned to hide my excitement from the other WACs by getting into water above my waist *before* she made her appearance, with her statuesque body threatening to explode out of the feeble restraints of the tight, little, clinging bottom of her bikini.

CAMERA ONE

A tremendous explosion wakes me. Rocks the house. Then the clatter of falling things. Heavy things. In the back, behind the house. The clock says ten. It's . . . Saturday. October. On the base.

Edith isn't here. . . . She has gone to Boston with her bosses, for a series of lectures on educating the prenatal infant.

I run out the back door, followed by Warren. Both in our pajamas. Len and Jeannie and Little Jo are fully dressed and already out in the field behind the house.

"What happened?" I ask, as we run up to them. But I can already see the smoke rising from down by the river.

"They blew up the bridge," Little Jo says. "What an explosion! Did you hear it?"

"No," Warren says, "we ran out here like this for a game of croquet on the lawn."

BULLETIN

Ecologist Sees U.S. On Suicidal Course

By GLADWIN HILL
Special to The New York Times

LOS ANGELES, Nov. 18— A scientist warned today that the United States was "approaching the point of no return" in its disruption of nature's chemical balances and had only about one generation in which to reverse its "suicidal course."

"Well, it's hard to see how they can go any further, if that's any consolation," I said.

"No, it isn't," Len said.

"It isn't?" Jeannie said.

"No," Len answered. "In fact, if you look over to the left, you'll see how they're already going further."

We looked to the left, downriver to the south, and sure enough, there were three small gunboats, fully manned and armed, moving up the river toward what had been the bridge to town.

"Now they'll be cruising up and down the fucking river all day," Len said, "to keep out B.C. infiltrators."

"Well, there's always a silver lining," I said, "the North Bridge up the river is still standing. We might as well use it while we can. How about a walk over to David's?"

"Count us out," Len said. "I've got the use of a truck today, and we're going to pick up some lumber."

"You building something?" I asked.

"Yes. It's for the scouts. Did Jeannie tell you? I've got the base behind me, now."

I nodded. "What are you building?"

"Oh, it's a kind of longhouse. We'll use it for our meetings this winter. It won't be much. Not very different from a simple recreation hall, but we've got to be careful to always refer to it as the longhouse. They already have a recreation hall for teenagers and they won't want to build another one."

"Will you finish it before winter?"

"Sure, we've got two months," he said. "Besides, the base engineers are going to help."

The three of them walked back to their house.

"Well, Warren, how about it? You want to come?"

"Sure, Jake," he said. "Shall we dress first, or go like this, in our pajamas?"

We dressed.

When we arrived at the North Bridge, we encountered a mechanized bedlam. A herd of cars and trucks of every size and species standing there honking and beeping at each other. None seemed to be moving.

"Jesus," I said, "look at this traffic! It was bad enough on Saturdays when there were two bridges."

"This is only the beginning," Warren smiled. "The last shall be first, Jake. The walkers shall beat the drivers. Soon it will be this way all over. The heads will be arriving at their destinations while the Americans are still tied up in traffic, having heart attacks."

He seemed unusually cheerful as we slowly walked up to the bridge, passing all the stalled cars.

"You faggot!"

"Hey, freak!"

A chorus of raucous cries began to emanate from the ranks of the frustrated motorists. Warren merely ignored them, a nonchalant, long-haired owl, gaily singing, "Oh, What a Beautiful Morning!"

"*Oklahoma?*" I said, in disbelief.

"You have to communicate with them in a language they can understand," he said rapidly, out of the side of his mouth, immediately picking up the lighthearted refrain again where he had left off.

Where the three approaches to the bridge bottlenecked, the traffic was worst. Cars and trucks were pointing in every direction, and the sound of their horns was almost deafening. Two separate collisions had occurred and angry people were milling around the dented cars shouting obscenities and pushing one another. On the bridge itself, a man viciously smacked his wife on the ear. Two men ran over. The first, a redheaded man in a suit and tie, punched the husband in the face, breaking his nose. The second, who was carrying a tire iron, seemed to lose his head at this point and he hit the redhead in the mouth with the iron bar, knocking out several teeth. He then hit the woman over the head with it, laying open her skull.

Halfway across we came upon a hot-dog stand on wheels (a hot-dog cart, really) with a large red, white, and blue umbrella over it. Stuck in traffic with all the motorized vehicles. It was tended by an old man wearing a World War I army uniform. The sign painted on the side of the cart read Doughboy Hot Dogs. Great War Veterans, Inc.

"Want to get a hot dog, Jake?" Warren said.

"Sure."

We walked over to the cart.

"Hello, Eben," Warren said.

"Why, hello there, Warren," the old man answered.

"You know each other?" I said.

"Sure, that's the advantage of having time. You get to know people. Everyone else is too busy working for the social good."

Warren introduced me to Eben. "You in the war, pop?" I asked.

"That's right, sonny. I sure was. The Great War. That was a *war*. Went overseas to get John Bull out of a mess. Fought the Kaiser for a while, straightened things out over there, went to Paris for a couple months, and finished—back home, where we started." He smiled to himself. "Yes, sir, Paris. Quite a town. Never forget it. Best year of my life."

Turning back to the cart, he opened the lid to the steaming water which held the hot dogs. "Well, you can't live on memories. What'll you boys have?"

"Want onions, Jake?" Warren said.

"O.K."

"Two with onions, Eben."

Eben speared two hot dogs with his fork and placed them on rolls. He pulled the lid off a metallic, red-stained compartment, which was empty.

"Sorry, boys," he said, "I'm all out of onions. This traffic jam has eaten them all. First time in the history of the stand," he shook his head.

"That's O.K.," Warren said. "Just some mustard will do."

Eben smeared the mustard on the hot dogs. I gave him two quarters.

"Just a minute," he said, "I can't charge you boys full price. Got no onions, you know."

"That's O.K., Eben," I said, but he forced a dime into my hand and wouldn't take it back.

As we walked away from the stand he opened up another metal compartment, peered in, and called after us, "You sure you boys don't want some liberty cabbage?"

"No thanks," Warren called back to him, smiling, and once again breaking into "Oh, What a Beautiful Morning," in a loud cheerful voice, over the cries of, "You Pinko!" and, "Hey, Fruit!" which came from the angry people inside the bellies of their crippled, steel hippos.

BULLETIN

Doing Their Thing Is Called Hippies' Way to Duck Life

CHICAGO (AP) — A psychiatrist on the staff of the Menninger clinic says that hippies refuse to face such adult responsibilities as marriage and earning a living, and refuse to admit their refusal, too.

CAMERA TWO

At David's cabin, the evidence of Sibyl's collecting days remained. In fact, before her incarceration, she had managed to fill the shower with broken furniture and, in several places, to advance the height of her junk piles to the ceiling.

David was seated in the corner on the mattress, wearing a Moroccan darrha, a kind of striped gray toga. He was talking to Walter Qwalters when we entered the cabin. We greeted each other and David passed us the hookah.

"Well," I said, "looks like you came into some nice stuff."

"Walter did," David said. "But things are getting really tight around here. This may be the last stash in Central Mass."

"By the time the chief took his share, there wasn't shit left for anybody else," Walter said.

"Now, Walter, take it slow," David said. "The chief has plans."

"Plans, my ass, pops. All the chief's got is talk. Talk and grass, because he cops nine-tenths of every lid we make. And what does he show for it?"

"Look," Daivd said, "The chief is reliable. You can count on that. When the action begins, the chief'll be on the field."

"Man, that's all I ever get from these guys," Walter said to us. "The chief sticks up for David, and David sticks up for the chief. And between them both they've smoked up enough grass to make me rich twice over. Grass don't grow on trees man. Especially now that the famine is on."

"The chief pays you for the grass he takes, and you know it, Walter," David said.

"Wholesale, daddy, *wholesale!*"

"Well, you just don't worry about it, you hear," David said, with a hint of force in his voice which hadn't been there when we'd first met him.

"I want to kick some ass, pops. I can't wait forever."

"The chief knows what he's doing. Just cool it."

"Tell me something," I interrupted. "Len Rainey buys grass from you, I know that, but is he the same chief that's involved in your movement?"

David said, "Len is *the* chief, man. Of everything. I thought you knew."

"Well, I'll be fucked," I said.

"Here," David said, handing me the hookah hose, "take a good drag, Jake. Catch up with the rest of us."

As I held the hot smoke in my lungs, I began to realize how obvious it all was. Had I been reading my life, instead of living it, I might have guessed it chapters before. But like Poe says, if you want to hide something from someone, put it right under his nose —there's a good chance he'll never notice it.

"Walter tells me you've taken my old job," David said.

"Yeah, temporarily, anyhow. In fact, I've got your stories here for you, Walter," I said, and I handed him the pile of army company punishment forms on the backs of which I had written the pieces for *Sado-Mask.*

"Thanks, man," Walter said. "We need you." Then to David, "This cat is dynamite. He's supporting the revolution."

"I had intended on doing some writing of my own," I said.

"I'm hip," David said. "Fiction, wasn't it? You getting any time for it?"

"What do you think he's writing for *Sado-Mask*, pops," Walter said.

"He means real fiction," David said.

"What's *real*, daddy?"

"It's hard to say, I guess," I said.

"What you're saying in *Sado-Mask* is real to my readers, pops. When your stories appear, the phone rings all week. They dig you, man. They dig you."

"That's not what he means, Walter," David said. "He's not talking about writing crap for the public, man."

"That's who buys the papers, pops. The public. And who do you think buys the books? John Q. Public. And if you don't like it, you're gonna lump it, man, cause John Q's got the bread, and if you want it, he's the man you got to talk to. Or else," he began to laugh, "you might as well clam up like Warren here, and let other people do the communicating while you smoke up all the grass."

Warren smiled and passed Walter the hookah which he had been smoking while the three of us were talking.

"That's not what he means, Walter," David said. "A real writer . . . well, he doesn't write for a public."

"Who does he write for, pops?"

"He . . . well, I think he writes for other writers. Not critics and scholars; they're all just genteel full-a-shits who think that when the day of reckoning comes along, they'll be allowed to hide in the stacks at the library."

"Yes . . . but I felt more like I was writing for the characters themselves. Like a kind of covenant. As long as I really listened, and tried to write what I heard, they would keep whispering their most private thoughts and fears to me."

"But your obligation is to real people, pops," Walter said.

"Well, that's just it, Walter. You see, I think the people who speak to me for my writing *are* real. As real as . . . you, for instance. Or David, or Warren . . . or even me."

"This is too philosophical for me, pops," Walter said. "You just keep turning out your two stories a week, and that's fine with me. Art's O.K. in its place, but the revolution needs bread, daddy."

"And grass," Warren added.

"You know it," Walter said. "If the chief didn't steal every lid we lay our hands on. . . ."

"Now, Walter, we heard this record. . . ."

"Don't put me down, pops," Walter shouted at David. "You're not the one to talk, man." Turning to me, "Do you know what this cat did? You hear about what he did to *Violence!*"

"No. . . ."

"Your friend David, here, I gave him full control over the last issue. I was in Boston, dig? Well, he can't just go ahead and put out the paper like normal. No. He can't just make up stories like we usually do—you know, 'Woman Gives Birth to Ape-Boy in Kashmir,' 'Vampire Strikes Again in the Andes' . . ."

"Wait a minute!" I said. "You mean you make it up! You guys just sit down and make up the whole paper, every week, out of your own heads?"

"Sure, pops," Walter smiled. "What the fuck do the readers know about Kashmir or the Andes?"

"But don't you have any basis? Anything to start with?"

"Fuck no, man," Walter said. "We ain't *The New York Times*, daddy. That takes bread, and we need all the bread we can get our hands on for the revolution."

"This is unbelievable," I said to Warren, who took it all in with his stoic gaze.

"It's fiction, pops," Walter said. "Like you said, man, art and reality."

"That's *not* what he said," David interrupted.

"You keep out of this, man. We had enough from you already. You fixed me but good, pops."

"What *happened?*" I asked.

"Well, everything's going just fine for *Violence*, see. Circulation rising, ads coming in . . . everything outasight, til I give Self-Sacrifice, here, control of the last issue, cause I think he's finally waking up again, dig? I think he's finally beginning to get his head back together. . . ."

"What *happened?*" I asked.

"Oh, nothing much. Except the Black Buddha, here, decided to run a contest. So right on page one he announces a contest for the reader who sends in the best violent story."

"So?"

"So, wait til you hear the prize, pops. The winning contestant gets to make up the whole next issue."

At this, Warren burst into laughter and I just couldn't keep a straight face myself, even though Walter looked so damn serious about the whole thing. So I cracked up and, when huge David said, from on the mattress where he was lying stretched out on his side in a pot-wrecked languor, "Well . . . shit, man, I can't write that crap every week," even Walter had to laugh, and all four of us sat there giggling and laughing until we cried, thinking of David's crazy contest, and the looks on the faces of the paper's loyal sub-scribers when they read about it.

We dug some sounds on the FM until David suggested we go over to the diner to get something to eat. Walter volunteered to drive us.

"I didn't know you had a car, Walter," I said, as we walked out of the cabin.

"I don't own it. I just rented it. That way I can write it off as an expense, pops. Keep the government from getting the money to buy bombs."

We walked down to the curb.

"This is it, man," Walter said, pointing to an enormous, new, copper-colored Lincoln convertible. "Hop in."

"Walter!" I exclaimed. "You said a car. This is a battleship!"

"It don't pay to be cheap, dad," Walter said. "Even a revolutionary's got to have some pride. Besides," he jumped into the driver's seat, "it's on Uncle Sam, so we might as well ride in style."

At the diner, I learned that Warren and David had previously agreed to go to a rock concert that afternoon. It was being held at a roadside club called the 1770, an old, converted, colonial mansion.

"Who's playing?" I asked.

"A local group. The Boston Braves. Why don't you come with us?" Warren said.

"I don't know. . . ."

"You'll make it, won't you Walter?" David said.

"You know it, daddy. We'll put the top up and drive over in my new air-conditioned."

He didn't refer to it as his "air-conditioned car." Merely as his "air-conditioned."

"You too, Jake?" David said.

"I have to be at work tonight at seven. The colonel's got some more fun and games on tap for the local citizenry, I guess. . . . But I don't see why I couldn't make it for a set or two."

"Far-out!" Warren said.

BULLETIN

Fighting at a Bonn Rally

BONN, West Germany, Sept. 7 (Reuters)—The police moved in to break up fighting at a rally sponsored here today by Adolf van hadden, leader of the rightist National Democratic party. At least 24 persons were arrested as the police dragged protestors from the Beethoven Concert Hall.

CAMERA TWO

When we got to the 1770 it was about 4:30 and the first set had already begun. The amplifiers were so huge we could hear the music quite clearly in the parking lot, where Walter left his air-conditioned.

We went into the main room room of the club. It was large for a roadside tavern, a kind of jerry-built, wooden dancehall which had been added to the original house in which the bar was situated. David and Walter ventured to talk to some friends at the bar while Warren and I went up front to a table for four. Above us, on the stage, the Boston Braves were wailing. All amplifiers up, all systems go. A local light show, the Minute Men, had their light machines spinning and strobe lights flickering on both the audience and the band, and, as the windows had been draped, we seemed to have entered a self-contained universe of music and color in which we and the musicians were welded into a unity within a winking rainbow of sound and light which held us all.

The musicians were wearing foot-long hair and loose clothing as varied and many-hued as the lights which flashed upon it. The Boston Braves. Five pieces—drums, electric bass, two guitars, and organ. We couldn't see the organist because our table was right down beneath the back of the instrument, but we could see the other four. And they were totally into the music they were making. Within it. And they were moving. And on lead guitar, I recognized a familiar face. It was Tommy Creetner.

Tommy was flying above the group, which was putting down a moving foundation that glistened with its speed. Faster and faster they chorded and drove while Tommy sailed out above them, going further and further toward orbital velocity on each run, riding with ice-skating grace out into inner space on a sheet of vibrations—of supportive organ chords which were only as thick and solid as thin ice. Only if he kept moving—only if his speed and daring held out—could he possibly continue his impossible glide and stay above, stay outside. And forward, forward he flew and swooned into mad dives of accelerated speed which swooped him down, down toward the earth, and . . . away, away on another tangent path of deafening speed, away from the ground and up, up again and along an arc of blind-flying speed which would once again have to support his soaring glide.

And out he rode, further and further, on long sustained notes, trembled and wavered with ecstatic energy of electric nerves, exploding into long single tremulous songs of dangerous bliss, a note at a time, and he helped the group to keep him up by laying out his own carpet a foot in front as he skimmed wildly over the surface, forward, forward to death, forward to bliss, forward to blessed ecstasy of bleached flight into the fire which doesn't burn the hot or cool but refines.

And only briefly would he stop. Only briefly to turn up his huge amplifiers even higher, extending the collage of his sound until it reached out to us, out of its bounds, out to us through the sweet-smelling smoke fog; it grappled with our innards, bending them in key, lending us the energy to leap and channeling the power shipped from great Niagara's grid through miles of singing wires solely so Tommy's fingers could send it back through the amps to turn it into crushed air, forced out to vibrate our guts and hearts and blow our minds until they redirected all that fabulous energy and sent it back to the source from which it originally came.

Violating the second law of thermodynamics which says the circle must be broken—simply by completing it.

And then it stopped.

And the crowd broke up the air with yells and applause and an Indian war hoop they used to let it out and Tommy pointed to each member of the group, who gave a nod or bow, and when he pointed to the organist, we stood up to see who was behind that cushion of sound that was being laid down, and we were aston-

ished to see that it wasn't a teenager or even a he. It was a she.
It was Moms.

And then the applause stopped. But like church bells whose ring
brings vibrations of sympathy long after their clang and chime
have ceased, the very walls seemed to unsponge the filtrate of
liquid music which they had absorbed, forming an electrical field
of pleasant hum around our ears. And the Boston Braves tuned
their guitars and turned up their amps for an encore. And in
anticipation I cried to the waitress, "Two double Grand Dads on
the rocks," and I said, "Will you join me, Warren?" and he said,
"Sure," and I shouted after the waitress, "Make that four doubles,"
and we laughed as the organized din and clamor began again with
a deep chord that seemed soft and substantial enough to sit on; but
Tommy began immediately to skim over its surface once again
with screaming Eric Clapton sounds and I thought of the great
eighteenth-century Swiss physicist Daniel Bernoulli who discovered that when a body is moving over a surface, the pressure it
exerts on the surface beneath is reduced as the speed of the body
is increased. The faster you slide, the easier it is to support your
glide. But you must *move*. And Tommy did. He was young
enough, strong enough, impossibly angry enough, to sustain his
faith in the thin ice on which he slid. And because of his faith—
because of his movement—the ice supported him. And it was at
that moment that I realized—that I knew for sure—that I had
been handed the secret of how to begin to swim.

After the set had ended, more drinks arrived, and as we gulped
at them, I chattered at Warren excitedly, still filled with the energy of the music, "Oh, Warren, who can remember what art is
capable of doing until you see it actually being done? Art is so
great, Warren. It's reality is more than you can imagine. It's the
hitching post in the universe that Einstein said no longer existed."

Warren smiled. "I guess I'm really rapping away," I said.

"It's great to hear you rapping again, Jake. But you have to hold
onto that vision. You can't let the base become your world, even
if you think you oppose it, because you won't be able to remember
the reason why it's worth opposing."

"You're right, Warren. It's what art does to you. Imagine, people
spending their whole lives trying to shape a shaft of air. Instead
of trying to scientifically break nature's code, they gently bend
her. They *work* at *playing*, and to see people who are so free of
the false practicality of earthly ends . . . well, it liberates you."

"Sure, it does." He smiled.

"Science will never be able to dominate nature," I said, rapidly. "Nature will only yield to love, not rape. It's art that redeems science, siphoning off some of its energies, like Tommy did with his amplifiers, and turning them toward holy inutility. Every vote against practical pig is a vote *for* the essential all-rightness of things as they are given to us. Not in a particular society, at a particular time, but in the universe, forever. What Tommy Creetner is into is not simply entertainment—it's the transubstantiation of electricity."

I swallowed a couple ounces of Dad so quickly that I began to cough and choke. "Take it easy, Jake. I know what you're saying . . ."

"I know you do, Warren, but it's *I* who had forgotten. But I know . . . I know. . . . Oh, Warren, I've got to stop this crazy *Sado-Mask* shit. It's no good. The revolution has to be fought with our own sensibilities, not with our societies. It's too late . . . too vast . . ."

"I know, Jake."

"The base is a world in which the soaring flights of the artist become unimaginable. But the making of art requires a faith in the possibility of imagining more than you ever imagined you could imagine. The phonograph is a dim light that can keep the *idea* of art alive, but it's only when you confront living artists that you remember that art is more than a few great works worth being preserved because they can bring relaxation and pleasure. Art is a special way of being in the world. The difference between art and revolution is ontological."

"*I* think so, Jake. I'm glad you came."

"So am I! I'd lost the ability to imagine myself as an artist. Dedicating one's whole life to merely plucking a string is senseless —until you see the look on the face of someone who is doing just that."

Warren opened up his smile at this, and I calmed down a bit, and we quietly sipped at our drinks and listened to the jukebox, which had been turned on at the end of the set.

"Have you noticed a change in David, lately?" I asked.

"Sure."

"What do you think it is?"

"It's the speed."

"David's taking speed?"

"Shooting it, now. Walter gets it for him."

"But look at Sibyl. Can't he see?"

"Sure, Jake. He knows better than anyone."

"Then what's the matter with him?"

"It's the only way he can get up, Jake. Without it, he's on a permanent down. It's the only way he can write. You've seen the results already."

"But it's not worth it, Warren."

"You don't have to tell me that," he said sadly. "As far as I'm concerned, everything we need is right here." He pointed to his head. "Listen, Jake, don't follow them. I don't care if you stay on the base or go AWOL or whatever. But write your book. Get off their crazy merry-go-round and simply walk over and take the brass ring. It's right there, waiting for you. I know you can write, Jake . . ."

"I don't. But I suspect I may be able to . . . Fuck it! This is absurd. You're right, Warren. I'm no good to anybody dead, and I'm killing myself in the name of something nobody'll even tell me about. They're all nuts! Each side needs the other. And Walter's giving David speed just proves it."

"You can't blame Walter, Jake. David's a big influence on him."

"I don't know . . ."

"Well, it's David's decision. Walter isn't pressing him. It's from the army, really. David says that since he got out of the army he needs to make up for something they took away from him. He doesn't exactly know how they did it, but they fucked up his head pretty bad."

"I know," I said, impatiently. "I know."

"And he says the last thing he remembers was Colonel Creetner. They had him at the hospital . . ."

"After he was fucked up?"

"He seems to think before."

"Before?"

"That's what he says. But he's pretty cloudy. Although the speed does seem to have cleared him up a bit."

"But he'll wind up in the state hospital. With Sibyl."

"He knows that, Jake."

"Well, then what's he doing? He's buying a present at the price of a future."

"He doesn't seem to care. And neither does anyone else around here. David knows exactly what he's doing—what he's giving up to write for *The Railroad* and to get ready for the action."

"What action?"

"That I can't say. Nobody seems to know, exactly. It has something to do with Len, I think, but as to specifics, I'm not sure. But I do know one thing, it can't be too far in the future, because the way these guys are popping pills and shooting up, the future's going to be a short one."

"David may be destroying his mind for the revolution, but he's doing what *he* wants to; Walter's supporting the fucking thing, but he's doing what *he* wants; you, Edith, . . . even Cal, you're all doing what you want to, but how about me? Where do I fit in?"

"I told you, Jake. Do what *you* want."

At this point Walter joined us, and then Tommy came over to the table to rap until it was time for the next set. After the set, I finished another drink, got a cab back to the base, put on my blue suit, and went to work.

BULLETIN

> ### Convict Falls Out of Jail
> PERTH, Australia. Dec. 3 (AP)—While working on a prison wall, a convict, Guiseppe Privitera, 29 years old, slipped and fell into the street outside yesterday. Privitera, an Italian, who is serving a four-to-seven-year sentence for rape, got up, limping on an injured ankle, and went to the front door of the prison where guards let him back in.

CAMERA TWO

When I arrived at the hospital, it was relatively empty so I walked over to the Bachelor Officers' Quarters to see which doctor had pulled O.D. The young doctors on O.D. always spent their free time at the B.O.Q., watching television.

It was Len's boss, Dr. Isenberg, a psychiatrist, in front of the TV, watching the game. We'd spoken a few times before and he seemed to be a nice enough guy. A little, round man, prematurely bald, with thick glasses. I didn't take him for the career officer type. He seemed too intelligent.

"Hello, Jake," he said.

"Hi, doc. Hey, I didn't know that shrinks pulled O.D."

"Oh, yes," he said. "We're M.D.'s too."

"I know, but . . ."

"But what, Jake?" He smiled.

"Well . . . when's the last time you sewed a man, doc?"

"You can speak frankly. We're trained not to resent it, even if your remarks are barbed . . . It was a couple years ago, I guess. Maybe five or six. When I interned at Presbyterian, in New York." Then, turning back to the TV, he said, "Don't worry, Jake. I spoke to the colonel. There won't be too much tonight. Just one small raid scheduled."

"Doc," I said, "tell me the truth. What do you think about what's going on around here? I feel like I'm trapped in a madhouse."

"I don't know, Jake. Madhouses can get pretty bad at times."

"But this isn't supposed to be in competition with them!"

"Well, as you know, I'm new here, like you—"

"Look, doc," I interrupted, "your job is to adjust people to this insanity, I'm aware of that—"

"No it isn't, Jake. My job isn't to fit people into ready-made niches. It's my job to help people become strong enough to find their own niches."

"Then, you don't think the colonel's psychotic?"

He smiled. "Psychotics can't continually function. A psychotic couldn't impress his superiors, get promoted, and run a three-hundred-bed hospital for a period of several years. He may be a little neurotic, more neurotic than most, perhaps, but we're all a little neurotic . . . Given the circumstances, the colonel, the whole army in fact, doesn't do such a bad job. Society drops its dirty business into their hands, and they just do the best job they can."

"And the B.C.? Do you think the B.C. are nuts?"

"Not 'nuts,' Jake. I don't like to use that word. In the case of the B.C., I think one has to differentiate between the leaders and the people under their influence."

"Which people?"

"Well, the crowd that puts out that puerile newspaper *The Railroad*, for instance."

He looked into my face. "What's the matter, Jake? You look

surprised. Are you so startled by the fact that I read *The Rail-road*? I'm over thirty, but I'm not in the grave yet." He smiled. "And I don't say those people who put out the paper are B.C., mind you. In fact I don't think they *are* B.C. But I do think that they're immature and, without realizing it, they're serving the interests of the B.C. That's the way these ideologues work."

"Then you think the leaders of the B.C. are dishonest?"

"Not dishonest, Jake, deluded. I've seen how these guys operate. There are lots of studies of revolutionaries, and the majority of them are psychologically maladjusted individuals who seek power because of their personal inadequacies.

"But I don't say they're hypocritical," he added. "Often they're perfectly sincere and even brilliant at rationalizing their goals in terms of social justice and freedom. That's what makes some of them so effective, particularly with young people who are idealis-tic and impressionable and impatient; who haven't learned the classic lesson that man must live within limits, regrettable as this may seem at times."

"Then you think *The Railroad* is misguided?"

"Well, I *did* think that. But now I think it verges on paranoia. It used to be merely jejune in a youthful way. It's taken a pecu-liarly paranoic turn in the last few weeks."

He looked inquisitively at me. "You don't look so good. Is some-thing the matter, Jake?"

"Oh, nothing much, doc. I had a few drinks this afternoon and I think I'm half-hungover and still half-drunk."

He laughed. "Well, we can fix that up. Why don't you take a walk down to the pharmacy there and tell Fergy to give you a Dexamyl. One won't hurt, and it's guaranteed to pick you right up."

"Thanks, doc. I will."

"And as for the B.C., Jacob, well I just feel sorry for the poor kids who follow them. They're going to get their little asses kicked."

"How can you be sure?"

"Because paranoia is based on guilt. It begins with, 'I'm guilty,' then it changes to, 'You're guilty too,' and then finally to just, 'You're guilty.' But you can't ever fully project your own guilt into others. Guilt that isn't faced becomes unbearable. Paranoic revo-lution is, in my mind, a form of inverted masochism."

As he turned back to the game, I said to him, "You're not plan-ning on staying in the army, are you doc?"

"I don't know, Jacob. Just out of residency, I could never have the responsibility that I have here—in charge of an entire mental hygiene service. So I don't really know . . . But Carol and I will work it out. We've still got over a year to make up our minds."

As he watched the TV, he said, "There's a lot of sick people in the army, Jacob. Somebody's got to take care of them too."

I walked out of the lounge and into the hallway of the B.O.Q. He called after me, "And, Jacob?"

"Yes."

"Let me give you a word of advice. You seem pretty disillusioned by what you've seen here in the army. But listen to me and don't put any faith in any human institutions or movements. In the army or out. Or you'll always get burned."

"I won't doc," I said. "I'll see you later at outpatient."

CAMERA TWO

The walk from the B.O.Q. to the pharmacy was about a quarter of a mile. When the hospital had been built in 1941, German air raids had been anticipated, so the hospital was laid out over as wide an area as possible to minimize bomb damage and to insure that part of the hospital could still function even if some of it were hit.

It was built in the form of an elongated H, its parallel sides being about three hundred yards long. The B.O.Q. and the pharmacy were at opposite ends of the building. Of course, it is an obvious shortcoming of specialized designs for specific purposes that they run the risk of becoming rapidly obsolete in changing circumstances, and this hospital, which had served adequately during World War II, was now incredibly inefficient. Yet, like a rhinoceros, it stood there, a massive representative of a species that looked like it should have become extinct years before.

The hospital required a large staff to run it because of all the time wasted walking between the offices and wards. The hallways were narrow as well as long, and, because the building had been built quckly, out of wood, on stilts, the walls had warped. In fact, walking between them was like enclosing yourself within the bending planes of a Juan Gris painting.

The fact that the hospital stood on stilts was not without its advantages, however, for the floor was rotting, and periodically the legs of the bed of some unsuspecting patient would break through the floor with a crack, and bang, his bed would drop down rapidly from under him. Then, crash, the patient, having been left unsuspended in midair, would suffer a similar fate. It was always good for a laugh.

At one end of the crossbar of the H was the main entrance and waiting room or lobby. The furniture in the waiting room was in much better shape than might have been expected, considering its age, because the colonel did not allow anyone to wait in the waiting room. He said that it gave the hospital an "unbusinesslike atmosphere" to have people just sitting around doing nothing.

Halfway down the crossbar of the H was affixed the surgical wing, with its two operating rooms. The operating rooms had been modernized after the war, and during the first few months that I was at the hospital, there was only one explosion in surgery during an actual operation. A light blew up, leading to an impromptu exit of doctors and nurses along with their Cuban brain-surgery patient, who had luckily just been stitched up before the blast occurred.

Not far from the hospital snack bar there was a little recreation center, set up as a small dance hall with a jukebox, for the off-duty WACs and GIs who worked at the hospital. Shortly after I became troop commander, however, it was my unpleasant duty to have the jukebox removed. The fat-assed XO had passed by there one night and he had me summoned to his office by Private Washington the following morning.

"I want you to remove the jukebox from the enlisted lounge, lieutenant," he said.

I was startled by the order and I said, "But sir, can you tell me why?"

"*Why*, lieutenant?" he snapped. "*Why?* I'll tell you why! They're dancing down there, lieutenant. That's why!" he said, triumphantly. "I caught them myself."

BULLETIN

Commercial Aircraft Use Of Military Fields Studied

WASHINGTON, Dec. 12 (AP) —The Pentagon said today that studies were under way into the possible use of military airfields by commercial aircraft.

The move is being considered as a means of relieving air congestion around major airports populated areas, a spokesman said.

Jerry Friedheim, the Pentagon spokesman, said that 57 military air bases are now being jointly used by commercial and general purpose aircraft.

CAMERA TWO

Sergeant Ferguson was pleased to see me when I arrived at the pharmacy. "Slow day, sir," he said. "Even the B-52s are out of town."

"Oh?"

"Yeah, they're dropping some big babies up in New Hampshire. Didn't you hear them take off?"

"No, I guess I didn't" And I realized why. Tommy Creetner's music had been so loud, it outroared the engines of the giant planes.

"Oh, ho," the sergeant said, playfully, "the lieutenant's been having a few snorts this aft. I can tell by his eyes."

"You've got me there, sarge. Isenberg says to give me a dexy."

"Coming right up, lieutenant," he said, grabbing a jar of little green pills from the shelf behind him. "Take a few. Uncle Sam's got no shortage of pills for commanding officers."

I put about four or five into my shirt pocket and, with a cup of water the sergeant quickly handed me, I swallowed one.

"Well, that should pick you up, sir," the sergeant said.

"I hope so, Fergy. What's new on the grapevine? Any action for tonight?"

He smiled in mock surprise. "I hope the lieutenant doesn't think I would trade aspirins and such for personal favors or information, does he?"

"Oh, far from it, sergeant. I know you wouldn't give away so much as a vitamin pill without the proper forms being filled out."

This was a private joke between us, since whenever anything was needed for the company, from volley balls to office supplies, Sergeant Ferguson would get them through blackmarket trading of everything from aspirins to darvon tablets with the other sergeants on the base.

"You know, sir," he said, getting serious, "it's a funny thing, about these forms I mean. The army has so many forms, such a ragged system of checks and balances and red tape in order to guarantee that nobody steals a fuckin thing, that nobody bothers to use the system at all. Too many headaches.

"Nobody but the privates," he added, smiling again, "and that's cause they don't know shit from shinola."

"I tell you something, Fergy, I think half the people in this country are getting paid to keep the other half from stealing. If an epidemic of honesty ever broke out in this country, we'd have a depression that would make the thirties look like a picnic."

He laughed, and then he remembered my earlier question about the raids that night, and he said, "The lieutenant might be interested in knowing that I gave Mooney eight-to-five that there'll be a small raid on the town tonight by a single squadron of Phantoms. Mooney thinks all fighter pilots got the weekend off, but I hear different, so stick around lieutenant, we may get some customers yet."

"I certainly hope so, Fergy," I said, and he laughed and turned toward a portable TV on which he had been watching the football game from the West Coast. "See you later, lieutenant," he called as I left.

I walked down the hallway, but when I reached the crossbar of the H, I stopped without making my turn. About a hundred yards ahead of me an iron wire screen with a locked door in it sealed off the rest of the wing. I had never ventured down this hallway, which I knew to be the service station area of the hospital where the immigrants were processed. The area beyond the metal gate was top secret, but as the hospital was nearly empty I decided I'd walk to the gate and take a look.

So I continued to walk straight ahead. I thought the wing was deserted until, when I reached the barrier, I heard muffled noises on the right, just beyond the fence. I peeked through and saw, through the glass panel in a door to a ward which had been converted into a classroom, a group of about thirty men, wearing a bizarre mixture of foreign-looking clothes. In a melange of accents, they were repeating, over and over again, the pledge of allegiance, led by an army instructor.

It surprised me to hear this because I had thought that kind of instruction was part of the later citizenship program, rather than the routine immigration procedure at the time of entry. I listened to a few rounds, got bored, and turned to leave when something caught my attention. At a knothole in a plank in the hallway's outside wall. It was an eyeball. Peering in at me. Someone was outside on the grass spying on the immigration center. As I walked away from the gate the pupil of the eye tracked my movement. Because the wall had no windows, I couldn't see who the eye belonged to. But I had my suspicions.

When I entered the emergency room the only patient there was a GI who had been hurt attempting to score in a touch football game behind the hospital. He had put his head down and tried a line buck, straight ahead from two yards out, and he had succeeded too well. Nobody laid a hand on him and he had run head first into a steel lamp post. He was sitting quietly, now, holding an ice pack on his head and watching the game of the week on one of the hospital TV sets.

If not for the dexedrine, which took away my appetite, I might have been at the hospital snack bar when we heard the Phantoms swoosh down over the hospital and deliver their packages somewhere over the town. I immediately dispatched two ambulances to the North Bridge, being certain that they would get tied up in traffic, and that, while stalled on the bridge, they would be able to locate where the jets had struck by watching for the smoke signals given off by the burning buildings. I sent a corpsman,

Specialist Brown, over to the B.O.Q. to tell Isenberg that we might need him in a half hour or so, and that the game was on TV at the outpatient clinic if he cared to watch it while we waited.

The first ambulance arrived about an hour later, coming to a screeching stop at the edge of the ramp which led up to the outpatient clinic and emergency room. Private Amalfi, a stocky, good-natured Italian boy from the East Bronx, was driving. I could tell by the tire squeal, for only Amalfi would drive the ambulance up to edge of the ramp at fifty miles an hour before hitting the brakes.

"What's up, Amalfi?" I asked, as he entered the clinic.

"Nothing much, lieutenant. I came back empty. Miller's got one. Some freak got his head busted is all."

"That *is* nothing. How come?"

"I don't know for sure, sir. Sergeant Powell of the MPs was over at the wreckage and he was saying they must've gotten tipped off. They must have, lieutenant, because those Phantoms really do a job on a place, I'll tell you. But no one was in when they hit, and on a Saturday that don't make sense. There must have been a tip-off."

"Where was it they hit, Amalfi?"

"Oh, this place on the edge of town. The 1770."

The second ambulance pulled up to the ramp and they wheeled in the sole casualty of the raid. Because he came up the ramp feet first, it was Warren's sandals that stopped my heart, even before I saw his face.

His face was covered with bright red liquid which had flowed down from the top of his head, as if someone had cracked an egg of blood upon it. He was only partly conscious and was confused about where he was and what had happened. But he seemed to have waves of frightening lucidity—as when he looked up into my face. I grabbed a towel and wiped away the tiny ponds of blood which had collected in the valleys around his eyes.

"Jake, what happened? Where am I?"

I took his hand and held it. I knew he had a great fear of hospitals and doctors.

"You're with me, Warren, at the hospital. It's going to be O.K."

"No Jake. . . . I want to go home. . . ." He faded back into a fearsome pool of silence.

"What happened, Miller?" I said. Then I yelled, "Shit! God

damn it, Amalfi, get your ass over to the B.O.Q. and get the doc. Fast!"

"Yes, sir."

"I don't know for sure, sir," Miller said, as we moved Warren into the emergency room. "They must have got out just in time —all except this guy, sir. The old part of the place took a direct hit and I think the impact on the dance hall knocked down a big chandelier on this guy's head. He must've been drunk or something. Guess he didn't get out with the rest."

We lifted Warren on to one of the tables in the white, bright-lighted emergency room. He faded in: "Jake! Jake, get me out of here!" he shouted, and then he faded back into incoherent little cries.

"You know him, sir?" Miller said, in disbelief, staring at Warren's hair and clothes.

"Yes, I do, Miller. He's a friend of mine."

"He's got a big gash there, sir. That thing really opened up his head."

"O.K., Miller. Thanks for your help. Get Brown and Zulicki away from the TV and over here, so they'll be on the spot when the doc arrives."

"Yes, sir," Miller said, and hurried out of the room.

Warren continued to moan softly and to mutter sad little sentence fragments which I couldn't put together. As I wiped away some blood from the top of his head, he turned his pained eyes up to me, and when they focused, he said, "Jake, take me home. Please."

"I can't, Warren. Your head is cut and the doc will have to look at it."

"No Jake. . . ."

"It's O.K. He's a friend of mine. I'll see that he takes good care of you."

"Will you stay with me, Jake?"

"Sure. Sure I will."

"Don't leave me, Jake. Hospitals freak me out. Stay with me, Jake, please. No matter what."

"I will," I said, and he faded back into his private agony. Now that the blood was wiped away, I could see the nasty gash. Its flaps opened into a pulpy pit of flesh, at which I couldn't bear to look. It would have to be closed.

Isenberg arrived at the same time as the two corpsmen whom I had sent Miller to retrieve.

"O.K.," he says to the corpsmen, "you two men will have to hold him down. He's still conscious."

"Jake!" Warren screams.

"Can I stay and lend a hand, doc?"

"You ever watch anyone getting stitched up, Jake?"

"No."

"Well, O.K., you might find it interesting. You can hold his feet. You think you can take it?"

"I guess so."

"Good. Go to the end of the table and grasp his ankles. Try not to hurt him, but hold his legs firmly on the table and keep him from moving. You two men," he says to the corpsmen, "hold his arms."

He takes a square piece of material with a hole in the center and lays it over Warren's head, so the bright gash shines through. And I've seen this before. On TV and in the movies. They cover the patient, except for the area on which they're going to work. To depersonalize the procedure. And on TV it always does. But here, on the table, on Warren, it doesn't.

"Jake!" He begins a feeble thrashing, his cries muffled by the cover over his face. "Jake, don't let them fuck with my head. Jake, *please!*"

"Hold him?" the doc says. And slowly, oh so very slowly, he begins to fill a big hypodermic needle with a clear fluid.

"What's that?" I ask, alarmed.

"It's just an anesthetic," the doc smiles. "Don't worry, Jacob. Everything's all right. I'm just going to anesthetize the area before I stitch it up."

Warren, half-delirious with pain, continues his ineffective resistance. And it is I, I who hold down his feet as he screams, "No! . . . David . . . no! Jake! . . . don't let them fuck with my head!"

No, it isn't like this on TV. For under the mask, under the wound which glares out through the aperture, there is my friend and he is screaming in fearful panic and pain. As we are struggling to hold him down. And it isn't a detached, scientific procedure, as I had imagined it would be. It's a brawl. It's a violent swinging, kicking brawl, three on one, to hold him helpless and still while . . . while. . . .

"What's the matter, Jacob? You O.K.?"

While in his hand he holds the long, shining needle and I suddenly understand what he is going to do with that column of glinting steel. And it begins to make me sick.

"I . . . I think so, doc. . . ."

He is going to inject the anesthesia by sticking the sharp needle beneath the open flaps of Warren's flesh, and into his head.

And it is not into an abstraction. Not a dummy replacing an actor in a medical drama. It is Warren. My friend. And we are pinning him to the surgical table while the doctor is fighting to steady Warren's skull with his left hand.

"Hold his head, Brown," he commands. "Hold his goddamn head still."

So Brown gets Warren's head into a kind of vise while Zulicki leans across Warren's chest with his body to hold both Warren's arms down and I press his legs against the table and, with his left hand, the doctor opens the lips of Warren's wound and slowly, while Warren screams wildly, slowly he inserts the needle into Warren's head—*"Jake!"*—and holds it there, slowly pressing in the pump, slowly releasing the viscous liquid, through the needle, under the flaps of flesh, and into Warren's head.

Then, more quickly, he follows the same path in bringing the hollow steel spike back out, while the surgical cover continues to thrash over Warren's shouts—"Jake! Help!"—and the white table sheet merges with the fluorescent glow of the surgical bulbs and shiny steel sutures and needles of viscous light brighten into thick white reflecting shrieks of pain and tight electric white torture lights. . . .

CAMERA TWO

When I woke up I was lying on a couch in the outpatient area. Amalfi was holding smelling salts in front of my nose to assault my senses until my self-protective mechanisms were shocked into pulling me awake and away. I pushed out with my arms. Felt a throb across my head. And looked up into Amalfi's eyes.

"What happened, Angie?"

"You passed out, lieutenant." He wiped my head with a towel which came back wet with red.

"What's *that*?"

"You cut your head when you fell against the table, lieutenant."

"No! No I won't. . . ."

"Don't worry, sir," he interrupted with a smile, "no stitches. Just a flesh wound."

I let out a sigh.

"I know how it is, sir. Just take it easy. You'll be able to go home in an hour or so. It's O.K. Your friend's O.K. He took a lot of stitches but the doc says you'll be able to take him home as soon as you feel up to it. The adjutant's volunteered to take the rest of your tour for you tonight. So don't worry about a thing. It's O.K."

BULLETIN

Doctor Says Sprained Ankle Is Worse Than People Think

SANTA BARBARA, Calif. (UPI)—People call almost any ankle injury "a sprained ankle" but the term is used too loosely, says Dr. Robert W. Olson, a radiologist here.

A truly sprained ankle, Dr Olson says, has one or more of the ligaments partially or completely torn, and it is nothing to pooh-pooh.

CAMERA TWO

By the time we got home, it was already past eleven o'clock and Edith had long been back from Boston.

"Jacob! Your head!" she exclaimed, as I entered the house, alone.

I had a small bandage on my head. Warren was in the car where I had left him in a painful, semiconscious state.

"What happened?" Edith said.

"I'm all right, but I'm only a preview of coming attractions. Wait until you see Warren."

"Jacob! What *happened?*"

"Warren had his head opened and then stitched closed tonight.

He'll be O.K. First help me get him in the house, and then I'll tell you."

Edith was shocked when she saw Warren's head swathed in bandages like the top of a mummy. Carefully, we helped him out of the car and into his bed, where he immediately fell asleep. Then I related the day's events to Edith. The fact that it was Warren who had been injured, rather than merely "a person," seemed to crack the shell of indifference into which she had withdrawn since getting her job in town.

"Jacob," she said, shaken, "you've got to do something. Now."

"What can I do? I mean it, you tell me what to do, and I'll do it."

She paced back and forth in front of me, unconsciously nibbling on her lower lip. "I know! You promise you'll do it?"

"If it's within reason."

"Jacob, I want you to go see the general, tomorrow. Sunday. At his home."

"That's not within reason!"

"Jacob! Won't you do *anything*? Do *I* have to go and see him?"

"A lieutenant can't just walk up to the general's house and demand to see him."

"Why not?"

"You don't understand. . . . You can't understand unless you've been in the army, yourself. A lieutenant can't even talk back to a captain, much less a general. They have absolute power over you. They can send you to Vietnam. They can put you in jail. They really can."

"Why you're so frightened, Jacob, is what I can't understand."

"It *is* frightening. *My* power is frightening. I can courtmartial people! And I don't even know the Code of Military Justice. I can ruin people's lives, break men who were decorated for bravery in World War II. Who've spent twenty-five years in the army. It's unbelievable."

"Well, if you don't go to see the general tomorrow, you'll only have yourself to answer to. I won't push you into it. I won't even be here tomorrow. But really, I can't see what's so terrible, Jacob. I met the general's wife at a wives' club tea. She's not so imposing. She's just a harmless old drunk."

"You might not think that if she invited you to Leavenworth for tea, and only she had the keys."

"Jacob, you exaggerate so. . . ."

"But it's *the general.* . . ."

"Put your exaggerations in your writing, Jacob. There, perhaps, they'll be more amusing. And maybe then you won't have to live your life within them, like some Quixote in rusty armor, which serves less to protect him than to keep him from moving."

We went into the bedroom and began to undress.

"I'm not kidding, Jacob," she said, "the time has come for you to act, if you want to be anybody at all."

We climbed into bed.

"Well, tomorrow's not here yet," I said. "We'll see."

She turned her back to me and buried her head deeply in her pillow, after casting one last cold frown in my direction.

"You say you won't be here?" I said.

"That's right. You'll be strictly on your own."

When I awoke the next morning, she was already dressed and she seemed in a better mood, perhaps due to the anticipation of an exciting afternoon in town. She was going to a dance concert, she told me. "It's an attempt to combine natural sounds with natural movement."

"What are they doing?" I asked, glad for the opportunity to turn the conversation away from the subject of the night before.

"Oh, several things. It's primarily going to be an attempt to bring the push-up, the sit-up, and the human belch into ballet, along with a soundtrack of frog croakings. It's very daring—the final assault on the old formalism."

"How about formalism in education?" I said, foolishly.

"What does *that* mean?"

"It means what do you think programmed education is?"

"Jacob," she said in exasperation that quickly turned to anger, "do you have any idea of what the state teachers' colleges are turning out? They're WAC sergeants with diplomas. And if that's the case in the East, can you imagine what it's like elsewhere? Any fool can see that the revolution in education stands or falls on the matter of the circumvention of the teacher.

"And don't think I've forgotten about last night," she added spitefully. "Before you go challenging the revolution we're creating, I'd advise you to get up the courage to speak to your own boss."

She stomped out of the house, slamming the door behind her.

"It's not my boss," I said quietly, to the empty room. "It's the general."

BULLETIN

Midget Held in Murder
Special to The New York Times
LOCKPORT, N. Y., Jan. 30—
A 31 - year - old midget was
charged here today with the
murder of his 34-year-old wife,
also a midget, after he walked
into police. headquarters and
surrendered himself.

CAMERA TWO

Warren didn't wake up until the early afternoon. When I heard
him stirring, I went over to him and sat down beside his bed.

His room was thinly furnished. A small bed. A door desk. Orange
crates against the wall, in which he kept his clothes. A rack of
records. A small bookcase, filled with paperbacks. Magazines scattered about. And, tacked to the wall above his newly turbaned
head, two large posters—Humphrey Bogart and Jean Paul Bel-
mondo.

"I'm sorry," I said.

He looked up at me from out of the tape and gauze.

"What, Jake? . . . What are you talking about? What happened?"

"You got your head cracked and then sewn up at the hospital."

"Oh . . . yeah." He looked around the room, to fix himself in
space. "What time is it?"

"It's afternoon. Sunday afternoon. You got hurt last night."

"Oh." He began to get up but lay right back down with a wince
of pain. "Wow, my head is sore."

"I can understand why! You got quite a gash. But it's O.K.—it's
sewn up now. Do you remember how it happened?"

"It must have been at the 1770. I remember someone leaped up
on the stage and yelled, 'Air raid! Air raid in one minute!' And
everybody ran out."

"What about you?"

"I'm not too clear yet," he said, with a puzzled look on his face.

He thought for a while, and then added, "I know Walter and David had left earlier, to go over to the Harlem. And then . . . then when this guy yelled and everyone ran out, I guess I just sat there. . . . Yeah, I remember now. I just thought that even if there was an air raid, I didn't want to join the herd of buffaloes stampeding around. It didn't seem to matter. For all I knew, I might have gotten killed just as easily running out."

"I'm sorry, Warren. I shouldn't have bought you those two doubles."

"Oh, it wasn't that. Besides, after you left a friend of Walter's came over to our table and broke out some opium-treated black hash. That made me feel a hell of a lot more content to stay where I was than the bourbon did."

I shook my head. "But why didn't you get out of there? What's the matter with you? You had a warning and you just sat there."

He was distracted for a moment by the bandages on his head, inventorying them with his fingers. "What was that you were saying, Jake?"

"Why didn't you move?"

"I don't really know," he said, pensively. "There didn't seem to be any place to go. I remember thinking to myself, 'Thy will be done.' That's the last thing I can remember—just sitting peacefully at the table, thinking, 'Thy will be done.'"

"I'm sorry, Warren. I'm sorry for picking at you even now, with your broken head. . . ." I got up from the chair and began to walk around the room, slowly, scratching my scalp. "And I'm sorry I deserted you."

"You couldn't have helped, Jake. I was content where I was, so I decided to take my chances at the table."

"I mean at the hospital. I'm sorry. I've been thinking about it all night. I hope you can find it in your power to forgive me."

"Were you at the hospital, Jake?"

For hours I had tossed over this confession. I feared I might be confessing to a deaf god. Now I realized that my situation was more like a blasphemer confessing to a deaf god. He hadn't been aware of my sin.

But I was aware of it. And confession was necessary.

"I failed you in the hospital."

"What happened there?"

"You were calling to me. . . ."

"Oh yeah. . . . I remember. . . . I saw you when they wheeled me in."

"You were imploring me to help you and I couldn't."

"Of course, you couldn't. You're not a doctor."

"No, you were asking me to get you out of there. And I stood by. I didn't do a thing. I knew how you hated being treated as an object—how you hated doctors."

"It must have been necessary, Jake. You made the decision for me. I might never have gone there if I had a choice, so it's probably better the way it worked out. . . . What was I saying? I don't remember."

"You were shouting about David. How you didn't want them to fuck up your head, too."

"I don't remember. . . . You did the right thing, though. I must have been delirious. They never physically violated David's head. They raped it, but . . ."

"Do you know how, Warren? Do you have any ideas?"

"No, I really don't. I can't figure it out."

"Neither can I. It sure beats me. . . . But I don't want to get sidetracked. I want to tell you that as you were lying helplessly on that table, I was at your feet, and you called to me for help, and I passed out."

He smiled.

"What's so funny?" I asked.

"I just noticed the bandage on *your* head," he giggled.

"Well, it should have been worse. I deserved a lot more than I got."

"Don't be so hard on yourself, Jake."

"I was holding your feet down, and at the critical point, I passed out."

"I'm sure it must have been only because you weren't involved in what was happening. You were a spectator and you left. That's all."

"I told you I was holding down your legs."

"That was just your arms, Jake. Your head was free to watch the show. And your imagination was free, too. . . . You have a vivid imagination, Jake."

I hit my fist into the palm of my other hand. "I still can't face what I did, last night. It's kind of you. . . ."

"Jake," he stopped me, "it was only because you were just an observer. If you had to sew up my head—if it depended upon you, and you had the skill—I'm sure you would have been able to do it."

"I don't know. . . ."

"I'm certain. Once you got started, once you began to get into it, I know you could have done it."

I sat back down in the chair beside the bed. "To be fair to myself, I have to admit that there did seem to be something indecent about watching your pain. Pain should be private; unless one can help, one should avoid intruding upon someone else's agony."

"Sure, Jake."

"There's really no point in being a spectator to the unavoidable torments of another human being."

"I know you would have been able to do it. Just by putting one foot after another, I know you could have walked through the valley of your fears and reached me—if you thought you could help, that is."

"How about one *stitch* after another? Into your head."

"You could have, Jake. There's no need to prove it. If you still want to dive into the full depth of the whole experience you could write about it."

"I don't know. . . ."

"Jake? Could you get me some orange juice? My mouth is really dry."

"Sure."

I went into the kitchen and took a can of frozen orange juice from the freezer. Ever since I had heard Mary McCarthy jokingly refer to "fresh frozen orange juice" on TV, I had never been able to open a can of the stuff without smiling. That's the power of wit —of words. They can haunt us—we are their natural house.

Were words my weapons? As my mother used to put it, when she feared I might do something immoderate, was the pen really my sword?

In business school, when I was studying economics as part of my course work in accounting, we were taught a parable which illustrated Ricardo's theoretical justification for international free trade. The point to be made was that even if a nation could make everything more cheaply than its neighbor, it would still pay for it to concentrate only on that which it could make best of all and trade for those products which it could make only slightly cheaper than other nations.

The parable concerned a lawyer who was the finest lawyer in

town and who was the finest typist as well. And the point was that since a great lawyer was more important to society than a great typist, he should hire a less worthy secretary to do his typing while being a great lawyer full time, rather than spending half his time being his own typist. Thus, for twenty hours a week the world would lose a great typist and gain a great lawyer.

I thought of this lesson as I mixed the orange juice. But how did it apply to me? Should I forget Walter and David and Len in order to write about what I was experiencing. Could I do it well? Could I be a first-rate writer as opposed to a mediocre revolutionary? Or was my desire to write merely a rationalization of a fear of violence? For I was not certain that words mattered any more. Do people want to learn about another's pain? Do they want to share it?

"Question marks!" I said to Warren, as I handed him his orange juice. "Everywhere. Question marks wherever you turn. That's the end result of this mad century of relativity and curved space. The exclamation point has been warped into a question mark."

He looked up at me and smiled and I had to join him, because I could not hide the fact that I was pleased with the way in which I had given form to my despair.

"That's the old Jake!" he said.

"I'm afraid the old Jake is dead, Warren, and what you've just witnessed is only a little rigor mortis," I said. "And stop smiling, you bastard."

"You did it again—you're still alive under that bandage, you devil you," he sparkled, pointing to my head.

"That's my curse."

"That's your blessing."

"Well, then I'm cursed with a blessing."

"How so?"

"When I was little my grandmother used to take care of me a great deal of the time. She used to read the Old Testament in Hebrew and she was always trying to teach me things. When I must have been two years old, she would look out the window with me and tell me how the green light was go and the red stop, and she'd teach me to read the signs on the stores, and even when I was older and the kids would play in the street, I would stay inside with her and she would patiently go through the comics in the paper with me, teaching me how to read."

I took the empty glass from Warren and placed it on the desk.

"And I remember each time that I would get a word right, she would kiss my head and say, in Yiddish, something that sounded like, '*A lebenach dein cupula.*'"

"What does that mean?"

"I'm not even sure. But the important thing is that I know what I *thought* it meant. I thought it meant, 'A blessing on your little head.'"

"Oh, wow!" Warren said, "That's great! *A baboner der krepelach.*"

I laughed. "That's close enough. But I think that's why I've never been able to put my head up when the bullets are flying. And that's why I can never go beyond a certain point with people like Walter and Len. When my grandmother died no one read a book in my house for ten years. So I felt it was up to me. She had passed something precious on to me, and I've always felt that I was chained to it—that it was my burden to hold onto it until I could pass it on to someone else. If this were a novel, I would have her give me the damn Bible on her deathbed or something, but it's not that corny. When it comes to violence I've never been able to go along with either side, though. Even when I played football, I was the quarterback—where I could use my head.

"And that's why I can't go along with all this craziness of revolution and Armageddon. I can't afford to get my brains blown out. I'm cursed, Warren. Because I think my head may be blessed."

"Not in my eyes."

"Oh . . . it's so hard, Warren," I whined, getting up and beginning to comb my fingers through my hair. "I feel like I'm living in a De Kooning painting in which the human form has been broken apart and smeared over with layers of blood. Everything is overlayed and fragmented."

"So?" he said.

"*So?*"

"That's right—*so.*"

"I'm not kidding," I said.

"I know that, Jake. But you can live with Charlie Parker's music. Why not with De Kooning's painting."

"Not *with* it, damn it. *In* it!"

"Bird lived in his music."

"Until he was thirty-five," I said. "This is too much for me. I can't bear it anymore, Warren. I think I'm going nuts. I need stability. Peace. I want to go to the ocean."

I sat down at the end of Warren's bed.

"You will, Jake. If you follow De Kooning far enough."

"Warren, where are you? What do you want from me?"

"We've gone too far to stop, Jake. But if we keep on, keep breaking down lines, conceptions, figures . . . keep fractionating reality into smaller and smaller bits, they'll eventually recombine. Lines will break down to points, if we have the courage to follow them far enough. I know they will. And points lead back to wholes —back to Georges Seurat, if you can get enough distance, Jake.

"If you're willing to let reality be, to keep your paws off of it, it falls back together again—the dots become wholes. Stay out of it, Jake. Write your book. Or stay stoned. Stay stoned and you're back with picnics and holidays. Back with Seurat, and every afternoon is Sunday afternoon in the park."

"I don't think I can live with that, Warren. I can listen to bop. . . ."

"Look, Jake, don't you see? That's what Coltrane was aiming for. What do you think his sheets of sound were? He was playing the notes so fast, breaking them up into such minute bits of sound, that they began to beat the ear. . . to become whole sheets by joining together. He was trying to play harmony with himself."

"But even Coltrane had to come up for air once in a while."

"Sure, he did. And even paintings have usually had edges to separate them from the ugliness around them. But you've got to learn to keep your mind within the frame. To concentrate. And grass will help you there, Jake. Not Len. And not Cal, either."

"And when the colonel napalms the grass?"

"Maybe by then we'll know how to concentrate without it."

"Oh, sure. Or maybe, as Edith would say, science will have come up with a cheap substitute."

"Science makes it possible for you to hear Bach whenever you feel like it. All things have two sides. Use the good one. Slow your life down, Jake, and perhaps you'll be able to catch up with it."

"I don't think there's time. It's too slow already."

"You should write, Jake. But if you won't, then I think you should begin to smoke seriously. I mean *before* you go to work as well as after."

"I don't have anything against grass."

"God gave us grass to help us. It's a natural plant."

"It's too late for kids' games."

"Lest ye be as little children, Jake. . . ."

"And it may be too late for that as well. You know what, Warren? I'm surrounded by people who believe I was sent here for a purpose. And strange as it seems, I'm beginning to believe it myself. But I can't, for the life of me, figure out what it is."

"Their sucking you into *their* game. . . ."

"Well, I don't know. I just don't know," I said, standing up. "And I'll tell you something, Warren, I have a feeling that by the time I find out it's going to be too late."

I started to walk out of the room.

"Where are you going?"

"Over to see the general," I said, with no spirit in my voice.

"Be careful, Jake," he said, as I left the room.

BULLETIN

Anti-Marijuana Law Sought
TOPEKA, Kans., Oct. 4 (UPI) —Gov. Robert B. Docking said Wednesday he would ask for legislation to destroy more than 52,000 acres of marijuana growing wild in Kansas. He said he would ask that marijuana be declared a noxious weed, thus permitting its eradication under existing statutes.

CAMERA TWO

Since all the officers lived in the same area of the base, the general's house was not far from ours. It could not be confused with our house, however, for just as the field grade officers' houses were much larger than those of the junior officers like myself, the general's house was proportionately larger than those of the field grade officers. And it was isolated. Even the field grade houses, though they were not duplex and had land around them, were still aligned in rows. But there were no other generals on the base. He was a row unto himself.

Because Edith had mentioned that she had met the general's wife, I thought I would try to see her first. And I did. She was outside the house, planting bulbs in her flower garden. Although I hadn't met her before, I recognized her from her photos in the base newspaper.

If you haven't been in the army, you can't realize what a violation of propriety it is for a lieutenant to walk across the general's lawn, enter his garden, and introduce himself to the general's wife. It isn't so much that it's wrong—it just isn't done.

When I was a boy I bought a dog, and I wanted to train him not to leap onto my bed. I did this by assuming an attitude more of frantic and exaggerated disbelief than of anger every time he leaped up onto the bed. As if it weren't merely wrong, it was unheard of. And rapidly the dog lost his ability to even conceive of being on the bed. It was as if the bed weren't there. There were many rules which he might break in a thoughtless or rebellious moment, but as for going on the bed, well, it just wasn't done.

But I did it. I walked up to the general's wife, introduced myself, and began to talk to her about tulips. She may have been an alcoholic but she seemed more batty than drunk. I spoke to her about Edith, whom she remembered, and about the weather, and gradually, I insinuated myself into her confidence.

She had downed her morning gins and, since I had been nothing if not amiable before joining the army, I was able to draw on this reserve to win her approval and to get her to consent to my seeing the general. It was her revelation of the general's interest in history, coupled with my assertion of some knowledge in this field, which finally turned the trick.

She entered the house and emerged a few seconds later. "The general will see you now, lieutenant. Go right on in. Second door on the left. I'll just stay out here with my bulbs."

CAMERA ONE

The general's study is a most comfortable place. Bookcases filled with books on military history, deep rugs, a mounted moose head, and evidence of work being done on an article or book. As I enter, he is standing with his back toward me, examining a large map of the Pacific Theater of World War II. It covers the major part of one wall of the room.

"Ah, lieutenant," he says, turning to me, "glad to meet you. Mommy tells me you're interested in history."

"Yes, sir."

"Good! Good, lieutenant. It's a fine subject. Awfully hard to find anyone who's still interested in it. Awfully hard. Sit down, son."

The general has not been seen in public since I arrived on the base, but I recognize him from his chain of command photo which hangs above mine in our company day room. He is what is called distinguished in appearance, with a deep suntan, silvergray hair, gray eyes, and a custom-made tweed sport jacket over brown pants. Yet something is missing from his expression. Perhaps it is the ability of organic matter to respond—to react to pleasures and irritations. One doesn't spend the better part of one's life in officers' clubs without paying one's dues.

Like his wife, he seems somewhat senile. Although it is probably unfair to blame this completely on the army. Maybe he had even been a bit senile before he joined the army. Perhaps this was why he had advanced so rapidly

"You see this map, lieutenant," he says, pointing to it with a wooden pointer, "World War II." He begins to light up a little, as if the mention of his favorite subject, even by himself, is enough to activate a relay somewhere deep inside of him which connects a few hidden circuits. "That was a war, lieutenant. A man's war. Where the enemy would stand up and fight."

"That's what I wanted to talk to you about, sir."

"What's that, lieutenant?" he says, surprised at my intrusion.

"It's about what's happening today, sir. All around us."

"Yes, yes, lieutenant, but getting back to World War II. . . ."

"Sir," I interject quickly, "the colonel is shelling the village."

"What? Shelling?"

"Yes, sir."

He thinks about this for a minute, facing his map, and then he turns to me: "Are the nips there, too?" then, turning to his map again: "Tough soldier, the nip. I remember back in the Second, on Luzon. . . ."

"Sir! It's Colonel Creetner! He's bombing our own towns. He's shelling the base."

"Ah, that's the ticket. Artillery will soften him up. He'll dig in —the nip. Have to flush him out."

"People are dying!"

"Back on Iwo they got a lot of our men, lieutenant. Vicious little fighters. . . ."

"But sir, these aren't the people you think they are! Yesterday a shell fell on the poor section of town and wiped out two entire black families."

"Black nips?" he says, scratching his head in wonder. "You learn something every day, lieutenant. Let that be a lesson to you. Times change. . . ."

"But . . ."

"Why, back at Guam, I was in G-4—light colonel at the time— fine people in supply, lieutenant, don't ever underestimate them, tough job, army moves on its abdomen, you know."

He turns to his map and begins explaining the supply aspects of the entire Pacific campaign in World War II. He talks for over two hours before his wife finally enters the study and calls him to dinner, stopping him in the middle of the replacement of boots and shoes during the battle for Okinawa, and giving me an opportunity to get out of there.

"Soup's on, daddy," she says.

"I hate to break this up, mommy," he says. "I like to stay in touch with the young people—especially if they're as interested in history as the lieutenant here."

I stand up.

"Stop back again sometime, lieutenant. We'll pick up where we left off."

"Yes, sir, I'll certainly do that."

But I never did.

BULLETIN

Man Missing Since '37 Prefers Cave to Family

YAMATOTAKADA, Japan (AP)—A 74-year-old Japanese, who left his wife and son in 1937 and was recently discovered in a mountain cave where he had lived for 20 years, has rejected pleas from his family to return home, police reported.

'I am much more comfortable living in the cave," police said Toyosaburo Sasaki, a former fisherman, had informed them. Authorities, however, took him from his 60-foot cave and placed him under the care of a Buddhist priest.

CAMERA THREE

We never got too friendly with many of our neighbors on the base. Most of them were of the order of Captain Lockhart and his wife Roberta, the people who lived across the street. They were too army for us, and besides, the fact that we spent a great deal of time with the Raineys seemed to scare them off. This was fine with me, since I'd only spoken to Roberta Lockhart whenever I couldn't avoid running into her on the street; and each time she had complained that the officers' club on the base was no comparison with the one at Fort Benning.

One exception was the couple who lived in the house next to ours, the Benutos, Frank and Donna. He was a young R.O.T.C. commissioned lieutenant in the infantry and she was the woman with the curlers in her hair who had run over to Len and me in the backyard on the day that Sibyl freaked out.

Frank and Donna were from New York City. They had one child, a girl of two, and Donna was pregnant again. Frank had been raised in Greenwich Village. The children of the Italian community there usually turn out pretty straight considering the neighborhood in which they grow up. In fact, while other parents have to warn their children against hippies in the abstract, the presence of an entire community of artists, hippies, and assorted other bohemain types right alongside the tightly knit, Italian-American group in the Village serves as a living and concrete example, a kind of audio-visual aid, for the parents to use in the instruction of their children in the group's taboos.

So Frank wasn't very hip. But on the other hand, he was not completely unaware of what was happening. In the long run it is much easier to hate and fear abstractions than people and, if Frank was not really very hip, he was at least fairly knowledgeable about, and tolerant toward, the ways of those who were. Since he had grown up with them, he did not have to get his picture of the American underground from television, which has portrayed them as a grotesque abstraction of what Americans most envy and fear—as America's devils. As America's Jews.

His wife Donna, being second-generation Astoria, Queens, was really more of suburban than of Italian descent. She was more mechanical, more afraid than Frank was. More American. In particular, she was afraid of Warren. But she was curious as well. The idea of a Warren, of a Warren living with the family of an army officer, was so contrary to her expectations that it aroused her curiosity.

After Edith got her job with Telecation, Warren did almost all our cooking and he was usually the only one home during the days. Because of this, Donna accidentally confronted him on the several occasions when she ventured over to borrow some sugar or flour from Edith. Slowly, she began to realize that not only was he a human being, but that he would listen to her when she spoke, and that he, more than anyone else on the base, appreciated the Italian recipes which had been handed down to her through her family.

In some ways, Donna was a great deal more afraid of the Raineys than of us. As Indians, they must have appeared to her as less real, more mythological figures than ourselves. But propinquity triumphed in their case as well, and she even progressed to where she was able to speak to Len or Jeannie without nervously fingering her scalp.

Of course, there was a point beyond which our relationship with the Benutos couldn't go. Frank was a very warm person and he loved animals. He owned a dog, a little white rabbit, and fish, and I enjoyed talking to him about them, but Donna played her radio all the time, tuned to a local AM station which featured songs like:

> You *need* love,
> You *want* love,
> If you don't have love,
> You think you're gonna die.
> You *need* love,
> You *want* love,
> You *need* love,
> You *want* love,
> And you don't need a reason why.
> You *need*. . . (etc.)

This made it imperative for me to avoid entering their house whenever I could manage it, but Warren didn't seem to mind, and he went over there often to play with the animals and the baby and to trade recipes with Donna. After a few months, Donna even let Warren babysit when she and Frank went out for the evening.

CAMERA ONE

Visiting David at the cabin. I get stoned. Browse through a book on hypnosis that I pick up off the floor. David drops off to sleep finally. He said he'd been up for forty-eight hours.

As I leave, I place the book on hypnosis in a vacant slot in David's bookcase. The open slot is in a set of Proust's *Remembrance of Things Past.* I check the other books. The one missing is *Swann's Way.* I now know where David and Walter have been getting their inside information about activities on the base.

CAMERA TWO

One afternoon, when I returned home from work, Edith and Warren were in the backyard. They were putting up a clothesline which would be suspended from five poles, forming an irregular pentagon.

A Big Brother LP was on the phonograph. Its sounds were thrown into the backyard by the stereo speakers at the open windows of the house. Janis was singing "Ball and Chain," while Warren sought the proper place for each supporting pole. Arms extended out in front of him. Hands twisted back to back. Holding the wishbone of a chicken pointed toward the ground. Dowsing for the special spot.

"What game have you two invented today?"

"What do you mean *game*, white man," Edith said, her face covered with sweat and dirt collected in the digging of the holes for the three shafts that were already placed.

"Well, what's Ki-mo-sav-vey doing over there, looking for water?"

"Everything in the universe has its place, Jake," Warren said. "It's just a matter of taking the time to locate it."

"O.K., Tom Sawyer," I said. "Always got to free Nigger Jim the hard way."

"Nigger Jim was *already* free," Warren said. "That's the point. He was free all the time and he didn't know it."

"Besides," Edith said, leaning on her shovel and looking over my head, "one Tom Sawyer is enough around here."

I turned, and there, sitting on the edge of the roof of the house with his legs hanging over the side, almost directly above me, was Little Jo, one finger on his lips to signal Edith to be silent.

"Drat it!" he snapped his fingers in disappointment. "Edith, that's not fair." And he jumped off the single-story roof into my arms.

"Hey!" I caught at him. "You'll hurt yourself."

But he didn't. I held him, and then deposited him back upon the earth. He immediately leaped back and began to tap-dance in a loose, dangling, scarecrow manner.

"What's this?" I laughed, and I began to chase him about, boxing with him, while he continued to dance and jabbed back at me.

"Hit de hand—hit de hand!" I Burt Lahred at him. And his dancing yielded to tighter delight as he planted his feet and began to punch excitedly at my palms, his face flowing over with glee. And I tackled him and toppled him over, pulling at his angel hair, tangled and curly and orange and ochre, and we rolled laughing upon the ground.

"Here!" Warren shouted.

"Stop! Stop!" Little Jo, still giggling, pulled back from my grip. "Stop it, you dodo."

I stood up. "Oh, dodo is it?"

Little Jo couldn't contain himself, and he rolled in the grass, gasping with laughter.

"That's right, Dodo," Edith cried, and began to tickle me.

"Cut it out, Edith!"

Little Jo jumped up and joined her.

"Cut it out, you two," breathlessly trying to free myself from their four flying hands.

"Here it is!" Warren shouted.

Little Jo moved away from me and looked toward Warren. "Hey, you guys, Warren found it. He dowsed it."

"He what?" I said.

"He dowsed it," Little Jo said, his face turning redder as he realized that Edith and I were smiling at *him* now.

"Aw. . . you guys," he said, throwing a long, slow, roundhouse punch into my hip.

I picked him up and turned him upside down, holding him by his ankles. Marbles, candies, and little CrackerJack toys spilled to the ground from his pockets.

"You people just go on fooling around, while I slave away here," Warren said, in mock exasperation.

As I put Jo back on his feet again, I heard Jeannie's voice: "I'll mark it for you, Warren."

"Hey! Jeannie!" I said. "I was just putting your protégé, here, through a few spins."

"*My* protégé?" she said. "You mean David's and Walter's, because he spends all his time at the cabin these days."

Little Jo amost spilled her drink, as he ran up to her and put his arms around her and hugged his head into her breasts, while she smiled and smoothed his hair.

CAMERA THREE

At no other time did I see Jeannie's face as radiant as it was at that moment. She had known loss, even before she had lost her baby —even before her father had lost his legs. It was a part of her. More than it was a part of her people, it was a part of her. For to love jazz is to be in love with loss, and only those with loss inside of them can afford to love such a mad effort to create on demand, to attempt each night to improvise pathways to heaven big enough for all the damned.

It's a hopeless business, jazz, and that's why even its most lyrical moments are tinged with sorrow. And why it can be so beautiful. Three centuries of loss leavened by the sharing of pain, which, when forced through a horn and infused with grace, freely given, can, once in a great while, flower out into the fruits of cornucopia.

For an entire generation, jazz groups were the last families of the lost, the last circles of introverted support for the freedom of each. And jazz lovers of today constitute a foreign legion of the lost.

That's why I was so glad to see the end of the blackout in the dark caverns of Jeannie's eyes. That's why it was so good, so awfully good, to see it, for inside Jeannie it was Times Square in September of 1945 and the lights were on again. And the war was over.

BULLETIN

CAIRO, ILL., NEGROES URGE MARTIAL LAW

CAIRO, Ill., Jan. 2 (UPI)— The predominantly Negro United Front Organization today asked Gov. Richard B. Ogilvie to impose martial law in this racially troubled river town.

The Rev. Charles Koen, executive director of the militant group, said in a statement that he feared militant whites might try to move against Negroes in the community of 8,500 at the southern tip of the state.

CAMERA THREE

During the month of October, the building of Len's longhouse proceeded in a manner which, I think, surprised even him. From the way he had brought together some lumber and surplus building materials, it seemed as if he had merely counted upon the base's approval of his project, rather than its full support. The longhouse he intended to build couldn't have been more than a slightly larger version of David's cabin, crudely put together by himself and the scouts of the King Phillip Memorial Society.

But one day, the base engineers showed up in force with new building materials and machinery, and they began to do the job for him. And, in a few weeks, they had constructed a building which was comparable to the social hall one might find at a children's summer camp. A simple rectangular building with a stage at one end. Before they left, they had insulated the walls to keep out the coming winter's cold and had installed, under the stage, a gas heating unit that they'd salvaged from one of the barracks which had been destroyed by a bomb hit in the spring.

When I congratulated Len upon the success of his venture, he invited me to the troop's first meeting in the new longhouse. It would be held on the evening of the eleventh of November. Veteran's Day.

CAMERA ONE

The eve of All Saints' Day. Halloween. The front of the house flickers in the light of hollow pumpkins which each hold a homemade candle. Warren has spent all week preparing. Making the candles in the kitchen and carving the pumpkins with a Bowie knife borrowed from Tommy Creetner.

The doorbell rings. I answer it. It's Little Jo, dressed in an improvised scarecrow costume without a mask. Behind him, a quartet of small boys, each wearing a grinning, blackface, Sambo mask.

"Trick or treat," he says.

I hand them each a colored bag of candy and trinkets which Warren has prepared.

"O.K., gang, take off the masks," Jo says.

And the four boys take off their Sambo faces, revealing three little white faces and one black one which is as dark as the Sambo had been.

Jo points to the little black face and cries, "I said take off your mask, Sambo!" and he and the little black boy crack up and Jo catches my eye and he beams into it and all five of them run off into the dark, giggling.

CAMERA THREE

In November my days fell into an hysterical sameness. Getting through my time in the army was similar to reading a long book by a novelist with a bad ear. Dragging yourself through the book as a whole may finally lead to your having learned something. But it's getting through each sentence that's the problem. I had conceived of the two years in the army as a small part of my life which might provide the material for a novel. But I was surprised to find that it was suffering through each day that was unbearable. ... And yet the hours did drag on by, between coffee breaks, which I began to take again after I found I could share them with Lorraine Washington. I fined people, inspected people, saluted people, and lectured people, and through it all, I thought of Cal.

The colonel would call me to his office almost daily, with new schemes and orders for me to impose upon the men under my command. I listened to Sergeant O'Mara's war stories and protected poor, drunk, Sergeant Mooney.

Mooney had worked in the hospital treasurer's office, but he was always so haplessly drunk the treasurer finally threatened to have him busted for fucking up the hospital's revenues (civilian patients were charged for their treatment). Since Mooney had only six months to go until he could retire at half pay, being demoted to the pay grade of a private would have been disastrous for him. So, with Cal's help, I was able to hush up the problem and to transfer Mooney to my company supply room where he would be out of the way and where I could keep an eye on him until it was time for him to retire.

Of course, he wasn't much use as a supply sergeant, since he screwed up all the records, let half the supplies get stolen, and once, when the colonel came around for a surprise inspection, he snapped to attention so briskly that he lost his balance and toppled headfirst into a big laundry basket filled with an odd assortment of foreign clothes. Luckily Cal was there and she was able to cover up for him. This was during the time when everyone in the army began to add the phrase "you might say" to the end of each statement they made, to relieve them of the responsibility of ever committing themselves to any definite assertion or point of view.

Not surprisingly, Cal had immediately picked up on this trend and she said it, too, as often as she could, but in her case it was not to avoid responsibility—it was just that she thought it was funny. So, when Sergeant Mooney fell into the laundry basket, Cal immediately said to the colonel, "Well, the poor man seems to have had an attack of vertigo, you might say," and she ordered three privates, who happened to be standing nearby, to help Sergeant Mooney back to his room.

The colonel never saw Mooney again, for when I told Lorraine about the problem she took it upon herself to call my office every time the colonel was on his way over so we had enough time to hide Mooney out in the woods behind the supply room and to put the company clerk in charge of Mooney's duties until the colonel left.

And, almost every day, I saw Cal. Even on the weekends, for she had befriended Warren, and, whenever she had some time off (quite often, it turned out), she would take him to the movies in Boston. Although Warren would have preferred to have gone to old reruns in Cambridge, Cal insisted on seeing only the latest movies which were shown in downtown Boston, and Warren, who was glad enough for the chance to go anywhere, didn't complain. So, even on weekends, I would hear the roar of her Jaguar pulling into our driveway and see her leap out in one of her tiny micro-skirts, and I would rush to greet her and look at her legs while she waited for Warren.

I was surprised to learn that someone as practical as Cal went to the movies as often as she did, and I asked her about it one day as she sat in my chair at the office.

"Movies are tomorrow's weather report," she said, "and that's what I need to know. They don't picture the world, they create it."

"A kind of self-fulfilling prophecy?"

"Right. The world on the screen defines the limits of the nascent world coming into being off the screen. And that's the world we're going to have to operate in, Jacob. Even scientists go to the movies."

And when she would leave the house with Warren, I would run to the window and peek through the closed venetian blinds so I could see her hair hanging out behind her, reaching out to me on the wind.

Although I continued my swimming sessions with Cal, they came to be less embarrassing for me after I had put the lesson I learned at Tommy Creetner's concert into effect. After I applied Bernoulli's principle. I would arrive early and pull myself against the side of the pool into the position one would use to begin a race without a dive. Both hands behind me, gripping the edge, legs drawn up under me to frog-kick me out with a single forceful thrust. To get me moving before I was swimming.

And, as long as I was moving, the water would support me. So, instead of thrashing about while Cal held me up, I began to take a few strokes. And I began to learn, to believe, that if I could use my strokes to *keep* me moving, after my initial thrust was spent, the water itself would support me.

But my lessons were short. Always interrupted by Cal's entrance, after which I couldn't concentrate on anything but the lines and bulk of her body.

And I began to fear that I was getting sick. Both in the head and the body. For I could not get her off my mind. I would daydream about being the general or even the president, appearing on national TV with Cal at my side, and being more envied for having her than for the power of my position. And when I attempted to write in my journal, I would drift into drawing pictures of Cal on the page—designing imaginary costumes in which to clothe her flesh.

And at night I couldn't sleep. Feared I was becoming ill as well as insane. Worried about the price to be paid for living in a constant state of sexual excitement, with its fevered brain heat and rapid heartbeat leading me toward death before I had really begun to live.

But I could not stop. And often, when I would finally get to sleep, I would be awakened just before the point of orgasm in a dream of Cal. And I would lie nervously stirring for hours, next to Edith, thinking of Cal and trying to calm myself enough so that I could safely go back to sleep without worrying about the need for impossible explanations to Edith in the morning, about the condition of the bed, should the dream recur.

I was sick. Sick with exhaustion. Sick with worry about my sanity. And sick with the realization that I could neglect my duties, even neglect to help the wounded who were carried into the hospital, for the chance to look at Cal.

Or to hear her say "we" when she spoke about the future with me.

C A M E R A   O N E

On the evening of the first longhouse ceremonies, I went next door to the Raineys right after I returned home from the hospital. They were both in the kitchen where Jeannie was cooking large kettles of something which smelled good.

"What are you making?" I asked.

"Corn soup," she said.

"It's a traditional dish," Len explained. "We'll eat it later in the longhouse. Our people always include it as part of the ceremonies. To us, beans, corn, squash, fruit, and berries weren't just industrial products, packaged in plastic for housewives to buy in the supermarket. We knew they were given to us by the Creator. Not by United Fruit. We watched them grow. And we knew that as divine gifts, they should be treated not *as if* they were sacred, but *as* sacred."

I turned to Jeannie, who was stirring the great simmering kettles on the stove.

"I didn't know *you* were involved with the scouts."

"I am now," she smiled.

"What are you, the den mother?" I joked.

"I'm a clan mother."

"A *what*?"

"A clan mother," Len said. "Now that we've got a longhouse and enough members, we're going to do it right. The Iroquois tribes have always been divided into clans which are each named after an animal. The various clans of the tribe were organized into two groups, each consisting of about half the members of the tribe— into moieties, as the anthropologists have termed them. But the main social unit was always the clan. So, beginning tonight, we've divided ourselves into clans. We're the wolf clan. And we've organized the clans into two larger groups as well. The Blacks and the Reds."

"But why a clan *mother*?"

"Indian women are in touch with the earth," he said. "They till the ground with natural implements and plant the seeds. And we've traditionally recognized this by having, as the leading figure in each clan, a clan mother. Iroquois society is matrilineal. Each male representative to the tribal council, and the sachems, or chiefs, are appointed by the clan mothers, and any of them who gets out of bounds can be deposed by his clan mother at any time."

"And you're a sachem?"

"Right."

"And the chief of the whole tribe, too?"

"That's stupid Walter's joke. We don't have a single authoritarian chief. We're democratic, just like the six nations of the Iroquois league. There are lots of equal chiefs. And nobody gets forced into doing anything against his will. Whoever is most capable in a certain activity steps forward and takes command, but he's got to depend solely on his personal abilities and his imagination to convince the others to follow him. Whether it's for war, or negotiations, or whatever."

I noticed that Jeannie wasn't saying much herself. I wondered if this was because she was involved in making the soup, or whether she was just going along with Len's Indian mania against her better judgment—humoring him, but declining to take an active part in it.

When Little Jo came in, we went across the field to the site of the meeting. At the longhouse, the various clans, half of them black, half "Indians," were led into the meeting by their clan mothers. We walked in behind Jeannie. It was austerely furnished with a large wooden table and some benches, most of which were set back against the walls. The stage at the end of the room was not being used. Above it someone had hung a banner: THE KING PHILLIP MEMORIAL SOCIETY. On the wall at the back of the stage a crudely printed sign stated:

AMERICA IS DEAD!
THE ONLY NATION REMAINING
IS CONSTERNATION.

We all sat down on the benches. After some prayers for the Indian dead, Len addressed the group. It was immediately obvious that he was a natural orator, and, as I knew was true of many of the actual Indian sachems, he seemed to be able to hold his audience with a kind of hypnotic power.

At that moment, I realized why the question of whether or not he was an Indian didn't interest Jeannie. For when Len spoke, he fell right into the ranks of the great orators for which the Indian tribes were famous. Men who led their people solely by the power and authority of their words. When Len spoke to the group, he *was* an Indian, a great Indian, and questions about his parentage or descent were irrelevant.

He spoke of the symbolic significance of the longhouse, how each individual longhouse represented the greater longhouse of the whole, original, Iroquois territory, which had been roughly rectangular in shape until it had been stolen by the white man. He pointed west, toward the stage, and spoke of the door behind the stage (the one which faced the river) as symbolizing the western door of the Iroquois confederacy, the end of the great longhouse of the six nations at Lake Erie, which was tended by the Senecas.

The eastern door of the longhouse (the one which faced back across the field, toward the officers' quarters) represented the eastern door to the territory at the Hudson River, and it was tended by the Mohawks. Then pointing to the east-west aisle which had been left clear along the center of the floor, he noted that this represented the Mohawk River, the great hallway through the territory occupied by the six nations.

He repeated what he had told me earlier about the sacred aspects of food, extending this to the musical instruments, all percussive, which many of the scouts were carrying. They were made only of natural materials, made by hand he said, of turtle shells, bark, gourds, sticks, and skin. Like the foods, these too must be regarded as sacred objects, their natural origins symbolic of the Indian's ties with the blessed nature around him.

And above all, this was true of tobacco. Tobacco burning and smoking had been associated with Indian ceremonies for centuries and God had given tobacco to the Indians for that purpose. And the pipes began to be passed around the cool, dimly lit room, and people would take a long puff and pass them on, and the room filled with the smell of the sweet, heavy, musty smoke that was so familiar around our house.

How had I been so blind? How could it have taken me so long to see what I should have seen chapters before? I finally understood what was happening to those large quantities of grass which Len had bought from Walter and David. He had been turning on all the scouts in the King Phillip Memorial Society. It was so obvious now. . . . But prior to this, it must have seemed so far beyond the bounds of probability that I hadn't even conceived of it as a possibility. And therefore, I had never looked for it. And so I never saw it.

And then the musicians, all of whom were boys, began to shake their rattles and to bang their instruments against the benches as the dancing began. There were eight of them—four white and four black. The white musicians were the four boys from the Boston Braves. And once again, leading them, swinging on rhythm this time, was Tommy Creetner.

And the dancing and smoking continued for exhausted hours into the frenzy-filled night. They did the bear dance and the buffalo dance and countless others as the rhythm section wailed away, and those who weren't dancing joined in the rhythmic chanting and pounding which shook the floor and seemed to turn the whole room into a pulsating extension of the wild dancers' bodies.

Deeper into the night they danced, finally reaching a point where the boys and girls changed into each other's clothes, doing steps in imitation of the manner of the other sex and, after this, the dancers removed their clothes and began to gyrate in naked ecstasy to the music together. And then the false-face society put on their masks (those twisted, grotesque, renderings of the human face) and did their dance, and the husk face dancers did theirs, and then we all sat around, energies spent, in our little sheltered ark of closeness and warmth in the dark, cold night, and we ate warm corn soup together, and we chanted quietly together, smiling happy-weary smiles at each other, holding each other, and feeling something for each other which I had almost forgotten how to feel for myself—openness—a love.

And as we quietly chanted and wrapped ourselves in blankets, Len began to recite, over the quiet, rhythmic chanting. He began to name the tribes which the white man had killed off. Which the palefaces had rendered extinct. Forever.

"The Micmacs, the Malecites, the Passamaquoddies. . . ."

And I could not remember the last time I had been so happy. Nor the last time I had been so sad: for happiness and sorrow are closer to each other than to that which opposes them both—lack of feeling.

"Abnakis, Nipmucs, Pennacooks . . ."

And I felt that profound hollowness which I always feel when

I think about the idea of extinction. Why? Why is the death of a species or a culture so much more terrible to contemplate than the death of an individual? Why does it release more of the terror of forever? Can it be that we still harbor chords which vibrate to the idea of the great chain of being, that mad attempt of man to impose a comforting completeness upon the universe and call it the design of God?

"Nausets, Wappingers, Niantics . . ."

Is it extinction that breaks down our feeling of the good fullness of things and puts us in touch with absence? With the anxiety-producing, zero-fear of empty forever, infinite sickening change? Terrible sea-nauseous change which pulls out our entrails and holds them up rotting and red-bloody in front of our faces on a platter of chilled silver, intricately worked.

"Conoys, Pamlicos, Nanticokes, Tutelos, Saponis . . ."

For if species can disappear, if an entire culture can die, then a rent is torn into eternity, and infinity is let in, and we step into a universe of vast nothingness and the mutability of ideas in which events on earth can change things so they will never again be the same. Never in forever time. Beyond years, beyond imagining. Never.

"I have spoken about the sacramental nature of the tobacco and herbs which the Great Spirit has given us to offer up to himself. I have spoken about their holy nature and their traditional usage amongst our people. But now I must say that once again the palefaces are acting to keep us out of touch with the Great Spirit who provides. Walter has told me he can no longer get the sacred grass. David, too, is helpless in the face of the government's sacrilegious attack upon our culture and our minds. Thus, my brothers, I want to appeal to a paleface among us. . . ."

"Len!" Jeannie cried out, in shocked dismay, but he silenced her with a dark glance, and continued.

". . . to a paleface who has shared our secrets and our corn soup, to a paleface who, I know, will not let us down in our hour of need. I want to call upon Jacob Klinger to act in our behalf. I want to call upon Jacob Klinger, who, I know, has a source of the blessed grass, far from here in the sunny Southland from which our people, the good Tuscaroras, were ejected over two centuries ago."

I couldn't believe my ears.

"I want to call upon Jacob Klinger, our friend, to atone for his faithful service to the powers of darkness each day by helping us to continue to serve the God of Light each night."

"I . . . I can't do that. . . ."

They were all looking at me. Peeking out from under their blankets, sweet faces in the dusky room, the young people who had held me together with them in the eye of the disintegrating society fashioned by their parents for them as well as for me.

"There's no grass famine. . . . Walter can get it, if he tries. . . ."

"We don't know that, Jacob."

"Len . . . you know that this Operation Interception is just another fraud. . . ."

"It doesn't matter, Jake. We're your friends. We want you to be with us. And we can't get grass without you."

"I can't. . . . This is madness. . . . I can't get involved in dealing. I'm in the army. They'll lock me up and throw away the key. This society of yours can't keep this a secret."

"We need you, Jake."

"I can't. (The faces—the faces of my fellow victims—my friends) I'll think it over. . . . Maybe once. . . . I'll write to my friend Randy. . . . That's all I'll do. I can't join with you, I'm sorry. I can't but hope that what you're doing, whatever it is, succeeds. I'm on your side. But I can't be with you. . . . Because I can't conceive of how any action you might have in mind could result in anything but your own destruction. . . . but I love you guys, and I'll respect your intentions and your right to your own choice. So if you'll respect mine—my feeling that this whole venture is a rudderless ship carrying all of you to a wasteful doom, and my decision not to join you, not to get involved with your ruinous trip—I'll write to Randy. I'll get you the grass."

"It's a deal," Len said.

And everybody relaxed.

BULLETIN

Colorado Cow Has Triplets

WIGGINS, Colo. (AP) — A Guernsey milk cow on an eastern Colorado farm beat high odds by giving birth to triplets, a bull and two heifers. A veterinarian said the chances of triple births among cattle are one in almost 107,000.

CAMERA THREE

I wrote to Randy, asking him to send us the grass. We had been roommates in college. He began in chemistry and I in physics. We did fairly well at first, but in the spring of the first year we both began to lose interest in science and we spent most of our time listening to records or going to places like Pep's and the Showboat in South Philly to dig jazz.

When I came to believe that truth was something that couldn't be learned in school, my disappointment turned into a cynicism which finally led me to switch to the Wharton School where I studied accounting. Business was easier than physics and left me more than enough free time to read and dig music.

Randy stopped studying altogether after Thanksgiving of his sophomore year. He failed two subjects that fall and was put on probation, but he was able to bullshit his parents into thinking that he was suffering from mononucleosis so they actually wound up complimenting him upon his passing three of his five courses while suffering from such a serious malady. They even came to Philly to see him. And they paid his tuition for the spring semester. And when they returned to their home in Charlotte, North Carolina, they left him a new Oldsmobile convertible to pick up his spirits so he would do better in the spring.

And when he failed all five of his subjects the next semester and was thrown out of school, they were surprised and disappointed.

CAMERA ONE

I am driving home for lunch. Standing in the middle of the road is an MP. It's Sergeant Adams. He signals me to stop and salutes my car.

From the right, a platoon of Mexican peons (still wearing their bright, tattered clothes and sombreros) marches across the road. And on the far side of their ragged formation, commanding them and counting out the cadence in Spanish, is Cal.

A stab of sunlight, reflected from the woods on my left catches my eye. There is someone there, kneeling in the fallen leaves. Partially hidden by the trees. He is watching the parade through binoculars and taking notes on a clipboard.

From my car I cannot be certain, but it looks like David.

CAMERA TWO

After lunch, I noticed Frank Benuto out in our backyard, running his dog in the snow. I put my coat back on and went outside to watch. Frank was using our pentagonal clothesline. He would shout, "Round, Bob, round!" and the dog would circle the five poles only to return to the point from which he started where Frank would give him a biscuit.

"Isn't it funny how he learns to do that?" I said. "He's standing right next to the biscuits in your hand and surely he can smell them—they're right near his nose—yet he follows the rules and runs *away* from the biscuits and all around the clothesline, just to come back to where he was originally."

"I don't think it's so odd."

"Well, it's not *odd*. It's just interesting that a dog will play a game like this—that he'll accept the rules as if they made perfect sense."

"As far as his needs go, they *do* make sense. He gets the biscuit in the end."

"I mean make sense outside of the arbitrary framework of the game you've constructed. It's like a home run in baseball. You begin at home plate and circle the bases until you wind up in the exact same place from which you started. Only everything's different then, because you're a hero."

Frank nodded his head in agreement. "Yeah, I see what you mean. Let's screw him up a bit."

He took a biscuit in his hand and called, "Round, Bob, round!" Then, when Bob returned, instead of giving him his reward, he called out, "Round, Bob, round!" once again, and Bob, after hesitating just long enough to give him a puzzled look, circled the clothesline again. It took three times. When Frank tried to send him around for the fourth, Bob put on an expression of weary disappointment, turned away, and trotted back across the lawn and into his doghouse.

"That's called not reinforcing," Frank said, as he turned to walk toward his house.

"I'm hip," I said, and I turned toward mine.

BULLETIN

> **Caspian Seals Bite**
> MOSCOW (UPI) — Dozens of vacationers have been bitten by maddened seals in Soviet Caspian Sea resort areas, Trud reported.

CAMERA THREE

In December, the colonel committed Frank Benuto's infantry company to the counteroffensive. After that I saw a lot of him at the hospital. He would stop by whenever he came to visit one of his men who had been hit by our artillery or bombers. He was obviously forlorn but I hesitated to speak to him about the madness in which we were trapped. I had few enough people to talk to on the base already, without seeking to alienate others.

Frank's father was a neighborhood dentist in Manhattan. He had sent Frank to college in the hopes that he too would become a dentist. The problem was that Frank didn't like to hurt people. He had read Albert Schweitzer and he felt that he had a reverence for life. I mentioned that Schweitzer, as a doctor, would have had to hurt people at times in order to cure them and he agreed in a vague way, opening his spaniel eyes and saying that he knew this, but that *he* couldn't do it.

So he studied and talked about animals. Frank loved animals, and he had constructed a dream future in which he would work in a zoo while doing graduate work in zoology. I encouraged him along these lines, suggesting that he write away to zoos to inquire about the possibilities for jobs and he always said he would—but he never did.

After a while I noticed that he would try to change the subject when I asked him about his future—he would reply that there were so few zoos around, and then, speaking in a monotone which seemed to fit the look of defeat in his face, he would turn to another less personal but still depressing topic, such as the proba-ble extinction of one or another species of animal.

He was a sad case, that Frank. He really didn't want to hurt life. I was convinced of that. But he was lost, and he was afraid that *he* would be hurt by those humans who didn't understand—the ones who didn't possess a reverence for life and couldn't feel the pain of others. So the security offered by the army appealed to him. And he could see that gleam in his wife's eyes when they drove past the spacious, ivy-covered houses allotted to the field grade officers.

Yes, he was a sorry case. And whenever I saw him I thought about General Ulysses S. Grant. For Sergeant O'Mara had told me stories about General Grant. O'Mara's grandfather had come over from Ireland in 1863 and had signed up in the un-ion army. He was with Grant at the battle of the Wilderness. And when O'Mara was a boy, he had told him about how he had tied a tag around his neck, like the other soldiers, telling where to ship his body after he was killed, so sure were the men that fighting under Grant was certain death. For Grant knew that he had a bigger army than Lee, so he reasoned that equal losses were in his favor and that the sooner both armies were depleted, the sooner Lee would run out of men, thereby ending the war. His men called him the Butcher.

Yet Grant would be moved to tears by the sight of a horse in pain. But I couldn't tell Frank about General Grant. No, I just couldn't do that. I wasn't cut out to be a dentist either, I guess.

CAMERA TWO

By the mischievous smile on her face, I could tell that Cal was up to something the moment she walked into my office. And I suspected that it concerned the administering of company punishment, which had become one of her favorite indoor sports because of the chance it gave her to involve me in her games.

And I was right. She said that she wanted to press charges against a WAC private named Myra Cranshaw. I hadn't heard the name before and Cal explained that she was a new recruit who had recently entered the army from Tennesee.

"Private Cranshaw," she commanded, in a loud voice, "front and center!"

I noticed that she could hardly keep from laughing, and when Private Cranshaw came through the doorway I could see why. She was a large, dumpy girl, about five feet, ten inches, and one hundred seventy pounds. An ungainly lump of a girl, with dull eyes and a sour face, and a mustache—a confused sea lion, floundering like a soggy sack in an unnatural element.

Stuck on her chin was a large bandage. And one on her cheek. And on her arm, a bright, phosphorescent bruise. And she limped. And she had a black eye.

I looked at her, and then at Cal, and although I knew I shouldn't I felt so much like laughing out loud that I had to bite my lips to hold it back.

"Private Cranshaw has been fighting," Cal said, her eyes twinkling with suppressed glee. "She assaulted a superior officer."

"What officer was that?" I said.

"Me, Jacob. Private Cranshaw assaulted me."

When I turned away from Cal and once more confronted poor, miserable, black and blue Cranshaw, the whole affair struck me as so absurd, so ludicrous, that I had to get out of my seat and pretend to search for the Code of Military Justice in the files in order to gain time to compose myself.

"Private Cranshaw," I said, "did you assault Captain Taylor?"

"With malice aforethought, Jacob!" Cal added.

"With malice aforethought, Private Cranshaw?"

"Ah don't rightly know, sah," she replied, in molasses-coated words. "Ah jes walked through a door and bumped into somebody and the nex thing ah knew, ah was in the emergency room here in the hospital, right flat on mah back."

"Are you saying that this was an accident, then?" I said.

"Ah guess so, sah. Ah don't rightly know *what* happened."

"Well, Captain Taylor, are you willing to accept that explanation and drop the charges?"

Cal just stood there for a moment, as if pondering a decision which would affect the fate of nations, and then, thoughtfully, she said, "I will drop the charges, lieutenant, on one condition: Private Cranshaw must promise never again to throw her weight around."

Cal swung around to the files, hiding her face and trying to control herself, as I bit my lip again and then said quickly, "Private Cranshaw, will you never try to throw your weight around again?"

And almost before she could answer, "Yes, sah," I blurted, "Case dismissed," spun Private Cranshaw around, bum's rushed her out the door, turned back toward Cal, and, as much as I knew it was cruel, as much as I knew I shouldn't have, I exploded into laughter along with her, and, laughing, we fell into each other's arms, and we held each other, laughing, and we didn't stop until we were out of breath and in tears.

BULLETIN

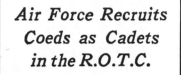

Air Force Recruits Coeds as Cadets in the R.O.T.C.

By JON NORDHEIMER
Special to The New York Times

AUBURN, Ala. — When seven Air Force cadets underwent six weeks of rigorous training at summer camp this year, their schedule included simulated parachute drops, long hours of precision drill under a broiling sun and classroom instruction in modeling and cosmetic makeup techniques.

"Lipstick is considered part of our uniform," said Leslie Farr, a honey-blond engineering student at Auburn University, who is a member of the Air Force's experimental program to attract coeds to a military career.

At a time when male disillusionment with the Vietnam war has thinned the ranks of the Reserve Officers Training Corps on college campuses, the Air Force is trying to recruit young women who are able to do a man's job in the service.

CAMERA ONE

Saturday morning. Awakened by the postman's ring. A package for me. From a W. Whitman. I check the postmark. Charleston, South Carolina.

Inside, a book. Walt Whitman's *Leaves of Grass*. I open it. The pages have been hollowed out. It contains about four ounces of grass. I look at the package in which the book had been wrapped. It was sent fourth class—book rate, to cheat on the postage.

Still the same old Randy.

CAMERA THREE

Once Frank Benuto found out that Cal often stopped by my office, he began to drop in more frequently. He was guileless enough to admit to me his attraction to her. And he was rather open about it toward Cal, too. She didn't take him very seriously, but she seemed to enjoy fooling around with him as though he were a sexually precocious teenager. If he chanced to come into the office when she was there, she would hitch up her skirt and take care to remember not to cross her legs as she sat. Then we would play an unacknowledged game in which Frank would sneak looks at her thighs and panties (although he knew that Cal was aware of what he was doing), and Cal would signal me with knowing smiles every time he did sneak a peek at her crotch (although she knew that Frank was aware of these looks which she gave me).

When Cal wasn't present, Frank would usually spend much of his visit with me describing what he would give up to sleep with Cal. He began in terms of money, but as he became more obsessed by his fascination for her (and as she became more open in her teasing—lifting up her tiny skirt at the precise moment when he was staring at her thighs) he began to talk about giving up other, more meaningful things than money, if it meant being able to sleep with Cal. Then, after he had seen her in a bathing suit at a swimming demonstration, he began to daydream aloud about living with her. And the things he offered to give up for this supreme achievement were, in the context of his life, meaningful indeed. In fact, it was hard to imagine anything that Cal couldn't have gotten him to give up or do, if she had felt it to be in the interests of her desires or needs. Or at least that's the way it seemed to me, from the way he spoke about her.

BULLETIN

De Kooning Suing Dentist To Get 3 Paintings Back

Willem de Kooning, the artist, is suing a Queens dentist to recover three paintings that the abstract expressionist claims are his "sole property and never offered for sale."

CAMERA THREE

And so the days got shorter, but the hours stayed the same as they passed me by, one by one. Continued exposure to wounds and madness had not rendered me immune to the contagion of their presence, but it did give me enough dullness and insensitivity to survive, as when your nose closes out the smell of putrescent flesh after you've had sufficient time to notice it.

I came to learn, however, that the gift of prolonged surface induration is not without its price. I began to find it hard to sleep at night. And when I did sleep, I would find that, along with my visions of Cal, I would have dreams of bloody violence and death which would shock me back into consciousness once again. So I would become more tired and irritable and less able to maintain my equanimity in the face of my days.

For instance, once, after a particularly bad night, the colonel called me into his office to tell me of a new plan he had conceived to save the army money.

CAMERA TWO

"You know how many dentists we have here at this installation, lieutenant?" he said.

"About fifteen, sir?"

"Sixteen, lieutenant. There are sixteen dentists, and do you know why we have these sixteen dentists here, lieutenant?"

"One for each two teeth, sir?" I whispered under my breath.

"What's that, lieutenant? Speak up!"

"Nothing, sir."

"Well, why do you think we have them, lieutenant?"

"To fix people's teeth, sir?"

"You bet your bottom dollar to fix people's teeth!" he shouted, pounding on his desk in excitement over my answer. "That's what dentists do! They fix people's teeth."

Then he asked, "And why do we need so *many* dentists on the base, lieutenant?"

The demon in me wanted to answer that it was because we had so many teeth on the base, but I held him in check and maintained a dumb silence.

"O.K., I'll tell you why, lieutenant. It's because when the shit hits the fan and starts to fly, it's going to knock out a hell of a lot of teeth. And when it comes to teeth getting shot out, we doctors have to yield to our confreres in the healing arts, the dentists. So here's the beauty of my plan, lieutenant: the B.C. didn't come through with his predicted fall offensive, right?"

"Yes, sir."

"I should say so. *Yes sir* is right! Our counteroffensive knocked the crap out of him. He couldn't get back on his feet, you might say."

"Yes, sir."

"But he's not out, lieutenant. He's down, no doubt about it, but he's not out. Possum, that's what he's playing. Possum!"

"Sir?"

"He'll be back, lieutenant, mark my words. Back this winter in double strength. Oh, he's wily, no doubt about it, you might say. He's a wily foe."

"But how does this relate to the dentists, sir?"

"Don't you see, lieutenant? You *blind?* Open your eyes, man!"

"Yes, sir."

"Look, the only reason we need so many dentists on this base is to be ready for his attack. We'll need them later, when the balloon goes up—when the shit starts to fly. But right now they spend half their time sitting on their asses. And that's not right, lieutenant. It's just not right."

"Yes, sir."

"You couldn't run an IBM that way! Or a General Motors. Could you now?"

"No, colonel."

"Call me doctor, would you lieutenant?"

"Yes, doctor."

"Well here's my plan: if we can balance production, so to speak, if we can balance our output, we can hold down employment, right?"

"Yes, sir."

"O.K., here's the meat and potatoes of it. In accord with my authority and responsibility as both base surgeon and service station commander, I am ordering you to tell your men they are to report to the dental clinic, in size places and alphabetical order, at a rate of five per day beginning tomorrow morning."

"What for, sir?"

"What's the matter with you, lieutenant? You thick today? To get their teeth pulled out, that's what for! You see the beauty of it. If we begin pulling their teeth out, we put all the dentists on the job now, when it's slow. That way we balance out the work load over time. And we won't be swamped when he begins his winter offensive. It's like in case of a bombing attack, you get down on the deck before they can knock you down. We pull their teeth out before he can knock them out. We can get rid of four dentists that way. You see the beauty of it, lieutenant?" he said, proudly.

"Yes, doctor."

"O.K., that'll be all for now. Don't forget: five men, tomorrow morning, lieutenant."

I saluted, but before I could go, he added, "And lieutenant, one more thing. Call me colonel, will you? This is the army, you know."

"Yes, colonel," I said, and I left the office.

BULLETIN

> **Bike Too Hot to Handle**
> JOHANNESBURG, South Africa (Reuters)—A local businessman has built a .V-8-engined motorcycle capable of 185 miles an hour, but it is so powerful he cannot ride it.

CAMERA TWO

Cal had noticed the bags under my eyes, and when she asked me about them I told her about the trouble I was having in getting a night's sleep. (I didn't tell her why, however.)

A few days later, she showed up at my office carrying a slim package which she handed to me.

"What's this?"

"Open it and see," she smiled.

I tore off the wrapping paper, revealing a phonograph record. Glenn Gould's recording of the Goldberg Variations.

"Bach!" I said, delighted. "What a surprise! I love the Goldberg Variations but I don't have it on record."

"You said you were having trouble sleeping, so I thought that this might help you make it through the night. Bach wrote it for just that purpose for Count von Kayserling. Goldberg was his clavierist, and he used to play them at night, when the count couldn't sleep."

I was happy to receive the record, but then I began to have second thoughts. "I appreciate this, Cal. . . ."

"What's the matter?" She stared deeply into my eyes, like a doctor looking for a mote.

"Well, I appreciate this . . . But to be honest . . . What's the catch?"

"How can there be a catch?" She thought for a minute and then added, "Is it Nietzsche you're thinking of?"

"*Nietzsche?*"

"Wasn't it he who said something about how much more important a people's music was in determing their basic spirit than the speeches they heard? Jacob, this is *Bach* I'm giving to you . . ."

"I know. It has nothing to do with Nietzsche. I guess . . . well, it's just that . . . sometimes I don't trust you. Sometimes, late at night, when I think about you, you still appear to me, to my imagination, as a kind of devil."

"Well, anyhow, I'm flattered to hear that you think of me," she said, and I couldn't help but smile. "But I can't see why you don't trust me, Jacob. Have I done anything to hurt you? Ever?"

She seemed touched, even hurt, by what I had said. It was the first time I had ever seen her reveal a dimension of dismay.

"I don't guess you have, Cal . . ."

"You know I haven't. You're always reading things into me that aren't really there. I pulled you out of the river—I've helped you whenever I could . . . Why I've even let you in on my plans and offered you a share in them. I've trusted you, I really have."

"I know, Cal."

"And you can't say I haven't been trustworthy myself. Look at that time I caught that Private Becker peeping into my window at night. That was a pretty low trick, and I could have helped my own career by turning him in. But I didn't, Jake. And only because you had mentioned to me that you liked him. That he was a college graduate, and he read, and he was the only enlisted man you could half communicate with. It was only as a favor to you that I covered for him, Jake."

"I know . . ."

"And any other officer would have busted your house for drugs long ago, if he knew what I know. Think of how I could have advanced my career at your expense, if that was what I wanted, Jake."

"I'm sorry," I said, as she rose to leave. "And I appreciate the gift," I smiled, uneasily.

She smiled too. "That's O.K.," she said. "An angel always looks like a devil when she's way up ahead of you and her back is all you can see. It's only if you have the faith to follow and catch up with her that you can see that she's been hoping all along for you to move up and join her."

She smiled gently and it was as if a cloud of mortality were passing over her face. Only when her face was washed in sorrow did its depths show against the gray, and they etched an image of her, of her tragic beauty at that moment, on my mind. An image of fragile strength—which nothing could ever erase.

And within a week, I began to sneak out at night and to hide in the woods and, with my army binoculars, to peek in her window at her as she undressed for bed.

BULLETIN

Mouse Frightens Elephant
SIENA, Italy (UPI)—A woman was injured when a crowd rushed to escape a circus elephant frightened by a mouse. The elephant reared and crushed a guard rail when the mouse ran in front of it during a parade.

CAMERA ONE

In the longhouse. Everyone is stoned on Randy's grass. Len is speaking about the history of the Indians.

"Don't believe what you read in the books, my brothers and sisters. The history of the Indians has been written by white men from white men's records. White men like the scientist Cadwallader Colden, who saw fit to report only our wars and not our achievements. White men like Francis Parkman, the American Francophile, who couldn't admit to himself what the French and the Jesuits had done to our people. But America, herself, has now taken over from the Jesuitical French. We drove out the French, and now America too must be driven out of our land. No, brothers and sisters, don't believe the white man's history.

"For we have been driven out of his history and into invisibility. But soon we shall be visible again, brothers. Soon our time will come. For as our prophet Handsome Lake has stated, it was the palefaces who killed Christ, not the Indians, and the palefaces will eventually pay for this crime. And they shall pay, as well, for what they have done to our land—our Eden. Given to us by the Great

Spirit, to be cared for, and to care for us. But it was stolen.

"For the white man has destroyed our forests and waters and poisoned our air. And it is because of this that from the first American president, George Washington, up until this very day, our people have referred to the president of the United States by an Indian term which, when translated into English, means, 'Destroyer of Villages.' This is the truth my brothers. For it was George Washington who sent the mad dog, General Sullivan, into the country of the Senecas to scorch the earth—to destroy the towns and burn the crops. But this disaster, like all disasters our people have suffered, only served to strengthen our resolve to carry on.

"You are all familiar with the great bridge disaster of 1907 in which thirty-five of our brothers were killed in a fall into the St. Lawrence River near Quebec City. Well, the white man thought that would end the Indian's desire to work on high steel. But the white man did not know the Indian. He did not anticipate that this would make the challenge of high steel even more attractive to our brave brothers. But it did. And this disaster was the beginning of the long history of Iroquois workers who went into high steel *because* it was dangerous. It took the disaster to bring the courage of our people out into the open once again. Yes, disasters have started our people going, not stopped them.

"This is the truth, my brothers and sisters. Listen to it. Hear it, for it shall make you free."

THIRD
QUARTER

Blessed are they who never read a newspaper
for they shall see nature, and through her, God.

HENRY DAVID THOREAU

Commercial

At the White House, President Sun announced today the incredible success of Operation Interception, which has been run by his brother Nick Sun.

"In the several weeks in which this operation has been implemented, we have achieved results beyond our wildest imaginings," the President declared. "Not one, I want to repeat this, not *one* ounce of marijuana has been seized coming across the border into the United States from Mexico. And the country has my brother, Nick, to thank for this splendid success."

It was rumored in high circles that the President might have other governmental duties in store for his brother, as his success in Operation Interception has catapulted him overnight into the national spotlight.

CAMERA ONE

Winter.

CAMERA THREE

In many respects (except for the ideological icing and the periodic violence) the army was not unlike socialist Russia. Daily life on the base had that same functional, stifling quality which army architecture shares with Russian modern. And the social arrangements were remarkably similar. In the army one has free medical and dental care for life, provided by the State. One is paid by the State for his work in service of the State. One shops in department stores supported by the State, buys one's groceries in commissaries run by the State, and one is forced to become a member of a social club which provides a State-owned golf course, bar, and restaurant, as well as parties with bands that play songs like, "I'll Be Around," and, "Don't Sit Under the Apple Tree with Anyone Else but Me." In the army clubs, one is back in World War II because that's where the army sensibility is. And the Russian, too.

One reads the semiofficial *Army Times*, submits to limits upon his Bill of Rights freedoms of speech and assembly, gives up many of the rights which have been built into the structure of Anglo-Saxon jurisprudence over the past seven centuries, and one has even the smallest details of his life watched and supervised by agents of the man who runs the area on which one lives—the general. And one cannot even vote for this man, for he has been given his job by the same power which sits upon the rest of one's life—the State.

Thus, if one wants to find out how it feels to live under a totalitarian regime, he can avoid the complications and expense of traveling to the U.S.S.R. by joining the American army. Or the navy, air force, or marines.

BULLETIN

> # Soviet Denounces U.S.Campus Rebels

CAMERA THREE

Time is that in which things change. One pleasant measure of my time spent in the army was the development of my friendship with the colonel's secretary, Lorraine. After I had seen the missing *Swann's Way* at David's cabin, I asked her to meet me for coffee at the snack bar and I told her about my connections with her friends. We began to meet more frequently, and by the coming of winter we were joining each other at the snack bar every morning.

Lorraine was from Manhattan. She had been born in Harlem but had grown up in the area northwest of Harlem known as Washington Heights because Washington had pulled his troops back to this high ground after they were driven from the Harlem Plains (the area around 125th St. and the Apollo Theater) by the British in a nearly disastrous rout in 1776. She had attended George Washington High School and, miraculously, she had emerged with an education. Of course, this meant that she was largely self-educated, but to me it was a source of her charm, for she had the large eyes and passionate reach of one who had known hunger for knowledge as a youth.

So every day, for the better part of an hour, we would meet to sip coffee and talk—about ideas, about books, and about ourselves. Unlike the people whom I usually had to speak to during my days at the hospital, Lorraine had not even been born before the end of World War II. This made it easier to communicate with her.

Along with novels, I found that she had been reading militant and revolutionary literature given or recommended to her by her friends at *The Railroad*. To balance this, I bought her a copy of Thoreau's *Walden* which included the essay on civil disobedience.

And she dug it. That's what was so beautiful about Lorraine. She was not so blind as to mistake prematurity with maturity—not unduly anxious to reach a point at which she could finally establish her maturity by beginning to speak with authority; it was authority that she instinctively opposed, for she sensed that authority is static—is opposed to process—whether it manifests itself politically or merely in one's speech.

I grew to like Lorraine more and more. And Warren and Edith did, too, once she began to drop by whenever she had some free time. Warren, who had nothing *but* free time, was especially delighted, of course, as he always was when he made a new friend. And they spent many hours together, listening to Warren's collection of 45s which dated back to the early days of rhythm and blues.

CAMERA TWO

On Christmas Day the air was clear and briskly bright and the ground almost free of snow. Lorraine, Warren, Edith, and I drove the short distance to Concord. We stopped first at Walden Pond. And the water proved to be as clear as Thoreau had said it was, more lucid than his own prose, but it wasn't the same pond. It was in the same place, spatially, but time had deposited tourists around its banks and one end of the lake had been converted into a public beach.

It made clear to me what is meant by the fourth dimension. For surely, the place we visited was not the pond at which Thoreau had lived, because his pond had existed in another age, more on the edge of civilization than in the middle of it. And the difference between these two ponds was as real as the space between Walden and the base.

We stayed at Walden Pond for an hour and then we drove into the town of Concord. Near Emerson's house we passed an old man standing on his lawn, looking up at the sky. We stopped to ask him for directions. The old man was surprised to learn that we were headed for the cemetery. Everyone else, he told us, always wanted to see the Concord battlefield and the old North Bridge where the American Revolution had begun and "the shot heard round the world" had been fired.

He gave us directions and we drove off, leaving him standing there on his lawn. When we arrived at the cemetery, we walked

over to Authors' Hill, where Thoreau is buried along with Hawthorne, Emerson, and the Alcotts. We were the only people there.
Americans don't pay much attention to artists or to death, and I
guess the combination of the two proved insuperable, especially
on such a perfect Christmas Day.

We walked from grave to grave. In a way, Bronson Alcott's was
more moving to me than Hawthorne's, for Hawthorne had carried
the hollow of his final home inside of him throughout his life, like
an abscess of antimatter, and death for him must have been sim-
pler than for Alcott. Because Bronson Alcott was something else
again—an American Quixote. Death to him must have seemed
external or irrelevant—and its arrival, a shocking surprise.

We looked at the enormous rock which distinguished Emerson's
remains and then at the cluster of slanting little stones that
marked the Thoreau family plot. Among them, one which was
whiter than the others, but the same size. And on it, a single word
—Henry.

So there it was: the inconspicuous, lovely little marker seemed
almost too appropriate. Almost corny. We stared at it silently, and
then Edith spoke.

"You know, Jake, I've just had an idea. You might write a book
about your days in the army and call it *Walled-In.*"

We all smiled and Lorraine said, "That's a good pun, but Thoreau beat you to it."

"Did he?" I said. "I don't remember that."

"He sure did," Lorraine replied. "I just read it last week."

"Well, I'm not surprised," Edith said. "He was always playing
with words."

Then Warren added, "When you've got nothing to do for a
couple of years, you learn to play with a lot of things."

"You know," I said, "I think a better idea would be to write a
book about life in the heart of the city. *Walled-In* would be a
better title for that kind of book."

"What would you write about?" Edith asked

"Well, maybe when I get out of the army, we could move to
New York. And sell the car and get a rent-controlled apartment
in the Village. And kind of isolate ourselves. Wall ourselves in,
right at the center of the modern madness."

"That sounds great!" Warren said.

"You certainly can't go backwards," Edith said, "so there's nothing to lose by going forward."

"Sure," I said. "And we'd have books and records, and we'd work only a couple days a week—just to have enough to pay the rent and buy some food."

"And to go to the movies," Warren said, smiling.

"Sure," I said. "And we'd have no auto insurance, and no gas, or repairs, or garages, or registration. We could walk to wherever we wanted to go. And we'd dig all the free stuff—concerts and off-off-Broadway revivals of the great plays."

"That sounds fabulous, Jake," Warren said. "Let's do it. How about it, Edith?"

"It sounds fine to me. As far as avant-garde film and dance goes, and multimedia techniques, New York is certainly at the forefront of the new developments. But tell me, Jacob, what does this have to do with Thoreau? With nature?"

"When Thoreau went out into the woods, he wanted to get close to nature, but it was really only a part of his larger goal, which was to simplify his life. To get to the heart of it and to find out if it was good or bad. And maybe today the best way to simplify life is to move ahead of it. To go to the heart of the city, and to wall yourself in where you can use the advantages of the city—like the subways and the possibilities of high-paying part-time jobs—to help you to get rid of cars and prying neighbors so you can concentrate and get down to the essence of your life."

"Where you can ride the railroad, instead of letting the railroad ride you," Lorraine said brightly, paraphrasing Thoreau and Emerson.

"I'm really serious about this," I said.

"So are we all, Jacob," Edith said.

"Why don't you enter a covenant with Thoreau about it, Jake?" Warren said. "A bond that'll keep you firm until you get out of the army and we can carry it out."

"O.K. But what shall I do?"

"We'll leave that to you," Edith said. "Why don't the rest of us go back up the hill here toward Emerson, and leave you alone for a few minutes."

The three of them disappeared over the top of the hill. I found myself leaving the path and walking across the grass to Thoreau's grave, where I laid my body along its length, on my back, my head against the headstone. And I lay there, my eyes upward, watching, through the bare branches of the trees, the thin, gauze clouds interrupting the pale blue sky.

And I thought of Thoreau. And I thought of Cal. And I thought of Thoreau to force out my thoughts of Cal. And I thought of the grave to force out Cal. And I thought of my own grave. Of being locked within it. With Cal. The two of us, sealed up forever with only the infinity of each other to explore.

And I thought of Thoreau. I wanted to find a way to be true to him. And to the others who lived in this splendid little town and turned it into the American Athens.

And I felt a bond between us. The gravity in my body pulled me down toward the gravity in Thoreau's bones. And I felt the beginning of a pull of faith. Faith in my being pulled back to the earth, in my making a bridge to the body beneath me, in my continuing to try to seek a way.

But I didn't find the way itself.

BULLETIN

London Circus Seeks Mother Lion for 3 Cubs

LONDON, Dec. 26 (AP) — The Robert Brothers Circus here needs a spare mother lion. Otherwise, they **fear,** three lion cubs born on Christmas Day may die.

Their mother has rejected the three cubs, Yule, Noel and Mary.

"The cubs urgently need the help "of a lioness who has recently given birth, a spokesman for the circus at London's Round House said. "Without a foster mother the cubs might die."

For the time being the cubs are being bottle fed by the lion trainer's wife. Their mother, Victoria, showed no interest in the cubs and was back performing in the circus today.

Zoos were unable to supply another lioness as a foster mother. So the circus is trying to find someone else with a lioness for loan.

C A M E R A   T W O

On the way home, as Edith drove us toward the base, I began to wonder aloud about my new commitment.

"There are so many people to be faithful to," I said, despondently, "so many ways to be true."

"So?" Warren said, smiling, but I didn't have the energy to follow down his path this time.

"Edith," I said, "do you remember what your brother said that time your father tore into him for goofing off at school?"

"No, but it must have been during one of my father's periodic rantings about how he would have given anything to have had a father who was rich enough to send *him* to college when *he* was a young man."

"That's it. And I never forgot your brother's answer. He said, 'I'm sorry dad. I guess I wasn't lucky enough to have had a poor father.' I've been thinking about these transcendentalists whose graves we've just visited, and I think that it may be hard for us to follow them because we weren't lucky enough to have been born into a bleak, Calvinist world.

"The presence of evil was real to their poor fathers, but they were the first generation of Americans to come into contact with the Asian teachings of being and nonbeing. Evil became lack of being, and this made sense to a nation of progress worshippers who could almost see the evil disappear as the nation brought its wilderness under control. And this was the beginning of America's denial of the existence of evil altogether—until recently that is."

"To Americans, evil is a European notion," Edith said.

"We started as Europeans," Lorraine said. "Perhaps we're going back now."

"It could be," I said. "Emerson and Thoreau lived in a world that could still believe in systems like Bishop Paley's natural theology. You know about that, Lorraine?"

"No. Tell me about it."

"Well, Paley wrote about the argument from design. For instance, since the human hand was so well suited to its functions, it implied the presence of a designer."

"Did Thoreau and Emerson believe that?" Lorraine asked.

"I don't really know. But they were certainly in the same ball park, because they were arguing on the basis of the correspondences between natural fact and human fact—between natural law and moral law."

"Darwin cut that string forever," Edith said.

"Good!" Warren said. "The less strings, the more freedom."

"Well, I don't know," I said, hesitantly. "But considering the things man is putting his hand to now, maybe Darwin's was the kindest cut of all . . . Melville must have thought so—I mean Thoreau went camping on the local pond while Melville was hunting great whales in the south seas. You know, when you think about it, it's not surprising that they came back with different answers."

"Melville wasn't read in his lifetime, Jacob," Edith said. "He died before his death, burying himself in the wretched obscurity of the New York Customs House. He had absolutely no influence on his times."

"I know," I said, wearily.

"I thought you loved Thoreau, Jake," Lorraine said.

"I do, but I love Melville, too. Do you know the story about Thoreau on his deathbed?"

"No."

"Well, Thoreau's aunt is supposed to have come to visit him as he lay dying and asked him if he had made his peace with God, to which he replied, 'I didn't know we had quarreled.' You see how typical of Thoreau that is, whether he really said it or not. Thoreau was such a prick, but only a quirky prick could have gone his own way against the drift of a madly materialistic age while still keeping the barb and sting of his wit alive—without becoming bitterly self-pitying. Emerson knew that—that was why he loved Thoreau. And I do, too. But I'm not sure that his path is still there for us to follow. The site of his cabin at the pond is marked, but the cabin itself is no longer there."

"Don't forget your covenant, Jake," Warren said, hastily.

"Oh, I won't. You don't have to worry about that."

BULLETIN

MOST BACK CALLEY IN A POLL FOR TIME

A majority of Americans are more disturbed over publicity given the alleged Songmy massacre than they are over the apparent killings, Time magazine reported yesterday.

Times aid that a poll it commissioned from the Louis Harris organization also showed "considerable sympathy for First Lieut. William L. Calley Jr., the platoon leader charged with more than 100 of the deaths at Songmy, United Press International reported.

"By a margin of 55 per cent to 23 per cent, they believe Calleyis being made a scapegoat by the Government," Time said.

The magazine said that 67 per cent of those polled "believe that the press and TV should not have reported statements by soldiers involved prior to a trial."

And, it said, "surprisingly, Americans are not particularly disturbed by the disclosure that United States troops apparently massacred several hundred South Vietnamese civilians reasoning that 'incidents such as this are bound to happen in a war.' "

CAMERA TWO

We stopped for dinner at an old New England inn, with a crackling log fire under a sign which told how George Washington had once stopped at the inn when it was young.

After a hearty New England boiled dinner of corned beef and cabbage and innumerable vegetables, we drove back to the base, but we were stalled near the main gate where we ran into an Eskimo Power demonstration. There were about forty Americans of Eskimo descent involved, carrying torches and signs and rhythmically chanting, "Blubber is beautiful."

To prevent a riot, the MPs gassed the demonstrators and then charged them with flailing nightsticks. The ensuing melee lasted for about fifteen minutes and resulted in about twenty hospital cases, with the final score: Eskimos 15, Army 5. (The team with the highest score loses.) However, the Eskimos did manage to burn down the MP booth at the main gate with a thrown Molotov cocktail and to set two MP patrol cars on fire. Our own car was damaged slightly by the head of a falling Eskimo, who was being clubbed to the ground by an MP. His skull and our right front headlight smashed each other.

Shortly after this, the med-evac helicopters landed on the highway (which had been lighted by flares for the emergency) and took away the wounded. The Eskimo wounded were herded into prison helicopters with wire screening on the windows to prevent them from escaping.

When the commotion finally died down and the street was cleared, Edith put the car into gear and we drove up to the gate where we were flagged down by an MP standing next to the charred, smoking remains of his little booth.

"What's the matter?" Edith said to him.

"I'm afraid I'm going to have to give you a ticket, ma'm."

"What for?"

"Violation of base traffic regulation 1782, ma'm."

"What in the name of heaven is that?"

"Driving after sundown with only one headlight, ma'm."

"Jacob!" Edith cried.

At that moment, another MP came over, looked at the car, and spotted the medical caduceus decal which I had fixed to the front window. Then he looked into the car and saw me.

"Wait a minute, Phil," he said to his partner. "I think I know this guy here."

He turned his flashlight onto my face. "Do you work at the hospital, sir?"

"Yes."

"I knew it! I knew I recognized you. Didn't you set my arm up there when I broke it, about four months ago, doc?"

Edith was about to answer but I silenced her by speaking first. "It's hard to tell," I said, with exaggerated modesty. "We set so many, you know."

The MP smiled. "I knew it! Forget it Phil. This is my doctor. He set my arm."

"O.K.," Phil said, "you folks can go now."

As we pulled away the one who had broken his arm called after us, "Take it easy, doc. And take care of that light when you get a chance."

"I certainly will, son," I answered, closing the window, and all four of us burst out laughing at the same time, and we couldn't stop, so we flooded our tight little car with waves of hysterical giggles and cackles all the way home.

BULLETIN

Indians Draft Plans For Alcatraz Center

SAN FRANCISCO, Dec. 25 (UPI)—The Indians who claim Alcatraz "by right of discovery" spent Christmas mapping plans for establishing a native American cultural and educational center on the former prison island.

CAMERA TWO

"Can you come to our winter ceremonies to celebrate the coming of the New Year?" Len asked me.

"I don't think so. I have to work on New Year's Day. The colonel's cooked up some plans to give extra hangovers to a few civilians. I think he's going to drop a bomb or two on the town that day."

"Well, you can come to some anyway. They take place on five

consecutive days. But it's a pity you'll miss the last day."

"What happens then?"

"We have a rite that's part game, part religious ceremony. It's a kind of Manichean contest between two sides which symbolizes the battle between the good Creator and his evil twin brother for control of the earth. A sacred wooden bowl is kept just for this game. We use it to hold the peach pits which mark the score. It's called the bowl game and always takes place on New Year's Day."

"You're kidding!"

"No I'm not. Our people have always done this. Look it up for yourself in the town library."

"I think I will."

And I did. And, for what seemed like the thousandth time since I had entered the base, I was surprised by what I learned: Len had been telling the truth. The Iroquois did hold their bowl games on New Year's Day. And I also learned that over one thousand years ago the Toltecs had built large masonry courts for the playing of sacred ball games. And that these sacred ball courts eventually diffused over the Mexican border to what is now Arizona.

BULLETIN

Divorce Issue Touchy

MADISON, Wis (AP) — Robert L. and Jeanne Wilde reached an amicable divorce settlement, except for one issue: who gets the tickets for the Green Bay Packer games in 1970. A judge settled the issue: each will use the tickets alternately.

CAMERA TWO

On New Year's Day, the colonel's Operation Hangover went off on schedule. Four Phantom jets zoomed down on the town like supersonic projectiles and bombed City Hall. And their bombs were extraordinarily accurate that day. Just one went astray, and all it did was wreck a downtown florist's shop that was closed anyhow.

There was only one mishap. One of the jets didn't come out of a dive and ploughed into a cheap hotel on Patton Street, killing the manager, the bellhop, the janitor, seven GIs, sixteen relatives and sweethearts, four whores, and two pimps.

The three remaining Phantoms returned safely back to the base.

CAMERA THREE

During the winter months, Tommy Creetner began to come into our house several times a week. He was giving guitar lessons to Little Jo, next door, each afternoon, and often, when the lesson was through, he would sit and listen to records with Warren and Lorraine. He and Lorraine began to get pretty tight, and I think one of the reasons each visited us so often was because there was a good chance the other might show up.

Tommy became friendly with Warren, too, although this was against Len's policy. But Len didn't say anything about it. I think he recognized that Tommy had a sufficient cumulative dosage of hate-rays stored in his bones to keep him militant for a lifetime, regardless of what Warren might say to him. In fact, he was, if anything, too militant. He was difficult for even Len to control because he seemed unwilling to accept external fetters of any kind. Len understood this and he allowed Tommy a lot more play than he gave to the other scouts of the King Phillip Memorial Society.

CAMERA THREE

Whenever I had some free time in the evening, I would walk across the field to the longhouse, turn on, dig the sounds and rhythms, and, often, listen to Len speak.

Once he talked about the origin of the League of Five Nations four hundred years ago. The principal architect of the Iroquois confederation had been the great statesman Deganawidah. The league had taken in the Tuscaroras in 1715, after this related tribe had been driven out of their homeland in North Carolina by the

Americans. For decades, the league held the balance of power in the northern colonies.

The American constitution, Len said, was based upon the federal structure of the League of the Six Nations. Benjamin Franklin, who drew up the Albany Plan of Union in 1754, upon which the U.S. Constitution was based, had been familiar with the design of the Iroquois League, and had incorporated its principal features into his proposal.

But the Indians had never needed to write down their constitution. And their society had never degenerated into a mockery of this plan, into a nouveau monarchy with a Madison Avenue king. They had never had a class of professional politicians, nor a police force, nor taxes imposed upon the people of the Iroquois six nations. The Mohawk, the Seneca, the Cayuga, the Onondaga, the Oneida, the Tuscarora. The Mohawk, the Seneca, the Cayuga, the Onondaga . . .

C A M E R A   O N E

David says, "How's the novel going, Jake?"

"Not so good. I'm keeping a journal but I don't seem to be able to get together the time and the concentration to organize it."

"What's it about? I mean, not the plot, but the mood."

"Suffering, I guess."

"In which sense of the word? Suffering as living in misery or suffering as allowing things to take their natural course?"

"That's right."

He looked blankly at me for a second and then he cracked up. "Too much!" he grinned, slapping me on the back.

C A M E R A   T H R E E

The first week of the new year was notable because of an innovation which Colonel Creetner announced at a staff meeting of the hospital officers. The meeting itself was prolonged by an argument between the chief of medicine, Lieutenant Colonel Bleekman, and the chief of surgery, Lieutenant Colonel Harris. Dr. Bleekman suggested that the members of the medical staff wear little red lapel pins and the members of the surgical staff wear green ones, so that anyone could quickly tell them apart.

Dr. Harris thought this an excellent idea and he was all for it, as long as there could be one minor change which would give the red pins to the surgeons, since red was the surgeons' traditional color.

Dr. Bleekman denied this, saying that while any color was appropriate for the surgeons, the medical doctors deserved to wear red because of their work with blood diseases and because of the diagnostic importance of blood tests.

Dr. Harris claimed this was unfair and added that green was inappropriate for the surgeons to wear because of its association with gangrene in the public mind.

Dr. Bleekman conceded that the surgeons didn't necessarily have to wear green pins, that they could wear white ones, or any other color for that matter, as long as the Department of Medicine got the red ones.

By this time everyone at the meeting had begun to choose up sides and private arguments multiplied throughout the room. Some of them even became rather violent, the most serious of which involved a urologist who punched an internist in the face, giving him a bloody nose and thereby making the color red, which was the subject of the dispute, even more vivid in everybody's mind.

At this point, Colonel Creetner called the room to order and recognized Lt. Col. May Grainger, the chief nurse, who claimed to have a solution to the problem. Colonel Grainger suggested that it was her nurses who ought to be given the red pins because of the traditional association of nurses with the symbol of the red cross.

Of course, this immediately returned the situation to its previous boil, and several fights and arguments erupted once again, the most serious involving the internist with the bloody nose who tried to get back at the urologist by kicking him in the balls (which I thought was most appropriate). Finally, Colonel Creetner calmed everyone down and appointed a committee composed of Lieutenant Colonels Bleekman, Harris, and Grainger to investigate the matter further, a decision of such Solomon-like wisdom it succeeded in ending the violence for the remainder of the meeting.

Colonel Creetner was then able to announce his new idea,

which he said would save the army men, money, and materiel (the three M's). It seemed that a good percentage of our attacks had fallen into a pattern. First a sweep by helicopter gunships, which strafed the buildings, followed later by med-evac helicopters, who would drop down to pick up the wounded. Attacks on crowds or people in the open were following a similar pattern. The helicopter gunship pilots were able to distinguish groups of B.C. from loyal civilians by the fact that the B.C. would run for cover when the gunships appeared, while the loyal civilians would have no reason to do so. Interestingly enough, intelligence had evaluated the reports of the pilots on civilian behavior during attacks, and the B.C. had turned out to have more support among the populace than was first imagined. When the gunships came over, almost all the people beneath them attempted to run away.

The colonel informed us that this whole procedure involved unnecessary duplication of effort and loss of valuable man-hours, for the gunships were coming home empty at the same time that the med-evac helicopters were going out empty. To eliminate this waste he was planning to arm the med-evac helicopters with large caliber machine guns and rockets so that the whole job might be done by half the choppers and half the men. And it would be done in less time, besides.

Under the colonel's plan, the med-evac helicopters would first unload their rockets on the buildings in the area, then they would strafe any people whom they might spot running, and, lastly, the choppers would land, pick up the casualties, and fly them right back to the Ellis Service Center for the finest medical treatment available, courtesy of Uncle Sam, as a propaganda gesture.

Only two questions were raised—the first by the chief of surgery, Lieutenant Colonel Harris. He was afraid that the heat of the machine guns would make the patients uncomfortable during the ride back. Colonel Creetner immediately noted that the helicopters could be air-conditioned, but Major Carson, the hospital supply officer, who had once commanded an infantry company and was the only officer in the hospital who had ever actually been in combat, stood up to assure the doctors that by the time the casualties were loaded the heat of the machine guns would be negligible. This made all the medical people happy, for, as doctors and nurses, their first concern was always for the welfare and comfort of their patients.

The second question was posed by Captain Beaumont, an internist, who wondered whether, in cases in which the choppers weren't completely filled with wounded, it mightn't be a good idea for them to make a short trip into Boston, where they could pick up a newly arrived immigrant for each empty stretcher before they returned to the hospital. This suggestion was enthusiastically received by Creetner and his staff.

So the colonel got positive feedback from everyone at the meeting and he put his plan into effect the following weekend, after leaving two days for the training of medical corpsmen in the use of helicopter rocket launchers and machine guns.

BULLETIN

Gen. Loan Back in Saigon

SAIGON, South Vietnam, Dec. 25 (AP) — Brig. Gen. Nguyen Ngoc Loan, former head of the South Vietnamese police, who became known through a widely circulated picture of him executing a Vietcong prisoner, returned today from seven and a half months of medical treatment in the United States.

CAMERA ONE

I arrive at the Hotel Harlem about midnight. There's a big commotion outside in the street. A large crowd has gathered. I join them and see, in the center of the circle, two young black men glaring at each other. One is slim, with sliced features and sharp clothes, wearing a yellow tie and bright green Nehru jacket and sporting expensive shades. The other is a big man in a plain short winter jacket with a turtleneck sweater showing at the collar. It is easier to read his anger because I can see his eyes.

He stares into the hipster's shades, stares at his head as if it were a slow curve ball, hanging up there temptingly in the air, and in his hands, as if ready at the plate, he is wielding a big baseball bat.

Both men are still, facing each other down. The only movement is in the light—the reflected flashing of the hotel's neon sign. The cat with the sunglasses slowly moves his hand toward his belt, and swiftly he flashes out a long knife with a short, quick sweep of his right hand. The action stops as they face off again. The big guy with the bat reminds me of Bre'r Bear. I expect him to say something like, "I'm gonna knock your head *clean off!*" But he merely concentrates silently on his target. And the cat with the blade doesn't move. He is scared shitless because he can't figure out how to both save face, and at the same time, save his own face from the bloody smash which is sure to follow any move he might make.

"Come at me, daddy," he says weakly, with a bravado so thin and false that you had to feel sorry for the guy, even though you never doubted he would use his knife if he got the chance.

"You take one move toward me and I'll break your fuckin head," the big guy says, and you can see in his eyes that he's not kidding.

At this point, the hoped-for finally happens. Out of the hotel swings the source of the trouble, a flashy black chick with a tight red knitted dress and a bouffant hairdo. She walks up to shades, puts her arm around his shoulders, and I sigh with relief as the eternal female principle is about to become manifest in the midst of this madness.

"Freddie," she says to shades, "what you want to fight like that for? You gonna get smashed."

Thank God, it's going to end. Even Freddie loses some of his taut strain and quietly sighs. Then she says, quite simply and in a matter-of-fact tone, "Here, let me hold your glasses," and, while the two men stare at each other in dumbfounded incredulity, she takes off Freddie's shades and steps back to a front position on the edge of the crowd to watch the fight—as if she had just laid out ten bucks for a ticket.

Freddie and the guy with the bat are looking at each other differently now. Neither will move but both recognize a new kinship between them—they have become brothers in puzzled disbelief.

At this point Moms comes out of the hotel and shuffles to a point between the two men. Her back turned toward Freddie's knife, she says, "O.K., Rudolph, you gimme that bat this minute."

"You get Freddie's blade first."

She turns. "You heard him, Freddie."

"Not while he's got that bat."

She puts her hands on her hips in exasperation and then she states with finality, "Now I'm gonna clap my hands and you two are gonna waltz on outa here, this minute, you heah, Freddie into the hotel and Rudolph down the street and on home, til you both cool off and get some damn sense into your fool nigger heads."

And immediately, she begins to clap out a beat, and they back off as the crowd parts to give them room as they leave the ring, and only at this point do I realize that Moms, ever the musician, is clapping *one* two three, *one* two three, *one* two three. She has told them to waltz out of there and I'll be goddamned if she isn't clapping her hands in waltz time—and she keeps up the beat until they are both gone.

Then without another word to anyone, she returns to the Moor Room, sits down at the piano, and begins to work out a version of the old tune, "Girl of my Dreams," to which she adds a new layer of delight by rendering it in waltz time, which she taps out on the floor with her shoe, and the old song shines like a long-forgotten necklace, removed from the drawer, dusted off, and exposed once again to the light.

CAMERA THREE

As the news of the meetings of the King Phillip Memorial Society spread over the base, the army officers who served as the board of directors of BATAC (The Base Teenage Club) began to worry about the future of their own activity. It was their belief that the scout group was taking away their members. In actuality, the scouts had only slightly increased their membership since moving to the longhouse, because they were extremely careful to admit only those kids deemed completely trustworthy.

But the directors didn't know this. Their president, Major Goldberg, won the attention of the colonel's mother by emphasizing the non-Christian nature of the King Phillip Memorial Society.

Of course, a direct move against the scouts could be interpreted (however falsely) as an example of racial prejudice, so this policy was ruled out for the present. Instead, they decided to fight back by making the teenage club more attractive to base teenagers. To find out how to do this, they hired a public relations man from Harvard.

The P.R. man (a Puerto Rican named José Rodriguez) recommended money as the answer. With the resources of the base behind it, the club would simply outspend the scouts by so much that the teenagers would be drawn back to it. Then, in line with the principles of participatory democracy, a meeting of all teenagers on the base would be called and the kids would be allowed to choose, by majority vote, which of the two activities should be permitted to continue as the sole representative of the teenagers on the base. The other activity would be closed. And once the scouts were disbanded, the base could cut back its spending on the teenage club to the usual amount.

This plan was accepted, and, in line with Professor Rodriguez's recommendations, the board began to hire top-ten recording groups to perform live at the club. Of course, the members of the King Phillip Society were not affected by this strategy, but many of the base teenagers did begin to drift back to see the pop groups that they had heard so often on the radio and the plan seemed to be working.

One night, late in January, the base was rocked by a single large explosion. The teenage club was totally destroyed by a homemade bomb. A suspect was spotted leaving the scene by an MP. He was commanded to halt and, when he didn't, he was shot at. One shot wounded him, slowing him down enough for the MP to apprehend him.

The suspect was brought to the hospital, where it was determined that the wound was not dangerous—the bullet had merely shot off three fingers on the suspect's left hand. The name of the accused was Creetner—Thomas P. Creetner.

BULLETIN

Violence in Young Laid To Inarticulate Students

SAN FRANCISCO, Dec. 13 (UPI)—Karl Shapiro, a Pulitzer Prize-winning poet, believes much of the mass physical violence by young Americans is a result of growing illiteracy.

"We have the most inarticulate generation of college students in history and this may well account for the mass outbreak of physical violence," said Mr. Shapiro, a University of California English professor. "They have no more intelligent way to express themselves." He spoke to members of the California Association on Monday.

C A M E R A   T W O

Len accompanied me to the hospital the following morning. The radio had been full of news about the explosion and he wanted to see Tommy. The act of blowing up the club was condemned by all the popular disk jockeys, who between commercials for pimple cream and for new out-of-sight hip boutiques in the local shopping centers, said that violence in the name of peace was a logical contradiction and therefore was self-defeating and that violence only breeds violence.

One station interviewed a psychology professor emeritus from the local junior college on the subject of the act of sabotage and on teenage violence in general. The professor said in no uncertain terms that psychology could no longer blame the actions of youths upon their parents or improper upbringing. Such an antisocial act as the one which occurred on the night before must be deemed an existential act, solely attributable to a chemical imbalance in the youth's glandular system which science has yet to isolate or explain.

When Len found out the details of what had happened, he was furious. He had known nothing about Tommy's plans.

"How could he? How could he be so stupid?"

"He's impulsive, Len. I'm sure he thought he was helping."

"Well, shit, this is going to be some help. And if they hadn't caught him, it would have been worse. They would've pinned this on our whole group. What got into him?"

It was the first time I had ever seen Len so upset. He had lost control of one of his scouts and, because he was always careful to plan his moves in advance, he wasn't accustomed to being surprised by events.

When we visited Tommy on the prisoners' ward, he looked up at us and said only, "I'm sorry, Len," before retreating into a silent depression from which he refused to emerge, even when Little Jo appeared, bringing him his personal belongings.

It was later that night I received word that Tommy Creetner had hung himself with a guitar string. By the time they found him and cut him down, he was dead.

I rushed up to the hospital and found an argument in progress between the nurse on the prison ward, the MP on duty guarding the ward, and the sergeant on duty at the emergency room. Nobody was willing to assume responsibility for Tommy Creetner's corpse until it was deposited in the hospital morgue. Each said that it was not within the area of his jurisdiction. So I assumed responsibility for Tommy's body.

I inventoried and listed his personal property on the form I found in the death kit which the ward nurse gave me. Nothing much. Clothes, pajamas, two bucks in his wallet, a ring, paperback books which Jo had brought him, along with his toilet kit and a guitar, electric, missing one string.

And one item which I didn't list. In his jacket pocket, wrapped in plastic, I found a lid of grass. I palmed it and put it into my pants pocket, quickly.

I filled out the identification tag—Creetner, Thomas P.; status: civilian dependent—and tied it to Tommy's toe, as the instructions in the kit told me to do.

At this point, the colonel arrived, followed by his mother. When they looked down at Tommy's corpse, the colonel couldn't seem to believe his eyes. He stared at the body for about a minute, not moving or saying a word, and then he turned to me and spoke: "Why . . . why, he's dead, you might say."

After this the colonel's mother demanded an autopsy, and when the colonel agreed they left to make arrangements for the funeral. I stayed at the hospital with the body. With a tag on a toe which contained the name of one of the finest young musicians I had ever heard. Creetner, Thomas P. Civilian dependent.

So this was was the way it all ended for Tommy Creetner. And it was my job to care for the corpse. To wheel it to the hospital morgue, which was in a small building located at the end of one wing of the hospital. To cover up all that music with a silent, white sheet, and to lift all that energy, now still, onto a steel surgical cart, and to wheel that piece of meat, as Sergeant O'Mara would say, along narrow, warped, ill-lit hallways to the hospital morgue, with its operating room sterility and autopsy cutting equipment and its metal freezer pulling at the body with its mouth. At the remains of this musical genius, this angry prodigy who would have swung Haydn and Mozart had he been born earlier. To push this corpse, already cold, into an electric stainless-steel grave.

When I reached the morgue, I pulled back the sheet to look at Tommy for the last time. And I understood why wax museums are so chilling to visit. It isn't because of the carver's skill in making the figures look alive. It's because the figures in wax museums look *dead*. Because that's the way Tommy looked. Like he was made of wax. Like a figure in a museum that you could inspect for a quarter.

But it wasn't a wax replica—it was what had once been the living body of Tommy Creetner, my friend, who had distributed his music equally among all who would listen, pressing rage coals of carbon-black venom into blue-white diamond ear-gifts for the world.

I began to pray for Tommy, and to weep for him (for all that music, never recorded), rocking dolefully back and forth above his corpse, watching the hot tears drop from my eyes onto the wax of his candle-skin, and I kept thinking of a single line he would repeat in a song he did, "Oh, yeah," filled with all the joyous energy of bound anger released, "Oh, yeah," over a guitar and Fender bass riff, "Oh, yeah," until it crowded everything else from my mind, "Oh, yeah," and after I looked down at this cheap imitation of a human being that was supposed to be Tommy, "Oh, yeah," I covered him up and slid him into the freezer, "Oh, yeah," and said good-bye to Tommy Creetner for the last time, and slammed the door closed.

"Oh, no."

And I walked into the dark woods, "Oh, no," and sat down on a dead tree in the snow, "Oh, no," and bawled until I was numb. "Oh, no."

BULLETIN

Girl, 16, Is an Elder

HOOSICK FALLS, N. Y. (AP) —Miss Laurie Shaw, 16 years old, has been installed as an elder of the First United Church, Presbyterian, here.

CAMERA TWO

When I returned home, I made no attempt to go to sleep. I poured myself a tall Dad and put the Goldberg Variations on the phonograph. Glenn Gould's classic recording of the piece, a performance that verges on technical perfection. But I found it could not give me what I needed.

The rendition was so flawless, so efficiently precise and mechanically swift, that under the woeful circumstances of that night it seemed *too* facile. There were no flawed interstices, no human gaps.

I was certain that the fault was not with the piece itself. For, as I had told Len that afternoon in the backyard, if Bach's music contained anything of the mundane, it was the fearsome reality of the awful chink in existence left by the death of a child. And if it taught anything, it was the possibility and the necessity of holding on—of not falling, yourself, into the fatal crevice. Of continuing, one note after the other, in spite of the open wound. But it isn't easy. Bach must be played with a certain arbitrary wilfulness, a difficult and dogged stubbornness that breaks up the music and makes it human; not like a long-distance runner, steadily pound-ing out the rhythmic miles, but with the forward movement of a broken field runner in football, whose every step must be in-dividually measured against the moves of his opposition.

When Warren and Edith woke up, I related the events of the previous night to them and we sat in the living room together, silently staring at the floor. After Edith left for work, I put on the Goldberg Variations once again and I explained my feelings about the record to Warren.

Like myself, Warren was glad for an opportunity to talk about anything but Tommy's death. And he dug what I was saying about the music. "I know what you mean, Jake. I heard a performance of it on the radio that you would have really gotten into. It was a tape of a concert in Czechoslovakia by an old woman pianist who lived in Prague. Her name is Madame Braun."

"I don't think I've heard of her."

"Sure you have. She was the one that they talked about on the news last month. The Czech government tried to arrest her for speaking out against the Russians' arrest of three young poets. She went into hiding."

"I remember now. She's that woman who got into trouble when she toured Europe in the thirties playing Bach in benefits for the Spanish Republicans."

"Right. And she's been in trouble with governments ever since. During the war she had to hide from the Nazis in an attic in Bratislava."

"And she hasn't turned up yet—since she went underground this time?"

"Nope," he smiled. "The kids spirited her away when the police busted one of her concerts and she hasn't been heard from since. There are even rumors that she's been smuggled into the U.S. but that she can't expose herself because she's spoken out against the war in Vietnam and they won't grant her asylum here. I think she gave a benefit for the Viet Cong once, in Prague."

"If she can play the Goldberg Variations as well as you say she can, I wish she'd make a record of the piece."

"She can't play well in the academic sense. She hits wrong notes and she's really too old to do the fast double-clavier fantasies very well. But she feels her way into the music. It's in the slow varia-tions that you can really hear her—it's her timing and touch that make the difference. You'd really dig her, Jake."

BULLETIN

*Popular Music Linked
To Rising Use of Drugs*

Special to The New York Times

UNITED NATIONS, N. Y.,
Jan. 6 — An article in the
latest issue of The United
Nations Bulletin on Narcot-
ics, covering the last three
months of 1969, says that
popular songs and those who
sing them are possible causes
of spreading drug addiction.

The, author is a Pakistani,
Sajjad Taqi, who besides being a freelance journalist is
described as a songwriter,
record producer and manager
of a folk singer, Steve Saks.

CAMERA TWO

Finally I went to my office. Once there, I could no longer think
about Bach. I thought about Tommy. And about myself. And the
hopelessness of it all. On a plane which has lost its way, and has
a mad pilot, and there's no way to get into the cockpit, and the
other passengers don't care anyway because the miniskirted
stewardesses are giving out free food and drinks. But we can't stay
aloft forever. Sooner or later we must come crashing down. So how
does one settle for a steak and a martini and a glimpse of a shapely
calf? How do you keep the anticipatory agony from driving you to
open the door and fling yourself out and thereby end the whole
demeaning trip? *Once and for all.*

I tried to write about my feelings as I sat at my desk, but I
couldn't. My office, and the whole damned hospital for that matter, was not merely stiflingly ugly—it was a sarcophagus of the
imagination. Then, almost with gladness, I remembered *Sado-*

Mask. Anything to get my mind away from the grave emptiness of the day.

I wrote about a colonel in the Green Berets who offered to fight anyone on the post for the championship. Only one person signed up, a Private Bobbie Walker.

On the night of the bout, the post sports arena was packed. Thousands cheered as the colonel, whose name was Charlie (Killer) Frick, entered the ring. And the crowd laughed as Private Walker came in to the ring alone, in a long purple robe, head covered by a towel.

After the preliminary instructions and a handshake, the crowd sat back to enjoy the slaughter. But then they gasped in amazement as Private Walker threw off the robe and shook out the long sleek black hair from under the towel. Private Bobbie Walker was a WAC. And, like the colonel, she wore only the bottom half of a tight bathing suit. Before anyone could intervene, the bell clanged and she leaped across the ring and onto the colonel with feline grace. Then she threw him across the ring with the sinuous strength of a tiger. And from that moment on, there wasn't a person in the crowd who didn't know that the post would soon have a new champion.

After this, there followed an account in which Killer Frick's abysmal defeat and submission was depicted in great detail. I signed it N. Ovid and mailed it to Walter. The writing of the story took only half an hour. Ten minutes less than the time of the actual bout itself.

Later, I learned from Walter that this was one of my most popular stories, especially in the area of the base. All copies of *Sado-Mask* were sold out within two days after the issue appeared on the newsstands in town.

BULLETIN

University of Florida Coed Is in Gun Club and R.O.T.C.

GAINESVILLE, Fla. (AP) — Miss Linda Lee Duke, who learned to shoot at the age of 13, now has a top position on the University of Florida's Rifle Club "A" team.

Since all members of the team are required to be in the Reserve Officers Training Program, the 17-year-old freshman from Cocoa, Fla., is the only "regular" Army girl on the campus.

With a score of 255 points out of a possible 300, Miss Duke is accepted as "a regular guy, but sort of a little sister, since I am the youngest on the University team," she explained.

She spends about 10 hours a week on the rifle range, an hour in R.O.T.C. class and two hours in drill. In her spare time she likes to sew.

CAMERA ONE

Stoned at the longhouse. Len is speaking.

"Against the rights given to our people in the Jay Treaty of 1794, we were later classified by the United States Government as Orientals. For years our people fought this designation, but today I accept it. I welcome it. We accept our Asian ancestors. We accept the word of the Buddha, as against the word of Madison Avenue.

"For, like the decent American, Henry David Thoreau, who told us that the way to go from a fraction of ourselves to a whole is to reduce our denominators rather than to attempt to increase our numerators, the Buddha teaches that the way to health and integrity is to reduce our desires. Meanwhile, the selfish mesmerists of Madison Avenue have as their motto precisely the opposite teaching: create more desire. And night and day they bombard us with repetitious clichés in order to hypnotize us away from the Buddha's teaching.

"But we reject this insane American romantic materialism. We only ask for what is due us as our birthright. Clean air, clear water, and the fruits of the earth on which to live—our share in the bounty of nature and our natural right to be free of the sickness, the madness, and the evil which the white man has brought from Europe.

"Our people have traditionally withheld their esteem from the man infected with the plague of accumulation. Besides a few personal belongings, we held our property in common—in trust. Property is theft and property ownership—in particular the lie of the ownership of the earth—has formed the basis of the social lie which is the white man's culture. It has led to the insatiable greed which has pulled them away from their souls and into the spreading madness we witness around us. We must extirpate the Destroyer of Villages from our land and avenge ourselves upon his lackeys, the hypnotized hordes of mad-grasping American robots."

BULLETIN

JUNK COLLECTOR, 72, MUST MOVE HIS PILE

KEYSVILLE, Calif. (AP) — Some people collect tin foil. Some save string. And then there's Al Coe.

He saves everything, and that is his problem.

Mr. Coe, 72 years old, has a belly-length beard and a peppery disposition. For 33 years he has been collecting junk and plastering it over a hillside in this tiny community near Lake Isabella in the High Sierra.

Now the Federal Bureau of Land Management says Mr. Coe and his treasures — including more than 350 automobiles, 20,-000 board feet of lumber and two tons of reinforcing steel— have to go. Even if it takes $30,000, which is the bureau's estimate of moving costs.

CAMERA THREE

Often when I walked through the streets of the town, I would get the feeling that I was being followed. Some movement occurring on the periphery of my visual field would trigger a response somewhere within me. After the first few times this happened, I learned to trust this feeling. For I discovered that it was Little Jo who would follow me whenever he saw me in town.

He would move long behind me, in the street, on the far side of the parked cars, darting from one car to the next as I walked along. After each forward dash, he would wait until I made up the distance he had gained and then he would run up to the next car.

Finally, I would notice him and he would burst into laughter while feigning regret at being caught. But, as we both understood, that was the point of the game—the joy of discovering that Little Jo cared enough about me to go through this playful procedure every time he saw me in town. And each time I would catch him at it, he would snap his fingers and say, "Aw, shucks!"—an expression so odd and dated that it would invariably bring out a grin on my face. Then he would punch me in the arm, smile, and run away.

BULLETIN

27 DIE IN STAMPEDE AT STADIUM IN CONGO

KINSHASA, the Congo, Dec. 25 (Agence Frence-Presse)— Twenty-seven persons were killed and 107 others, many of them children, were injured Thursday when a crowd stampeded outside a football stadium in Bukava in this former Belgian colony, the Kinshasa radio reported tonight.

The stampede occurred shortly before the arrival of President Joseph D. Mobutu at the stadium in the western Congo, where he was due to watch a football match.

The radio blamed Bukavu city authorities for the accident. It said that they had insisted that the whole crowd wait outside the stadium until General Mobutu arrived.

Just before he arrived, they allowed the crowd to start going through the gates and the stampede started and hundreds were trampled, the radio said.

All doctors in the city of 235,000 were mobilized to treat the injured, the radio said. General Mobutu later toured the hospitals where the victims had been taken, it added.

CAMERA ONE

Cal stops by my office just as I am preparing to leave for the day. She is wearing a maroon velvet cocktail dress with a plunging neckline and carrying a fur coat on her arm.

"Wow! What's the occasion?"

"The colonel's asked me out. We're eating at the club and then he's promised to take me dancing."

"You're kidding."

"Don't you think I'm attractive enough to get a date, Jacob?" she says, leaning forward until her breasts swell out of the dress in front of my face. She laughs, "I told you I'm serious about this. When are you going to wake up to that fact?"

"I don't know what facts are anymore."

"Well, you better find out, Jake. I'm not kidding about this. Do you think I'd go out with that old fart if I wasn't serious? Wake up. Time is getting short, Jake."

"I know. Hey, would you mind doing me a favor?"

"What do you have in mind?"

She leans forward again and smiles.

"It's for Little Jo," I say, trying not to look down the front of her dress. "He's been pretty broken up since Tommy died, and I thought you might be able to use your influence with the colonel to get hold of Tommy's guitar. It would make a nice present for Jo if you could get your hands on it."

"*If?* Jacob, I don't know which you do more—underestimate me or overestimate me." She smiles and turns to go. "Don't worry, I'll get him the guitar. See you."

And she leaves to go dancing. With Colonel Creetner.

BULLETIN

Pink Elephants Resisted

LONDON (Canadian Press)— Telephone operators protested when the post office brass suggested girl telephonists should hang a toy pink elephant on their chairs when they go to the powder room, to save the girls the embarrassment of asking if they could leave the switchboards. Their union suggested an "Oscar for daftness" for the idea.

CAMERA THREE

Once I went skiing at Big Bromley in Vermont. And I didn't do badly for the first time. By the end of the day, I was on the intermediate trails.

When you ski down slopes which are beyond your ability,

you learn to proceed by indirection. Instead of moving straight down the slope, you zigzag across it so you're going down at a much smaller angle than the angle of the hill itself. In fact, if you turn so you're skiing across the slope on a line parallel to the level ground at the base of the mountain, your angle of descent is actually zero and only your momentum keeps you moving.

But the catch comes when you must turn yourself around. If you're heading down the slope to the right and you want to turn to cross back to the left, you must pass through an arc that's shaped like a C. And when you're at the midpoint of the arc, you're facing directly downwards and your angle of decline is the same as that of the slope and you're picking up speed at an alarming rate.

Yet, if you hang on in spite of the fact that you're rushing down at a speed beyond your ability to sustain, if you fight the pull toward the base of the hill, you'll swing through the drop of the arc and soon be slowing as you head across the slope once more. As long as you hold on to your balance and your path. If you prepare to fall as you pick up speed, you will fall. But if you risk a serious spill you'll find that you won't have fallen at all.

BULLETIN

Bill Cracks Down on 'Speed'

WASHINGTON, Dec. 24 (UPI) —A bill that would set a mandatory fine of $5,000 and a five-year prison sentence in the first conviction for manufacturing or distributing a drug known as "speed" has been introduced by seven members of the House Select Committee on Crime. Speed, which is the chemical methampehtamine, is said to cause many fatalities among youthful experimenters.

CAMERA ONE

Cal drives up to our house in her Jaguar. When she gets out of the car, she is carrying Tommy's guitar.

"Well, you got it."

"I told you I would. Although, I'll have to admit, sometimes that damn colonel surprises even me."

"Oh? What happened?"

"Haven't you been into town today?"

"No, I haven't left the house."

"Well, I would have been here an hour ago if *I* hadn't left the base either. The colonel's set up a checkpoint on the bridge. They're searching every car for guns and dynamite."

"They searched your car?"

"Jacob, be serious. But they searched every other car and I was tied up in traffic for almost an hour. Can you imagine what it's going to be like on a working day, when the people from town who work on the base try to get across the bridge?"

"Well, don't look at me. He's *your* boyfriend."

"Very funny," she says, yet she can't help but smile. "Here's the guitar. Say hello to Little Jo for me. I've got to run."

"The colonel taking you dancing again tonight?" I joke.

"Don't be funny," she says as she walks toward her car. Then she turns her head toward me and says, smiling, "He's taking me bowling."

And she drives away.

CAMERA ONE

I stop in the town diner for a cup of coffee. Walk to an empty stool at the counter. Seated on my right is a thin fellow with a tiny head, short haircut, and simple look on his face. And he strikes me as a type—the buck sergeant who will never get promoted but who will not be thrown out of the army either; because of his simplicity, he will obey the rules and look up to his superiors.

Mashed potatoes with gravy, corn, and meat loaf. Holding the fork in front of him like a shovel, he scoops the food into his mouth.

"Good," he says, vaguely in my direction, as he mashes the gravy into his potatoes with his fork. Then he takes a bite, smiles, and says again, this time to me, "Good."

I smile back and nod politely. He seems the kind of person who feels privileged to be associated with the men in his outfit. There are many sergeants like him. They are the docile, happy ones—the bat boys of the army. They seem perpetually stoned, so glad are they to have security, to have a bed and a job, and to be a part of something as powerful and far-reaching as the U.S. Army. It's like living in a dream to them. It's like real life.

I drink my coffee and as I rise to leave I realize that the sergeant is still playing with his potatoes. He looks up at me and then he begins to jabber out an incomprehensible but good-natured stream of consciousness monologue, all the time smiling directly into my face. I listen for a while and finally sort out the message. He's warning me to beware of dope because he says he heard that the Chinese are trying to spread it through the army.

As I watch him grin and play with his food while he rambles disjointedly in his speech, I realize that he's not in the army at all. He's the town fool. I get up to leave and pat him on the back. "Thanks, chief. I'll keep my eyes open for any dope."

And I wonder about my Henry James's writer's eye, on which nothing was to have been lost. He wasn't in the army at all.

BULLETIN

Clerk in India Gives Up Job To Grow Giant Fingernails

CALCUTTA, India (AP)—It is not hard to see what Murari Aditya has been doing for seven years as the results are growing on the fingers of his left hand.

In 1962, for want of a better idea, Mr. Aditya quit his job as a government clerk and began producing what he claims have become the world's longest fingernails.

He constantly guards against accidentally breaking off the 7-inch nail on his ring finger or the 6½-inch nail on his middle finger or any of the other three, all between 5 and 6 inches long.

His secret? Nail polish and plenty of it.

Having suffered through two accidental breaks, Mr. Aditya has learned to be careful, but he travels freely on buses and streetcars.

CAMERA TWO

Warren was worried about David. He asked me to go see him before he did anything foolish, for David had been talking more militantly than ever lately.

"They put Sibyl away, and they tried to put me away. And they almost succeeded," David said to me.

"It was the speed that put Sibyl away. And it's going to put you away, too, if you don't slow down."

"No, it was the man who tried to put me away. And I'm going to prove it."

"You better stay away from the base. They know who's writing those editorials in *The Railroad,* and you can imagine what the colonel will do if he gets his hands on you."

"I said I'm going to find out. Or rather, I'm going to prove what I already know. And when I do, it's going to turn American history upside down."

CAMERA ONE

A snowball crashes against the picture window of our living room. I leap out of my chair, fling open the back door, and shout, "Son of a bitch!"

It's Little Jo. He looks at me with a pout-angry face and shouts, "Oh, I wish you were on TV—so I could turn you off."

Then he laughs and begins to gallop toward the longhouse, smacking his ass in rhythm as he runs.

CAMERA TWO

One evening Edith and I went out to eat with Frank and Donna Benuto, but afterwards I discouraged Edith from accepting any similar invitations in the future.

We ate in the restaurant of the local hotel in town. I didn't mind Donna's preoccupation with her electric garbage compressor and other new products because Edith was also interested in anything new, and she was able to field Donna's conversation while I talked about animals with Frank, a subject on which he always had something interesting to say.

It wasn't until we had finished the main course and were preparing to order dessert and coffee that Donna finally got to me. She hopped up out of her seat and began to stack the dishes and clear the table. Edith and I must have worn our astonishment openly, for Frank quickly explained, "Donna can't stand dirty dishes."

She buzzed about us, busily collecting and organizing, and then she took an unused tray from a waiter's serving stand and carried the cups and plates into the kitchen. The next time the kitchen doors swung open we could see her in there—she had put on an apron over her cocktail dress and was standing over the sink, washing the dishes.

About ten minutes later, she returned to our table, saying with a satisfied smile, "There, that's a lot better isn't it. Now we can drink our coffee in peace."

Of course, when we told Warren about this, he was delighted and he insisted on accompanying us the next time we went out to dinner with Frank and Donna. I told him that he could take my place—that I would just as soon stay behind to babysit for the rabbit and the fish.

BULLETIN

Safe and 2 Vehicles Stolen From School for Retarded

Four or five men early yesterday stole a safe with $500 and two rented station wagons from the Edenwald School, which is operated for retarded children by the Jewish Child Care Association of New York at 1250 East 229th Street, the Bronx.

C A M E R A   O N E

The hospital chapel. A converted ward, used during World War II to isolate infectious disease cases, located at the far end of the front ramp.

Major Charles, the hospital chaplain, returns to the chapel late at night, looking for his wallet which he had misplaced. He opens the back door and before he can get to the light switch, a GI and a WAC who have been making love on the altar leap down, grab their clothes, and run out the side door into the darkness.

The following day, he calls me into his office. He is deeply disturbed about the desecration of his chapel, but he is more worried about the possibility that the sinner may return some Sunday morning and profane the services by his unsuspected presence.

So the major has me inform my men that, to prevent this sacrilegious possibility, he is declaring the chapel off-limits to all GIs.

He says nothing about the WACs.

BULLETIN

Evangelist's Tent Slashed

COCOA, Fla. (AP)—A North Carolina evangelist says he does not want to prosecute, but he does want to find out "who slashed God's tent." Vandals cut a dozen long slits in the revival tent of the Rev. Bill Bowman of Kannapolis, N. C.

CAMERA THREE

In accordance with the matriarchal tradition, the chief authority in the Handsome Lake religion was a woman. Her title was Keeper of the Faith. When Len suggested that the King Phillip Memorial Society ought to have a Keeper of the Faith, a young black girl stood up and suggested Jeannie. There was a chorus of seconds and Jeannie was selected unanimously. So Jeannie Rainey, whose attitude toward the society was more tolerant than enthusiastic, became the Keeper of the Faith.

It was in regard to Handsome Lake (or Ganyodieyo), the eighteenth-century Iroquois visionary and prophet, that I caught Len making statements which were clearly untrue. I had become aware of Handsome Lake when I worked for the Society of Friends in Philadelphia. He had been heavily influenced by the Quakers and there was a lot of material on him scattered about the office. So I knew that although he had a separatist side to his thinking (for instance, he advocated keeping the Indian children out of the white schools), he had a conservative side as well. His teachings regarding children's duties to their parents were almost Confucian in tone, and he was really more of a Christian-pacifist in orientation than a red power militant.

When I mentioned this to Len, he readily admitted the truth of my contentions. But he argued that Handsome Lake had been a figure of another time and that circumstances had changed as nonviolence had been proven futile. Nonviolence had to be the *result* of violence now. Only if the Destroyer of Villagers and his zombie lackeys were destroyed could the Indians return to a non-violent world.

He also claimed that he wasn't violating the true spirit of Handsome Lake's thought, for his Indian teachings had to be separated from the teachings of the Quakers, who had turned his thought away from its essence, which was not Christian but Indian. And that, he said, was what he was trying to do.

BULLETIN

About 1,000 Asians Ordered to Close Concerns in Kenya

Special to The New York Times

NAIROBI, Kenya, Jan. 10— Nearly a thousand Asian traders in Kenya have been ordered by the Ministry of Commerce and Industry to close their businesses by June. The ministerial notices informed the traders that their lisences would not be renewed.

Many of the traders affected are noncitizens, although of 400 in Nairobi, a large number claim to have Kenyan citizenship.

One Asian shopkeeper with Kenyan citizenship noted Government assurances that all citizens would be treated alike in their applications for trading licenses. But he added, Kenya appears to be treating Asians as second-class citizen.

CAMERA ONE

The colonel decides to continue checking cars at the North Bridge for another month. Not one gun or cache of explosives has yet been uncovered. This is evidence of the operation's complete success, the colonel says.

BULLETIN

> ## Model T Is in Living Room
> SANTA MONICA, Calif. (AP) —A fully restored Model T Ford looks out the bay window of James Hoskinson's living room. "It's been through hell for 50 years; why not just let it sit and look pretty?" Hoskinson said. "It seemed a shame to keep it locked up in the garage."

CAMERA ONE

At the Moor Room bar. Slumped in the seat next to me is a white woman in her fifties, buxom, double-chinned, knotted wine-red hair. Sorry looking, as if she's been drunk longer than she likes to remember. And she doesn't have a single tooth in her mouth.

She braces herself, sits up, pulls open her blouse, and plops two heavy bare tits onto the bar.

Red, the bartender, does a double take. "Ruthie, what you doin? You puttin your tits on the bar again. You know you ain't supposed to do that. This here's a classy place."

She doesn't move.

"What you want, Ruthie? What you want that makin you so crazy?"

She turns toward him slowly and she says in a despairing, drunken drawl, "I wanna bite the world."

BULLETIN

Beauty Contest Covers Up

PORT ELIZABETH, South Africa (AP) — Under pressure from clergymen, a local motor club changed the name and ground rules of its beauty contest. What was the "Miss Mini" contest became the "Miss Motor" competition for women clad in slacks and jackets.

BULLETIN

South Africa Police Use Copters to Find Fields of Marijuana

Special to The New York Times

JOHANNESBURG, South Africa, Jan. 10—Teams of policemen, aided by South African Air Force helicopters, have seized and destroyed tons of marijuana valued at $70-million in a remote area of the Drakensberg Mountains in Natal.

Policemen, using specially trained Alsatian dogs to smell out marijuana, which is called dagga here, discovered whole plantations of the illegal plant in the remote area, it was reported here this week.

CAMERA TWO

Then Edith was arrested. By the town police. Warren and I had to get up a hundred bucks to bail her out.

It was nothing very serious, although Edith and her girlfriends were infuriated by the whole affair. The reason that her girlfriends (most of whom worked at Telecation) were angry was because they had been arrested, too.

It had to do with their women's rights group. They had decided that as their first confrontation project they would attempt to integrate the men's room in the town bus terminal. So they held a shit-in. And they were arrested. Although they almost got away with it because the policewomen who were called in to make the arrest—in order to avoid any charges of police brutality—refused to go into the men's room to get them because they said they were too embarrassed. At the last minute, however, the mayor of the town solved the problem, by hiring a painter to print the letters WO in front of the MEN on the door, thereby turning it into a ladies' room and removing the only obstacle to their arrest.

The following week they had their day in court, pleaded innocent, made a few speeches, and were fined fifty bucks each. There was some talk of an appeal to the higher courts but it died down and the incident was closed.

CAMERA ONE

Driving along Main Street with Walter Qwalters. Looking for a parking space. Then he spots one, about a block down on Patton Avenue to our right. But Patton Avenue is one-way, against us.

So Walter drives past the intersection, stops, and then begins to back the car wildly down Patton toward the space.

If driving the wrong way on a one-way street is dangerous, driving the wrong way in reverse is ten times worse. But I know Walter may avoid a ticket by doing so. The man doesn't care which direction you're going in as long as he can see that you're facing the right way.

CAMERA ONE

The white man believes Sigmund Freud was a genius because he discovered there were meanings in people's dreams. Like Columbus, however, he is honored for finding that which was never lost. For our people have known, for hundreds of years, that dreams have meanings. That the soul has needs and desires of which the conscious mind is unaware and that it reveals these needs in our dreams. And we have also been aware of the harm, both physical and psychical, which the repression of these needs can bring. They tell us of the desires of our soul. And these desires are real. We cannot ignore them.

Let me speak to you about our brothers, the Ojibwas (whose name the white man has corrupted into *Chippewa*). The Ojibwas would dream of a great bird—the thunderbird—who came north each summer, bringing the thunder, and migrated south in the fall, so that there was no thunder in the winter. And all of Ojibwa culture and lore was centered around dreams of this bird.

Until the white man came and took away this holy bird. He said that the thunder was caused by another god, a being that no one has ever seen. And the name of this god was electron. And that, mysteriously, it was both matter and wave at the same time.

For this chimera, he took away the Ojibwas' sacred bird. So Ojibwa dreams are empty these days, and Ojibwa life is not the same.

BULLETIN

CAMERA ONE

In the living room, alone. Warren and Edith watching TV in the bedroom. I'm listening to Janos Starker play the Bach Suite Number Three for unaccompanied cello.

The volume of the TV increases for a commercial and pulls my mind away from the music. Spray starch. Spray it on. Spray it on. Gets whites, whiter. Blues, bluer. Aquamarines, aquamariner. ... What kind of a man wears H.D.T. deodorant? The kind of man who marches to the music of a different drummer. . . .

On with the earphones. Hermetically sealing my head in a plastic bag of Bach in which my ears can breathe.

CAMERA TWO

I dreamed of the bout between Colonel Frick and Private Walker. Only I was the colonel. And Cal was Private Walker. And the audience in the arena was composed of the greatest thinkers and scholars of the last three thousand years of Western civilization. And when she threw off her robe, revealing her grand and lovely body, almost bare, not one of them could take his eyes off her.

When she turned and approached me with a fierce look in her eyes, I was scared shitless, more because of what I saw in the faces of the audience than because of the threat of Cal's approach. For it seemed to me that everyone in the audience—every one of the great scholars—was secretly rooting for Cal.

I woke up shivering in sweat chills. And I couldn't get back to sleep. So I spent the remainder of the night wrapped in blankets on the living room couch, nervously seeking solace in my record of the Goldberg Variations.

BULLETIN

Few in Tribe Speak English

NAPLES, Fla. (AP)—Only 10 per cent of the Miccosukees living along the Tamiami Trail between Naples and Miami speak English, according to Dr. John Rehbein who administrates the government program among them.

CAMERA ONE

Len and I are in the backyard with Frank Benuto, watching an artillery attack on the southern part of town. The big guns are behind us, out of sight, so we can only see the flame-bursts across the river.

Before the attack started we had been watching Frank run his dog around the clothesline while he informed us of the sad possibility that the gorilla would soon be extinct. The big apes seemed to have lost their will to survive as a group. They had even begun to foul their own nests. Frank said that when a species did this it was a clear sign that they were headed for extinction.

CAMERA ONE

Night. Alone in the house. Thinking of Cal with my journal open in front of me on the desk. Walter Qwalters stops by to pick up my stories for *Sado-Mask.*

"You working on your book, pops?"

"I'm trying to."

"Tell me something, daddy. You gonna have anything about black people in that book?"

"I think so."

"Well, how you gonna write about black people when you've never been black yourself?"

"I can write about death, can't I? But I never died."

"You got a point there, pops." He picks up the stories from the desk. "You want to dig some music at the Harlem?"

"Sure."

"Well, let's go, man. Get your coat. I'll give you a lift back here when we leave."

So I don't get to work on my journal one more night. But I do hear Moms play the blues once again. And that's one of the few things that can always be depended upon to help me forget about Cal.

BULLETIN

Repeated Gas Bills Go To House Without Gas

STOURPORT ON SEVERN, England (AP)—Mr. and Mrs. David Fortey have been living in their new home for eight months and have received eight gas bills, three demands to read their gas meter, two threats of legal action from the gas company, a warning that their gas will be disconnected, a visit from a gas engineer and hints of a court warrant.

"There's only one problem," said Mr. Fortey. "We don't have gas in our house. We cook on electricity and we don't even have a gas meter."

"There seems to be some confusion," said a spokesman for the gas board.

CAMERA THREE

I began to watch the news on TV whenever I could. Once Warren asked me why I bothered and I was unable to explain. He said that it was because I was afraid they were going to announce the end of the world one day, and I didn't want to miss it.

And I couldn't say he was completely wrong. But as I thought about it, I came to believe that it was really because I couldn't get myself to give up the idea that if you watched the news often enough something good would eventually happen. So I watched every day. But it never did.

BULLETIN

'Dixie' Bill Voted in Florida

TALLAHASSEE, Fla., June 4 (UPI) — The Florida House passed a bill Wednesday prohibiting county school boards from banning the playing of the song "Dixie" at school events. Schools in Dade County (Miami) have banned the playing of the song because of racial turmoil and objections of black students that the song connotes slavery and Negro subservience.

CAMERA THREE

It was at this time that *The Railroad* editorials began to elaborate on David's ideas about American history which he had only hinted at when I'd spoken to him that day at the cabin. It turned out that David had constructed a kind of conspiracy theory of acculturation. He had combined some of Len's ideas about culture as hypnosis with his reading of the revisionist writings on the American reform movement in the years prior to the beginning of World War I which pictured it as a basically conservative effort on the part of the old-American WASPs to regain control of the newly emerging urbanized America under the banner of good government.

One aspect of this movement was the Americanization drive—the attempt to rapidly acculturate the new foreign peoples to the old American values, and, when this proved insufficient, to steal their children by getting them into the WASP-run, Americanizing public schools. David noted the coincidence in time between the first stirrings of this movement in the 1890s, and the move by the U.S. Government to turn Ellis Island into the giant immigrant receiving center of the United States in 1892.

Len had merely pointed to the *functional* identity of the hypnotic relationship and the parent-child relationship. But David, who had often spoken to him about the idea, took it literally. And as I read his editorials in *The Railroad*, the backbone of his revolutionary thesis began to emerge: David literally believed that the U.S. Government had created Ellis Island as a center for the mass hypnosis of immigrants—for the immediate indoctrination of the ethnic minorities with American values and beliefs by teams of trained hypnotists using post-hypnotic suggestion. He felt this was a calculated final effort by the WASP ruling elite to conserve the selfish American capitalistic spirit (as embodied in the Protestant ethic) and thereby to negate the effect of Southern and Eastern European immigration upon the stock of those who had originally opened up (and raped) this virgin land.

BULLETIN

Police Chief Arrests His Son
NORTHVILLE, N. Y., Nov. 6 (AP) — Police Chief George Scunziano Sr. has arrested his own son in the investigation of vandalisml at the Northville Central School.

CAMERA ONE

Night. I'm alone in the house. The doorbell rings. It's Little Jo, standing alone in the weak street lamp's light. A mischievous look on his face.

Before I can say a word he begins to sing, in a loud voice, to the tune of "The Star Spangled Banner," "O-fay can you see?"

Then he quickly runs off, laughing, and disappears into the darkness.

BULLETIN

> ### Imitation Grass Stolen
> CHICAGO (UPI)—Daniel Parvis complained to the police that someone had stolen a 3-by-20 foot strip of imitation grass from the front of his hotel.

BULLETIN

> ### Women Go for Barbering
> ANAHEIM, Calif. (AP) — A survey of Orange County's two barber colleges indicates that nearly half the students are women.

C A M E R A   T W O

"Don't give me any of that *functional* shit, Jake. I'm not being metaphorical. I mean what I say," David told me.

"But you know that not everybody's susceptible to hypnosis."

"You're not going to find a more susceptible group than immigrants who've just made a long, disorienting journey to a strange land, leaving their roots and identities behind. They wanted to become Americans, Jake. That's why they came over here. And when they finally arrived, imagine how suggestible they must have been. Helpless like lost children. Open to anyone who'd tell them what they needed to know to get along in a totally new land."

"Even so, only one in five under normal circumstances can be put into the deepest hypnotic state. And another one in five can't be hypnotized at all."

"That's what I'm saying, Jake. These weren't normal circumstances. And how do we know what drugs the government has at their disposal to help him get into their minds?"

"But surely, not *all* could be hypnotized."

"No. . . . But how do you think they selected which aliens to deport during the Red scare after World War I? Everyone agrees the people deported were innocent. So how did they decide who to deport? I say that the people arrested were chosen from among those who had proven invulnerable to their hypnotic advances."

"Still, David, there must have been thousands who didn't bite."

"Right. I agree. Twenty million people came through Ellis Island during the fifty years it was open. How many does it take? Six or eight million indoctrinated with the insane Protestant ethic would be enough. They'd become the models of success for the others. The adaptable ones in the group who, because they were hypnotized with American values, would be able to make it on the outside. Who were, in fact, helped to make it by the very WASPs who controlled the American institutions and who were behind their hypnosis in the first place.

"So, they became the model citizens of their communities. And they helped to indoctrinate the next generation. To see to it that only those who had internalized the WASP value system (with its mad drive to work and succeed and its racist overtones) were able to get out of the ethnic ghettoes and into the mainstream of the sick society around them. Couple this with the schools' drumming into the kids' heads that their parents are obsolete, the American youth worship which makes the less-Americanized parents *feel* obsolete and . . ."

"Then the hypnosis just begins the process? The hypnosis itself ended on Ellis Island?"

"No, Jake. They had to get to the kids *before* they were old enough to go to school. That's the insidious part of it. Part of the hypnotic message commanded these people to hypnotize their children with the same message."

"Then how did it fail? Where did the King Phillip Society scouts come from?"

"Don't you see, Jake? It worked too well. They were so successful in hypnotizing the immigrants that they destroyed the family that was supposed to perpetuate the message by hypnotizing the kids. Poppa worked sixteen hours a day, so he was never home, and Momma was so affected by the same drives and values that, as soon as she could, she began to leave the house to find a job. It took about two generations. World War II was the coup de grace. A whole generation of kids grew up without much contact with their parents. And after the war, the parents never really came home. Momma couldn't go back to housework. She wanted to be active, to make money—she wanted to succeed, too. It's the old American story. Did you know that in the 1642 Code of Laws for the colony of Massachusetts idleness was a crime?"

"But the kids did go to school."

"Sure. But it was too late. They could teach the kids, but it was too late to really hypnotize them. They had lost their children. Not all of them, of course, but enough so that the kids could form their own culture. A single freak doesn't stand a chance. The community will define him as nuts and he'll come to half believe it himself. But if all his friends are also defined as nuts, they'll get together and set up their own ideas about what's nuts and what's sane. To them, society will seem nuts."

"But what about proof of this? Do you have a single shred of evidence?"

"Look around you, Jake. Are the zombies that run the base hypnotized or not?"

"But that's not proof."

"Well, I'll tell you something, Jake. I'm going to get some proof real soon. Because I think that's what happened to me at the hospital. I think those bastards tried to hypnotize me, but it didn't take. It fucked up my head and they had to throw me out into the rubbish heap instead. But that's what they're doing there now. They're still hypnotizing the immigrants they process."

"I don't believe it."

"That's your problem. But I'm going back there soon to get my proof. And when I do, it's going to show this rotten country to be the shit-heap we know it always has been."

BULLETIN

Conspiracy Charged

Special to The New York Times

CHICAGO, Feb. 6 — Dr. Charles B. Huggins, winner of a Nobel Prize for cancer research who is a member of the University of Chicago faculty, today described student disorders at the university as part of an international Communist conspiracy.

CAMERA ONE

The WACs are issued dual purpose spray cans. Each has two spigots: one for deodorant and one for mace. The idea is that the deodorant function of the can will tend to make the WACs place it on the shelf where it will be readily available in case an assailant sneaks into the room of one of the WACs at night.

The idea is the brainchild of Sergeant Mary Rourke, the heavy-set, tough-talking, veteran first sergeant of the WAC detachment. Sergeant Rourke is given a letter of commendation from the secretary of the army for her suggestion.

BULLETIN

Naked Briton Stops Traffic

LONDON (UPI)—Graham Kane pleaded guilty to obstructing traffic by running out into the street stark naked and grunting like an ape.

CAMERA ONE

Sergeant Rourke of the WAC detachment attempts to spray under her arms but pushes the wrong button and maces herself. She is admitted to the hospital with serious burns of the eyes.

CAMERA ONE

In the backyard with Frank Benuto.

"Hey, Jake, why don't you come with Donna and me over to the show at the officers' club tonight?"

"Who's there?"

"They've hired an Irish couple—a husband and wife singing act."

"What are their names?"

"Faith and Begora. Can you make it tonight?"

"I don't think so, Frank. We'll take a raincheck."

BULLETIN

DRAFTED STUDENT A SUICIDE IN PARK

A 21-year-old college student who reportedly was depressed since receiving a Selective Service preinduction physical hanged himself yesterday from a tree in Central Park.

CAMERA ONE

Walking along the street. I run into Colonel Creetner. He is wearing two hats. I wake up.

BULLETIN

BROOKLYN BUTCHER IS SHOT BY WOMAN

A Brooklyn butcher was shot
in both wrists yesterday afternoon when he was slow in preparing a half-pound of chopped
meat for two women bandits,
one of them armed with a gun.

CAMERA ONE

Walking along the street. I run into Colonel Creetner. Once again
he's wearing two hats. But this time it's O.K. Because he has two
heads.

BULLETIN

3-Year-Old in Britain Gets Note on His Military Duties

HORSFORTH, England (UPI) —A letter arrived and advised Pvt. Simon Richardson that, as a member of the Army General Reserve, he was liable for service in any part of the world on orders of the Queen.

Simon was not particularly perturbed, but his mother, Mrs. Anne Richardson, "could hardly believe my eyes."

Simon is 3 years old.

CAMERA THREE

In February the days began to get noticeably longer. Winter is funny that way. The sun begins to return just before Christmas, but because of the weather's momentum, the days get colder as they get longer. If one judged merely by the obvious presence of snow and cold, one might be led to conclude that the sun had frozen stuck in the sky and could not come back.

CAMERA THREE

About one evening a week, swimming meets were held in town at the athletic club pool. The presence of Cal in these meets, which were open to the public, created a new breed of swimming fan— paunchy, middle-aged men, with floppy shirts and shiny pants, who would come to the matches alone and sit in the front row and sweat a great deal.

In fact, Walter, whom I often ran into at the matches, picked up on this by initiating a sports section in *Sado-Mask*. In it, he featured large pictures of Cal and announced the date and time of swim meets in which she was scheduled to take part. From the evidence of the letters to the editor, it quickly became one of the paper's most popular features.

In February, the swim meets were transferred to the state college pool, which had the facilities to accommodate the large crowds that were showing up each week.

BULLETIN

3-YEAR STUDY FINDS THE GORILLA IS SHY

WASHINGTON — The gorilla is one of the most maligned animals in the world, according to an American woman who reached this conclusion after three years of studying wild mountain gorillas in Africa.

Beneath their fierce appearance lies a shy and gentle nature, Miss Dian Fossey believes. These peaceful vegetarians would rather spend the afternoon sliding down a mountainside than charging a hunter, she said.

BULLETIN

OMAHA ZOO GORILLA KILLS HER OWN BABY

OMAHA (UPI)—Casey the gorilla became a father, but his wife killed the baby because she did not know what it was.

Zoo officials said that maternal instincts were alien to Benoit, the mother of the three-pound male gorilla. She carried her baby with its head in her mouth and would occasionally shake him vigorously.

Zoo gorillas born in captivity do not know what a baby gorilla is because they have not been raised in a family-type atmosphere, officials of the Henry Doorly Zoo said.

CAMERA TWO

The hospital adjutant was a tall, thin guy who was about thirty-eight years old and had never risen above the rank of captain. He was inept at everything except volleyball. This created a problem for me because it meant that every Tuesday night I had to come back to work in order to cajole and threaten anyone I could find to make up a volleyball team so the adjutant would have men to feed him at the net and to watch him spike.

Edith suggested that I complain to the colonel about this, saying that it interfered with the Tuesday night raids on the town. In February I tried it.

"Then we'll have to cancel them," he said.

"The games?" I said, expectantly.

"No, the raids. Every team needs a time out once in a while, lieutenant. It'll do the men good. We'll just step up our raids on the weekends. Inform the men, lieutenant, that we'll be expecting them to stick around on the weekends from now on. There'll be no more weekend passes. We'll be needing all the manpower we can muster to counter His late-winter offensive."

CAMERA ONE

Two books of grass arrive from the South. Again, fourth class, book rate. One is *Coriolanus*. The other is *Tender is the Night*.

CAMERA THREE

The volleyball continued into early March until, late one Thursday evening (the night on which the basketball league used the gym), a single one of our shells scored a direct hit on the fieldhouse, knocking in the roof and killing nine players, three spectators, and two referees.

CAMERA ONE

It is now March. And I am sick. Getting more sick each day. I have begun reading the Bible at night. And composing suicide notes in my mind during the day.

CAMERA THREE

All he and his wife wanted was to be able to pursue their own interests. He was a writer and she was attempting to create radical children's games. Both were bored with their social life and re-sented their jobs—they felt that earning a living distracted them from their more important private projects. From their callings.

Then they met Vivian, a large, dark, strange woman, who taught horseback riding for a living. Vivian was a purely physical crea-ture, energetic and unreflective, and they were both attracted to her by her robust beauty.

Vivian found them interesting as well. She appeared to like the soft, sedentary quality of their life, and she became good friends with them. Vivian began to visit with increasing frequency until she was spending all her free time with them; finally, Emily asked

John whether they might ask her to come live with them and John quickly assented. Shortly thereafter, Vivian moved into their spare room.

Vivian's total lack of modesty surprised them at first. They were far more conventional, even when just the two of them were in the house, and it came as a shock to them to see Vivian walking around the house in just her panties or completely nude. And it was hard to get accustomed to the exercises which she performed on the living room floor each night, as they worked on their respective projects. Both John and Emily were lured away from their work by the physicality of Vivian, by her energy, her sweat, the sweet glow of her skin. Both found themselves falling in love with her presence, and as they did, each became proportionately less attractive to the other.

Vivian's horseback riding instruction paid her well, and one day she suggested that both Emily and John quit their jobs and stay home doing their true work—all three could live on the money Vivian made. She dared them to do it—to quit their jobs in the name of their real projects, and, as each feared to admit a lack of courage to her, they did it, although they both realized that the abrupt manner in which they quit, coupled with the reputation they were getting in the community, would make it difficult for them ever to get a good job again.

But John stayed home and worked on his novel and gradually it became impossible for him to even consider going back to a daily job in the straight world ever again. And Emily, too, got involved in her work at the expense of her ability to function in society. Their world shrunk until they became totally dependent on Vivian. They would rarely leave the house; Vivian's return was enough to bring them the joy and excitement which they missed from society. They would make dinner for her. They would clean her clothes and straighten her room. Then, when she came home, they would sit with her and talk about the events of her day, but they had trouble concentrating on the conversation for each was secretly counting the minutes until Vivian would begin to remove her clothes, walking in front of them with less and less on until, finally, when barely clothed at all, she would begin her exercises on the living room rug as they looked on.

As the weeks passed, they began to do less work and to spend more of their time talking about Vivian. They spent hours discussing what time she would return home from work and what she would say and what she would wear for her exercises that evening. They would only leave the house to buy food or to purchase clothes for Vivian—leotards, bikinis, costumes for her to clothe herself in when she appeared on the stage of their nightly theater. And they began to compete with each other in praising her. And then, to feel her body when she moved; to touch her as she strained to complete her workout; to caress her as she performed her nocturnal ritual.

And as their infatuation for her increased, their own sex acts began to diminish in frequency and importance until it was only Vivian each cared about, and their private sex life died. At this point, Vivian demanded that they turn their savings over to her and they vied for the privilege of being allowed to pick it up at the bank and bring it to her. With the money she bought a huge, king-size bed for their bedroom and had the room redecorated with soft fur pillows and deep rugs and mirrors on the walls and ceiling.

After the alterations were completed, Vivian moved into the bedroom with them, all three sleeping together on the king-size bed, John between the two women.

Then, beginning at a rate of twice a night and steadily increasing, she would order John to roll over on top of Emily and, as they began to screw for her, she would start to remove whatever clothes she was wearing, and they would watch while they fucked as she put on her leather riding boots, and then she would climb up onto the bed and stand over them as they moved together, until she would mount upon John's back, riding them both as they writhed beneath her, digging her boot heels into Emily's thighs and buttocks, squeezing John's body with her powerful thighs, as he struggled to support her weight, to move in and out of Emily with this creature on his back, and Emily struggled to breathe beneath the weight of the two of them, struggled to reach around John to touch Vivian, to feel and caress the body of this marvelously vibrant animal who rode them both, hour after hour, time after time, into exhaustion and the wasted blackness of collapse.

Yet Vivian kept increasing her demands, until John and Emily spent almost all of their time in the bed, screwing on demand or recovering and resting up for the toil of the night ahead. And John found that he had neither the energy nor the time to continue working on his novel, while Emily forgot about her interest in radical games. And both strapped themselves to a wheel of delicious enervation on which they spun and copulated beneath the weight and gaze of their lover, who seemed to grow still more desirable and more indispensable. And they sank into a quicksand bed of sexual pleasure and sweet sensuality which sickened them even as it sucked them in, until day and night and outside and inside lost their meaning for them. Until there was only Vivian, bold, exciting Vivian, fierce, fiery Vivian, dominating their lives. They existed only in Vivian, and for Vivian, in a sultry morass of Vivian's flesh and commands, until they were no longer able to imagine a life without her, nor to remember, or even conceive of, a life before her.

N. Ovid

CAMERA ONE

I dream of First Sergeant Rourke. She walks into my office, slams the door behind her, rips off her skirt, and pulls down her panties.

But she has two boxes.

And each has a sign above it: IN and OUT.

CAMERA ONE

Edith waves to me from the kitchen. I've got the earphones on. Listening to Jimi Hendrix's "Purple Haze."

"Are you talking to me?" I remove the phones.

"Yes. There's a phone call for you. Long-distance. Someone named Irv Feldman."

"Good God!" I pick myself up off the rug. "What now?"

Irv Feldman is an optometrist. The only doctor of any kind that our block in the Bronx ever produced, he has been, as far back as I can remember, the oracle my mother referred me to on any problem I might have had, from acne to advanced algebra. He still lives on the same block in the Bronx, has fat twin daughters and a baby son, and always complies with my mother's requests— however inadequate he may be to carry out the missions she sends him on—because he's "nice."

"Hello."

"Hello, Jake? Irv. I hear you got a problem."

"More than one, Irv."

"I can understand how you feel. I was in World War II, Jake. It wasn't any picnic either, believe me."

"I believe you Irv, and I'm sorry my mother put you up to this."

"It's O.K., Jake. She's worried. It's understandable. She's a mother. You don't write to her, you won't speak to her, a mother doesn't hear from her son, she gets worried. That's the way they are."

"I know, Irv."

"Look, Jake, they don't care about you as an individual, right? They never did. That's the army. Your sergeant bosses you around. . . ."

"I'm an officer, Irv. I boss the sergeants around."

"It's all the same. They're not your kind of people, that's all. They're not what you call mental geniuses."

"I'm hip."

"I remember how it is. The college guys always had it tough. They make you hike, they make you wash the floors, they inspect your stuff all the time."

"But, Irv . . ."

"You got to learn to live with it."

"I'm not sure I can."

"You got to, Jake. Then you get out and believe me you feel you learned something. Tell me the truth, Jake, can you honestly say you haven't learned something already from that *meshugina* army?"

"I can't say I haven't."

"You see what I mean? Well, I'll get off. I don't want to be a bother. Just stick with it. We all went through the same thing. Some day you'll look back on it and laugh at it all."

"Thanks, Irv. Good-bye."

"Good-bye, Jake. . . . And don't do anything foolish. It's just life, Jake."

After he hung up I thought of the Dylan line, "It's life and life on-ly," and I said into the dead telephone circuit, "That's what I'm afraid of, Irv."

BULLETIN

Goldwater Praises Youth

Senator Barry Goldwater, Republican of Arizona, said last night that the current crop of young Americans is "the best generation I've ever known in my life." The Republican Presidential candidate of 1964 made the statement after receiving the Good Scout Award at a fund-raising dinner for the Greater New York Councils of the Boy Scouts of America.

BULLETIN

GOLDWATER AIDE TURNS ANARCHIST

Karl Hess, 'Idea Man' of '64, Assumes Role of Radical

CAMERA ONE

At the longhouse. Stoned. Len begins to speak. A kind of sermon based upon the authentic text of a eighteenth-century American nursery rhyme about a famed Indian fighter of the Massachusetts Bay Colony—a Captain Lovewell.

The two lines which Len has selected from the children's rhyme are the following:

He and his valiant soldiers did range the woods full wide,
And hardships they endured to quell the Indians' pride.

BULLETIN

Jersey Mother, 23, Charged With Killing Her Daughter, 4

PATERSON, N. J., Dec. 26 (UPI)—A 23-year-old mother of three children was held without bail today, charged with beating her 4-year-old daughter to death with a shoe.

CAMERA ONE

A single boat moves up the river, near the bank. Spraying chemicals along the shore. Poisoning the ground so that the trees and delicate wild flowers, which have bloomed beside the river for centuries, will not grow there any longer. So there will be no natural growth to provide cover for the B.C.

BULLETIN

Trap Built to Catch Poodle Traps British Grandmother

FARNHAM, England (UPI)— Mrs. Mora Tilley, a 65-year-old grandmother, built a trap to catch a poodle running through her garden.

She caught a blackbird, then a cat and a neighbor's dog.

When she checked to find what was going wrong, she trapped herself.

Mrs. Tilley sat and waited while her 4-year-old grandson opened the cage door.

She caught the poddle later. It was undergoing "dog psychiatry," authorities said.

CAMERA ONE

Another package of grass arrives from Randy. This time it's packed in a hollowed-out copy of Theodore Dreiser's *An American Tragedy.*

CAMERA ONE

The colonel's mother is disturbed at the drop in attendance at the Sunday services in the hospital chapel. An outside consulting firm is called in and paid twenty thousand dollars to make an objective study of this matter. After a month, they conclude that the problem is related to the chaplain's order which placed the chapel off-limits to the GIs. The order is rescinded.

The colonel orders me to come up to the hospital every Sunday morning at seven thirty to individually wake up each GI and ask him whether he wants to go to chapel.

I tell Cal about the problem.

"Well, just pass it on, Jake. Give an order to a sergeant to do it."

"I hate to use people like that. I don't like to use my authority."

"Don't be silly. The sergeant will pass it on, too. And everyone else will pass the buck until it reaches someone who has no authority and is looking for a chance to get some. It'll be a pleasure for *someone* to do it. Why deprive him of his joy so you can torture yourself?"

I pass it on. And I never hear mention of it again.

DO-IT-YOURSELF BULLETIN

(Paste in your own favorite,
which you have clipped from the pages
of your local newspaper.
I recommend *The New York Times*.)

CAMERA TWO

When the lunch hour arrived, I went home. The house was empty, so I went next door. Only Len was there.

"Len, I need help. Forget the Indian bag for a while and help me. I need a psychologist. I'm going nuts."

"No you're not, Jake. *They're* nuts. You're O.K."

"No, you don't know about it. I'm really going nuts. I'm a sick person. I want to be put away somewhere."

"You just want to get out of here."

"Well, then I'll run away. I'll go AWOL. I want to go where it's warm."

"Take it easy, Jake. We need you."

"Everybody needs me. But I need, too. I need to go away."

"Why don't you? Get away for a couple of days."

"That's not enough."

"Try it. What've you got to lose? If it's not enough, if you feel you can't come back to face what's happening here with the rest of us, then fuck it. Don't come back."

"But where can I go? How can I get leave?"

"Look, Jake, I've been meaning to talk to you anyway and I guess this is as good a time as any to do it. Things have reached a head around here. We've all reached the limit. We're all going through the same changes you are."

"You don't know. . . ."

"Yes! All of us. The time is getting short. Soon we'll have to make our move."

"What?"

"Don't worry about the details. Just take a few days and go to Charleston. We need some grass. A lot of it. Fast."

"We can get it through the mail."

"Not anymore, we can't. I have an Indian GI, a Sioux, working at the base post office. They know something's funny. They're checking every package. Why not get out of here for a couple days. Cool off. It'll do you good. I'll even pay your fare. This way, even if you're not with us, you can do something to help us out. We need you, Jake. We need the grass, *now*. Think of the scouts. They're depending on you. It's the least you can do for them."

"But how? How can I get leave?"

"Not leave, Jake. Get a three-day pass."

"*How?*"

"Use your friend, Captain Piece-of-Ass."

I knew he was right. Cal could easily get a three-day pass for anyone she chose. And I knew she would do it for me.

"Take the bus down. Relax by yourself. Dig the scenery and get your head together. Then you can pick up the stuff and fly back. I'll pay for your tickets. Even as a psychologist, that's the best advice I could give you, Jake. Get away from here for a couple days. Maybe it'll help you to see where things are at for you."

I thought of the South. Of civilian life again. Of traveling. Of warmth.

"O.K. You win. I'll do it."

"Great! I'll pay all your expenses."

"No. I'll take care of that. Cash isn't my problem right now."

"You'll feel a lot better for it."

"I don't know. . . . But it's the least I can do for the kids. I don't know what you've got planned for them, but I have a hunch that if I want to do anything for them, I better do it now. I'll get you the grass."

"I appreciate it, Jake. If you get the pass this afternoon, you can leave on the bus to New York tomorrow morning. Then, an overnight bus to the South, spend a day with your buddy, and on the third day, catch a plane back. I'm going to fast until you return. Then I've got a surprise for you."

"I don't want any more surprises. I want stability."

"You'll like this one. On the night you return, we're having a concert at the longhouse."

"Rock?"

"No, classical. I've gotten in touch with Madame Braun. She's in the area, and she's agreed to play."

"Madame Braun!"

"I knew you'd be surprised."

"But . . . but how did you do it? How . . ."

"Don't waste time with questions. Get your ass on up to the hospital and get that three-day pass. Let's just say Madame Braun's performance is a present for you, from the scouts, if you decide to return."

BULLETIN

Movie Is 'Continued'

KETCHIKAN, Alaska (AP)— On the opening night of "Mackenna's Gold," the screen at the Revilla Theater went blank with the story's climax yet to come—three minutes of the final reel were missing. Refunds or rain checks were offered. When the missing film arrived the next day, the patrons returned for the conclusion of the picture.

CAMERA TWO

The bus to Charleston didn't leave New York until late that afternoon so I had about three hours to myself in the city. I took the AA train up to Eighty-first Street. To the Museum of Natural History. Walked past Teddy Roosevelt's statue and went inside.

The building itself is part of the show, a gloomy, cavernous structure in which the ancient bones seem to belong. It's as if they had been there for millennia, just waiting for the opportunity to provide young people with material for recurring night mares.

I followed a path which moved forward through time. Beginning with the bones of primeval sea creatures and working up through the age of the dinosaurs to the skeletons of creatures not yet extinct. There it is again: the idea of extinction. It, too, seems to have been waiting for centuries in the caverns of this mammoth museum. Waiting for the nightmares and daydreams of malleable imaginations like my own. For the museum is steeped in extinction; it hangs in the air like dust.

Yes, there are spaces in that museum which exhibits can't fill. But there are connections, too. Evolution. One can see it all around him. All creatures look so much more alike when you get down beneath their skin. So obvious, the ties of fish to bird—the similarities between tyrannosaurus and tiger. So clearly marked, the connections between the mammals—until . . . until the break. The hiatus. You follow the chain step by step through the apes until the museum slaps two creatures side by side: the skeleton of a baby chimpanzee next to that of a human child.

It knocks you out to see it. Something has happened to the skull —to the head. Every head in the place seems a product of the same gradual evolutionary process until you come to the single, big-headed freak.

The child's bones were so delicate and fragile. So finely wrought. Except for his enormous balloon of a head. Just seeing it drives theories of missing links from your mind, for the child is so weird —the strangest creature in the whole museum, the one alien freak-headed outsider. And you can see in a second it's his head that will give him whatever power he may have. (And that will make it so terribly dangerous to have him for an enemy.)

But he looked so lonely. So odd. Like what? What did he remind me of? Then I knew. I thought of all the science fiction comics I had read as a boy, about people who come to Earth from another planet (usually Mars). And they're always little frail creatures, with enormous heads, who are separated from the indigenous life on Earth by their vast intelligence. And they pose a threat to the Earth and its inhabitants because of their tremendous brainpower and technology.

Yes, we are the Mr. Bigdomes who have somehow appeared on the surface of the Earth and subdued it with our bulbous head-power, eliminating some species and enslaving others, while poisoning the water and air and scaring the shit out of every natural being on the planet because they know we will follow our big domes wherever they lead us, even if it means the destruction of the Earth itself—because the earth is not our natural habitat and we don't know how to live on it or preserve it.

CAMERA ONE

I walk out of the museum, into the sunlight. Over to Broadway to get a sandwich. But there's a crowd of people blocking the sidewalk on Eighty-first Street. They form a semicircle with the curb as diameter. And they are all shouting excitedly in Spanish.

In the center of the half-moon space, there is large, dark man who appears dangerously silent in the midst of the jagged babble. Against a parked car, a Puerto Rican woman, short and stocky, about thirty-five years old, heavily made up and wearing a tight, red satin dress that clings to her big ass. The man she is comforting is short, and through his hands, in which he holds his head, I can see that his nose is running blood. Suddenly, he straightens up, throws out his arm knocking the woman aside, and charges the dark, silent figure in the center of the half-ring. The woman screams and clutches his jacket tail, but he moves forward, pulling her along.

The big man watches his opponent's rush and, without saying a word, he throws a single vicious right which crashes into the little man's jaw, knocking him down in his tracks like a dropped sack of potatoes. The woman stops, shrieks out in furious grief, and then throws herself at the big man, screaming wildly and cat-swiping at his eyes with her nails as she rushes forward. Her prey takes one step back, giving himself enough room to throw a single left hook which clouts her so solidly behind her ear that she seems to turn horizontal in midair before dropping like a log right on top of her stunned little defender.

Then the big guy slaps his hands together, barks a few short, angry epithets in Spanish, spits once on the jumbled heap of pain below him on the sidewalk, and walks away.

Slowly, like two clowns painted red with blood, the damaged losers help each other up. Her dress is torn and she's holding her ear with one hand while trying to support him with the other. His face is bleeding profusely. Like two drunken pals on the Bowery, they weave down the street unsteadily, leaning on each other.

CAMERA TWO

I was surprised by the fact that no one in the crowd (all of whom seemed to know the three people involved in the brawl) made any attempt to intervene or, after it was over, to help the victims. I thought that perhaps I shouldn't have remained a passive spectator. That at least I could have tried to get the police.

But I quickly changed my mind. On the other side of the parked car, against which the woman had been leaning, I noticed a patrol car, double parked. Inside sat a single policeman, who was quietly looking at the crowd on the sidewalk. He must have seen the whole fight, too. And he hadn't attempted to call the police, either.

BULLETIN

Human Head Is Called Too Weighty to Hold Up

LOS ANGELES (AP)—Are you having trouble holding your head up recently?

You should, according to a medical man who says that the average human head weighs 14 pounds and it is not easy to hold it up all day day long.

The weight of the head, in fact, contributes to that nagging pain in the neck or shoulders that often is blamed on tension, said Dr. H. H. Campbell, director of the Institute of Traumatic Plastic and Restorative Surgery in Toronto.

CAMERA TWO

I left for the South that evening. On the bus, I sat next to a guy who played defensive end for the Citadel. I don't know if he was a good end, but he had the size to be one. It wasn't easy trying to sleep in a shared bus seat with a person of his width, but it seemed like it might be a hell of lot easier than trying to run around his end of the line. I finally did get a couple hours sleep, covering my legs with my coat to take the chill off the night.

I awoke in Durham, North Carolina, and it was almost spring. When we got off the bus for breakfast, a warm sun was coming up and the sky was clear. The air had a bright sting to it, but it seemed more friendly and open than the ice air of the North—more hospitable. And inside my scratchy head, music began to spin, as it always does on mornings after too little sleep. And it was old music. Nothing could be finer than to be in Carolina in the morning. Songs were so trite before kids began to write their own that we forget how true some of the old ones can be. But these lyrics told me to leave the bus terminal and to walk on the grass of this state, so near to Kentucky blue. To smell the turf.

And to return to eat a big breakfast of fresh ham and eggs and grits, and to hear the heaviness of the morning quiet, and to languish in the slowness of the honey-haired waitress who, just a year or two before, might have been twirling a baton for Durham High. With her chipped tooth actually adding to her smile and dreams of Duke boys with fast cars gleaming in her eyes. No, not Temple Drake, but a poor girl, with two first names, looking for a young law student from Raleigh or a business manager who'll take her away with him to the tobacco company in Winston-Salem. Looking for a house on the edge of town with three baths and two kids.

Carla Sue, Betty Jean, Amanda Mae. Nothing is impossible in this sleepy, warm land, where guys wear names like Darrell and Rodney and Buford, and the earth really does smell as fresh and inviting as your mother once did, and the girls speak with maple syrup on their tongues, and they tickle your ear with their words when they talk, and *Gone With The Wind*, though it never existed in the antebellum South, has come into being since the movie came out.

And I thought of Len. For this earth, this beneficent mother, as he would call it, was never owned by any Indians, but it did provide for the Tuscaroras for centuries. This fertile land, sloping into the foothills of the Blue Ridge, this heavy-smelling loam and sweet green of trees and grass once supported a noble people until the ancestors of Rodney and Buford and Betty Jean and Amanda Mae kicked them out and took it for themselves.

Does Eula Jane's father know that his precious state's rights, the backbone and bane of the ill-fated Confederacy, stem from the League of Six Nations?

An ancient Negro comes out of the kitchen wearing a white uniform and baker's cap, and he begins to sweep the floor while whistling a tune so familiar nobody even hears it:

> If you white,
> All right.
> If you brown,
> Stick aroun'.
> But if you black . . .

Yes, the South, in Carolina, in the morning, is impossibly lovely and winsome, and it will offer you all the hospitality and graciousness it has withheld from half its inhabitants for three hundred years. . . . Oh, the contradictions, the gross and exacerbated fissures upon which this country is built would stagger the mind of a Karl Marx. How does this lush, magnificent, sunny southern land appear in the harsh light of the New England imagination? New England, with her ground still frozen and bandaged with patches of dirty snow. The bones are closer to the surface up there. And if the air is less redolent, the eyes are more acute.

One can hate the people of the South—all army bases are, in a real sense, extensions of the South—but one cannot hate the South itself. Not the mother of the Tuscarora nation, who still lives . . . on the reservations in northern New York State . . . if only in Tuscarora dreams.

The bus entered the city limits of Charleston and headed for the terminal along the L. Mendel Rivers Boulevard. Charleston was a much smaller city than I had anticipated. I understood now why it was possible to write to Randy simply in care of his apartment house—the Pickens' Manor—with no street address on the envelope: it was the tallest and newest building in the city, and it towered over the town like a rocket on a launching pad.

I got the apartment number from his mailbox. Apartment 62. Over one of his aliases: S. W. Jackson. It was, I soon learned, no more audacious than the rest of his operation. My old physics lab partner had not given up a promising career in science to become a mere bank teller of a crook. He had always had a dash, a verve which he wanted to manifest. He was operating illegally for the love of the style of it, not just to make a few dollars.

A playmate-styled chick in a shorty nightgown answered the door.

"I'm looking for Randy," I said.

"What time is it?" she asked, through the buzz of her sleep.

"It's about two."

"Oh," she said, and she turned toward the living room. I followed her into the apartment. From the bedroom I could hear Randy shout in that remnant of a southern accent which he saved for cursing, "What in the goddamn, motherfuckin, hell time is it?"

He popped his head out the door and saw me. "Jake! My man!" And still nude, he rushed over to me and shook my hand. "Well, I'll be goddamned, if it ain't Jake the Flake."

Then, remembering the woman, he turned to her and said, rather formally for a man with no clothes on, "Pamela Lou, meet my oldest and best buddy, Jake."

He reached for a terrycloth robe which was on the top of an armchair and, putting it on, he said, "What's up, Jake? Anything wrong?"

"Can I talk?" I said, giving a slight nod toward Pamela Lou.

"Oh, Pam's a hustler from the word go." She smiled proudly at his compliment. "She's been with me for about a week, now. Ever since her old man ran out on her."

"Were you married?" I asked her.

"Not that kind of old man," Randy grinned. "I mean her *real* old man. Her father. I met them last year, at the Darlington 500. You ever hear of that?"

"No."

"It's the big auto race down here. I was running a crap game behind the outhouses, doing right well with the crackers and hillbillies, when I met her and her old man. They were turning a few tricks of their own."

He whacked Pam's ass. "About a week ago, she and her old man dropped in on me. I was on my way to a big blast at the house of one of my associates, Fast Eddie, so I took them along. Well, someone brought a case of scotch he'd picked off a truck, and we drank the whole damn thing. The party got a little rough after that.

"It started when this stripper I know, named Georgia Moon, showed up, packing a .45 that looked like a small cannon—it probably would have knocked the damn house down if she'd gotten to fire the fuckin thing. Seems she thought she had some kind of claim on my life, and that while she could travel around showing her tits to half the fuckin state, I was supposed to stay home and play solitaire, right? Luckily, I was at the side of the doorway when she came storming through, so she ran right by me, holding the cannon out in front of her like she'd just thrown a left hook that didn't connect. I grabbed her arm from the side, banged it on a table, she dropped the piece, and I began to smack some fuckin sense into her when some stupid shit decides that he's going to defend her honor, so I pop him one and the next thing you know people begin swinging at each other and throwing furniture and all hell breaks loose."

He smiled, relishing the vision of the scene. Then he sat down and lit up a cigarette. "It was quite a night. By the time the cops got there everybody had split except for one chick who got cut pretty bad, a guy who was out cold on the floor, and another guy who somehow had gotten his leg broken. And that night was the last time anybody saw Pam's old man.

"It was during the middle of the fight. I was squared off with this big ugly cat when I spot the old bastard slinking out of the house with Eddie's turntable under one arm and his TV under the other. Nobody else even noticed him in the confusion. Well, I laughed so hard when I saw him that I dropped my hands and this big cat caught me with a right up here (he touched a small cut above his left eye) that came so close to putting me out of business I was forced to hit him over the head with one of Eddie's lamps. He was the guy who was out cold and, in fact, the only one who got busted.

"Eddie's well known around here. We all pay off the man. So he got off clean. In fact, Eddie had seen the big ugly cat slug me, so he dropped a few bennies in the guy's pocket before the police took him away. We won't be bothered by him for a while, anyway."

The doorbell rang. Randy glanced at the clock and said to Pam, "That's Toledo with breakfast."

She opened the door, letting in a haggard man, about forty years old, with clothes that were flashy but disheveled. He was carrying a big paper bag from which he took out paper cups of coffee, cheeseburgers, and french fries.

"Toledo Jack, meet my man from the north country, Jake Klinger. Toledo is one of my associates."

Randy picked up a cheeseburger from the table. "Help yourself, Jake. Hey, I never did get to hear what's on your mind."

"I came to pick up a load of grass. We need it all, right now. I can't stay, Randy, I'm going to fly back. I brought an empty suitcase we can fill with kilos."

"Same old Jake," Randy smiled. "Mr. Conscientious. When do you have to leave?"

"Tomorrow morning at eleven."

"Good enough," he said. "We'll have a ball till tomorrow and then put you on your plane. Eddie and I'll get you to the airport.

How about it, man? I'll show you my town. Mix some pleasure with your business."

"Sounds fine, only I'm pretty tired. I didn't sleep more than an hour or two on the bus last night."

"No problem at all. Just let Dr. Jive fix you up," he said, dropping about a dozen green pills into my hand. "These will wake you up fast enough."

"O.K. I'm game," I said. I swallowed a bennie and washed it down with a shot of Jack Daniels I poured for myself from an open bottle on the table.

After the meal, they each dropped a bennie and we went out to groove on the sights.

The clocks in Charleston appeared to have stopped during the Civil War. It was a charming, sleepy little city of narrow streets and antebellum houses. And the many quaint shops gave even the business area a nineteenth-century ambience. Seeing the slave market shook me up, though. One can read about slavery, but encountering the actual market is something else again. For I could see David up there on the platform, wearing almost no clothes, surrounded by a large, noisy, market-day throng, while Grandma Creetner climbs up onto the block and checks his teeth and muscles, and feels his balls, and then signals to her son down on the floor and he, in his most businesslike tone, ups the bid twenty dollars.

Then we passed the Francis Marion Hotel and its Swamp-Fox Room and drove down to the shoreline park facing Fort Sumter.

The fort was on an island, much farther from the mainland than I had imagined. And in the lovely park at the water's edge there stood a statue of William Gilmore Simms. I was the only one of the four of us who had heard of him. I had read his novel, *Woodcraft*, about the irregulars fighting the guerrilla phase of the American Revolution in the southern woods. He had written his novels about the same time that Henry Thoreau was living in Concord, hundreds of miles to the north.

After this we drove to what seemed to be the fanciest men's clothing shop in town. Randy had ordered a custom-made suit there. Toledo seemed anxious to get out of the place, but Randy took his time, even requesting a few last-minute alterations before he would accept the suit. When the salesman took the suit into the back to the tailor, I whispered to Randy, "Isn't a place like this kind of expensive?"

"Don't worry about it, man. I charge it."

I couldn't see how that would make it any cheaper, but when the salesman came back with a box and said to Randy, "Here's the suit. Will that be charge, Mr. Jefferson?" I got the picture. I also understood why Toledo looked so anxious to get out of the store.

The only question remaining was whether Randy had had the audacity to sign up for a charge account under the name of Thomas Jefferson. So when the salesman brought the charge slip for him to sign, I watched him write out his full name: John Quincy Jefferson. I joined Toledo in getting out of there as fast as I could.

Later in the afternoon, Toledo Jack dropped Randy and me off at the apartment and left to drive Pam to Columbia. We sat down in the living room again, broke out a new fifth of Jack Daniels, lit up a joint, and began to talk.

"Do you have the grass here?"

Randy just smiled and opened the bottom drawer of his desk. It was completely filled with brick-shaped kilos of grass.

"How'd you get that stuff across?"

"Jack and Fast Eddie. I go into Mexico and buy the stuff. It's not hard making contacts. I provide the capital, then I let my *associates* risk their asses getting it across. Although, I must admit, they have a pretty sophisticated system," he laughed.

"What's that?"

"Well, Eddie is called Fast because he once ran on a track team in high school, but between you and me, he can't run worth a shit anymore. But the beauty of it is that he doesn't know it. He drops a few bennies and, man, as far as he's concerned, he's Jesse Owens in Berlin.

"So what these two geniuses do is Toledo stays in Mexico with the grass in a big laundry bag and then he and Eddie meet each other at the fuckin fence, just down a ways from the border patrol station. Then Toledo throws the damn bag over the fence to Eddie, who puts it on his back, turns north, and hotfoots it all the way back into Texas."

"You're kidding!"

"No, I'm not," he laughed. "I sit in my hotel room and all I've got to do is revive the crazy fucker when he comes whizzing in the door and collapses. It's really not a bad system. The man has all kinds of sophisticated devices at the border, but they can't conceive of a thirty-five-year-old, raggedy-assed, rummy track star catching a screen pass at the fence and *running* into the States with the stuff."

"Are you going to keep this up?"

"Just til I get enough capital saved up to open a little club here in town. Though I would like to pull one final caper that would top off my career as an international dope smuggler."

"What do you have in mind?"

"I'd like to buy a big sack of grass one Christmas Eve, you dig? Then, I want to dress Eddie up and have him run into the States at midnight, carrying his pack on his back, decked out in an authentic, red Santa Claus suit."

"You're kidding!" I said, laughing. But I wasn't sure that he was.

He put a Brubeck record on the box. It was old Brubeck, a red plastic LP on the Fantasy label. *Jazz at the College of the Pacific.*

We each poured some more bourbon and, as we listened, Randy saw me watching his right hand unconsciously beating out the time, as if he were driving the group, while, with his left foot, he kept up a rhythmic beat on the sock cymbal. We both smiled and we were back in college nights of Isaac Newton and Robert Boyle and jazz records piled up on the box, playing one after another as we sat over our books trying to study, feet tapping, heads nodding, Randy's left hand on the physics text, his right holding a drumstick, tapping out the rhythm on the desk lamp above his book.

"I wore out a lot of lamps that winter," he said.

"That was a long winter."

"I'm hip."

"Do you still dig Brubeck?"

"I still play him a lot. The old stuff. Mainly in bunches. When I get nostalgic, I guess. How about you?"

"I do too," I said. "But I've come to listen to Desmond's solos more and more."

"So do I. Brubeck doesn't swing as much as I once thought he did, but Desmond wears better. That cat still knocks me out."

"Same here. I've been thinking about Desmond a lot lately. I have a theory about him: I think he's the reincarnation of Franz Schubert. A man of infinite melody."

Just then, Desmond broke into, "For All We Know," and Randy broke out another joint, and we began to float upon the smoke, upon the profound but agile sadness of airwaves jammed into music through a gold horn. Of visions of Desmond, seeming to hide in the hook of the grand piano (looking like a bent hook, himself), stepping higher and higher while dancing a delicate pas de deux with Brubeck, and I took another drag and I saw Desmond setting down patterns of sparkling liquid music upon which Franz Schubert (syphilitic, hairless, dressed in the discarded finery of his friends) waltzed. Against the doctor's orders, against his friends' advice, against the best interests of his own health and life, Franz danced, and it was like the time he carried a torch at Beethoven's funeral, and I saw him dance with a maiden and I saw him dance with death until he was beyond happiness and beyond unhappiness as well, upfloating sideways above the linden trees, to where green is bleached by the sun.

And as we sat there, I felt I was out of the army and I could conceive of a life of my own, with my friends Paul and Franz and Jack Daniels and my grass, and Randy looked at me with an old smile upon his face and said, "Listen to that fucker's tone—just listen to it."

And Desmond's sound was so spring-water clear, his melodies so lyrically overflowing like a snowfall of diamond runoff from a single cloud on a summer day, that I thought maybe this is what we're looking for—not nature, but purity. Artistic purity. Simplicity. Clarity of line. Maybe melody is what we must learn to believe in—not fixed melody, but bursts of spontaneous song, infinitely varied and always new.

When the record turned itself off, we sat staring blankly at the smoky air. Randy turned the record over and I said, "You say you may buy a club around here?"

"I think so. I'm looking around. I make a little extra money playing cards and gambling and I thought I might dig having a place of my own. You know, a back room, with blackjack, a roulette wheel, some chicks dealing, a bar in the front. Maybe a nice jukebox with jazz on it."

He took a drag on a joint and then continued, "You know, Jake, in whatever I do there's always room for you."

"I don't know . . . I'm tired of dealing with the law."

"You're new around here, Jake. In the South, the law is for the spades. I mean you have to pay a few people, but it's not much of a hassle. You'll see tonight."

"I don't know . . ."

"You don't have to go back. Change your name, stay here with us, and they'll never find you."

"I think I do have to go back. . . . But I don't really know what I want. I'm tired of dealing with the law. In any way."

"You think a straight business is any different? There, Mr. Clock becomes your boss. And the bank. And the customers. You can't get away from it."

"I know."

"Well, it's up to you. If you want to be masochistic and go back into the army, it's your funeral, not mine."

"I know."

"It's easy to make it down here. The people are kind of slow and the town's filled with soldiers and sailors, bringing in a fresh load of Uncle Sam's green every payday. I like it. I don't get to read much anymore, or have many really bright friends—don't have any, in fact—but I get up in the afternoon, stay out all night, gamble, make out. . . . I'm doing O.K. for myself. Just like to make enough to get out of the dope business. I got busted once, and I don't kid myself, they'll eventually get me again if I don't quit while I'm ahead. You can't keep playing double or nothing with your winnings. Any gambler knows that."

Randy had been busted in New Orleans, three years before. He'd been dealing in California, hiding his stash in a golf bag he had checked at an exclusive golf course. But he got into some trouble because he'd taken a pistol shot at a Mexican who'd attempted to rape his woman, so he left for New Orleans in a hurry.

He stopped to pick up a hitchhiker in Nevada who was kind enough to pay Randy back for his free trip by arranging for him to make a big drug sale to a local narc. Because of Randy's father's influence and money (he owned a big auto agency in Charlotte and was a prominent Democrat), the charge was reduced from dealing to possession and he got one year, suspended, which was fortunate in that it got him out of the army without getting him into the Louisiana State Prison at Angola.

"I like dealing with people who are outside of the mainstream of life," he said. "The people I know tend not to operate in the clear light of day. They're not so fast in making distinctions. The world's just a game anyhow, so why not make your living at gaming. People are coming to recognize this. Gambling's one of the great growth industries in America today. From where I stand, life looks more like a ramp than a staircase, Jake. I can't ever think in terms of finding my own particular step. There'll always be action and risk, and that's the way I like it. People who think they've found a level step for themselves can't afford to experience any joy. They can't get high, because they're scared to death they'll see another step above the one their on."

"The bastards I work for don't want *anybody* to get high."

"Right. Because they've invested too much in convincing themselves that they're already *there*. Well, I don't believe in any *there*. And I dig people who've been knocked around so much they've forgotten any dreams of security or stability they might have had. Cats for whom the clear light of the sun is the lie."

Randy put on an LP by Wardell Gray, the great tenor man who was found in a Nevada ditch with a broken neck at the age of thirty-three. We snorted some cocaine, drank another bourbon, and then drove out to a suburban-style ranch house where a divorcée named Rhoda was fixing dinner. She was a tall, average-looking woman (taller than Randy, who was well built but was only about five feet eight) but she had nice legs and a good ass. When Randy told her that I was staying for dinner, she nodded compliantly and brought out a bottle of bourbon with three glasses. She had a new stereo console and surprisingly good records.

"I pick them out," Randy said, when he saw me looking at the titles. "There's not much interest in music in these parts."

He put a Charlie Parker side on the box and explained to me that Rhoda worked for the army at a depot in town. She had no kids and her ex-husband was a welder at the navy base.

"Doesn't anyone in town *not* work for the government?" I asked.

"I don't," Randy smiled.

He was probably not only the hippest man Rhoda had ever slept with, but the smartest, most worldly person she had ever met. She said little while we ate—just served us and gazed longingly at Randy. When we finished dinner he said, "See you," and got up to leave.

"Aren't you going to stay here tonight?" she asked.

"No. Got some business to attend to in town."

Our first stop was at a club near the old slave market. It was called the Green Jade, a nicely plushed cocktail lounge with a circular bar served by two pretty barmaids in leotards. There were a few soldiers but almost all the customers were sailors.

As we sat down both barmaids came over to say hello to Randy.

He introduced me as a poet friend from the North and ordered two bourbons.

"What's this poet jazz?" I said, after the women had left, one to service a young hick sailor who was buying drinks for her as well as for himself and the other to fetch our bourbons.

"I mean it, man. I've read some of your stuff. That army haircut's a piss-poor disguise."

"You seem pretty tight with these chicks," I said, to change the subject.

"Oh, I've slept with each of them a couple of times. . . . And once, with both of them together," he smiled. "They're pretty good. You want to meet one?"

"I don't have much time. Let's stay loose and look around."

"Suit yourself," he said, as the first barmaid, Diane, returned with our drinks. Her face turned soft as she placed mine in front of me.

When we finished the drinks and got up to go, I reached for my wallet.

"Forget it," Randy said.

"No, this one is on me."

"I said forget it, Jake. These are on the house."

I must have thrown him a puzzled look.

"I'm known around here, man. I don't pay for drinks at any of these bars. The chicks make the money for the house on these smart-ass sailors who think they're hip. They don't know shit and the chicks really soak them. There's a community of the night around here, Jake, and we take care of each other. I lay some grass on the women once in a while and they dig me. They dig you too, I saw it. This is a great town when your in on the inside because there's always that tide of Uncle Sam's green coming in once a month and we just help ourselves to it. Then, when the sailor boys go home to their cots, we start to ball."

The barmaids smiled at us as we left through a curtained back door. It led into a room where there was a small bar and about five gambling tables tended by chicks in bunny costumes. We had another drink and the story was the same at this place and at the two others we stopped at. Everyone knew Randy and accepted me immediately because I was with him. And sailors, who had been putting on cool faces and sucking in their gut to impress the barmaids, stared at me in bitter wonder, as I immediately got the inviting smiles they were playing for so desperately.

By the time we got to the Peek-A-Boo Club, the drinks (on top of the joints we'd smoked earlier) had us pretty well wrecked. We went up to a table where a man was sitting alone. About thirty-five years old, wearing the kind of clothes people wear when they dress up to go to the track (the flats) but won't pay the extra buck to get a seat in the clubhouse.

Randy introduced me to his associate, Fast Eddie. I felt that I knew Eddie, that I had met Eddies before. And I could understand how he could literally run dope into the country, for he had a boyish quality about him, a kind of threadbare naiveté. Eddie would be loyal—extremely loyal—to a few people, to the crooked. And he would be totally amoral toward the rest.

As I sat down at Eddie's table, Randy said, "I'm going to leave you two for a while. Got some business with Carl at the Twenty-one. See you there in about two hours?"

"Right," Eddie said, I nodded, and Randy left.

"What's up?" I asked.

"It's Georgia Moon," Eddie said. "She just got back in town and she's working here tonight."

"The chick with the gun."

"Right. You heard about that scene, man?"

"Randy told me."

His face crinkled with delight. "That was wild, man. Oh, hey, here's Carolina."

A very tall blonde, Hollywood regal, heavily made up, with a long fall of finespun hair down her back and a low-cut golden gown which seemed both too cheap and too expensive at the same time, sat down at our table.

"Jake Klinger," Eddie said, "meet the belle of the South, Miss Carolina Nice."

I was going to say, "Pleased to meet you, Miss Nice," because I thought it would sound funny, but when I looked into Carolina's lusterless eyes I quickly saw that irony was not a part of her otherwise abundant equipment, so I just stood up after Eddie introduced me. I sensed this would impress her as being somewhat chivalric.

"Where's your little friend?" she said to Eddie.

"He's not around right now."

"I can see why. After the way he treated Georgia."

"Is she still gunning for him?" Eddie grinned.

"Don't be silly, Edward. Georgia wouldn't hurt a flea. She cried during our whole trip. When we played Memphis and Augusta, she could barely perform."

"Georgia and Carolina are . . ."

"Exotic dancers," she finished the sentence for him. "We travel together. But I'm terrified for Georgia. She's been out of her mind with grief since Randy jilted her."

"He never was going with her," Eddie said.

"Maybe that's what you think. But Georgia thought he was. She's a wonderful girl, really she is. And she was so devoted to him, really. Now she'll never be the same."

"When she came through the door with that cannon in her hand, I didn't think any of us would be."

"Well, you just forget about that unfortunate instance. She was hysterical with grief. She probably wouldn't even have known how to use it."

"I'll bet," Eddie said, sarcastically.

"But let's talk about something more pleasant," she said, signaling to the waitress. "Dottie, dear, give me a bloody mary, and give each of these gentlemen a Jack Daniels on the rocks."

Then she turned to me, batted her long false eyelashes, and said in a soft-throated, cello tone, "Tell us about yourself, Mr. Klinger."

At that moment, I sensed that she, too, had been drinking heavily, and I began to tell her about myself, heavily editing the manuscript of my life and becoming more the poet and less the accountant with each swallow of good Jack Daniels' Tennessee sour mash. And Carolina ate it up, because, although she was one of the hardest looking chicks I had ever met, she thought she was sentimental. And every once in a while she'd return to the subject of poor Georgia, and how Randy had been so cruel to her, and how sad a poem she could write about their brief love affair, if only she had the time.

At one point, she even began to weep. And that made her eye makeup run, and the realization of this seemed to make her weep even more. Then, as the show began on a small stage above our table and Georgia came out and began to strip, Carolina reached over the table to me and kissed me, pushing her tongue deep into my mouth and moving it with snakelike expertise. And as she kissed me, her right hand reached under the corner of the table and began to rub my crotch, and the friction made me hotter and hotter until we were hit by something flying through the air. We separated, and I took an elaborate, black-laced bra off my head. It was Georgia's. She had spotted us and thrown it at us from the stage.

Georgia Moon was a statuesque, wild-looking woman, very tall, with something crazy in her eyes. It was more than grief, real or imagined; her eyes were slightly askew—not angry or woeful, but insane. And one could see that it had always been there. Before Randy, before she was even born, perhaps.

The band broke into "Big Maryanne" and the words passed through my head:

> Big Maryanne
> She's tall and nice
> She can do what you can
> And do it twice

And big Georgia stood above us, scowling defiantly at Carolina while gyrating her unsupported, but naturally cantilevered, tits directly at me.

"Shake it on out!" Eddie yelled to her, and after she had finished her number and left the stage, Carolina began to kiss me again and to tell me of the pathos of Georgia's unrequited love, and we drank some more—we were so drunk, in fact, that when Eddie suggested that we go to meet Randy at the Twenty-one and take the two women with us, it seemed like a reasonable idea.

A short while later, Georgia showed up at our table, in a se-quined gown she had slapped on herself, and, sure enough, with mascara-teared eyes. She barely had time to throw down two doubles before the four of us left for the Twenty-one.

As we walked out (without paying) I asked Georgia about her next show. "Fuck that!" was all she said.

The Twenty-one was marked by a simple electric sign—21—on a small, dark street. The door had a glass peephole and it was necessary to be viewed before being let in. The door was opened by an aged Negro who moved so slowly I thought I could hear his joints creak.

"What's new, Lightning?" Eddie said to him. "You seen Randy?"

"Yes, sah, Mr. Eddie, he in the back with the boss."

"Thanks," Eddie said, and led us through the gambling tables up to the bar.

Behind the bar, a second-rate rock band played. Just playing for pay, a nine-to-five job, at night. But on a platform across the bar from us she was dancing. The platform reminded me of the one we had seen that afternoon—in the old slave market.

She was ample. Not hard like Carolina, or Lady Macbeth–sly like tall Georgia, but ample bodied in soft-firm flesh. She wore only a G-string, a tiny patch of velvet gold between full thighs which supported a torso that was stocky in an appealingly girlish way, and her skin was vividly filled with color as if her blood and tissue were trying to make contact with things outside of herself. She was snub-nosed and would be called strawberry blonde in that her hair picked up a pale rosé tint from the flushed tone of her skin.

And she could really dance. Not in the too-smooth style of ballet dancers trying pop, but in a frantic, jerky-beautiful way which fitted the funky atmosphere around her. Not a go-go girl (that species of human basketball invented by TV) but a bluesy dancer, a natural fool, acting out her belief in the possibility of perfection for those who ask for it. And the audience of sailors didn't understand what they were witnessing but were caught up by her enthusiasm—by the evidence of that risky flirtation with nothingness, sustained by innocence, which they could only interpret as an invitation to rape.

Our two strippers had withdrawn into a dark alcove leading to the ladies' room and Eddie said to me, "That's Billie. She's cute, isn't she?"

"She's beautiful."

"I dig that plump little ass."

And her generous breasts, pulled tight by their skin cover, and the curve of the line which channeled her chunky thighs down into her knees, and her ankles, and those last ingenuous remnants of a time when nudity was blessed—her bare feet.

"She says she's nineteen, but I'll bet she's younger. She's got *some* tits, though. You want to meet her, Jake? She's easy. We've all made it with her."

"Yes, I'd like that."

As she ended her dance (giving herself to it with an abandon that was pathetically lovely in view of the pedestrian musicians she had to carry), the sailors began to applaud and cheer wildly and one drunk navy captain reached over the bar and handed her a five-dollar bill, which she placed in the only pocket she had, between the soft patch of gold and her sweet cunt, and she smiled, not at the officer or at the audience—not *to* anyone, in fact—but from the gratitude she felt for the grace which allowed her to succeed once again in exhaustively filling the form of the dance which the second-rate music allotted to her.

She pulled a simple shift over her head and it seemed supported solely by her breasts, they were so firm and protruding. Eddie caught her eye and she climbed down and joined us.

"Billie, I've got someone I want you to meet. A friend of Randy's from the North, Jake Klinger. He's a poet."

"Oh, I'm pleased to meet you, Jake. I think I like poetry."

"Baby, you *are* poetry," Eddie said, pinching her ass.

She smiled at him, and I asked if I could buy her a drink.

"Oh, don't spend your money, Jake. I can get free drinks here. They try to get me to put the touch on sailors, but I guess I'm not very good at it. I'm a dancer, that's all."

"That's enough," I said, as the barmaid set a double gin in front of her.

"It's gin that'll make you sin," Eddie said, rising from his seat. "I'll leave you two for a while. I'm going into the back to check on Randy."

His mention of Randy reminded me of the two sweet things who had come in with us. I telescoped a glance at the alcove and saw them still huddled there, Georgia holding a handkerchief up to her face, probably on another crying jag. When I turned back to Billie, I realized that she was shorter than I had thought. And more fragile. Short, slightly plump girls always seem more vulnerable to me than tall wiry ones. Perhaps it's because they're softer—more malleable.

"I really liked your dance, Billie. Where'd you learn to dance like that? It was beautiful."

"Oh, I made it up, I guess. I just do what comes into my body. I let it dance for me. The people seem to like it. Do you think people will appreciate what you do if you're sincere?"

"Sometimes. But it takes more than sincerity, unfortunately."

I praised her again and I noticed that she averted her eyes; that was the secret of her charm, I thought. This lovely girl, whom everyone had made, and whose body was so lush and generous that she could be paid for wearing it without clothes, was shy. Or was she? (Was it merely the bennie, grass, and alcohol medium in which my sleepless mind had begun to float?)

"Do you know much about poetry?" I asked her.

"No, tell me about it."

I didn't imagine *that*. That quote from Walt Whitman, who,

when Thoreau asked him if he knew about Eastern philosophy, answered simply, "No, tell me about it." And so I told her about it.

In my voice, I could hear the intoxication talking. And her eyes kept sucking me into their sky-blue candor. We talked about her dancing. And about music. And about how we both loved the Beatles and the Stones, and I drank some more bourbon and dropped another bennie and went on rapping madly about Bach and Mozart, and about how in her dancing she was doing what she could to keep them alive and how whenever anyone performs with grace they are in fact within grace, for they are playing in the theater of God, and I told her some poetry which I had written in Philadelphia, and once she was so moved I saw a sunshower begin in her eyes and I reached toward her cheek and dried it with my handkerchief and smoothed back her hair and pulled her toward me and kissed her gently, and I could feel the soft of her cheek on my face, and I could feel her feeling the touch of my flesh to hers, and I could feel the outreaching life within us both.

And then the record scraped and everything around me became taut and crystal-cold, as Carolina's nails flew, scratching wildly across my lap and toward Billie's face on the floor where she had been thrown, but before I could get my fog-bound brain into contact with my arms, Randy had grabbed Carolina and pulled her violently back and several people had stepped between the two women as Randy twisted Carolina's arm in a hammerlock until she began to cry out. The band began the next set and Billie lifted herself off the floor and, looking up at me at an angle which showed shadows around her eyes which hadn't been penciled in, she downed her drink with a gulp and said, "Will you meet me at four when I'm through? I've never talked to a poet before," and I said, "Sure," and I kissed her cheek where it showed the mark of Carolina's slap, and she returned to the stand and removed her shift, to begin once again, her dance.

Randy released Carolina and she veered off toward the alcove to join her sister in sorrow, who, when she spotted Randy, collapsed onto the nearest chair in such a dramatic fashion that she seemed less a stripper than a drag-queen playing a stripper in an Italian opera.

A man in an undistinguished but expensive suit hustled toward us and said to Randy, "Look, either you get those two broads out of here or you got to leave. I'm not kidding, Randy, friends or no friends. They're nothing but trouble and I don't want them in here."

"Cool it, Carl," Randy said. "I'll handle it."

He walked to the table at which the two were now seated, signaled the waitress for fresh drinks, sat down with them, and began calmly talking to Georgia while Carolina, like a maiden aunt chaperone, listened carefully to every word and frequently nodded approvingly. Soon Randy had put his arm around Georgia's shoulder, and I could see her wipe her eyes and look deeply into his as he spoke, and then he smoothed her hair and kissed her cheek and said something which made both women chuckle and brighten. They went to the ladies' room to freshen up their faces, and when the women returned the three of them came up to me at the bar.

"Jake," Randy said, "Georgia and I are real tight again and the four of us are going to paint the town to celebrate."

"I can't, Randy, I . . ."

He grabbed my arm, pulled me toward him, and hissed, "Ixnay," into my ear. I was his guest. There was nothing I could do but follow as both women raised themselves to their full stature (each at least four inches taller than Randy in their high heels), straightened their dresses, took one of Randy's arms apiece, and paraded toward the door with him between them.

Lightning opened the door and when I reached it I saw Randy lift his arms off their shoulders and quickly grab a clump of hair in each hand which he used as a handle to slam their heads together with a muffled thud. Then, while they were still dazed, he grabbed each one by an upper arm and, like a pitcher simultaneously snapping off curve balls from both sides at once, he flung them forward and they tumbled off the curb in a tangle of arms, legs, heels, and gowns. Before they could figure out what had happened, he turned with businesslike abruptness back to the club, saying to the incredulous doorman, "Lightning, call a cab for our ladies." As he handed Lightning a five-dollar bill, he added, with an aristocratic detachment, "And Lightning, take care to lock the door. I believe that one of the ladies may be armed."

Randy walked up to the bar. "Let's have a double Jack Daniels here, Marie. I believe I need a drink." And he broke into a big smile.

We left the Twenty-one and spent some time on the outskirts of town, stopping at several places that Randy was thinking of

buying when he had enough cash. At a club called the Roost he
and Eddie got into a card game with some people who agreed to
continue the game at Eddie's apartment. On the way over, we
stopped to pick up Billie and they dropped the two of us off at the
Pickens' Arms.

When we got up to Randy's apartment, I was so drunk and
stoned that I couldn't even get the key in the lock. Billie finally had
to do it for me. We went directly into the bedroom and, without
saying a word, I began to remove her clothes. I remember that as
her face reappeared from a sweater which I was lifting over her
outstretched arms, she looked at me and said, "I hope you won't
think badly of me because of this."

"I won't," I said, reaching awkwardly around her to unhook her
bra and, in my sodden clumsiness, failing, until she reached back
and released it herself, exposing her large breasts, which were full
and firm and resilient when kissed.

We lay in the bed together and I kissed the mound of her
abdomen, the round swell below her navel, and her breasts and
thighs, and we twined around each other, wrapping ourselves in
a blanket of each other's arms and thighs, and we rubbed against
each other and caressed our bodies together and moved and kissed
and rolled in the bed. And I kept moving, for each time I stopped
the room began to spin, but I was sober enough to sadly realize it
wasn't working because, although I was larger than when I started,
I wasn't really erect and even when I rolled Billie over and
climbed upon her ass and rubbed myself between the soft rounds
of her rump while knotting my fingers into hers, with arms outstretched on both sides across the bed like wings, and kissed her
neck and moved upon her and into her, I knew I couldn't make
it, for in all my drunkenness I could not forget that my hair was
short because I was in the army, and I had lied to Billie by not
telling her this, and that I was married, and I had lied to Billie by
not telling her this, and that I wasn't a poet at all, and that she
wasn't in bed with me but with some glamorous, fictional character that I had created out of my wasted imagination, and I felt that
my fucking was a lie and that my being in South Carolina was a
lie and that my whole goddamn life was a tissue of thin fiction
which I could too easily see through. And I thought to myself, what
am I doing here in this crazy gangster movie world where people
have names like Toledo Jack and Fast Eddie, and then I thought
what am I doing anywhere, with my wild undisciplined imagina-

tion that is turning Billie into a kind-hearted whore from a nine-teenth-century novel, and I thought maybe that's the sad truth—maybe I can't make it in this world because I'm lost in the wrong century and maybe that's where I belong, in a nineteenth-century novel, and maybe I'm a fictional character myself, the product of the fevered imagination of some frustrated author who can't fit into the modern world and who belongs in a nineteenth-century novel himself.

And if this was true, I felt sorry for both of us, for we were both lost—both cowards and fearfully sick sinners.

I rolled Billie over and put myself into her from the front and struggled to move but it was no use; like the time I had tried to write in my office and finally had been forced to turn to my story for *Sado-Mask,* I could not rise to fill the required form.

Finally Billie spoke. She was tired and it was no use and maybe we should stop and she was sorry, and I said no it wasn't you, you were fine, it must have been the booze, and she said it was no-body's fault, and I said it was nobody's fault and that I was sorry and that she should go to sleep and she did.

The ceiling began to brighten as I lay on my back. I rolled over and switched on the radio which was set on a table near the bed. It was tuned to a local black station and it softly sounded the blues. A simple cone of paper, moving the unseen air across to my ear, bearing the music of the always lost and rarely found. It was a solo piano and I immediately recognized the unmistakable style, the audacious toying with time, accen-tuated lags behind the beat followed by light-legged runs ahead of it again, and I thought of Eddie and Randy and every other guy in Charleston who had made it with Billie, and what did that make me, and in how many ways had I failed Billie, and failed my friends, and failed myself, and even failed my goddamn author (if there was such a sorry person as he), and what did I breathe if not failure? And the ceiling, which was light now, began to move, and to keep myself together I forced these thoughts out of my poor head and listened to the energy of the piano singing out to me across the dawn electronic sky, and I listened to the soft beat of Billie's breath, and I listened to the rhythm of my own familiar sobs, and it was as if I was in the cone of the radio and every tear seemed to drop upon the piano and strike a key, and I fell asleep listening to the music, which, in spite of everything, had never failed me.

The next thing I remember was hearing a voice and noticing the direct sunlight falling into the room. Randy was in the bedroom doorway and I could see Eddie on the couch behind him.

"We've got to get going or you'll miss the damn plane," Randy said. Then, nodding toward Billie who was just beginning to stir beside me, he said, "Need a towel?"

"No thanks," I said.

Randy looked puzzled for a second and turned away saying, "I'll make some instant coffee."

He left the door open and Eddie began to tell us about the card game which had just ended. I got out of bed, gathered up our clothes which were strewn about both rooms, separated Billie's and brought them in to her, and she got out of bed, and we stood there for a second, naked in front of Eddie who continued his story, and then, without saying a word, Billie put her arm around my neck and pulled me to her and kissed me deep and long until Randy yelled, "Soup's on!" and we put on our clothes, and when I was fully dressed Billy turned her back to me and let me clip on her bra.

Billie came with us to the airport, sitting snuggled against me in the back of Randy's big Buick. When we arrived we all got out of the car and Randy removed the suitcase full of grass from the trunk. He handed it to me and said, "The offer still holds. You don't have to go back."

"I think I do, Randy. But thanks anyway. I won't forget how nice you've been."

"Suit yourself," he shrugged. "It's your choice."

As I picked up the suitcase, Billie looked up at me and she said, "It's been so nice, Jake . . . so nice," and I turned toward the terminal and said, "Well, see you all," and she said, "Will you, Jake? Will you send me letters and poems? Will I ever see you again?"

"Yes," I said, and I kissed her forehead as she stood motionless on the sidewalk, and I turned guiltily away. I shook hands with Eddie and Randy, and Randy said with a sincerity which, in all the years I had known him, he had reserved solely for me, "There's a vacant life here, Jake, and you're always welcome to fill it."

"Thanks, Randy. Take care of Billie."

And I walked into that series of doorways and buildings and vehicles which began in Carolina and ended in the army.

When I arrived back in Boston, Edith and Warren were at the airport to meet me. I saw Warren's hair through the terminal window before I went inside and I recognized Edith's walk as they came over to greet me—there was a brusqueness about it, as well as a briskness, a kind of plodding purposefulness.

"Jake!" Warren said. "You look awful."

"I haven't slept more than a few hours since I left."

"Wow, you look it. Your eyes are wild."

"That's the bennies. I dropped another one on the plane with some bourbon. I couldn't sleep, anyway."

He continued to stare into my face as Edith and I exchanged greetings. "Did you get the grass?" she asked.

I nodded yes. We went to pick up the suitcase and when we got it back to the car Warren began to sniff it and smile, although we all knew he couldn't smell a goddamn thing.

"It's there, all right," I said, as I took the car keys from Edith and unlocked the door. "Kilos on top of kilos."

He hugged the suitcase to his chest and took it into the back seat with him. I got in behind the wheel and, as Edith sat down next to me, I wondered how in hell I could tell her about what had happened.

But she began to talk immediately. Rodger had worked out a new system that would eventually use a single computer complex, not merely to keep the records for an entire school, but to grade all the exams as well. The exams would be made up by the computer from randomly selected questions programmed into the computer's memory in advance by the people at Telecation. Wasn't it wonderful that this would increase objectivity in grading and obviate the effects of the inadequate testing programs taught at the teachers' colleges by eliminating the subjective pupil evaluation and eventually, when the system was in widespread use, Objective Achievement Testings (OATs) would lead to accurate college admissions policies and eliminate the inefficiency of the present system which supported the archaic social structure inherited from an unconsciously elitist system of social organization, etc. She talked all the way to Concord and beyond.

So she solved my problem for me. Because she was unable to

imagine that anything more important could have happened to me in my hundreds of miles of drunken traveling than had happened to her in a couple days at Telecation. I was so tired, so drunk and wrecked, that keeping the car on the road and humming some Desmond solos in my bleary head seemed enough for me to do. When Warren handed me a joint, I took a drag. I knew it would make no difference. I was already wherever I was going to be this time around. I couldn't go any further.

It was not until we were almost back at the base that Edith was reminded of some news that was actually relevant to me. "Oh, yes, Jake, Len's become further insane. He's had some crazy dreams and I believe he's going to do something drastic at the concert tonight. Don't get involved, Jacob. I think he's really flipped this time. Don't go to that concert tonight."

"Is it tonight? When is it?"

"It's at eleven. And, oh yes, I forgot to tell you, Mary and Gloria and the other women who were arrested with me at the shit-in are forming a permanent protest group. We've calling ourselves the FART CREW."

"The FART CREW?"

"Yes, it's a rough acronym for Female Artists for Civil Rights for Women."

As we passed through the gate to the base (it had been rebuilt since it was burned down in the Eskimo-power demonstration on Christmas Day) the MP noticed the officer's bumper sticker and saluted the car. Warren, who was wrecked in the back seat, returned his salute but he didn't seem to notice. When we arrived at our house, Len was waiting outside for us, pacing up and back in front of his door.

"Len!" I shouted to him from our driveway. "What's up?"

Mysteriously, he turned without speaking and signaled for me to follow. I walked into his living room but only Jeannie was there, drinking something on the rocks. Len called to me from the bathroom, "I'll be out in a minute, I'm taking a piss."

From the second bedroom of the house, I could hear guitar music. "What's that?" I said.

"That's Little Jo," Jeannie beamed. "He's taking lessons again. On Tommy Creetner's guitar. The kids in the Boston Braves got him a teacher."

"That's great."

"He's really gotten into it again in the last few days. We can't get the guitar away from him. I think the fact that it belonged to Tommy has him spooked. He sits with it hour after hour."

"Who's teaching him?"

"A friend of David's. He's beautiful—plays jazz, rock, you name it. He says Little Jo has a great ear."

"Tonight's the night." It was Len. He looked not only distraught but distracted, and it was fearsome to contemplate what might be on his mind, he looked so strange.

"Len, you're not going through with this," Jeannie said.

"You damn well better believe it," Len said. "I've had the vision." He turned to me. "I fasted and stayed awake the whole time you were gone, Jake. And early this morning, as I sat out on the lawn and watched the sunrise, it came to me."

"What the fuck are you talking about?" I said.

He spoke in a monotone, directly into my face. "I saw a great white serpent squeezing the life out of my people. And then I saw a great red serpent coming from the north, and the two serpents began to fight, and the battle was terrible in its fury, neither could win, but in the chaos my people were able to sneak away to the hills. Then, from out of the south, a black serpent appeared, and he entered the battle and vanquished the other two war-weary serpents. Then a terrifying bright light appeared, and the black serpent grew frightened and withdrew back toward the south, and the red serpent went back to the north, and the white serpent split in two, with the larger part disappearing into the sea while the smaller part joined my people and lived in peace."

"What was the light?" I asked.

"Revolution!"

"That's not true!" Jeannie snapped. She leaped up off the sofa and began to plead with me, "Jake, stop him. That's not his vision. That's the story of Deganawidah. It's an old legend of our people. It's been passed down through the longhouse for centuries."

"I saw it!" Len shouted.

"It's just an old legend, Jake. Don't listen to him." She began to weep and she came up to me, pulling on my sleeve to turn me away from Len. I looked down into her eyes. The bright pupils softened by tears—like wet almonds. "It's not true, Jake," she cried. "You can stop him."

"Me?"

"He wants you, too. Don't join him. He needs you, Jake. He's counting on you."

"On *me?*"

"There's nothing he can do to stop me," Len snapped.

"What about the rest of the legend?" Jeannie shouted at him. "What about the young seer who shows up to guide his people? He's a boy, Len. Not you! A boy!"

She turned to me. "Jake . . ."

"This is a family matter," I said. "I don't want to get involved in this mad business of tribal legends and visions."

"We have two months to go, Len," Jeannie said. "Just two more. . . ."

"Everyone's involved," Len said. "They've arrested Lorraine."

"Oh . . . I didn't know. . . ." Jeannie stammered, and she sat back down.

"I've got an Onandaga corporal working with the MPs," Len said. "He called me up about an hour ago. She's in the stockade. ▮▮▮▮▮ her with David, spying on the secret immigrant ▮▮ ▮▮ the hospital from the outside. He got away. But in her case, it'll be all over. They'll throw the book at her and Cal will do the pitching."

"What can we do?" Jeannie said softly.

"*We* can't do anything," Len said, and I had to force myself to look toward him, for I knew he would be looking at me. "*He* can," he said.

"Jake?" she said.

"That's right, Jake."

"What can *I* do?"

"Give her an Article 15."

"*What?* What are you saying?"

"Give her company punishment. You know you can do it. Hit her with an Article 15 and they'll release her, if you do it now. They won't court-martial her after company punishment's been administered. It's double jeopardy. They won't try her for the same crime twice."

"Is that right, Jake?" Jeannie asked.

"Yes, I'm afraid so. But where does that leave me?"

"Don't worry about the future," Len said. "There isn't going to be any. We've reached a break in history."

He poured us each a tall glass of Dad. "Jeannie, you take the car and get it filled with gas."

She got up out of her chair, slowly, and left without saying another word, stopping only to take a last long swallow of her drink.

"Look, Jake," Len said, "remember what Frank Benuto was telling us about the mountain gorilla? That one of the signs that it's headed for extinction is that it fouls its own nest? Well, look at America's nest, Jake. Look at Lake Erie. Look at the rivers and the air and the highways lined with auto graveyards. Look at what they've done to my people. You can't pay for a crime like that so easily, Jake. That's not death, that's genocide —social murder. And there's only one way to pay for that—social suicide. And that, my friend, is what we're presently witnessing all around us."

"No. . . ."

"Yes, Jacob."

"I don't believe this. I can't."

"Look around you, Jacob."

"I won't. . . ."

"Open your eyes."

"Then Warren is right. . . . Drift with the stream. Give in to chaos."

"No! He's not!" Len shouted, grabbing my collar. "No, he's not right, Jake. The answer is to move. To get the momentum to move over the chaos."

"Leave me alone, Len. . . . I feel like my world is falling apart. I'm worse than when I left. . . . We're locked in a madhouse. And there's nothing outside . . . because the world is becoming America."

"That's right."

"Then what can we do?"

"Tear the fuckin place down, Jake. Do to them what they did to my people. Tear their fuckin sick civilization apart."

"No. . . ."

"We're brothers, Jacob. I know it."

"We don't have any power, Len. We can't do anything. It's hopeless. Warren's right. I don't have the strength to fight. I can't get a foothold on reality. That's what I've been trying to tell everybody. I'm not a fighter. I'm nonviolent. That's why I get along with Warren. We've been together for years. I'm not a fighter, Len."

"You played football in college."

"You too! You've been through my personnel file, too. Who hasn't? Everyone knows more about me than I do. Everyone was 'fated' to meet me. How did I get into this mess? Where did it begin?"

"Well you did play . . ."

"I played quarterback, Len. I was able to use my head. I passed. I hardly ever ran. I like violence, Len. I like it when violent people do it to each other. It's justice. But I can't participate anymore, because I can't believe anything—football, war, *anything*—is real enough to be worth it."

I took another swallow of Dad. "Don't you see, Len? If I thought there was a chance—if I was sure the bag was real, and I felt there was a chance, I would try to break out of it. But I'm not sure there is any reality outside of myself. I think my problems are *mine*. In *me*. And I'm scared. And I don't want to join those who are sure that all their problems are external. I don't see how you can win."

"You won't, until you get outside. Until you turn the corner. Remember what I told you that day in the backyard? They've given us the ball, now. They've invented the B.C. They're so hipped on winning that they needed an enemy and now they've created one to beat. But we've got the ball, Jake. We're moving to the outside. We can't run against their strength so we've got to go outside. Beyond their definitions. Beyond what they can conceptualize as possible, much less as feasible. We're young, we're adaptable, and we're going to turn their corner."

"But who can believe in directions anymore . . . Why, *you* believe in winning, too. *You're* hypnotized, too. You still believe in winning and losing. That it's still possible. But that's part of *their* game. It's *all* a game. Go on, deny it—you want to beat them for what they did to your people. You want a bloodbath. Revenge. It's all part of the same game. I'm trapped in games. Surrounded by psychopaths. What's happening to me?"

"You'll have to decide, Jake."

"You're a psychologist—analyze *yourself!* You know it's just part of the same action-reaction pattern that's been going on for thousands of years. You're all hypnotized!"

"You'll have to decide for yourself. But remember one thing, Jake. You're on the field now. Forever. One way or another, you *will* have to decide."

"I'll be getting out in a year from June."

"There is no out. . . . *Out* is a vestige of a bigger world."

"But you don't have anything going for you, Len. No programs, no plans, no visible following besides a few disgruntled heads among the kids on the base. It's like playing against a pro team without even a game plan. And worse, without even knowing if there's still a goal line."

"You're right. I don't. But I'm not going to sit on my ass any longer. I can't bear what's happening around us. I can't stand it anymore. So I'm going to move, Jake, to the outside. Only then will we know if I've been right or wrong."

"And you don't care if you kill every kid on the base in the process. This isn't revolution—this is a masochistic farce. And I can't play."

"It's up to you, Jake."

"Why didn't you act earlier?"

"I let them do it for me. I wasn't ready yet."

"I can't do it, Len."

"We want you. I've got the kids and there are Indians all over the country. Thousands of them. Just waiting for revenge. They'll join us, as soon as we move. They're waiting for a leader. The time is ripe, Jake. My people need me."

"This is madness, Len. There aren't thousands of Indians. . . ."

"There are! I know my people."

"I can't. I won't. My whole world is spinning. . . . Leave me alone. . . ."

"You were sent, Jake. I know it. Sent here, from all the millions, to live in my house. One of the few white men who aren't hypnotized."

"No, Len. I don't even know what you've got planned, but count me out. I'm not well. It would be like sawing off the last branch I can sit on. We'd be promoting the fall into chaos."

"Maybe. But there is no solid ground. Einstein told us that. America is beginning to sense what's happening. They're beginning to sense that this country was built by hypnotized, greedy zombies, and that they've lost their children, and that there'll be no one to pray for them when they're dead, and even if there were it wouldn't matter because they've sold their souls for washing machines, just like their grandparents sold theirs for washboards and their great-grandparents for the furs and land that led them to kill my people.

"They stole Mother Earth, and divided her up, and ploughed her, and now they're so fucked up all the Viennese psychiatry in the world can't help them. And they can't face this, and they're going to try to kill themselves and take us all with them so there'll be no one left to remember their crimes after they're gone. Look, Jake, you'll have to decide, but at least get Lorraine out. That's the least you can do."

"O.K. . . . I can't say no to that. Besides, I'm so damned tired and wrecked, I don't give a shit what happens to me anyhow. I just want to get some sleep."

I moved over to the phone and called the stockade. The night sergeant was already on duty. It was Sergeant Adams, the MP sergeant who had taken us to our quarters when we first arrived on the base. I identified myself and told him that I had just been advised of Private Washington's heinous offense. He said that they'd been waiting for me to return to file formal charges and the court-martial request. I told him that I was going up to my office at that moment and he agreed that under the circumstances it would be best to bring Private Washington there at once so I could question her about the crime and establish the necessity for pressing court-martial charges against her. I quickly placed a call to my own office, caught Sergeant O'Mara as he was leaving for the day, and told him to wait there for me.

I walked back to Len, swallowed another drink of the Dad, and said, "It's been quite a couple days. I haven't slept more than an hour or two, myself."

"Did you get the grass?"

"It's next door, if Warren hasn't smoked it all, by now. . . . Well, I'd better get going if I'm going to get up to the office."

I walked into our house, past Edith and into the bedroom. She sensed something was wrong and came in after me as I began to change into my dark blue suit with the bars on the shoulders.

"Jake, what are you doing?"

"Lorraine's been arrested."

"You're kidding!"

"No, I'm not."

She hesitated for a minute, just standing there, watching me dress, and then she said, "But what are *you* doing?"

"I think I can get her out."

"Jake! That's not you. That's Len talking. What crazy idea has he put into your head?"

"I have to go."

As I brushed by her, she clutched at my suit. "Jake! He's nuts. Insane. He's your friend, but he's flipped out. He needs help. Face it, Jake."

"I have to go, Edith."

"He'll bring you down with him. He's no Indian. He'll destroy everything that you and I . . . and the kids are trying to build. He's a monomaniac who's adopted a cause that isn't even his, so that he can have an excuse to destroy."

"I have to get Lorraine out of there. I'll talk to you when I come back."

As I walked past her, she handed me a white envelope. "Walter left this for you. It's money for your stories in *Sado-Mask*."

"I don't have time now," I said, putting the envelope in my pocket. As I left the house, Edith called after me, "Don't do anything you'll regret later."

Sergeant O'Mara was alone in my office when I arrived. Before I could even sit down the MPs arrived with Lorraine. Sergeant Adams preceded her into the office, and she was flanked on either side by two MPs armed with sawed-off shotguns.

The sergeant took off her handcuffs at my command. I informed Lorraine of the offense she was charged with and of her rights under the Code of Military Justice and then I said, "These are serious crimes, Private Washington, but in view of the fact that you are a first offender, and of sound character and mind and body (I looked at the contours of her breasts pushing against her blouse —she reminded me of Billie), I am prepared to offer you company punishment as an alternative to court-martial."

"Sir!" Both sergeants shouted at once.

"Sergeants!" I admonished.

"But sir," Sergeant Adams said, "have you any idea of the seriousness of this offense?"

"Yes, sergeant," I answered, at which Sergeant O'Mara leaped up and blurted, "Sir! It'll be your ass!" and then, realizing what he had said, he blushed and said, "Begging the prisoner's pardon, ma'm," to Lorraine, who stood dumb in wonder at it all. Both sergeants began to jabber at once, so I banged the book containing the Code of Military Justice down on the desk and shouted, "Silence, men! This is a court of law! Cease and desist!"

And as soon as they had ceased and desisted, I offered Lorraine the alternatives of company punishment, administered by myself, or the risk of a court-martial. She was so bewildered, she didn't know what to say, so she answered, "Whatever the lieutenant suggests," and the sergeants leaped at me again, but I silenced them and said, "I'm not allowed to tell you my sentence beforehand, but I'd suggest taking the company punishment."

"Then that's fine with me, sir," she said.

"Good. Private Washington, how much money do you have with you?"

"None, sir."

"You can dock her pay, sir," O'Mara volunteered.

"No, I have a better idea." I reached into my jacket pocket and pulled out the white envelope which Edith had given me as I left the house. There was two hundred dollars in twenty-dollar bills. I handed Lorraine the money.

"Private Washington," I said, "you are fined two hundred dollars. You have the right to appeal. Do you waive this right?"

"Yes, sir."

"Good. Case closed. Give the money to Sergeant O'Mara to hold in the name of the U.S. Government. They're the ones who really earned it anyhow."

I turned to Sergeant Adams. "Well, sergeant, I guess that's that. You and your boys can go now. The case is closed. Private Washington has paid her debt to society and is free to begin a new life of honest virtue."

"This is highly irregular, sir," he said. "Highly irregular. There'll be repercussions." But he turned and walked out of the office with his two flunkies, shaking his head and muttering to himself as he left.

"You started at the bottom in this man's army, didn't you, O'Mara?" I said.

"Yes, sir. E-2 company clerk."

"Good, I thought so. Then you can type up the Article 15 forms while we wait. I want to sign them and close this matter tonight."

"I hope the lieutenant knows what he's doing," he said.

"I hope so, too, sergeant," I said.

At that point I realized how fast I had been talking and how excited, even hysterical, I'd become. The days of smoking and bennies and lack of sleep were collecting their fee. I needed a drink. Sergeant O'Mara began to type the forms. "Wait here, Lorraine," I said, "I'll be right back."

I decided to take a chance. Down the hallway I hurried, over to the NCO barracks and into Sergeant Mooney's room, flinging the door open in front of me.

"O.K., nobody move. This is a raid," I yelled. Mooney looked at me as if I were an abysmal apparition, but I had guessed right. He was in long-johns, sitting sloped on his bed, watching TV over his enormous gut. And there, on the windowsill near his head, was a fifth of cheap bourbon, half-full.

I began to shout about drinking in the barracks (although I didn't know whether it was illegal or not) and I guess I scared the shit out of poor Mooney because he began to stammer and apologize, "Begging the lieutenant's pardon, sir," and so forth.

"Well, O.K., Mooney," I said. "You've been a pretty good supply sergeant. I'll overlook it this time."

"Thank you, sir. Thanking the lieutenant's pardon. . . ."

"Of course, I'll have to confiscate the bottle."

"Oh, yes, sir," he said, handing the bottle to me. And as I left he said, "Thank you again, sir. I won't forget the lieutenant's kindness in this matter."

"That's quite all right, Mooney."

I took a long pull at the bottle and returned to the office. When O'Mara saw me carrying the bottle, he smiled the smile of a man who has thrown up his hands and given in to the fates. "God help us," he said.

"Don't worry, O'Mara," I said, "the CO won't catch us, because I *am* the fuckin CO around here." Then I quickly turned toward Lorraine, and said, "Oh, begging the private's pardon for my abusive language," and we both cracked up. And I handed her the bottle and as she took a long swig I could see the release come into her face—the breaking of hours of fatigue and tension—and when she finished, she said, "That's fuckin A-O.K., lieutenant, but don't let it happen again," and we both exploded into laughter as Sergeant O'Mara forced himself to fix his attention upon his typewriter, with an effort of will which only a man of faith who has entered a valley beyond human understanding can attain.

After O'Mara had finished the forms and found that the roof was still in place and that he wasn't struck dead by lightning, he seemed to relax, and he even took a nip from the bottle himself and smiled once or twice. I was certain that he drew upon that saving grace which is possessed by writers and bullshitters, the ability to turn any disaster into a scenario for a future story which gives one the will to hang on, just so he can tell it to others when it's over.

After he left for home I turned to Lorraine and said, "Well, now what?"

"I don't know about you, Jake, but I'm going over to David's to get ready to go to the concert tonight."

"You're going?"

"Sure."

"And Thoreau?"

"It's like you said, there is no Walden Pond anymore."

"Well, we'd better get going." She walked with me to the parking lot. "Want me to drop you off at the cabin?"

"No, I'll walk. It may be my last chance to spend a peaceful hour or two."

"Good luck, Lorraine."

"You too, Jake," and we moved toward each other and pulled each other into ourselves and kissed, and as I held Lorraine against me with her head on my shoulder and I looked above it at the clear evening sky, I realized how much she meant to me, how much it meant to have someone else who saw what was making you sick, and she looked up at me and I kissed her again, and I hated to let her go for, in a sense, I was already inside of her, my books in her brain, my ideas in her head, and, after all those hours of soul-searching talks we had had at the hospital, my vision in her eyes.

When we finally separated she said, "I'll never forget you, Jake," and as I drove home alone, I thought of how deep our friendship had grown, and I thought about David, and about all the kids in the scouts with whom we'd had such free, such decent times. And a line by Antoine de Saint Exupéry (who had been killed during World War II) kept popping up into my head like a gyroscope you can't knock down: "You are always responsible for that which you have tamed." And I thought to myself, "That's very true. But what is our responsibility to those whom we have helped to free?"

And I realized that I didn't even know what Len had in mind for that evening, and that the reason for my ignorance was that I had purposely avoiding asking about it, because I didn't want to know.

When I walked into our house, swinging Mooney's bottle by the neck, Edith's eyes widened. "Jake! You look like a walking horror."

I turned to a mirror and saw what she meant. My skin seemed pasty, like unbaked dough, and what little hair I had was standing up on my head as if I'd been electrically shocked.

"Jacob, you've done something crazy. I can tell."

"It's O.K. It's nothing."

"It's not O.K. You look half-mad, Len next door *is* mad, Jeannie's crying, Warren's wrecked. . . ." She tore at her hair in exasperation, "And it's going to get worse, I know it."

She walked up to me and looked directly into my eyes. "Jacob, don't go." She joined her arms around my neck. "Please don't go."

The telephone rang. Edith picked it up.

"Jacob, it's your Uncle Bernie."

"This is incredible!" I screamed. Bernie was my mother's brother, a used-car salesman who drank a lot and had a joke for every occasion.

"Hello."

"Hello, Jake?" he said.

"Hello, Uncle Bernie. Look, it's too late. Tell my mother I can't talk now."

"Jake, wait a minute. What's going on? Your mother's not here. She told me that your wife told her you're having some problems."

I didn't answer.

"Look, Jake, that's the way things always are. It's not only now. I remember in World War II, when they started taking fathers. It was really terrible. I had to send mine."

And I couldn't help but laugh. Who provides these jokes in times of agony and bitter lament? And why? To cheer us through? To give us the little detachment we need? Or to further humiliate us by topping our tombs with cap and bells.

"You see, Jake, you're laughing. If you can still laugh you're O.K. Am I right?"

"I don't know, Bernie. I think I'm too tired to ever laugh again."

"You just stick it out, Jake. You're a bright boy. You've got a future ahead of you. And if you still want to write when you get out, well, you just go ahead and write."

"I don't know. . . ."

"Jake, listen to me. Just do what they tell you, and before you know it, it'll be behind you, like a bad dream."

"I've got to get off now, Uncle Bernie. Thanks for calling."

"O.K., Jake, but promise me one thing, you won't do anything foolish, will you? You're a married man now, Jake. You've got responsibilities. You've got to think of more than yourself."

"I know Uncle Bernie. So long."

I hung up the phone and Warren came into the room, carrying the suitcase of grass. "Wow, Jake," he said, "what great dope! This stuff is gold, man. Gold!"

I took the suitcase from him. "I'd better bring this in to Len."

"Jake, no!" Edith cried, and as she grabbed for my sleeve, I pulled my arm out of her reach and carried the suitcase out the door, saying, "I can take care of myself, Edith."

Len was in front of his house, loading cartons of food and containers of water into his car. In the doorway of his house stood Jeannie, watching him, looking deflated and forlorn and yet as winsome as ever under the weight of her woe.

"Len," I said, "I don't know what's on your mind, but you've got to stop."

"I can't. It's too late. I've had the vision and the plans are all set."

"What plans? What's going on?"

"Oh, we're going to have a little tea party," he said.

"What are you talking about?"

"Tonight, after the concert, we make our move. The end run I was telling you about."

"Len, what *are* you saying?"

"It's tonight. The word is out. They're going to raid the concert right after Madame Braun finishes playing. We're all in the longhouse and they move in during the confusion when everybody's applauding."

"How do you know?"

"I've got a private, Big Bear, a Seneca, down at base headquarters. He read the secret message from Creetner to the general. There's no turning back now."

"Don't go, Len. Just stop. That's all. Just don't go."

"We have to. They'll still bust Madame Braun."

"But . . ."

"There are no more buts, Jake. Everything is set."

"But what are *you* going to do? What about weapons?"

"We have bows and arrows. And spears. Tomahawks . . ."

"Are you *crazy*?"

"There won't be a big force against us. We've got to fight him with our weapons, not his. There are Indians all over, just waiting for someone to strike the first blow."

"But you'll be sitting ducks."

"No we won't. They've got the firepower but they're trapped by their own narrow conception of possibilities. We'll stun them with speed and the grotesque."

"The *grotesque*?"

"During the performance we sneak out of the longhouse through the back door. We move down the bank to the river's edge, split into two war parties, move in both directions along the river, and circle back around behind them while they're waiting on the outside of the longhouse for the concert to end. On our way back, we'll have enough time to stop in the woods, pick up the weapons we've hidden there, and get into costume."

"*Into costume?*"

"Right. We can't hit their line so we go around it, out of bounds, beyond their conceptions. That's the beauty of it, don't you see? It'll give us the few seconds of stunned surprise that we need. They won't know what the fuck hit them. Standing there for an hour in the chilly moonlight, alone with their thoughts, and then, just as they're about to bust the place, being charged by a band of hooting, wild Indians, in full regalia and war paint. They won't be able to believe their eyes. They'll be paralyzed, Jake, shocked into inactivity by visions of the ghost buried deepest in the American psyche." His eyes angled off my shoulder and the moon picked up their gleam. "It'll be justice. We'll hit quick, and run. And when the news gets out, thousands of rage-throttled Indians all over the country will join us."

"Us?"

"You and me, Jake. And David and Walter and all the kids. . . ."

"Oh, no. Not *me*. Count me out."

"You're in, Jake. I saw you there in the vision. You're the leader of the part of the white serpent that breaks off and joins the red men. We're counting on you."

"I'm sorry," I said, and I stood there for a while, saying nothing, just watching Len as he packed the car. Then, as I turned, and walked unsteadily toward my house, I heard the sound of softly amplified guitar notes floating on the cool evening air, and I stopped dead.

I turned back to Len, who was putting the suitcase of grass into the car, and I said, "Len?"

"Yes."

"What's the car for? Why are you packing the car?"

"It's for Jeannie. She's going to wait for us with the supplies at the old North Bridge in Concord, where we're going to regroup after the attack."

"Oh," I said, nonchalantly, hoping against what I knew, afraid to say the next words that I knew I had to say. "Oh, Jeannie and Little Jo will wait for you at . . ."

"That's not what I said, Jake."

"You can't be serious!"

"He has a right to be in on it, just like everyone else. We need every man we can get."

"*Man*, Len. *Man!* Little Jo has a right to grow up, too. You can't do this."

"I can't spare anyone," he said. And then, as if acting in a play that I had previously memorized, I thought I heard his next word before he uttered it: "Unless . . ."

"I can't Len. I can't do it."

"Suit yourself. You have to decide. It's either you or the boy."

"You son of a bitch!" I cried, grabbing his collar and pulling him toward me, but he remained impassive.

"You'll have to decide. It's up to you," was all he said.

"But what about my writing?" I said. "I could write about all this."

"There'll be time for that later, but not now."

"There's never time for art in a revolution."

"That's not true, Jake. But how can you stand it? You see what they're doing here. How can you bear it any longer?"

"I can't. That's why I want to write about it."

"Well, I can't bear it either!" he shouted at me. "That's why we have to do something about it. *Now!* Before they destroy any more of us. Who do you think we're going to be listening to out on that field tonight while we get ready to strike the first blow for our freedom? Bach, goddamn it! Johann Sebastian Bach. And who do you think we're going to try to rescue in there? Not some half-assed writer who daydreams about finishing a book some day, but one of the world's greatest artists, a woman who's devoted her life to art and to keeping up the spirit of oppressed peoples all over the world."

After this outburst, he stopped, and the silence seemed deeper than ever before. Only the sound of the guitar punctuated the approaching night.

"O.K.," I said. "You win. It's a deal. One veteran righthander for one rookie."

"I knew you'd help us, Jake. We have to do *something.*"

"Little Jo goes with Jeannie?"

"You have my word."

"O.K., Len," I said, with weary resignation. "I'll be at the long-house at eleven. I'll do whatever you say."

"Good," he said. And as I walked away, he called after me, "I didn't mean that about your writing, Jake."

"I know," I said, without enthusiasm, as I walked into the house.

Warren and Edith were waiting for me, facing the door when I opened it. They stood there, shoulder to shoulder, as if their toes were touching a line on the floor and they were presenting themselves for an inspection in grief. And they leaned forward, as if they were restrained by some invisible physical object set down in front of them.

I stopped and looked at them, snapping a picture which I would keep in my mind. Earnest, dumpy Edith, who had so many plans and meant well and was always crying and had plodded off each morning to support us for so many months in Philadelphia, while I read and wrote poems and wandered about the streets with Warren. And skinny, bedraggled, Warren, looking more like a perplexed spaniel than a wise owl at this point. We'd been through a lot in our years together. We'd fought and laughed and argued and cried, but we were a family, we three. We'd never betrayed each other.

"Jacob, why. . . ." Edith said, beginning to weep again. And she looked so helpless when she cried, perhaps because she seemed so far from her normal efficient self. . . . "Jacob, don't go. Please don't. Why must you do this? You don't belong with them. Jacob, stay here. We'll get out in time, and you can stay home with Warren and. . . . Jacob, why? Why must you go?"

"I don't want to, but I can't *not* go."

"Oh, Jacob. . . . We need you."

"I ran and ran, but it seems that history has finally caught up with me."

And as I looked at her, she seemed like a once-proud snowman, wilted by the late winter sun. I walked up to her and kissed the tears off her eyes and then I stepped back and firmly shook her hand and turned to Warren and moved toward him and pulled him toward me, and I held him tightly against me, and then I turned his face toward mine and I kissed him on the forehead and let him go.

As I turned toward the door, Edith seemed to fall apart, grasping desperately at anything which floated by in her brain. "Jacob! The year isn't up yet. . . . It's not complete. The story needs a whole year. . . . Like Walden. That's it, Jacob, like Walden. Wait until June. Just til the four quarters are up. A natural cycle, Jacob. . . . Like Thoreau. In another day it'll be spring. It isn't time yet for this to end."

"Time moves more quickly these days," I said, as I walked out the door.

And I thought of the two of them standing there, like a sad Laurel and Hardy in drag. And it was strange, for I'd always felt that Warren was a kind of son to Edith and me, but now it was they who seemed the parents, and I the son, leaving home to make my fortune in the world. And it was like a nineteenth-century novel again. Only the world I was entering wasn't the same.

There is a point you reach, when you are doing long-distance running, at which your body seems to take over. When you enter a world which is neither reality nor dream, but is, quite simply, *other*—an alien world in which you watch things happen with only a vague sense that they are happening to you. By the time I reached the WAC officer barracks, the bennies, grass, bourbon, and lack of sleep, coupled with the montage of miles and events through which I had just traveled, seemed to have bombarded me into an insensitivity of the ego in which universals seemed body rather than mind. I was moving simply because I was standing on a slope and I lacked the will not to. And the slope led down, down to the barracks and into Cal's room.

So I rolled forward, into the barracks, and into her room, the door flying open in front of me and bouncing back off the wall. I slammed it shut behind me, stopping for only a second, when I saw her. Combing out her long, sleek, black hair, her back toward me, she swung around, like a dancer, in slow motion, her hair and breasts swinging around after her. And I looked at her for a second, in her bikini panties and nothing else, looking anything but vulnerable. And that single second seemed to explode open, it contained so many possibilities.

She was so damned beautiful. Not just good-looking, but actually beautiful, like a painting. Like something that should be preserved for our grandchildren to see. And seeing her full stature, almost unclothed in front of me, staggered me for a second, nearly throwing me off my stride, for it seemed like confronting a Greek statue, but I had started down the slide, I was moving forward, and I lunged toward her, and before she could raise her arms I seized her around the slim center of the trunk of her body, pinning her arms, and my momentum drove us back into her dresser, jamming it against the wall, and as I reached down behind her, my hand creeping in between her ass and her panties and ripping them away, I heard the tinkle of spilled glass falling from her mirror and the smash of her clock which fell to the floor from the dresser top.

"Jake!" she cried, with startled sharpness, her body immobilized by surprise. "Jake!"

But I pushed forward, locking my arms around her, pressing myself against her, against the dresser as bottles broke and toppled, and I held her there. As she began to resist, I could feel the athletic vitality of her body against me, but I held on, and we pressed together, electrically seized, like hugging the third rail til you can't let go, and I thought my heart stopped, but I held.

She twisted within my grip, and she was big, as big as I was, but I grabbed onto the dresser behind her, and pinned her to it, and as our faces were forced into each other I kissed her mouth and kept on, kept on going forward, kept on holding, and I jammed my tongue into her mouth, and she stayed taut, braced . . . and she gave me her tongue, and I continued to hold on and kiss her, and she looked directly into my eyes, as if to say O.K., Jake, you asked for it.

And I loosened my grip as she moved me toward her bed, caressing my body with her hands as she helped me off with my clothes, and when we were both naked, she reached around me and moulded the curves of my back and buttocks with her hands, like a sculptor, and I became totally stiff.

We swung onto the bed and held each other and kissed each other's most private parts, and she opened herself to me, taking my erect dammed blood and flesh sex in her hand and placing it inside of her, and we looked through each other at the level of our eyes and she began to work me, to drive me back with the muscles and sinews of her thighs and to suck me down in the magnetic vacuum of her attraction, forcing me up and drawing me back, caressing my sex in a strobelike flash of the muscles within her like a snake coil tightened around me, letting go together, pulling tight together, up and back, together, moving in and holding back, each against the other and each with the other, holding back . . . until it begins to happen, together, and together we slide into the smooth shell of the sea and sink in the foam of release, together, as we float and swim together, and rub our crotches together til the sparks fly out and the room smells of hot flint burnt, together and apart, passive and active, each and each other, separate and together.

And then, as it begins to die, the wave drains back into the sea, leaving us suspended, naked and in each other's arms, on the sodden sand of the cool beach of sheets. Together.

As I lay there beside her, she turned to me and lifted up her head, and as she stroked my hair with one hand and touched my unshaven face lightly with the other, she kissed me on the lips with a gentleness of touch that I hadn't imagined she could possess.

And we remained in the pastel tones of each other until time began to be drained of color by reality's wash, and as I rose and slowly pulled my pants over my legs, she said, wistfully, "Stay with me, Jacob. Don't go."

"I've got to run now."

"Don't go, Jake," she softly implored. And she rolled over onto her side, and lay there naked and beautiful like a Matisse odalisque. "Things have changed, Jake. I can tell you now. The colonel's proposed to me."

I straightened with a jerk.

"He has, Jake. Don't you see? We can win now."

She sat up on the bed, bringing her face close (so impossibly close) to mine as I sat there lacing my shoes, with her eyes reaching out to mine, as she quietly said, "Jake, the world you want is over. It simply is no more. Mozart, Vivaldi, Brahms, they're gone for now. It's all over."

"What's finished? What's over? Do you know something you're not telling me, Cal?"

"Oh, God, Jake, look around you. I don't have to say it. It's over, that's all. Tonight is the beginning of the end. It's total war now. The government is going to write the music that the people will dance to from now on, and it'll always be a march."

"What?"

"It's going to be a 2/4 world. The era of complexities will soon be over."

"You've been talking to the colonel about Nietzsche and music, haven't you?"

"Why do you say such things? [I had really hurt her.] Why do you read these things into me? You should read Nietzsche, Jake. He was a beautiful man. You know what he said once, about love? 'Let it be your aim always to love more than the other, never to be the second.' Please stay with me, Jake. Join with me. Please."

I stood up. "I'm sorry, I can't."

"We'll have power, Jake. You can't do anything good without power. We'll still have art. You and I will keep it alive. We'll still be able to have Mozart for ourselves. And we'll preserve it for others."

"This is all an ego trip and I'm sorry but I can't make it mine. I can't believe in it."

"Remember what I told you about Handel that time. Sometimes the pathways to humility seem like the biggest ego trips of all. Someday things will change back. Art needs stability, Jake. We'll go along for now, and as I get control of the base we'll begin to move. First we can limit the casualties around here, and then we can begin to deal with the big boys."

She lifted her naked body off the bed and walked over to me, and she seemed to exude a damp cleanliness. Her arms hung like drapes along her sides, parallel to her hair, and she had never looked so lovely, and when she asked me again to stay, her voice seemed to roll to me over pubic down, it was so soft and unpretentious, and she seemed like seaweed being buffeted about. Fragrantly tired and fragile, and even, for the first time, a girl.

"I can handle these guys. It's the only way. There is no choice. I love you, Jake," and she took me in her arms and held her vulnerable nakedness against me. "I'll do anything for you, Jake. I'll marry the colonel. I'll put out for the general. I'll even screw the goddamned president of the United States if it will help. Don't you believe me? I don't want to, but I will. Don't you believe me?"

"Yes."

"And you do love me, don't you? You do feel something for me?"

"You're the greatest woman I could have imagined."

"Then you'll join me?"

"I'm sorry, Cal, but I can't."

"Then get out!" she screamed. "Get out of this room!" And she picked up her pillow and swung it at me with such force that it tore open and scattered feathers into the air. "Get out!" she screeched, hitting me with the pillow on each cry, "Out! Out! Out!"

I backed out of the room, hurried down the hallway, and as I was about to walk through the outside door, she called to me with a sudden resignation in her voice, "Jake."

"Yes," I turned.

"Jake, don't go to the concert tonight." She stood there in the doorway for a second, wearing only tiny pillow feathers resting on her hair like a snowflake tiara, and then she disappeared into her room.

I walked out into the air, into the darkness lighted only by the glisten of the moon's milky tinsel, but before I left, I circled around into the trees, back to a spot on the edge of the woods opposite her window. She had knelt on the floor, resting her chin on the windowsill, and she stared at the moon, in a trance of unblinking despair. And then, with a drained finality in her voice, she said aloud, without inflection, "I'm alone again. And it's forever, this time. In this whole foul, ridiculous, shitty world, I'm the only one who has the courage to stand up and face you. To hold the world up to your face as a one-way mirror in which you will be forced to see yourself and through which you will know that I, that I alone, am witness to what you are."

She raised herself up and as she moved the window down its runners to a close, I could hear her say, wearily, but with that determination that was so deeply a part of her, "O.K. . . . Thy will be done."

BULLETIN

Vietcong Attack Delays Bicycle Race for 3 Hours

DINHQUAN, South Vietnam, Jan. 21 (AP) — The Vietcong delayed the Tour de Vietnam bicycle race for three hours today by attacking South Vietnamese troops clearing the highway. One Government soldier was reported killed.

After the fighting, the more than 70 cyclists rode about 40 miles of the course by truck.

The Government-sponsored race is intended to show that the country's roads are safe.

Commercial

In Washington today, President Sun announced his desire to remove Vice-President Herbert Hubert from office and to replace him with his brother, Nick Sun. The move, which would require a constitutional amendment, was termed highly irregular by some of the dovish senators on Capitol Hill, but because the president has stated that he is acting in the interests of national defense, immediate approval of the measure was expected in the Congress and the required number of state legislatures.

CAMERA TWO

I passed through the officers' quarters area and entered the field behind our house. It was about a hundred yards long and shaped like a football field, a level plateau about twelve feet higher than the river. Behind the longhouse, which was situated at the river end of the field, the ground dropped sharply down to the water at about a sixty-degree angle. The field was bounded on both sidelines by woods.

When I let myself into the longhouse, the process of filing out the back door had already begun. I moved next to Len at the rear of the group; although he said nothing, and his face remained expressionless, I could sense his relief at my arrival.

We passed through the door opening on the river side, squatted on the ground at the edge of the drop, and lowered ourselves down the bank as quietly as possible. At the bottom we split into two files, the blacks turning toward the left and moving along the river bank to the south and the rest of us turning to the north.

Someone tapped me on the shoulder. It was David, his finger to his lips to signal for silence and a look of excited expectation on his face. He gave my shoulder a squeeze, smiled to me, and turned away into the darkness.

I followed Len and the kids several hundred yards north where the bank began to level off. We climbed back up, entered the woods, and proceeded to a pile of equipment which had been hidden away beforehand. The kids with us were about half boys and half girls. Quickly and unself-consciously they removed all their clothes and began to put on their Indian costumes. Len handed me a costume and he and I changed out of our clothes along with the kids. It was only after I was dressed and was painting my face that I wondered how far in advance he had arranged for my disguise. Many of the kids had bows and arrows and spears. Some carried war clubs. Len took a tomahawk and I randomly picked up a spear. One young boy, not older than fourteen, unfurled a red flag and fixed it to a wooden pole.

"What's that?" I whispered to Len.

"It's our flag. The spades have a black one."

"Len," I said, "there's still time to stop," but he didn't answer. He walked away and became involved in checking equipment and in helping the kids paint their faces and bodies. As a final touch, we all put on feathered headdresses. This wasn't an Iroquois custom, it had come from the plains Indians, but by this time I knew enough not to question this. It was a myth we were fulfilling, not a historical reality, and we were the Indians that lived in the white man's mind, the specter that had haunted, and would continue to haunt him, for as long as he lived on this continent.

And this is crazy, I thought. But it was too late. Events have a momentum of their own and they carry the human flotsam along. I began to fade into private visions. The days of sleepless riot were taking their toll. I saw history as a great steel ball, rolling down the street, crushing everybody in its path, and up above, balanced precariously on the rushing, heavy globe, I saw Len, trying to walk it like a log roller walking a log, and whether he would make it hung in the balance—whether he would be a hero or a clown. And up there alongside him, dancing wildly to fight the effects of the ball's roll, I saw another ludicrous, painted fool. And it was me.

We all gathered around Len in a huddle. He was bent over a large cardboard carton and he spoke to us in an intense whisper. "The white man is our enemy. He has taken our land—our mother, the earth. He has taken away the woods of the Pequot and the plains of the Sioux. He has taken away the farms of our brothers, the Cherokee. He has taken our dreams and turned them into machines.

"It is time to turn the white man's power against himself. The grass sent by the Great Spirit has freed our minds and ennobled our hearts and given us clear sight and moments of peace. Now it is time to free our consciences for the bloody tasks ahead. The time of grass is over. We are about to begin the battle for the minds and hearts of thousands of our brothers across this once-great land, the thousands upon thousands who are waiting to join us, waiting for someone to stand up and strike the first blow. History begins tonight. Here. Drink up. The time has come."

He reached into the carton and began to hand out bottles to everyone. I held mine up to the moonlight. It was a pint of Thunderbird wine.

And in the complex but somehow elementary logic composed of bennies and the moon, it seemed only right, even axiomatic, that this should be happening. And I no longer bothered to think about it, for I knew we were heading full speed for the sidelines, for that area beyond the everyday playing field where anything goes and old logics must be thrown away with old weapons, thrown back beyond Ellis Island, back into the sea.

We approached the field through the woods and stopped on its edge. Far from the longhouse, at about our own twenty-yard line.

And the field was no longer empty. Down at the longhouse end, I could see them. About forty soldiers. And their bayonets, unsheathed, licked through the moonlight. And just outside the door to the longhouse I could see Frank Benuto, in command. And then, on the step above him, another figure, staring out over the dark field. It was Cal.

To our left, at the other end of the field, I could see our house. I can still go there, I thought. I can still turn away. But I was moving now, moving at last, and my movement was carrying me in the other direction. Len whispered to me that the attack was scheduled to begin at about eleven forty. He had timed my Glenn Gould record of the variations and added three minutes because of Madame Braun's age. The kids had been instructed to nurse their wine until the time of the attack and then to move as soon as the troops rushed into the hall.

So I opened my bottle and sipped on the thick, sweet liquid as I lay on the grass and watched the moon and listened to Bach, the Goldberg Variations, played as I had never heard them played before. There were no blinding flashes of pure speed, no unbelievable runs of dazzling technical brilliance. In fact, as I lay there in the cool night air, I could hear obvious mistakes, especially in the fast passages, some of which threw Madame Braun off so that she had to stop and begin the entire phrase again.

But she had something else—understanding. Understanding of the music, and of things beyond the music as well. A comprehensive grasp of where things were at. And a gravity of insight—a muted hint of the awful weight which knowledge brings—filled the music she sent out to us over the brisk March air. And it touched my ears with the delicacy of gnarled fingers, and in the light-heavy slowness of her lines she carried sadness beyond itself and into the region where pain turns into ecstasy and the cadence of the piece cracked, releasing the notes and the rhythms as she pushed Bach's music until its bounds were so joyously broken that listening to it was like watching a cripple who has learned to dance.

But something was wrong. I stared at the moon until it hurt my eyes as I tried to put my thoughts together—What was it? What was wrong? . . . And then, with a frightening clarity, I knew. The attack was scheduled to begin at eleven forty because that was the exact moment when Len expected Madame Braun to finish her performance. The soldiers would make their move, the kids would be ready to make *their* move, and Madame Braun would have a few seconds to sneak out the back door before the fighting started.

I looked at my watch and saw that the attack was scheduled to begin in approximately two minutes and I realized that of all the people on the field only I (and possibly Cal) knew what was happening and that certainly I was the only one aware of its disastrous effects. Madame Braun was playing the repeats. She was playing the music as Bach had written it, repeating each variation one more time after she finished it. Who could have predicted that anyone, and especially a seventy-year-old pianist, would attempt to play such a technically demanding and exhausting piece as the Goldberg Variations with the repeats as Bach had written it? It was incredible. And around me, on the edge of the field, the kids were restless and confused. They had finished their wine and were ready to move, but the music was still hanging in the air. The anticipated silence hadn't come.

I whispered the information to Len and he signaled to the kids to stay down and wait. I decided I might as well make the best of the situation, so I lay there on my back and dug the sounds until midnight tolled on the base headquarters' clock. At that moment I realized two things. One, that it was March 21, Johann Sebastian Bach's birthday, and two, that we had no way of communicating what was happening to the black kids across the field.

When the twelfth gong sounded, they broke out of the woods and charged the longhouse. They were drunk and they war-hooped wildly as they ran, but our kids, who were confused because the music hadn't stopped, hesitated. The few seconds of indecision was crucial. Instead of confounding the troops with a simultaneous, two-pronged attack from both sides of the field, we witnessed a disorganized half-charge, right into the strength of the troops who had not yet begun to move toward the door of the longhouse, and, in war, a half-charge is far worse than no charge at all. The troops were surprised, but they were able to see the direction of their enemy and they had time to respond reflexively, getting off bursts of automatic rifle fire before the blacks, in their weird Indian getups, had a chance to slash and hammer at them with their hand weapons.

At this point, some of our kids stood up and began to shoot arrows at the troops. A couple soldiers fell, but the ultimate confusion, the chaos which we had counted on to compensate for our lack of firepower, was lost.

As Madame Braun began to play one of the fantasies for the second time, Len leaped to his feet and, swinging a tomahawk over his head, he shouted, "Let's move! Let's go! Let's. . . ." CRACK.

I watched him fall, and in the moonlight he seemed a costumed figure from a black and white TV show dropped into life to die. And as our kids began a scattered charge toward the longhouse to help the blacks, and some of the chaos we needed finally appeared, and the Bach was drowned out by gunshots and war hoops even older than the music itself, Len lay at my feet, dead. His face was turned up toward the moon which bounced pale light upon the dark hole where the bullet had violated his skull and ripped through the tissue of his brain and ended his short, unhappy life on earth. And as I stood there, above the body which lay still on the cold silver ground, I heard myself speak a single sentence into the cool moonlit air: "When the gun goes off, the game is over."

I picked up my spear and turned toward the fighting when someone grabbed my arm. It was Lorraine. We began to run toward the longhouse together.

"Where's David?" I shouted at her over the din.

"He's been, shot. A sucking chest wound. He'll never make it."

"Walter! Where's Walter?"

"He's not here, Jake," she said, with a sudden gloom in her voice. "He never showed up."

It was then that I heard myself begin to shriek, to scream out a cracked, macabre cry as I ran toward the longhouse, faster and faster toward the center of the fight. I shrieked out my grief at the fact that I was the only adult our side had left on the field.

On the steps a soldier moved toward me with his bayonet. I ran him through the middle with my spear. His intestines spilled out and his pimpled face looked terribly surprised as he fell at my feet and I thought, oh God, he couldn't have been more than eighteen, and I screamed another wild-animal scream and ran through the fighting and carnage and into the longhouse where the frenzied slashing continued in a packing-house butcher bath all around me. And as I passed through the doorway, screaming madly, I glanced at the stage and I saw it happen. It simply appeared. Still. It simply *was there.* Through her neck. Sticking out in the front. A red-stained arrow, through her throat.

Its force jerked her violently around as I ran—toward the front of the stage. And as my momentum continued to carry me forward through the hall in a slow, floating run, I could see her face as she fell.

I couldn't believe my eyes, for over the heads of the people battling in front of me, over the spilled blood and screaming children, I could see her topple off the piano stool. And it was Moms.

In a long black satin gown, with her hair pulled back in a bun, her bulky black neck pierced by the crimson shaft, she hung over the edge of space, impossibly suspended for a second in time, and then she fell to the floor, spilling the stool on the stage.

It was Moms.

And by the time I leaped up onto the stage the music had stopped, and I felt some terrible thing inside myself that had to get out, and I hung my head into the open piano and vomited onto the strings.

Then, with my head still dangling over the piano's guts, in the midst of all the mournful calls and hysterical kill-shrieks, I had a vision. An image of Jeannie, shivering in wait for us at the Concord bridge, and next to her, Little Jo, quietly strumming on Tommy Creetner's guitar. But it made no sound, for he no longer had a place to plug it in.

Bracing both hands against the piano's hook, I lifted myself and turned to the furious disorder below me on the longhouse floor which looked like it had been mopped with the blood of children, and to those of us that were still alive, I pointed to the back stage door and shouted out one mournful cry: *"Retreat!* Retreat everybody! R-E-T-R-E-A-T!"

And you. You had your breakfast and you read your morning paper. You read the news:

> In a weird series of events last night in Massachusetts, the details of which are still largely secrèt, it appears that a minor rebellion was staged on an army base in which several officers are reputed to have taken part. It is reported that both sides suffered heavy casualties in fierce fighting.
>
> Although the army has released few of the details, usually reliable sources indicate that about a dozen of the rebels are still at large and they are rumored to have regrouped their forces in the wealthy suburban community of Concord, Massachusetts, and to have taken refuge in the nearby woods.

And you remembered that there had been an exhibition baseball game the night before. The Yankees *versus* Cleveland. So you turned to the sports. You wanted to find out the score.